FATHER OF CONTENTION

by
Lanie Mores

Tellwell Talent
www.tellwell.ca

ISBN
978-1-77370-908-6 (Hardcover)
978-1-77370-906-2 (Paperback)
978-1-77370-909-3 (eBook)

For my parents—I couldn't have done this without you.
And for my boys—
Lee, Erik, and Batman (my dog, not the superhero).

One does not become enlightened
by imagining figures of light,
but by making the darkness conscious.

- Carl Jung -

Prologue

The smog is thick—in my head, out on the streets.
Desperation obscures my view, disembodied sounds
Of engines running, honking horns, people's voices,
The only evidence of their existence.
All is grey, an underdeveloped photograph
Like the London "pea soupers" back in the '50s
With smog so dense, it coated the lining of your nostrils,
Rested on the skin like a toxic shroud.

All is a blurred smudge of continuous motion,
A film projector stuck on high speed.
Until invisible fingers reach out, grasp the film, so it slows,
Now sliding through frame by frame.
As my perception shifts, I see the people now.
Grey mist separating, snaking through and around each individual,
As they stare forward with numb expressions, no sense of purpose,
Marching forever forward on a path to nowhere.
I'll give you purpose, my forever enemy.
For as much as I loathe you, I need you.

You're a complex creature, I'll give you that.
Mortals, dissatisfied with this station, you dare to create.
Building blocks of life, rearranged,

For self-preservation, prolonging the life span.
Incapable of keeping up with the consequences,
Limited minds with incomplete awareness.
One day, to be surpassed by your own creations,
Your ultimate, inevitable end.

Yet, this type of pride I understand.
Selfish ambition led to my current allotment in life.
Draped in shadow, with others like me, I'm forced to abide.
Wandering back and forth, pacing to and fro, like a caged animal,
Searching for the perfect one.
I had a home once, riches beyond measure.
Everything I could have ever wished for.
Respect. Adoration. Status.
Until all that was snatched away from me,
Awarded to others less deserving.
As punishment, forced to live with these inferior creatures,
Mindlessly defacing, destroying their own home,
Weakening its supportive pillars and beams
With their disrespect and neglect.

I feel displaced. Dispossessed. Restless.

I don't bother with the shelters or warming centres,
For I am not welcome there.
It is not a place for my kind.
And I'm not interested in something so tentative or fleeting
Like a sidewalk house of cardboard turned limp and soggy should it
rain.
I seek something more permanent.

I watch the people floating past with their blank, unseeing eyes.
They try to ignore me, but I see them. I see right through them.
We've heard that the eyes are the windows to the soul.

Peering past white scleral curtains, through dark glassy pupils,
You truly can see into the depths of each man, each woman.
What they are made of. Who they are. What they are capable of.
Are they missing something? Love? Spirituality? A sense of purpose?
An empty vessel waiting to be filled?
Then I could slither into that emptiness,
Donning vestments of bone and flesh,
Filling that void with my spectacular, substantial presence,
Able to fully live once more.

If only it were that easy.

On cue, a distinguished gentleman glides by my field of vision.
Wearing a white suit with wide lapels,
Crisp polka-dotted shirt unbuttoned to his sternum.
Hair of golden honey-brown worn long, lightly feathered back.
Leather briefcase clutched firmly at his side
Like it contains his sense of worth, self-respect.
Attached to his wrist—a thick, gold Rolex,
Not unlike the bejewelled sceptres and crowns
I've seen on Pharaohs and kings in times past.
Opulent objects bestowed upon mere men
Giving the impression they are above the others around them,
Like gods.
An aura surrounds him, but not one of light.
One I recognize. Tainted.
Drinking in the beauteous vision of this man,
Jealousy punches me in the gut.

I was once beautiful. A beauty so bright and glorious
I was compared to a morning star.
My great presence would have caused this man to cower before me in shame,
Made him feel inadequate.

But my glorious countenance was also stripped away from me.
Now I am hideous, vile, repugnant even.
It is common to take for granted the gifts we are given,
But once gone, we mourn, lament for them and I do so now.
The frustration of my losses ferments and grows
Until it is replaced with a fury that drives me,
Compels me to get back what I deserve.
Determination clears my mind,
Outweighs any limitations I might have.

I was a leader once. And I still am.
The other transients that slink with me in the darkness,
They follow me. They do my will.
We work with one accord to reach a common end.
The earth crumbles beneath my feet, my time runs short
To rule this dying world, to prove to the worlds beyond
That I am worthy.

For I am already the Prince of the Power of the Air,
The Prince of this World.
But, without a true following, these titles mean nothing,
They are words in a vacuum, less substance than air.
No longer satisfied being trapped in shadow,
I crave permanence, for my presence to be known throughout the
masses,
To expand my following.

My eyes remain glued to the fine gentleman,
Not letting him out of my sight.
I reach forward, but as light strikes my fingers,
They disperse into a thousand particles of ash.
I flinch, retracting my hand, where my fingers reform in the darkness.
Not yet but soon.

This man, this human—could he be the one?
My supplicant. My salvation.

It all starts with one.

—The Prince of this World

PART I

Chapter 1

It was ironic that the body rested below Renner's favourite apple tree in the yard—the only place he had ever associated with a sense of safety and peace. Now, the tree appeared tortured. Long robbed of its verdant armour, bared arms reached up to the sky in supplication for the secret buried between its knobby roots.

The night the body was both buried and exhumed was on an unnaturally long November night in 1952. The moon and stars became completely obscured by a heavy mass of clouds, and a palpable darkness drifted into the small municipality of Flein. Flattened shadows raced across the land, pressing up against every surface, the breeze a secret accomplice to the silent invasion, shifting and spreading the darkness like a disease.

Renner's frail cottage was not immune. Easily slipping passed the drafty wooden door and window frames, seeping in through the splintery hard wood floors, the darkness entered his home and dashed straight into *Vater*'s heart. After the deed, the darkness fled outside with the body, lying atop the freshly dug earth, alongside dried and rotting apples. A sounder of wild boar was instantly drawn to the scent of fresh blood but before claiming their reward, they were frightened off by Alberich Winkler, the nearest neighbour, showing up at the front doorstep with 12-gauge in hand.

Later, in his report, Alberich would say it was the sound of a woman screaming that made him call the *Volkspolizei*—the East German police force established by the Soviet Union after the

Second World War—before grabbing his gun and rushing over to the Reinhardt's home. Unsure of what he was going to discover, he approached the cottage with extreme caution.

But, when he kicked open the front door, nothing at first seemed amiss. Ulrich Reinhardt approached him in his usual drunken state.

"Hey, what the hell do you think you're doing?"

"Where's the wife and boy?" Alberich demanded, while trying to sneak glances passed the burly man blocking his view.

"None of your business," he sneered.

The neighbour caught sight of nine-year-old Renner poking his head out from beneath the sink, eyes stretched wide, terrified.

"Why is he hiding, then?"

Ulrich's muscles tensed, and he looked as if he was going to go for the gun. Luckily, the Volkspolizei pulled in or there might have been two bodies to dig up instead of the one.

Once the Volkspolizei were finished taking the neighbour's statement, Renner was questioned. The source of the screams was identified. The location of the body discovered.

With shovels in hand, the police extracted the body from its shallow grave. Looming over the hollow, it took four officers to reach in and pull out the rolled-up, flat-weave, chenille rug with yellow flowers. The rug that had so faithfully lain on their kitchen floor was now stained with a halo of blood that radiated outward from where Renner's mother's head was swaddled. The rug would forever become a symbol of the event, etched deeply into Renner's mind.

The rug was unfurled, and he saw his mother for the last time, although she vaguely resembled herself in life. Eyes the shade of weak tea, a wide nose set between high cheekbones, now eerily misshapen, the right side of her skull sunken in. The tight bun she always wore, a usually perfect ball of yarn, was now frayed and matted in blood.

Renner searched inside for the sadness that should have surrounded the event, but mostly what he felt was relief mixed with guilt.

Vater was a hostile and cruel man, made even more so after serving in the war. The drink always drew out his darkest impulses, swiftly weakened his moral compass, if in sobriety he ever had much of one. This day was destined to come.

But, all things happen for a reason. Renner would never know why his mother decided to put up a fight that night. To finally stand up to her aggressor. But, as Renner watched the Volkspolizei shackle his father's wrists and cram his massive frame into the police car and wrap his mother in a clean tarp to be transported to the morgue, he realized this was a necessary evil that Vater was meant to commit.

For the first time, Renner was free.

Free from the constant fear and brutal beatings. Free from being trapped under his father's thumb for the rest of his life.

Renner was shipped off to the nearest orphanage, where children his age were rarely adopted. His case would prove to be one of the exceptions.

He was given a second chance, free to live a different life.

★ ★ ★

The summer was experiencing its final heat wave as Renner boarded the train, his life's possessions in tow. Twenty years had passed since the day he lost his mother and starting this new chapter in his life brought back the memories of that day, how he had watched his cottage shrink in the distance. He wondered if he could finally leave those memories behind. The memories that, no matter how hard he tried to shake, to block them from his consciousness, remained stuck to his heels, a stubborn shadow, trailing behind wherever he went.

But, perhaps this time would be different, never travelling this far before. The train was just the first leg of his travels. Next, he would board a plane and fly overseas for the first time. Patting the plane tickets folded in the front pocket of his white t-shirt, he felt a glimmer of excitement radiate throughout his nervous system.

The train car he was assigned was already cramped with six other passengers when he finally located it. They occupied themselves in various fashions: reading, napping, and two scruffy kids played War with a deck of old, beaten cards. Besides the few initial exchanges of pleasantries, nobody spoke.

Settling into the narrow portion of the seat he was allowed, Renner felt a jolt as the train started to move, and then watched the parcelled landscape race past him in blends of green, yellow, and brown from the vast plains of grasses and interspersed farmlands.

The train's rhythmic pulse on the tracks—*clang clang, clang clang, clang clang*—coupled with the unchanging scenery was lulling Renner to sleep. His head rested against the window, the glass cool on the side of his forehead. Eyes finally drifting shut, an image of his tearful adoptive parents saying their goodbyes projected onto the back of his eyelids. The memory was fresh, a mere few hours old, and still painful.

"Renner, my *Liebchen*, do you have to go?" his short, generously proportioned mother had clung to him. "You could always complete your graduate studies at the Universität Leipzig, the same university where you received your medical doctorate. It's so close. And the professors there couldn't praise you enough." As she pulled away, he noticed her moist, blue eyes had aged, and her once jet-black curls were now salted with white strands. His father, also, had somehow aged before his eyes in one brief moment. The signs of illness more pronounced. It was a new clarity that leaving had bestowed on Renner, an unsettling clarity, making it much more difficult to leave than he had anticipated.

"I know, but my interests are more in line with the research being conducted at the Barbora Institute of Technology. I couldn't pass on this opportunity. And I'll be back before you know it," Renner consoled.

In truth, he didn't know when he would be able to return, the option depending largely on his curriculum, and then there was the possibility of being offered a job directly upon graduation. What then? Perhaps a few brief visits would be possible. Even though he loved his parents with every cell in his body, leaving them was a necessary sacrifice on the road to fulfilling his dreams.

Dreams that started all the way back when he was allowed to attend school for the first time, after his biological mother was murdered. A passion, a drive was awoken in him: to learn, to create, to succeed. In the land of opportunity, Barbora Bay, Washington in particular, he would be able to attain those goals.

What awaited him there?

His anticipation swelled, wiping away the heavy feeling of tiredness he had been fighting. Re-opening his eyes, he sat upright, and smoothed out his t-shirt and hip-hugging flared slacks. Patting his front shirt pocket, buried beneath the plane tickets, he located his KS cigarettes, withdrew an ivory lighter from the same pocket and lit up. Renner offered the other adult passengers a smoke, and an older gentleman accepted. Their carriage, previously filled with the odours of food, stale breath, and sweat, was now replaced by a sweet nicotine cloud, a surprising reprieve.

Sixteen hours, three naps, and four meals later, Renner finally found himself at the Seattle-Tacoma International Airport.

Inside the airport terminal, Renner grabbed his suitcase from a pyramid of multi-hued luggage, and then threaded his way through the thick crowd of travellers, angling towards the subway. At 6'2", he could easily see over the sea of heads, and locate the signs to guide his direction. Not only was his height impressive, but his physique as a result of regular weight training and playing on his university's soccer league garnered many a glance from the travellers rushing past. Few could resist his confident swagger, his smouldering eyes the colour of smoked turquoise. The women gawked, even tripping over each other to get a better look, embarrassing themselves in the process. But, Renner hardly noticed.

The subway entrance was congested with potential passengers. Waiting briefly in line to purchase his ticket, he then manoeuvred his large frame through the turnstiles. The floor vibrated as the subway pulled up on the opposite side of the terminal, forcing him to jog to reach the doors just as they opened with a pressurized whoosh.

Throughout the ride, Renner fought the nausea from the stench surrounding him. Too much wet fabric trapped in a small space, too much inconsistent motion, too much fatigue. When the subway decelerated at the BIT terminal, he heaved a sigh of relief. He had made it.

The Barbora Institute of Technology. BIT for short.

His new home.

The sprawling campus housed castle-like buildings, ancient trees, vibrant gardens, and hordes of people. Some strolled in groups, as couples, or solo, unmindful of the moist climate. With so many umbrellas swirling and floating around him from every side, he felt as if he was in the middle of a traditional Chinese umbrella dance.

Using the campus map sent to him in his acceptance package, he located the registrar's office in the Forsythe building. Forced to wait in line for another inexhaustible amount of time, he literally fell asleep on his feet.

A gentle nudge from behind broke his slumber. Renner snapped to attention, the secretary's desk now right before him.

"Do you have your proof of registration?" a charcoal-haired woman with thick bifocals requested from Renner. He handed over the forms he had received in the mail. The heavyset woman thrust the bifocals up higher on her bulbous nose with an index finger, scrutinizing the paper like an FBI agent searching for discrepancies but then looked up at him, impressed.

"You've been busy, Doctor Scholz," strong emphasis on the doctor. She smiled, acknowledging his academic achievements.

"That's merely the foundation for my real aspirations. I still have a ways to go."

"You sure have travelled a long distance to study here. Is this your first time in America?"

"In fact, it is," he smiled.

"Let me get your file," she said, as she lumbered to the filing cabinets at the back of the office. Within seconds she was back in front of Renner, rifling through the paperwork. "Here it is, the amount owing for the year and the dorm rental." She slid the paper over to Renner, then added, "You can pay in full or do monthly payments."

"I'll pay in full. My father gave me a signed cheque." He jotted in the amount owing and then slid the cheque over to the secretary.

"Konstantin Scholz?" she read the name on the bottom of the cheque in recognition. "As in, the creator and owner of KS cigarettes?" she asked incredulously.

"That's the one. I'm surprised you've heard of him." Of course, his father's name was well-known back home, but he hadn't realized that even in the U.S. the brand was recognized. Renner's heart swelled with pride.

"Are you kidding me? Those are my favourite cigarettes. They're so smooth," she gushed. "There's a special ingredient in there that I can't put my finger on, but it separates your father's company from the rest."

Renner nodded. "His lab technicians are magicians. I used to sneak into the laboratory at my father's factory and watch them for hours, breaking down materials into their base components and then recombining them in a way that made the final product far more superior than its original form. It's what inspired me to go into the sciences."

"Are you planning to carry on your dad's legacy? Working at his company? He's such an amazing success. I read his biography in the newspapers. A real rags-to-riches story."

Back in the 1950s, Konstantin Scholz had developed KS cigarettes, which practically exploded overnight into an empire, becoming one of the most successful cigarette companies in Europe.

Despite his enormous riches, his father managed to remain humble, and could be even quite frugal at times. The main lesson he wanted to instill in Renner was to work hard, earn his keep, and appreciate everything he had.

"No, I'm more interested in using science to further medical advancements. Create therapies. That sort of thing."

The secretary shuffled the paperwork into a pile, slipped the sheaf back into Renner's file, and handed him a receipt.

"Here's your room number and key. You'll be staying in Leighton House, which is facing the Barbora River. One of the oldest residences in the United States, the dorm actually used to be a hotel for movie stars and the elite, so the decor is quite elegant. Mostly graduate students in there. There's even a library that has a reputation for containing a unique selection of books. Originals, not found anywhere else in the world." She handed Renner the dorm room key and a simple map leading to Leighton House.

"Thank you," he said as he grabbed the key and map. "Sounds interesting."

"I believe your roommate has already moved in."

"My what?"

"Your roommate. Paul Barrington, I believe is his name. Checked in a few days ago. He's a real charmer that one."

"You must be mistaken. I requested a single."

"No, I'm positive. Obviously, this isn't what you expected, and I'm sorry to have to be the one to tell you, but, due to the fluctuation in attendance this year, we have a limited number of rooms. Most residents have had to double up."

"I don't understand. I paid the price of a single." Frustrated, he ran his hand through his shoulder-length golden hair. *No, this could not be happening.* The last thing Renner wanted was a roommate—someone to distract him from his studies, get in his way. He was used to being on his own, having his own space. There must be a way to rectify the situation. But, what the secretary told him next shattered that thought.

"You're lucky you got a room at all, to be honest. A lot of students have had to find shelter elsewhere. And the prices have sky-rocketed due to the Vietnam War and inflation. Not ideal, but I'm sure you'll make the best of the situation." She smiled encouragingly.

Renner shook his head in denial.

"Hey, don't blame the messenger. If I could help you out, I would. Otherwise, you're all set. Good luck with your studies, and welcome to America."

Still clearly disappointed, Renner snatched his suitcase off of the floor, and mumbled a less than heartfelt thank you to the secretary.

Back outside, the dorm map led Renner through the rain drenched streets straight up to Leighton House—his new residence. And the place did not disappoint.

The dormitory was palatial, covered in red brick with white concrete accents, a wrought iron fence and perfectly shaped hedges circling the property. A domed peak adorned the highest point of the structure, reminiscent of a filigreed crown. Inside, the main lobby housed a colossal oak desk sandwiched by concrete pillars, a crystal chandelier, and ornately carved banisters and door frames. The building still resembled its original form as a hotel and was as formidable as the secretary had promised. An ideal place to stay while engaging in his studies. If only he had gotten a single.

Renner dragged his feet up three flights of stairs and found the room he would be staying in. As he reached out to turn the circular doorknob, a lanky female brunette threw open the door and stepped out of the room he was about to enter—*his* room. Startled at first, she froze with doe-brown eyes wide. Regaining her composure, she ran off down the hall barefoot, shoes dangling from her fingertips.

Renner grasped the door handle, the door not fully closed, swinging it inward. The room was small. Two wooden beds hugged the outer walls on opposite sides of the room with matching oak desks. There were two chest-high dressers, filing cabinets, book-cases, and in the middle, separating the room, was a desk flanked by comfortable looking mustard armchairs, a round sitting table and a floor lamp. A window overlooked the courtyard.

But that's not what caught Renner's attention. The left side of the room was already occupied. Clothes littered the floor, and a sexy Elizabeth Taylor poster was crudely taped above the bed. A tall, handsome, naked man lay propped up in bed smoking a post-coital cigarette, his privates thankfully concealed by an awfully small, white sheet. The space smelled of smoke and male sweat.

"Lucky thing I didn't come a few minutes earlier," Renner stated.

The man's chiselled features were split by a huge grin. "I'm Paul Barrington," the naked man introduced himself, proffering his right hand.

Renner hesitated to grab his hand, knowing where it had been. He shook it, anyways, not wanting to be rude, barely suppressing the urge to wipe his hand off on his pants afterwards.

"I'm Renner Scholz. You must be my flat mate." He pointed to the tidy vacant side to the right of the room, raising his eyebrows in question. "Mine, I suppose?"

"Hope you don't mind, brother. I came in two days ago. I've already settled in."

"I can see that." Renner eyed the mess, and remembered the girl fleeing the room moments earlier. *Settled in, indeed.*

Thick plumes of exhaled smoke circled above Paul's mussed, brown curls. "Where are you from?" he asked, noticing Renner's thick accent.

"Erfurt, Germany."

"Ah, a German," Paul responded in a terrible mock German accent while administering an animated Heil Hitler salute.

"Excuse me?" Renner frowned.

Paul started laughing. "Hey, don't get all bent out of shape. I'm teasing you, brother. Is this your first time in the States?"

Renner nodded. "This is my first time anywhere. I needed a permit to come and study here. Getting permission to leave East Germany is extremely difficult."

"Bet that cost a pretty penny."

"It wasn't cheap. I'm lucky my father has connections." Renner set his pewter luggage on the floor next to his new bed and threw his wet jacket over the desk chair.

"What does your father do?" Paul asked.

"He developed the KS cigarette company."

"Never heard of them."

"More of a European thing, I guess." Renner felt the front pocket of his white t-shirt, extracted the opened package of cigarettes, and flung it over to Paul. "Here, I have a few left."

"Thanks." Paul caught the package mid-flight, and immediately slipped a KS cigarette from the wrinkled package and used the cigarette he was presently smoking to light the new one. He nodded in approval, "Not bad, not bad at all." He hocked up some phlegm and spit the wad into the trash can beside his bed. "So, I guess you're some kind of hotshot back home?"

"No, not at all. Nobody knows who I am. My interests are vastly different from my father's. I have no desire to take over his company once he's gone." Renner paused, regretting his choice of words, feeling his throat tightening against his will. Attempting to ignore the flood of emotion, he carried on. "I'm focused on the sciences and genetic engineering."

"They didn't have anywhere for you to study in Germany?"

"Yes, of course, but things are different over there. Not as much opportunity or freedom. Also, I wanted to come here, so I could work with Dr. Shubally, who's focusing on a similar project as I am. Have you heard of him?"

Paul's face soured, and he sat forward on the bed, placing his feet on the floor. Leaving the small sheet over his lap for privacy, he drew on a pair of boxers that had been discarded on the floor. "You could say that."

"Sorry, did I hit a nerve?"

Paul huffed. "Hardly. He's overrated, that's all. Lots of buzz about nothing, if you ask me." He swaggered over to a blue cooler at the foot of his bed and pulled out a Pabst Blue Ribbon beer. "Do you want one?"

Renner declined.

Using the edge of his desk to smack the cap off his beer, he took a long pull from the bottle, and then settled back against the pillows on his bed.

"So, how is the experience of being a German in America so far? Do people treat you any differently? Harbour anti-German sentiment against you after causing World War II and having millions of humans' blood on your hands?"

Renner's fur bristled. "I'd hardly say I specifically was to blame." He couldn't help but feel defensive. Besides being irrationally accusatory, Paul's words stirred up the old feelings, the unwelcome feelings. Reminded him of his biological father. "That was a long time ago. Most people have moved on. Besides, the German people paid their dues. There were millions of Germans slaughtered following the war."

"Yeah, but they deserved what they got. It was justice being served." Paul gave him a challenging look.

"What's that supposed to mean? A lot of innocent people were killed as well."

"Hey, look. I'm just rambling." His features smoothed over, and his voice turned to honey. "I don't want to get off on the wrong foot. It's great that you got permission to study here. I'm sure you're right. Most people have probably moved on. There's another war to concentrate on, another group of people to blame. Forgive me for being so blunt. It's one of my worst traits." He flashed a cocky smile, perhaps most people fell for. But Renner knew his kind. Clearly saw the fakeness behind it. Still, they were roommates and some sort of relationship needed to be formed and maintained if they were going to survive living together for the year.

"And you, where're you from?" Renner asked, unzipping his suitcase and unloading his folded clothing into the dresser on his side of the room. He left the smaller items in the bag, suddenly too tired to completely unpack. Collapsing onto the firm bed, the weariness fully settled into his muscles, his brain. He promised himself he would finish unpacking later. Now, all he wanted to do was sleep.

"You might want to wash that first," Paul indicated the bed. "Mine was pretty grungy when I came. Dust and mice poop. Not sure how great the housekeeping is around here."

Renner, so tired, normally would have flown off the bed, disinfecting the surface immediately, but now he simply lay there, semi-conscious.

"I'm from New York," Paul finally answered. "You look wiped. Long trip?"

Renner merely nodded, eyes now closed.

"Well, don't let me keep you up. Look, I feel bad about my rudeness earlier. We're heading out to the pub in a few hours. If you're not too tired, you're welcome to join us. Let me make it up to you."

Even though Renner rarely frequented bars, pubs, discos, or even dated for that matter, due to his intense focus on his studies to achieve his future career, his classes wouldn't be starting for a few days. Not wanting to alienate the first acquaintance he had met, and the person he was forced to live with at least for the next year, he nodded once more.

"Sure. Wake me up...in a...little..." Renner mumbled, his sentence dissolving into snores of exhaustion.

He missed Paul's repeated gesture of the Heil Hitler salute. "Will do, sir."

Chapter 2

One month after Renner came to live at St. Anthony's Catholic Orphanage (Katholisches Waisenhaus St. Anton), the snow arrived on the same day as his soon-to-be adoptive parents. The orphans instantly ditched their daily chores and rushed outside to play, throwing soft snowballs at each other that disintegrated before reaching their targets. Renner watched from inside the brown, brick building, still practically a stranger, not even sure how to play or interact with the others.

When the sleek maroon Cadillac pulled up in front of the orphanage, the children stopped, checking out the potential for adoption. Normally, the couples who showed up looked straight passed the older ones, seeking out the babies and toddlers who remained inside.

The affluent couple, giving the gawking youngsters a cursory glance, strode straight passed them, up the concrete steps and then opened the front door of the orphanage, letting in a shower of flurries. Renner froze, staring at the beautiful man and woman, so elegant and well dressed.

Mona and Konstantin Scholz. Man, they looked young, he thought, as he looked at them in his dreamscape, not only as the nine-year-old child he was back then, but also as the adult he had become. Tears welled up in his eyes.

The Scholzes approached the main office, where Schwester Gertrude welcomed them with a lilting voice. Mona explained their plight, her not able to carry a child, suffering miscarriage after mis-carriage. The couple was desperate to become parents.

Schwester Gertrude nodded empathetically, clutching Mona's right hand, the left hand busy blotting tears with a handkerchief. Spotting Renner still anchored by the window, the nun called him over, introducing him to the Scholzes. The couple's eyes instantly lit up. Despite his age, his tattered clothing and scraggly knotted hair, they were interested. Immediately, they arranged for him to come to their house for a trial period.

The Scholzes house, humble for them and their burgeoning wealth but an ultimate palace for Renner, was intimidating at first. So much space, so many rooms, such expensive furniture. But after baking gingerbread cookies with Mona and eating them until their stomachs ached, and Konstantin teaching him how to write his own name, and how to properly roll a cigarette, the palace felt like home.

With the trial period a massive success, the Scholzes returned to the orphanage to complete the paperwork, making the arrangement legal. Renner officially became their son, and for the first time ever, he felt a new emotion, totally foreign to him until that moment...happiness.

* * *

Not enough hours later, the Rolling Stones song "(I Can't Get No) Satisfaction" blasted at a thousand decibels jerked Renner out of his dreams. Opening his tear moistened eyelids, he felt momentarily confused. Where were his avocado green walls, beige gossamer curtains, and goose down comforter? Where was the delicious aroma of bacon and eggs wafting up the staircase from his *mutti's* kitchen? Then realization dawned on him—he was at BIT in his new dorm room.

He glanced at his Rolex, which he had adjusted upon landing at the airport in Seattle. The watch read 9 p.m. With the nine-hour time difference, it was actually 6 a.m. Germany time. His brain struggled below the weight of it. Groaning, he sat up, peeled himself off of the bed, realizing he was still clad in his white t-shirt and slacks, now a wrinkled mess.

Paul was rummaging through his disordered desk, knocked a lamp over, placed it back upright, and finally located what he was looking for—cologne. He generously squirted the fragrance onto his polyester dress shirt, leaving behind a spattering of tiny dark circles.

"How'd you sleep, brother?" he yelled over the music, in a haze of eye stinging scent.

"I still feel as if the earth is moving underneath me, and my head is made out of concrete, but, other than that, not too bad."

Renner rubbed away his tears, hoping Paul didn't notice, while contemplating his next move. His muscles were stiff from hauling his weighty luggage around the previous two days and sleeping in uncomfortable positions. The new bed, as lumpy and hard as a bag of walnuts, didn't help.

"Can you be ready in a half hour? I don't want to rush you, but there's a group of us going together to the bar tonight, and the other guys can get a bit impatient, if you know what I mean?"

Renner didn't know what he meant as he hadn't met these people. But still, he nodded. "Sure, no problem. I'll be quick."

Rummaging through the folded clothes in his dresser, he grabbed a taupe three-piece suit and was about to pull it out when he was interrupted by a loud cackle.

"Where do you think we're going, to a wedding or something? If you wear that, people are going to think you're a freak. Try something a little more casual." He pushed his way in front of the dresser, tossing aside shirts and pants he clearly disapproved of, finally settling on a tight baby blue dress shirt and flared denim pants. Yanking them from the dresser, he tossed them at Renner. "Here, these will have to do, I guess."

"Thanks a lot," Renner replied sarcastically, but Paul appeared to take it as legitimate gratitude. Renner shook his head, while fishing out of his luggage a clean pair of underwear and socks, a towel he had brought from home, and the rest of his bathroom essentials. "Where can I find the lavatory?"

"The what? We call it a bathroom here. It's down the hall, and to the left. We're one of the lucky four units that have to share a communal bathroom on this floor."

"Great."

"I'll wait for you here." Paul popped the top off of a Pabst Blue Ribbon beer, and sucked on the opening long and hard, as if he couldn't get the contents into his system fast enough.

Completing a short jaunt down the hall, Renner reached the communal washroom that was thankfully empty. At least, for the moment, he would have a modicum of privacy. The toilets and faucets were relatively clean. Just a few traces of soap scum left behind in the showers. The scent of pine and minty toothpaste lingered behind the last person to use the facilities.

Renner disrobed, and submerged himself in the warm, forceful shower spray, grateful the water was taking the grime away from his body and washing it down the drain. It re-alerted him, invigorated him. Gave him a second wind. Excitement burbled up in his belly once more. *I'm finally here.* He couldn't believe it. And tonight, he would get a taste of the night life, his first night in Washington State.

Drying off with his soft olive-green towel, he caught a whiff of his home in the fabric. The familiar scent tugged at his heart strings, reminding him of what he left behind, but there was no time for nostalgia. Quickly, he blow-dried his golden brown hair into soft feathery waves, and upon examining his chin and upper lip, decided a shave was in order.

When Renner returned back to the dorm room, Paul was downing his third beer of the night, the empties accumulating at his feet. "Finally. Another few minutes, and I was going to send out a search party. Let's go," he said. The two men grabbed their jackets and wallets and headed down to the main level.

Three men waited for them at the lobby entrance, which Renner promptly learned were Dennis, John, and a short, stocky fellow with a moustache that was almost as wide as he was tall named William. They also lived in the same building, just on different floors. From their alcohol-laced breath, Renner surmised they, too, had already been drinking.

They agreed on walking to the nightclub, the night balmy and the bar only several blocks away. The concrete was still darkened from the earlier rain and glistened in the streetlights. The fresh scent of moist earth tinged the air.

The group of men crossed the Hancock Bridge over the Barbora River, which gave them the ultimate view of the Seattle skyline. The city lights and skyscrapers were lit up in shades of cobalt, burgundy, and amber that bled onto the surface of the water below.

"Renner, wait until you see how easy the women are here. You don't even have to give them your name, and they're raring to go," Paul informed.

"Yeah, not like at NYU. Those girls were tight, man. And stuck up," William added.

"Did you attend the same university?" Renner asked.

"Known these boys my whole life," Paul responded, throwing his arms around Dennis and John's shoulders and drawing them in close.

William tugged a flask out of his jacket pocket, took a swig and passed the booze around to his comrades. Renner politely declined.

"What about you, Renner? Do you have a girlfriend back home?" John stared expectantly with raised eyebrows, worried their fun would be dampened by the prospect. His long forehead squished his facial features together, giving him a cartoonish appearance. "Well?"

"No, not anybody special," he responded, noticing a collective sigh of relief from the assembly.

"I find that hard to believe," Paul interjected. "Handsome guy such as yourself. Filthy rich. Women must flock around you, ripe for the plucking."

"I don't have time for a relationship. I've dated girls, but I'm too focused on my studies to have anything long term. I'm not the marrying type."

When they reached the nightclub, cleverly named The Seattle Outpost as the location was on the outer edge of Seattle, Renner was surprised. From the outside, the squat building looked as if it were a regular automotive garage, the patrons oozing out of the building and onto the sidewalk the solitary clue that there was a discotheque in full swing within its brick walls.

Renner and his companions weaved through the permeable membrane of patrons, slipping inside the building already thick with cigarette smoke. They climbed a wide staircase leading them into a cavernous room bathed in flashing lights. Disco music blared from the speakers.

Renner's platform shoes stuck to the booze-soaked floor with each step. Bodies were packed from wall to wall, some standing and drinking, others gyrating to the music underneath a giant mirrored ball on the dance floor.

Relieved he wasn't claustrophobic, Renner moved with his group as one, heading straight towards the upstairs bar. The atmosphere was stiflingly hot. Damp, sweaty bodies pressed against him as they squeezed through the throng, leaving behind dewy patches on his clothes and arms. The heavy cigarette smoke saturated his hair and clothing. He pined for the shower back at the dorm, destined to revisit it again that night.

At the bar, Renner and his new friends all purchased beers and the frosty suds instantly cooled him down.

Surveying from their higher vantage point, he could see that the nightclub was separated into three levels: the uppermost level had VIP tables surrounded by high-backed chairs, the middle level was cluttered with standing tables, which encircled the lowest and most popular level, the dance floor. The establishment's walls were stone grey, the floor, varnished hardwood.

Women were everywhere. Tight, shiny hot pants, bared midriffs, garish makeup. His companions eyed up the assortment, as if they were entrees at a buffet.

Paul elbowed Renner in the ribs, and then yelled into his ear over the raucous noise, "I think she fancies you." He pointed with his beer at a small, skinny red-haired girl wearing silver tights, platform shoes that did little to heighten her tiny frame, and a peasant blouse that exposed her pale abdomen. Makeup caked her eyes and mouth as if she had broken into her mother's cosmetic bag. She looked to be about twelve-years-old. With huge eyes sparkling, she licked her lips in what she probably thought was a seductive way but made Renner feel embarrassed for her. Her tiny hand came up in a playful wave.

Renner turned to Paul. "No thanks."

"Her friend's kind of hot, though," Paul acknowledged. The friend was auburn-haired, a bit taller and equally young looking.

"Go for it," Renner encouraged, taking another swig from his Heineken. He pulled out a cigarette, lit the end and took a deep haul. He offered Paul a smoke, who graciously accepted.

"In a minute. Let them pine away for a bit."

The girls continued staring, smiling, unashamed.

"Sorry we didn't get to talk too much when I arrived…well, for falling asleep mid-conversation. I was so exhausted," Renner apologized, exhaling cigarette smoke.

"No problem."

"So, what are you taking?" Renner asked.

"Just a bit of weed here and there. I tried LSD once. Didn't enjoy the feeling. Scary stuff," Paul smirked.

"Very funny. I meant at BIT." Their college dorm was strictly for graduate students. How could this partying womanizer come so far in his education?

"Genetics," he replied. He grabbed a handful of salted peanuts from a bowl atop the bar, munching open-mouthed.

Genetics? This surprised Renner even more. "Really? I didn't realize we were in the same field. What part of genetics are you interested in? Genetic diseases, genotyping, forensics?"

"None of those. I'm focused more on genetic enhancement. Specifically geared towards the military's use one day," Paul answered smugly. He crammed another handful of peanuts into his maw, winking a blue eye.

"What kind of research?" Renner had to ask.

Paul pressed his finger against his lips. "Shhhh. It's a secret. If I told you, then I'd have to kill you," he said. "But, wouldn't you like to know."

"You're kidding, right?"

"How do I know what side you're working for? Maybe you're a spy? You are German."

"You're such an ass," Renner stated, defensively. Now he could tell Paul was teasing him, but he had heard enough barbs about his nationality.

"Take it easy, man. You know I'm just joking. If you're going to hang around with me, you're going to have to grow some thicker skin."

"Well, maybe you can figure out a genetic enhancement that will help me to do that."

"Touché." He nodded, smiling.

Even though he was annoyed, Renner was equally intrigued about Paul's research. "So, what kind of enhancements are you talking about?"

Paul continued in a hushed tone. "What do you think would happen if our soldiers fighting in the war were larger, stronger, smarter and faster than our adversaries? What if they could heal themselves, block out pain, last days without food or sleep, even have the ability to defy death itself?" Paul paused for dramatic effect.

The answer was obvious. The American soldiers would annihilate their competition. Renner knew exactly what Paul was hinting at. There were rumours swirling around about covert military-based genetic research being conducted to develop a super-soldier by enhancing certain favourable attributes in humans: endurance, strength, size, improved healing capabilities, increased longevity. But, this could only be at the hypothetical stage. The concept was so riddled with moral, social, and ethical considerations that it was merely a rumour, right? He wondered.

"But, how?" Renner questioned. "The Research Ethics Board would never approve of such a thing, especially not at the BIT campus."

"Oh, but they have."

Renner looked at Paul skeptically, brows furrowed in disbelief.

"With animals, of course," Paul added.

Renner's eyebrows relaxed. Well, that made more sense. "What kind of animals are you working with?"

"Mainly rats, but we have dogs at our disposal as well."

Mice and rats were most commonly used in animal research as they were abundant in supply and highly affordable as opposed to monkeys, dogs, pigs, and other larger mammals, all of which have anatomy resembling humans' but were more difficult and expensive to provide. The drawback to using rodents was that the findings to these studies were not always able to be generalized to human beings. It was fortunate that Paul would be able to use canines in his experiment for this reason.

Renner experienced a sudden pang of jealousy, and even a bit of panic. He still had to write his research proposal, let alone have the proposal submitted and cleared by the ethics board. He wondered how Paul had managed to have his proposal finished and approved even before the school year had commenced. Before he had a chance to ask him, Paul interrupted.

"Well, I think those lovely ladies have suffered long enough. Let's go show them a good time." Extinguishing his cigarette into a metal ashtray on the bar, he sauntered up to the young girls, in full swagger mode.

The other members of their group had peeled off during his and Paul's intriguing conversation and gone mingling in their own separate ways. Not wanting to be left alone, Renner begrudgingly followed Paul and the two child-like women out onto the dance floor, finding a millimetre of space to squeeze into.

Bumped from all directions by adjacent dancers, Renner pondered what Paul had said. Renner's favourite place on earth was to be in a lab knee-deep in beakers, test tubes and chemical solutions. However, he wouldn't be able to start his research for weeks, until he got the final clearance from the ethics board. Meanwhile, Paul would be starting immediately.

Paul's research was extremely progressive—cutting edge—and even though the concept was still in the hypothetical stages, he could gain vast recognition, maybe even win a Nobel Prize if he were able to help the government develop a super-soldier. He would have several job offers immediately upon graduation, and his career path would be set. Renner's ears burned, his stomach tightened. His mood completely soured.

It wasn't fair.

The young red-head continued to leer at Renner as she danced, making him even more uncomfortable. Paul, oblivious to Renner's inner turmoil, flailed rigorously to Abba's "Waterloo." Renner tried to shrink down into his dress shirt as he awkwardly stepped side to side. He wasn't much of a dancer, but the red-head didn't seem to mind. She inched closer, until her hips rubbed gently against his pelvis. Any attempts at his backing away were thwarted by the surrounding dancers, and if anything, they pushed him even closer to her. He subconsciously slowed down and then eventually stopped moving altogether. Sweat trickled down the side of his face, his neck.

"I need another drink. I'll be right back," he politely excused himself.

"I'll come with you," she stated a little too desperately, grabbing his arm.

"No, no. You stay here. Keep my spot. I'll be right back," he lied. Disappointment ravaged her pretty features. As he walked away, he didn't have to look back to know that her emerald eyes followed him the entire way as he escaped back to the bar.

Ordering another Heineken, he took a deep breath, running his hand through his sweat dampened hair. He was ready to leave. Keeping his eyes averted from the dance floor, he devised his plan of exit. He had a relatively good idea as to the route that would lead him back to Leighton House. And even getting lost would be better than this blessed hell.

Dennis sidled up to Renner with his bloated face and vein-riddled nose already exhibiting the classic signs of alcoholism. He ordered another round of drinks for himself and a chubby woman at his side, whose cheeks were flushed from dancing. Dennis leaned over, and yelled too loudly into Renner's ear, breath rank from beer and residual garlic from whatever he ate for dinner, "Are you having a good time?"

"Yeah, great," Renner replied without conviction. "But, I'm pretty tired. I think I'll head out soon."

"Are you sure? The place is just starting to pick up."

Renner couldn't imagine how the bar would be at full throttle. He was sure the establishment was already violating fire safety laws by being well over capacity.

"Sorry, I don't want to be a downer, but I'm feeling a little jet-lagged. I need sleep. I'll see you around, though."

"Yeah, of course. We're going out tomorrow night too. You should come."

Another night of raucous congested partying and drinking? He thought not but nodded anyway. "Sure. See you tomorrow."

One more stop before leaving—saying goodbye to Paul—proved harder than he anticipated. Women, emboldened by the liquid courage they had been consuming all night, approached Renner, attempting to engage him in conversation, and although he was unresponsive, that didn't stop them from trying.

At present, a blond stuffed into the most gravity-defying bra he had ever seen, boobs hiked up to her chin, was glued to his side chattering in a squirrelly manner, interrupting him every time he attempted to make an exit. As she continued her mundane monologue, the main door to the pub swung open. He's not sure what it was, the door opening and closing all night reminiscent of a western saloon, but something provoked Renner to look up at that precise moment.

Three women stood at the opened doors. Renner specifically noticed one of them—the one with long raven coloured hair, dark smoky eye makeup framed by long fan-like eyelashes, red pillow-y lips. She wore a strapless black jumpsuit that fit tightly over her curvaceous, lean figure. Suddenly, she laughed at something her friend said, her large white teeth momentarily lighting up the bar's atmosphere.

Renner took a sharp intake of breath. She was the most exotic, strikingly beautiful woman he had ever seen, with an olive complexion, and almond-shaped azure eyes, catlike, dangerous. He temporarily forgot about his desire to flee.

"Are you even listening to me?" Chin-Boobs squeaked, her pink cleavage glaring at him accusingly. "I bet you haven't heard a word I said!"

"Ah, yes, of course, I'm listening," he stammered, eyes still riveted to the exotic woman now gliding effortlessly through the bar.

The blond noticed where his attention was focused. "Forget it!" she blurted as she stormed off.

Renner took his eyes off of the exotic woman for barely an instant, his eyes flickering to the pissed blond as she hustled away. But that was long enough. When he looked back up to find the black-haired bombshell, he couldn't find her, swallowed up by the crowd.

Frantic, he scanned the premises. A few times, he thought he spotted her in the distance, a flash of wavy, dark hair, but when he would finally reach the woman he was following he would realize that it was a false alarm. It wasn't her after all. Walking in circles around the nightclub, he searched and searched for over thirty minutes without success.

On one of his rounds, he ran into Dennis again, who was now totally plastered.

"Arrreyou sssttill 'ere? I thought you 'ere leavin'?"

"I was, but…hey, did you happen to see a gorgeous woman with long black hair come by?"

"There're lots of pretty women 'ere. Could 'ou be more ssspe-cific?" he spat in Renner's face.

Wiping the spittle off of his cheek with the back of his arm, he said, "Trust me, if you saw her you would know. She's stunning."

"Well, then, if I see 'er, I might have to keep 'er fer mmmyself." Elbow to the ribs.

Renner must have displayed a look of panic because Dennis quickly replied, "Hey, relax. I'm just pulling yer pubes. I'll keep a look out for 'er, and let you know the second I see 'er." He flung a sweaty arm around Renner's shoulders in a friendly manner, stumbled a little drunkenly then regained his footing. "You gonna try hook up with her tonight, you little devil?" His face was mere inches from Renner's nose.

Renner tried not to gag. "I…never mind."

He peeled Dennis' sweaty arm off of his shoulder and squeezed back into the crowd, Dennis yelling behind him, "Good luck. I 'ope you find 'er."

Renner wasn't even sure of what he was going to do once he found the exotic woman. Sure, she gave him something more exciting to focus on, had even slightly improved his night, but he didn't want a relationship, didn't want any distractions from his studies, and she didn't look the type to pursue for a one-night stand. Yet, he was so drawn to her.

Peculiar.

He had never experienced this before, especially not over someone he had seen across a room. Balked at the idea of love at first sight. But he couldn't ignore the bunched feeling in his gut, and butterflies—yes, butterflies—whenever he thought of her voluptuous figure framed in the entranceway.

So, perhaps he would find her to admire her beauty once more. That would be enough to make him happy. No talking or contact, for that would be dangerous. Too tempting. One final look and then he would be on his way.

But, after searching for over an hour, he finally gave up. She was nowhere to be found. She probably left at some point during his rounds, and here he was searching for her in idiot fashion when he could be back at the dorm by now, sleeping like a baby.

Time to say his goodbyes.

Wobbling sideways, penguin style, he squeezed between the patrons to get back onto the dance floor, back over to Paul, who continued to thrash maniacally. They almost head-butted as a result of his roommate's spastic dancing. Grabbing him by the shoulders, holding him still enough to avoid a concussion, Renner announced he was leaving. He was relieved to see the young red-head had finally disappeared. Her friend was still dancing with Paul, looking beyond a little tipsy.

"OK. See you back at the room. Don't wait up," Paul yelled back, barely breaking stride.

Renner abruptly turned around to leave and collided into a raven-haired woman carrying an armload of drinks. It was her, the woman from the door, the one he had been searching for most of the night. She hadn't left after all.

She stood before him, soda and beer cascading down her ample cleavage all the way down to her platform boots. Her face first expressed surprise but then quickly morphed into fury.

"Hey, watch where you're going!" she fumed.

"Ah, *scheisse*. I—I am so, so sorry," Renner stammered. He grabbed the empty glasses and beer bottle from her hands. "I'll be right back."

Sprinting as fast as the throng would allow, he reached the standing tables, dumped the empty glasses onto an already overflowing surface, yanked a handkerchief from his pocket and raced back to the woman who still stood frozen, arms stiff and outstretched at her sides dripping onto the dance floor. The dancers around her, including Paul and his conquest, had stopped to watch.

"I am so sorry," he repeated, all he could come up with as he tried to mop off the liquor and pop with his handkerchief.

"What do you think you're doing?" she demanded in a thick Polish accent.

Paul guffawed.

Renner realized then that he was wiping off her bosom. His skin flashed crimson.

"I think I got it," she hissed and grabbed his hand to obtain the soiled handkerchief, to clean her own bosom. As their hands touched, her facial features changed, registering first surprise as her eyes grew wide, and then confusion as her face softened. She looked into his turquoise eyes, penetrating his very core with her gaze. Suddenly, she pulled him towards her, her lips pressed against his ear. He inhaled deeply her sweet, spicy scent, which immediately clouded his head, warming him in all the right places.

Huskily into his ear, her breath warm on his skin, she whispered, "One day you will be my husband."

He watched her smile—a fabulously rich, warm and mysterious smile—then spin around, and disappear into the crowd once more.

Chapter 3

The following morning Renner awoke with a pounding headache and the lingering smell of cigarette smoke in his hair despite the second shower he took before bed. He didn't feel as disoriented when he opened his eyes this time. Knowing exactly where he was, remembering everything that had happened the day before. Most importantly, he remembered his encounter with the mysterious woman.

What did she mean that one day he would be her husband?

Was she teasing him? Or was the phrase some sort of pick up line or saying that he wasn't familiar with?

Would he even see her again? He didn't know her name, where she was from, if she was a student at BIT, where she worked if she had a job or if she was even single for that matter. And if he did find her, would she be upset with him over the spilled drinks, her ruined clothing? She hadn't appeared upset when she walked off, but maybe after thinking more about the incident, her anger would be re-ignited.

He crawled out of bed, rummaged through his luggage and found the Aspirin his head sorely needed. Attempting to dry swallow two pills, they lodged in his throat. After several failed attempts to get the pills to complete their journey to his stomach, he finally slunk over to Paul's disordered side of the room.

"Hey, Paul. Do you have anything to drink?"

Paul pulled a rumpled pillow over his head, blocking the sound of his roommate's voice.

A glance at the clock on Paul's desk indicated the time was already 10 a.m., hours after Renner would normally get up. He didn't feel it was too early to awaken Paul. Plus, the pills were starting to dissolve at the back of this throat, causing him to gag.

"Paul!"

Paul peeked out from beneath the pillow. "What the hell?"

"Sorry, but I'm choking on some Aspirin here. Do you have anything to drink?"

"There's beer in the cooler." Rolling over, he went back to sleep.

Desperate, Renner grabbed the beer out of the cooler, the ice from the previous night now a pool of water. Downing the luke-warm suds, he noted the irony of taking his medication with the very culprit for causing his headache in the first place. Hair of the dog, is that how the saying went?

After pulling on a clean pair of jeans and a brown turtleneck, Renner glanced at his comatose roommate. Briefly, he'd imagined them navigating the vast campus grounds together, Paul helping him find his way as he'd already been there a few days. Not that Renner wasn't used to doing things on his own. He was a bit of a loner, with many acquaintances but no real friends.

Guess I'm on my own today.

Ravenous, his first objective was to find some sustenance. Slipping on a pair of sunglasses, and pocketing his class schedule and campus map, he left the dormitory, venturing down the same path the boys had used the previous night when walking to the bar. He had seen many cafés along the way.

The morning was mild, rain-free, the clouds fanned across the aqua sky in ribbons of white. Sailboats bobbed in a line chasing the wind across the Barbora River as Renner passed over the Hancock Bridge.

Within several minutes he found a quaint eatery that wasn't too busy, the Coffee Maker Café. He purchased an apple strudel and large black coffee. Other patrons, some probably students, checked him out as he walked to a round table towards the back of the café. He felt self-conscious, not an abnormal feeling for him, his places of comfort restricted to his home, the school or the lab.

Trying to ignore the stares, he shifted his focus onto his future, and how his success would bring him a different kind of attention, where he would stand out in a revered and admired way. He had achieved that attention during his medical studies back in Germany but realized it might be a tad more challenging at the prestigious university of BIT and at the graduate level, no less. But he was determined.

His pastry tasted bland and dry, his coffee watery. Disappointed, he choked them down, and returned the dirty plate to the front counter where a pimple-faced boy was taking an order from a new customer.

Renner glided out the door, ready to explore his new environment. Fishing a cigarette out of his front pocket, he lit up, and took a few deep hauls. He always craved a cigarette following meals. Loyal to KS cigarettes, smoking always made him think of his father.

Konstantin Scholz—a self-made man running the most successful cigarette company in Germany. Even the advertisements for KS cigarettes were popular back home. Everybody knew the KS brand jingle, had the song memorized, even children. He remembered the secretary at the admissions desk the day before. Even in America, his father's brand was known.

Renner still thought of his father as the strong, virile man that launched the company and made it an enormous success. However, the man that he'd left behind in Erfurt no longer fit that image. Konstantin Scholz was now frail, walked with agonizing difficulty, and occasionally suffered from relentless coughing fits leaving bloody sputum on his handkerchief, although he tried to hide this from his wife and son. Konstantin Scholz was dying. This fact was obvious despite his efforts to act as if nothing was wrong. Renner had a gut feeling that, ironically, the cigarettes had sickened his father. Lung cancer was his guess. The phlegm rattled breathing, coughing fits, shortness of breath with even the slightest activity, the dramatic weight loss.

Yeah, definitely cancer.

Recent studies were showing the correlation between nicotine use and diagnoses of lung cancer and other cancers, indicating that cigarette smoking and chewing tobacco had carcinogenic effects. *Who'd have thought?* Renner continued to take drags from his own cigarette. He barely smoked, intended to kick the habit but resisted as it was a link to his father. Sometimes he could be loyal to a fault.

It saddened him to think of his father so ill, and his mother, incapable of being on her own. She didn't even know how to drive, relying on Konstantin as her chauffer.

Thinking of his parents, Renner felt a pang of guilt. Perhaps he was selfish to leave them in such a state. But, what he planned to do at BIT—with his studies and his research, with his future career—was also for them. He wanted to help find a treatment or even ultimately a cure for cancer—maybe not in time to save his father but at least to make him proud while he was still alive. To know his son was making a difference in the world. This line of thinking always reassured him about his decision to leave his parents behind.

Grinding his cigarette butt against the pavement with the heel of his boot, he placed his feelings on the backburner and retrieved the school map and schedule from the back pocket of his jeans. He had retraced his steps, coming back over the Hancock Bridge to the BIT campus and now stood in front of Kings Court. Created by surrounding interconnected university buildings made from limestone, the courtyard was a square space of green grass, perfect for students wishing to hang out and catch some sun. Now was no exception. Four young women sat upon a quilt, legs splayed out in front of them, trying to catch the few rays that managed to squeak past the cumulous clouds. Two men tossed a Frisbee back and forth. One of the men tripped while diving for the Frisbee, and the women giggled.

From the map, Renner discerned that most of his classes were on the east side of campus, so that's where he headed, turning right and walking down Brassard Road, and then left onto Abbey Drive. As he approached the cluster of science buildings, his heart leaped in his chest.

He couldn't wait for classes to begin.

Strolling a little further, he found where his first class was to be held, The Research and Academic Center. The three-story rectangular building looked ethereal, the sun bouncing off of the windows creating a glimmering effect. Etching the location in his brain, he looked back down at the map to locate the next building on his list. Bromley House, a little further up the road.

As he drifted down the sidewalk, a gentle wind patted his back with phantom fingers. A sudden deep chill settled into his bones as if he was locked in a meat freezer. He had an impulsive urge to look behind him.

Was he being followed?

Despite the strange sensation of another presence, when he turned around there was nobody behind him.

Renner, the wind sighed.

The hairs rose at the nape of his neck, and he shivered. He shook his head as if that would get rid of the strange feeling. Was he hearing things?

He took a few more steps forward. And again, distinctly, he could hear a noise behind him, a shuffling set of second footsteps. But when he looked behind him, there was still nobody there. Just the shadows snaking, and undulating along the grass and concrete, and up over the buildings and trees.

Was somebody playing tricks on him? He wouldn't put it past Paul. Perhaps his roommate had roused from his coma and was attempting to pull a prank on him.

Hyperaware of his surroundings, he again continued forward but after hearing the sound of shuffling behind him and choosing to rule out auditory hallucinations, he spun around.

"Show yourself!" Renner demanded. He wasn't one for games or to let himself get spooked. A young couple walking on the other side of the street looked at him as if he had lost his marbles. They visibly picked up their pace, scurrying away in the opposite direction.

"Is anybody there?" Renner demanded again.

"Who are you talking to?" Suddenly, the petite red-haired girl he had met at the bar the night before, appeared on the path ahead of him.

Renner looked behind him once more. Nothing was there. Even the shadows had stopped moving.

"Were you following me?" he asked. Up close, in the cloud filtered daylight, he noticed that her hair was more strawberry-blond than red, and she was somewhat cute. Freckles dusted the bridge of her nose. She wore a bright pink jacket over a black miniskirt, and tights. The garish makeup from the night before was wiped clean, replaced with a dab of blusher on her cheekbones and peach gloss on her thin lips.

"No, silly. I was coming from the other direction. I heard you yelling at someone, and then recognized you from last night. I thought I'd come and say hi." She gazed at him adoringly. "I'm Wendy Scott." She thrust out a tiny freckled hand.

"Renner Scholz." Accepting the hand, he gave it a gentle shake, careful not to crush her little carpals and metacarpals. The second their skin made contact, she blushed. Looked down at her knee-high boots. Looked back up and batted her barely-there eyelashes.

In a voice high and nasal, she asked, "Where're you headed?"

"I was going over my schedule and finding the location of my classrooms, so I'm not scrambling to find everything on the first day," he answered, already bored of their conversation. Why did this seemingly harmless girl annoy him so much?

"So, you're a BIT student as well?"

Renner nodded.

"What're you taking? I'm starting my first year in writing and humanistic studies, majoring in creative writing. I was also going over my schedule. Do you mind if I tag along?" she asked excitedly.

"Well, I…"

"Thanks. I'm headed towards the west side of campus. That's where most of my classes are held."

He breathed a sigh of relief. "Well, my classes are mainly on the east side, so we might as well go our separate ways."

"Oh, well, that's OK. I'll join you anyways," she shrugged, smiling. "My dream is to be a poet. I've already written ninety poems, and I'm going to publish them as a book one day. Do you want to hear one?"

Before Renner could object, she began reciting a short haiku. She began: "Eyes of crystal glass, Cut right through my defences, Takes my breath away."

"Well, what do you think?" she asked.

He couldn't tell her the truth, so he simply nodded.

"I made that one up right now, off the top of my head," she proudly exclaimed.

"I couldn't tell," he replied sarcastically.

"The poem is about you," she blushed again.

That made the poem all the worse. Now Renner was annoyed and uncomfortable.

The next hour was spent walking from science building to science building, through subterranean tunnel systems jam-packed with students, and walls decorated with artwork, banners, and flyers. All the while, Wendy babbled incessantly about random thoughts that popped into her head, while trying to rub up against him every chance she got.

They paused for a break in an underground domed atrium, three stories high.

"This is Veteran's Lobby," Wendy announced, admiring the stained-glass ceiling depicting soldiers at war. She pulled Renner over to get a better view. "These engravings in the walls are the names of all the American soldiers, once alumni, who have fallen in each of the wars."

Renner walked up closer to the names and quickly found the wall displaying the soldiers that had sacrificed their lives fighting in World War II. He studied the names, there were so many of them. Gently tracing the rough grooves etched deeply in the concrete with his fingertips, he wondered if any of these brave soldiers had died by his biological father's hand.

"Renner?"

"What?"

"Are you OK? You look a little funny. As if you're a million miles away."

"No, I'm fine."

Finally completing the tour of Renner's classes on the BIT campus, he wanted to jump for joy. The constant drone of Wendy's nasally voice was scratching away at his nerves. But, she had attached herself to his side like a boil. She quickly proved that lancing her from his company wasn't going to be easy.

"What do you want to do for lunch? I know the best places to eat. I am from Seattle, you know. There's Francesco's Pizza, The Terrace, Café Desjardin. So, what do you think?" She waited for a response this time.

He was famished, the lack of food back at the dorm a reminder that there wouldn't be any sustenance for him unless he ate out. The distasteful breakfast had long been burned off by the extensive morning trek across campus. He supposed he could endure Wendy's company for a few more minutes. Perhaps he could use her for more information on the area, besides the best places to dine. He would also avoid having another meal alone with people gawking at him.

"Sure," he responded against his better judgment, her pleasure instantly obvious.

"Wow. I love your accent. Where are you from?" she asked.

"Germany."

"I once knew a girl from Germany. Well, I didn't really know her, but she lived on my street. Or, maybe she wasn't even from Germany. Was she from Austria? Anyway..." And off she went with her disconnected blathering for the remainder of the walk.

They climbed over the Hancock Bridge, and then down a small alleyway lined with restaurants and cafés. Mouth-watering aromas floated to Renner on the breeze, causing his stomach to rumble.

"Oh my gosh. I almost forgot about Loretta's. We should totally eat here. This is my absolute favourite place to eat in the whole wide world," she professed.

The savoury smells of garlic, tomato sauce, basil and oregano wafted into Renner's nose. Glass doors framed by a red, green, and white awning opened up to a stairway that descended into an authentic Italian restaurant. An older Italian fellow with slick black hair and a potbelly led them to a vacant table.

Renner had been gone from home a few short days, but he already missed his mutti's cooking. This would be the first home-style cooked meal he would have upon arriving in America.

They sat at a round table donned in a checkered tablecloth, where a waitress swiftly filled their glasses with chilled water. The restaurant was sparsely decorated—mainly wrought iron tables, chairs, and artwork depicting Sicilian landscapes adorning the walls. The servers wore identical uniforms, crisp white blouses tucked into pressed black dress pants. They all looked to be of Italian descent and were probably related. A family-owned business.

After a quick perusal of the menu, Renner ordered spaghetti and meatballs, Wendy a thin-crusted pepperoni pizza. The food was delivered piping hot within minutes.

Wendy paused briefly to take a bite of her order, and then continued talking with a full mouth. He had long ago lost track of her conversation. Tuning her out was the only way he could handle being in her presence. He planned on ditching her after lunch.

When she directed a question towards him, he attempted to pick up on what she was talking about.

"Are you going to the bar again tonight? I'm going with some of my friends. You know Tammy? She was dancing with us last night. I think she hooked up with your friend." She took a messy bite of pizza, sauce dribbling down her chin. "Anyhow, she'll be there. And Lois, and Jan. Maybe Teresa."

It exasperated him to no end how she would ask him a question and then neglect to leave him time to respond.

"Your friend Paul said he was going to be there. And tonight, there's a live band playing, The Tortured Minotaur. Have you heard of them? They're a local band, not very good in my opinion. But the bar should be pretty packed. It'll definitely be a great time. I hope you come."

Renner remembered the stifling heat and congestion from the bodies. The overwhelming noise. His annoying companions.

What about the raven-haired woman that he had doused in drinks? Would she be there?

As if to remind him, his head started pounding again whether from the effects of the Aspirin wearing off or from his new acquaintance's banter.

"I think I'll stay in tonight. I should get back to the dorm. I haven't even properly unpacked yet. I should probably get some rest too. I have a bit of a headache."

Dabbing his mouth with a linen napkin, hoping she'd take the hint and do the same, he then stood up, reached into his back pocket for his wallet and threw down on the table enough American bills to cover both of their meals, plus a hearty tip for the waitress.

"Oh, sure. Too bad, though. I'll miss you tonight, Renner," she blushed flirtatiously, batting her sparse strawberry-blond lashes.

"Goodbye, Wendy."

She looked surprised. "I can walk you back to your place," she offered, hopeful.

"Thanks, but I could use some quiet time right now."

"OK," she replied, crestfallen. "I'll see you soon." She reached her face up to kiss Renner, to his horror, on the lips. He deftly turned his head in the nick of time, her lips landing on his cheek instead, leaving behind a trace of pizza sauce. Cringing, he swiped it away.

Her face transitioned from the shade of roses to plums. Fleeing the restaurant, she sprinted up the stairs back onto the street and took off down the alley.

The resultant silence was glorious. Renner strolled back to the dorm, his headache already diminishing to a dull throb.

Back at Leighton House, upon entering his room, he noticed Paul was no longer there. Prime time to unpack. Pulling out a drawer from the bottom of the wardrobe, he stuffed his underwear and socks inside. He hung up a few shirts and trousers, now wrinkled from being left in his suitcase too long. The desk drawers were small but were able to hold most of his papers, pens, and other school supplies.

Once unpacked, a glance at the room in its entirety displayed an imaginary line separating Renner's immaculate side from Paul's disarray. Renner would attempt to put up with the untidiness of his roommate but thought that type of disorder was inexcusable. A disordered living space meant a disordered mind.

Sitting at his own desk, he pulled out a piece of paper and plucked a pen from the metal pencil cup holder he had unpacked and started writing a letter to his parents as promised, ensuring them he had arrived safely. His mutti and *vati* would already be checking daily for his correspondence. Folding the paper, he then sealed the letter within a white envelope, ready to be sent the following day.

Shuffling through papers from his undergraduate studies, he found the one he was looking for. "Genetic Engineering and Forced Mutations: Implications for the Future Study of Human Disease and Treatment." This was his focus in genetics, and the research that he was planning for his graduate thesis, working alongside Dr. Shubally.

Paul suddenly walked in the door, causing Renner to jump.

"Hey, Renner my man, where've you been?" he asked, blinding Renner with his brown and white, flower print short-sleeve shirt tucked into tight periwinkle trousers.

"I took a tour of the campus, and finished unpacking. You?"

Paul deposited a case of beer on his desk, and then sat on the mustard-coloured lounge chair in the middle of the room.

"Just out. You look better today. Are you still up for tonight?" he asked.

"I'm going to decline this time."

"All right, suit yourself. There'll be loads of chances in the future, I can assure you of that," he winked.

"I heard you lucked out with that brown-haired girl last night. I ran in to her friend, Wendy."

"Oh, really? I don't remember," he replied, uninterested. "What are you doing, studying already? School hasn't even started."

"I'm going over one of my old papers. On Monday, I'm meeting with Dr. Shubally, to go over the research that I'll be doing here. I want to get my head on straight," Renner explained.

"Oh, you're one of those." Paul rolled his eyes.

"What's that supposed to mean?"

"Nothing. Hey, there's a group of students meeting in the lounge on the second floor. Have you met the headmasters?"

Renner shook his head in the negative.

"They'll be there. We're ordering Chinese food and we'll get to meet the other students staying here at Leighton House. That apparently is an important component here, socializing with our own kind. Do you want to come?"

Renner, still not sure what to make of his roommate, glanced over at the wind-up alarm clock on his desk. He couldn't believe the time was already a quarter past six, supper time.

"Alright," he accepted Paul's invitation, not ready to write off a free meal.

They shuffled down the stairs, joining other students heading in the same direction. They entered the lounge, which was already half full. The smell of Chinese food and fresh brewed coffee filled the space. There was a long table lining the far wall filled with boxes of steaming rice, beef and greens, egg rolls, Cantonese style chow mein, coffee, cream and sugar, and even some home-baked chocolate chip cookies. The two men stood in line behind the other students that were already stacking their plates full of delicacies. After grabbing their food, they found some empty sofa chairs, and sat down to eat.

Dennis, from the night before, appeared at their spot. A huge grin erupted on his bloated, red face. "Renner, did you find the woman you were looking for last night?" He pulled up a chair beside them. His hair was dishevelled as if he'd recently woken from a nap, his weak chin sporting stubble.

Renner looked embarrassed, cleared his throat. "Um, I did, yes."

Paul's interest piqued, he nudged Renner with his elbow, "Are you holding back on me, man? Did you meet a woman last night? Come on, spill the beans."

Renner confessed his humiliating story, how he ran into the exotic woman causing her to dump drinks all over herself by accident.

Paul responded by laughing hysterically. "Oh, that girl. I saw the whole thing. You should have seen the look on her face. She was pissed!" He almost fell out of his chair he was laughing so hard. "That's so embarrassing, man. I think you blew your chances."

Renner felt Paul was enjoying this a little too much. He didn't appreciate being the butt of a joke. He also didn't appreciate to hear that he might have ruined his chances with the beautiful woman. Not that he was looking for a relationship. But, still.

"Well, there was more. Something kind of weird. At first, she looked furious, and I thought she was going to slap me."

"That would've been even more awesome," Paul chortled. Dennis chuckled in agreement.

Renner ignored them. "But then she grabbed my hand, and something happened, something changed in her eyes, her expression.

She said one day I will be her husband. What do you think that means?" he asked, plunging a fork full of rice into his mouth.

"I think that means you should run in the opposite direction. You haven't even taken her on a date yet, and she's already trying to chain you down? Run. Don't look back," Dennis replied, eyes wide.

"He's right. You don't even know her name. Sounds crazy to me," Paul affirmed.

"Ah, I don't know. There's something about her."

"Oh no. Sounds as if you're already under her spell," Dennis said.

"I've never seen anyone like her. I just have a feeling."

"Well, you asked for our advice. It's up to you if you want to take it," said Paul.

"It doesn't matter either way. I'll probably never even see her again."

Their plates were almost empty, a few crumbs left. Renner slurped down the last of his coffee and placed his cup on the end table.

"Time to get ready for tonight," Paul exclaimed, standing up and brushing the cookie crumbs off of his trousers. "I got the beer," he addressed Dennis.

"Let's meet in my room, have a few drinks and then we can go. John and William will meet us there too. Maybe in twenty minutes or so?" Dennis suggested.

"Are you sure you don't want to tag along?" Paul asked Renner once more.

"Nah, I'm good. I'm going to turn in early tonight. I think I have a bit of residual jet lag. Plus, I have a lot of things to do tomorrow. I haven't even picked up my textbooks, and school starts in two days. I want to make sure I'm prepared," Renner answered bracing himself for more of Paul's criticism. This time, none came. "Do you know what time the bookstore opens?"

"The Text-Mart and Supplies? The store should be open by 9:30 or 10 a.m. I still have a few more books to grab. Maybe we can all go together?" Dennis suggested.

"It's a plan," Paul responded. They agreed to aim for 11 a.m., not too early. The boys would be partying again tonight.

★ ★ ★

The following day, the clock read 1 p.m. by the time Paul rolled out of bed. Renner had kept busy organizing his room, escaping for a quick bite to eat at the horrible café he had visited the previous morning, and then relaxed in their "living room" with a book on genetics.

Paul took all of ten minutes to get ready and then they climbed a floor to knock on Dennis's door. He, too, had recently awakened. His stubble was now progressing to beard stage. "Let's go," he announced. Apparently, showers weren't big here.

They headed out into the rain, each of the men pulling up their hoods to protect their long tresses from the dampness.

The Text-Mart and Supplies Store was in the Student Center at BIT. Once inside the building they pulled off their hoods and separated in search of the textbooks they required for their classes. Renner and Paul headed towards the section on genetics, while Dennis disappeared in search of the neurobiology texts.

"I'll grab a cart," Paul suggested. Seconds later, he returned with a metal push cart, the left wheel gone rogue, spinning erratically as he pulled up beside Renner. "You can share with me."

Renner had already found the first text on his list, "Principles of Biochemical Analysis" and plunked the heavy book onto the top shelf of the cart with a metallic clang.

In no time, lopsided textbook towers were teetering precariously, threatening to tip over whenever they pushed the cart forward. They kept their books on separate shelves so as not to mix them up. Renner noticed some of the books they grabbed were the same, meaning they shared more than one class.

Once his book list was completed, Renner grabbed other miscellaneous items he had left back home but would be requiring here:

a stapler, paperclips, notepads, and a calculator. He also grabbed some nonperishable snack foods and cola for their dorm. Finished, they headed towards the till to purchase their items.

As they pulled up to the till, Renner froze, the blood draining from his face.

Paul immediately noticed his roommate's pallor. "What the heck's wrong with you?"

"The cashier—that's her! The woman from the bar!"

She was stunning in a long maxi dress, white cotton with yellow and orange flowers. Her silken hair was pulled to the side and secured with an elastic band, a white gardenia blossom tucked behind her right ear.

"This should be interesting," Paul chuckled.

Renner hastily unloaded his books and other items, hoping she wouldn't notice him. Head low, eye's averted.

"It's you." She stared at him with such intensity that he grew uncomfortable. He wasn't sure if she was happy to see him or still upset about the drink incident.

"Hey, I'm sorry about the other night. You left so quickly, I didn't get the chance to properly apologize. Were your clothes ruined? I can pay for them to get dry-cleaned."

"That's OK," she replied, waving her hand in dismissal and smiling confidently. "Black doesn't stain very easily." She continued entering the purchases into the till. "Are you normally so clumsy?"

"Not usually, no."

"That's a relief. Just wondering what our future kids are going to inherit," she giggled as she loaded the food items into a paper bag.

"I beg your pardon?"

Paul stood in line behind Renner, first-hand seats to the conversation. As she looked away to type more prices into the cash register, Paul caught Renner's eye, and drew an imaginary circle beside his head, mouthing the word "crazy." She looked up, catching Paul in the act of mocking her. He attempted to act casual, scratching his head, but her eyes pinned a death glare on him, her jaw tensing.

Renner laughed sheepishly. "Yeah, I was wondering about that. The bar was so loud, I wasn't sure if I heard you properly. But, you're kidding, right?" he asked, laughing again nervously.

"I would never joke about one of my visions."

"Visions?"

Face softening, she looked deeply into Renner's eyes, causing his mouth to go dry. "Don't you believe in psychic abilities?"

He looked back at her in confusion, temporarily at a loss for words.

"By the looks of these books you're buying, you must be a scientist. Which suggests your mind is too narrow to believe," she answered her own question in a challenging tone.

Finally able to form sentences again, he asked, "Is that we're talking about here? You're a psychic?"

She nodded, sliding a package of Ding Dongs into the paper bag.

He shook his head in disbelief. "I don't mean to offend you, but if there's no logical, empirical way to assess psychic abilities, quantify them or observe them, then they can't exist. So-called psychics are simply people who're talented in pulling the wool over the eyes of weaker minded individuals. In my opinion, it's pure nonsense. And I don't need to be a scientist to know that."

She looked stung. "Well, I'm sorry you feel that way." She continued to process the order, but her mood had become sombre.

"When I think of a psychic, I picture an old lady with moles all over her wrinkled face, hovered over a crystal ball inside a circus tent. Definitely not someone like you."

She ceased putting the purchases through, and stood, hand on hip looking at him sourly. He couldn't help but notice how beautiful she looked when she was angry.

"Well, I am one…and one of the best, not to toot my own horn."

Renner was starting to think that she wasn't joking after all.

He ignored the growing line forming behind him, and the harrumphs that vocalized as he stood in place. If this was anyone else, he would have finished buying his items and simply walked off shaking his head. But, he couldn't fight the attraction he felt for this strange woman. He was feeling even more jazzed up by their debate.

"Again, I'm sorry if I've offended you. That's not my intention. I thought you were pulling my leg. There's just no proof that psychic abilities exist."

"OK, skeptic. If proof is what you need, why don't you come and sit in on one of my readings? See if you still think psychic abilities are nonsense after that," she said defiantly, a sparkle in her azure eyes.

"OK, I will."

Finishing his order, she flipped over the receipt and scribbled quickly on the back before handing the paper to Renner. "I'm Milena, by the way. Meet me at this address on Friday at 6 p.m."

He nodded in agreement.

"And I don't want to hear you say a peep during the session. You'll simply be there to observe. Do you understand?"

Again, he nodded.

"Good. I'll see you Friday night…" She paused, waiting for him to proffer his name.

"Renner. Renner Scholz," he awkwardly replied. Milena was proving to be quite the assertive woman. She had a little fire in her, making him feel challenged in a good way.

"See you Friday night, Renner Scholz."

Renner pulled his cart to the side while Milena tended to Paul's purchases. She did not look at him anymore. He felt dazed after their conversation, intrigued by Milena more so than anyone ever before and he didn't even know her. In fact, what he was learning about her so far went against the very fabric of his belief system.

A psychic.

But those sensual eyes, berry stained lips, luxurious black hair. She was stunning. He couldn't quit staring at her.

What was he getting himself into?

Chapter 4

Monday morning Renner awoke to bright sunshine streaming through the curtains, playing on the back of his eyelids like a disco ball. A tall balsam stood outside their dorm window, and a bird chirped gleefully from the tree's branches. A wake-up call. Renner turned to face his desk clock. It was exactly five minutes before his wind-up alarm was set to chime. *Perfect timing.*

Switching off the alarm, he slipped out of bed. Today was the first day of classes and Renner's stomach was packed with butterflies.

Paul still slept in a tangle of arms, legs and sheets. Head not even visible. They were starting their day off in the same class, Genetics for Graduate Students, and Renner wondered if he should bother waking Paul.

Before he could make up his mind, Paul's alarm blared, causing Renner to jump like a startled cat. An arm shot out of the sheets, slammed the snooze button and disappeared again. Paul continued to sleep.

Renner escaped to the showers, which were packed full of naked men wiggling around each other, reminding him of pigs in a pen. No luxury of privacy today.

Returning back to the dorm room, clean, fully dressed, and ready for the day, Renner saw that Paul was still in dreamland.

"Paul, wake up," Renner whispered, "it's almost time for class."

Grumbling was heard beneath the sheets, and then a few decipherable words from lips stuck together. "Five more minutes."

Renner shook his head in disappointment. Paul's priorities were not on the same level as his own, and again he wondered how he'd gotten into BIT in the first place, at the graduate level to boot.

Pillaging through his nonperishable stash of snacks, Renner was rewarded by a granola bar, which he consumed in three bites. Next, he threw his beige jacket over a long-sleeved shirt the shade of a Portobello mushroom, grabbed a leather satchel containing his school supplies for the day, and left the dorm. Racing across campus, he reached the Research and Academic Center with only minutes to spare.

Entering the filled classroom, he found an empty chair close to the front, and unloaded his textbook, a pen and notebook. He glanced at the neighbour to his left, a man with longish, curly hair, an upturned nose, dark rimmed glasses, and bushy eyebrows. His odour was a combination of a freshly opened bottle of vitamins and a musty, old basement, and he already looked bored out of his wits.

The professor entered, creating an immediate hush in the crowd of students. The brown suit he wore was a size too small, the thick, brown tie around his neck a little too short. White hair sat erratically around the crown of his pink scalp.

Professor Shubally wasn't solely Renner's Genetics for Graduate Students professor but also his research supervisor for his graduate thesis. Renner would be joining him after school that very day to commence what had inspired him to study genetics in the first place. Using recombinant DNA technology, they were going to attempt to engineer a rat model that would develop different strains of human cancer. These rats would then serve as disease models on which scientists could more accurately test new lines of cancer treatments and medications than the current methods would allow. The research was groundbreaking, the results of which could even change the course of how other diseases were studied.

There was a race towards the finish line before they even began, as other researchers were conducting similar studies. If Renner and the professor didn't work hard to develop a functioning model to support their hypothesis, then somebody else would beat them to it. Get their results published. Get all the recognition. Renner wasn't about to allow that to happen.

"Can I have your attention, class," the professor sternly announced despite the now dead silence his mere presence encouraged. "Welcome to Genetics for Graduate Students. I am Professor David Shubally." Nobody stirred. Somebody in the back of the room coughed uncomfortably. "Please turn to page thirty-five in your textbook. I assume you have all completed your pre-assigned reading?"

Of course, Renner had, reading what was considered a review of what he had learned during medical school. Still, he enjoyed re-reading the chapters as this was his favourite subject.

The professor flicked on an overhead projector and within seconds had set up on display the familiar diagram of a DNA strand—a three-dimensional double helix, which matched the picture on page thirty-five but lacking the labels of each component. Difficult to believe, but it was only in 1953 that Watson and Crick had discovered that the DNA strand had this particular structure. Since then, the field of genetics had proliferated at an accelerated pace to where it was today. The developments that had transpired since then were staggering.

"Give yourself a moment to review the diagram in your text, and then close your books. We will label the overhead diagram together." After a brief pause, he continued. "DNA. Deoxyribonucleic acid." He spoke slowly, dramatically annunciating each syllable. "Can somebody tell me what DNA is?" He pointed to a fellow in the front row who had his arm raised.

"It's a molecule that holds within it all of the hereditary information, found in humans and most organisms. Each cell essentially carries this information or blueprint, located mainly in the nucleus of the cell."

"What are the four chemical bases that make up the DNA molecule?"

Renner thrust up his hand but was disappointed when another student was called upon to give the answer, a mousy brunette with her hair parted down the middle, thick bifocals and the shadow of a moustache.

"Guanine, thymine, adenine and cytosine."

"Correct. What chemicals pair together to form the bases on the helix?" he asked the same girl.

"Adenine pairs with thymine, and guanine pairs with cytosine." Using a red marker, the professor scribbled the labels onto his overhead picture of the DNA strand.

"And what is the backbone of a DNA molecule composed of?"

Just then a dishevelled, pillow creased, unshaven Paul stumbled into the classroom interrupting the teacher, and rushed over to a vacant seat three rows behind Renner.

"Nice of you to join us. You are aware class started ten minutes ago, young man?" the professor scolded.

"Yes, sir." Paul's face was flushed.

"I do not tolerate tardiness in my classroom. Do you understand? That's your solitary warning. And that goes for the rest of you as well. Don't think you can come late and disrupt my class. Ever! If you're late again, you're out! Do you understand?"

"Yes, sir," Paul replied with a glare, jaw clenched tight.

"Can you tell me what makes up the base of the DNA molecule?" the professor grilled Paul.

Paul answered cockily. "Yes, the base is made of sugar phosphate."

"I need more. This isn't elementary school, you know." The professor waited.

"Deoxyribose and phosphate."

"Correct."

Apparently, Paul did know something after all. Renner was surprised, even though they were starting with the basics. That was the first remotely intelligent verbiage that Paul had uttered since he met him.

Throughout the class, possibly as punishment for entering late, the professor picked on Paul, calling on him for almost all of the answers, which became increasingly more complicated as the class progressed.

"Organisms are made up of different sequences of these base pairs, and the unique traits that they have also arise from these different sequences. Genes, therefore, are parts of the DNA strand that are responsible for the coding of a specific biochemical function. What does it usually produce?" the professor again asked Paul.

"A protein?"

"Is that a question?"

"It produces a protein," Paul asserted.

"Yes. And the arrangement of the DNA sequence would dictate the protein's structure, and that in turn would dictate its function. So, what then is the genetic code?" he again addressed Paul.

"It's the code that establishes what proteins an organism can make and what the function of the proteins will be. The proteins will then make up the organism."

"That's right. Can you give me more detail?"

"All organisms are made up of the four base pairs, adenine, guanine, cytosine, and thymine, but the sequence of these pairs and the number of these base pairs is what makes the organism unique, is essentially its genetic code. It's what determines whether an organism will develop into a banana or a human being."

"Now, what is recombinant DNA?"

This is where the class was going to get interesting. Recombinant DNA technology was a relatively new area of study, and still largely theoretical in application. Again, Paul was put in the hot seat, all the other raised hands ignored.

"Recombinant DNA is when the DNA of an organism is combined with a different DNA strand in order to develop a new strand of DNA, usually involving the combination of genetic material from two distinct and separate organisms."

"And what would be the purpose of doing this, from a scientist's perspective?"

Paul replied, "Primarily, the DNA of an organism could be altered to produce a unique and unnatural trait in the host organism in order for that trait to be studied in more depth."

The class carried on in this fashion, the professor concentrating most of his questions towards Paul, the tardy, disruptive student. Paul unflinchingly answered all of them, without error, without hesitation. He definitely knew his stuff.

Despite his interest in the topic at hand and his shameless enjoyment of watching Paul get attacked by the professor, dodging academic bullets shot at him left and right, Renner found his mind constantly straying. Milena had cast some sort of spell over him, something he couldn't shake. Didn't want to shake.

On Friday night, he would be meeting Milena at the address she had scrawled on the back of his receipt in her loopy handwriting. Five more days. Time couldn't pass fast enough.

She was so mysterious and exotic. He felt compelled to learn more about her, and more about her so-called abilities.

Before he knew it, class had finished. The professor closed the day's session with an assignment.

"You'll have one month to write a paper on Recombinant DNA and the possibilities for future research. This paper will compose thirty percent of your final grade for the class. Do not disappoint me." He glared at Paul.

Renner gathered his belongings, depositing them into his satchel, and sidled up to the front of the room to properly introduce himself to the professor. He always thought having a good relationship with his professors and supervisors was important. Back at his former university in Germany he knew them all on a first name basis. Here, the other students, including Paul, merely walked past the professor with eyes averted, exiting the classroom.

Dr. Shubally switched off the light from the overhead projector, and then realized there was a student still present.

"Can I help you?" he looked at Renner, mildly annoyed.

"Excuse me Professor Shubally, I'm Renner Scholz. I'll be doing my research with you after school."

The professor's face noticeably lit up, all traces of annoyance replaced. "It's nice to meet you, Renner. I've heard fantastic things about you. I'm excited for us to get to work." He enthusiastically shook Renner's hand. "I read your undergraduate thesis on Genetic Engineering and Forced Mutations. Fascinating work, I must say."

"Thank you, sir. That's a huge compliment coming from you. You're a legend."

"Ah, I wouldn't say that. But, I have a feeling that together we can do wonderful things."

"Yes, sir. I can't wait."

"I'll see you after classes, then, in the lab. Around five o'clock sound good to you?"

"That would be perfect, sir."

"Do you have the room number for the lab?"

"It's in my syllabus. I'll be there at five sharp."

The professor gathered up his notes, filed his projector sheets inside a manila envelope, which he then deposited into his briefcase and exited the room.

Satisfied with his first encounter with Professor Shubally, Renner left the room, surprised to see Paul waiting outside the door. Had he been eavesdropping?

In answer to his own unspoken question, Paul blurted out, "Not too ashamed to brown-nose, I see. *I'll be there at five sharp,*" he mimicked in an unflattering falsetto tone. "Sir," he added after a slight pause. His words were said teasingly, but Renner detected a note of hostility.

"I think being respectful towards my professors is important, especially with Dr. Shubally since he's my thesis supervisor."

"I think being respectful towards my professors is important," Paul continued to mimic Renner.

Renner frowned, and shook his head. "What are you, ten? You know, I don't have to defend myself to you."

"Aw, is Renner getting all upset now?" Paul adopted a pretend sad look. "Are you mad that I figured out that you're a suck up? Is that how you get your good grades?"

"What's gotten into you? Maybe if you showed up to class on time, you wouldn't have gotten picked on so much. But you don't have to take your anger out on me."

"Not all of us can be as perfect as you, Renner."

"I don't have time for this. I'm going to be late for my next class."

"Better run along. God forbid you show up late!" Paul's voice receded into the distance as Renner rushed off.

Renner was disconcerted over their altercation. Where had the hostility come from? He thought they could at least be civil to each other being roommates and all, but now he realized their relationship wouldn't be that easy. Paul was no ordinary roommate.

The rest of the day flew by without incident. Renner enjoyed all of his classes, and soon forgot about Paul's rudeness.

At five o'clock, he located the research laboratory without any problems thanks to his campus tour with Wendy. The laboratory was fully stocked. Several cubicles lined each side of the room, allowing numerous students to work conjointly on different projects. Layers of shelves lined each cubicle holding test tubes, beakers, goggles, Bunsen burners, dissection instruments and trays, graduated cylinders and other glassware, sphygmomanometers, chemicals, compounds, and microscopes.

The professor's pinkish white head was bent over a microscope in the last cubicle on the right side of the laboratory. Dr. Shubally glanced up, muttered hello, and then returned his eye to the ocular lens while adjusting the slide on the stage, securing it with a clip. Rotating the coarse adjustment knob, and then the fine adjustment knob, he finally motioned for Renner to take a look. "Renner, you're just in time. Come and look at this."

Renner looked into the eyepiece and saw a preserved specimen of a cancer cell on the glass slide, obvious with its familiar oat-shaped appearance.

Renner cleared his throat, looked up at the professor. "It's a tissue sample of a small cell lung carcinoma."

"Very good. It's a sample from a tumour that was grown using a tumour transplant model."

Tumour transplant models were the current method for studying human and animal cancers. This method involved transplanting the cancer tissue of a cell line underneath the skin of an animal, usually a mouse or a rat, with a compromised immune system. The cells then developed into lump-like solid tumours, adequate for studying the parameters of tumour growth. Using these models had expanded the knowledge base in the cancer field but had its limitations. Most predominantly was the issue that the cells didn't act as they normally would in a human body where cancer starts to grow spontaneously from healthy cells within specific organs.

When studying or testing new treatments for disease, scientists were put in a difficult spot. On one hand, it was often difficult and even unethical to study and test new treatments on live humans when the outcome was uncertain, such as efficacy of treatment and side effects. On the other hand, the use of animals to study human diseases was difficult in the sense that animals didn't get most human diseases. The tumour transplant models done with mice and rats were a means to mimic how cancer acted in the human body, but the cells were placed there in an unnatural method, and so studying therapies on these cancer cells didn't always accurately predict how well a treatment would work in humans, especially on specific cancers arising in specific organs. It didn't display how the cells could metastasize to other areas of the body, it didn't give any information about the genetic aspects of cancer. It had too many limitations.

But, if a rat could be genetically engineered to get human cancer, having the malignant cells arise out of healthy cells as it would in the human body, then the genetically engineered rat model would serve as a great platform for testing the efficacy of treatments and medications, and also for studying how the disease arises from seemingly normal cells, how it progresses to malignant cells, how it spreads through the body, heredity factors and so on. That is what Renner and Dr. Shubally were proposing to develop, and what had lured Renner all the way from Germany to study.

"When we succeed in recombining rat DNA with the human cancer virus, we will finally be able to study the disease more closely. Today we'll focus on writing the research proposal for your thesis to submit to the ethics board for approval. I've already submitted my proposal to get the ball rolling so that we can start as soon as your proposal is approved. I can see, Renner, how this breakthrough will lead to more discoveries in cancer research, and even for other illnesses as well."

"I'm so excited to work with you on this experiment." Renner looked down, shuffling his feet uncomfortably. "Before we begin, though, I do have a suggestion. Something I've been think-ing about."

"Fire away."

"I know that we were planning on introducing the cancer virus to adult rat DNA, but what if we were to inject the virus into embryonic cells of developing rats? If we were to change the DNA at the embryonic phase…"

The professor interjected, while standing up taller in a moment of inspiration, "Yes, yes. Then the rats would contain the virus in all of their cells, and also be able to pass the genes on to their offspring, giving us a wealth of information about the heredity of the cancer strains, and also save us from having to create the cancer rat models each time we study them as some of the offspring will be born with the engineered DNA strain ready to be studied. This is brilliant, Renner."

Renner beamed with pleasure. Accolades from Dr. Shubally were the biggest honour he could ask for. "Thank you, sir. I have suggestions for the procedure as well. Do you think we'll have any trouble getting this change past the ethics board?"

Dr. Shubally paused in thought. He sat back down on the metal lab stool going through the scenario in his mind. Rubbing his chin, he paused.

"I think it'll be fine. It's not that much more invasive than we were predicting. Rats have commonly been used in experimentation with the intention of helping the human race, and using embryos isn't that much different than what we originally planned. Animal testing is a small sacrifice with the intentions of saving thousands, even millions of human lives. Worth the sacrifice, I'd say, although there are animal rights activists that would heartily disagree with me. But we've never had an issue with them here."

Renner's eyes flicked over to the preserved tissue sample displayed on the microscope slide, the tissue sample of the disease that was ravaging his father's body. The sacrifice would have to suffice. The possibilities that this discovery would present were limitless and could go towards the treatment and cure of countless different diseases besides cancer. Diabetes, Muscular Dystrophy, Alzheimer's. The discovery would be considered miraculous.

"I'll have to tweak my proposal, adding in our new approach— injecting the rat DNA at the embryonic phase. Let's focus together and get these proposals hammered out so we can submit them immediately. Then we'll go over what preparations to do in the meantime while waiting for the experiment to be approved. There's more research to do, we need to compile a list of required equipment, and make sure the lab is adequately stocked before we commence."

Several hours later, they had drafted a decent proposal. Renner left with rough notes in hand, planning to type them up back at his residence.

As he walked down the long white hall of the research laboratory department, he passed a cubicle with another professor, working diligently with Paul. Renner had been so deeply absorbed in his discussions with Professor Shubally that he had been unaware of the other researchers present in the lab.

Paul glanced up as Renner passed by. They made eye contact. As a reflex, Renner almost waved, the word "hello" frozen in his throat, but then remembered their hostile exchange that morning and refrained. Paul must have also harboured this thought as he turned to face the opposite side of the cubicle, continuing his experiment as if Renner didn't exist.

Chapter 5

Over the next four days, Renner fell into a routine, with Paul an omitted factor. Paul conveniently woke up long after Renner had left the dorm and returned at night long after Renner was fast asleep.

Today was no exception. As Renner tugged on an orange sweater, bell bottom jeans, a black leather jacket and boots, he glanced over at Paul, still unconscious. Always tardy, how hadn't he been kicked out of school yet? But, at least it limited their exposure to each other. Less awkward this way. Renner accepted it as their new norm.

The dorm room window displayed a morning that was downcast, clouds piling up in front of the sun in a battle formation shield. Hopefully he would reach the campus cafeteria before the rain started to pour. Rushing out the door and down the stairs to the main lobby, his plans for a quiet breakfast were interrupted.

Wendy was waiting, large plastic Barbie smile on her face. The mauve knitted toque she wore sat on her head slightly off kilter. Oversized mittens and a stretched-out cable knit sweater draped over her tiny figure again gave the impression she had raided her mother's closet.

Renner groaned. How did she figure out where he lived? After not seeing her all week, he assumed she had forgotten about him, finally picking up on the various hints that he wasn't the slightest bit interested.

"I hope you don't mind, but I thought I would walk you to class today."

"Well, actually…"

"I ran into Paul at the pub last night," she cut him off, "and he told me you were living in Leighton House and that you have a class together this morning."

So, he had Paul to thank for the unwelcome visitor. Paul, who hadn't spoken to him since Monday. If his intention was to further piss Renner off, he had succeeded. But, he still didn't understand why his roommate had turned on him.

"Don't you have your own classes to get to this morning?" Renner asked.

"My English class starts at ten, so I have an hour to kill." She thrust a brown paper bag towards him and a steaming paper cup of Joe. "Here, I brought you some Dunkin' Donuts and coffee."

"Thanks." He wouldn't be escaping her so easily, again.

Starving, he opened up the bag, the aroma of freshly baked doughnuts tempting his stomach. He dug out the powdered treat, and took a hearty bite, decorating his lips in confectioners' sugar. Licked it off. Sheer heaven. The coffee was even better.

"What do you think?" she asked expectantly. Her smile was too wide, both her upper and bottom rows of teeth fully on display, however, her incessant desire to please him mainly produced feelings of pity.

"Yeah, it's great, thanks. Do you want some?"

"No thanks. I grabbed a muffin before coming over. You missed The Tortured Minotaur performance. They were better than I thought they would be."

Together, they walked across the BIT campus. Renner took another bite of doughnut. He needed to tell her he wasn't interested in her romantically but wasn't sure how.

"Are you enjoying your classes? Mine are great, so far, except for Writing and Reading the Essay. The teacher is soooo boring. His voice is hypnotizing and puts me right to sleep. It's one of my earlier classes, too, so it's soooo painful to sit through, when I'd rather be at home in bed. You know what I mean?" The verbal diarrhea continued until Renner reached his building.

"Well, this is me."

"Oh," her shoulders dropped. "Well, have a great class. Can I see you after? Maybe grab a bite to eat?"

"Sorry, I have other plans." He thought of Milena. That evening, at six o'clock, he would finally get to see her again. His pulse quickened.

"Oh, I see," she couldn't hide her discontent. "See you later then?"

"Ah, sure. Thanks again for the donuts."

"No problem."

Renner hustled up the concrete steps, slipped through the entrance and then slowed down to a casual stroll as he made his way down the hallway to his classroom. He was thirty minutes early, but he would rather sit in the empty classroom than listen to more of Wendy's drivel.

The remainder of the day progressed smoothly, minus Paul's continued cold shoulder, avoiding eye contact with Renner during their first class together.

When his final class terminated, Renner sprang from his chair and he fled back to the dorm to get ready for his meeting with Milena. Startled, he found Paul lounging on the mustard armchair in the middle of their room, chugging a beer.

Renner shucked his leather jacket and boots. Turning around to face Paul, they made eye contact for the first time all week. His roommate looked as if he was struggling to swallow a horse pill. "Hey, sorry I've been a bit of an ass," he finally spoke. "I don't want us to have to avoid each other. We're roommates. The least we can do is to try to make this arrangement work."

Renner was surprised by the impromptu apology. He wasn't sure if he should accept it, still uncertain of why they weren't talking in the first place.

"Of course I want to make this work. But, you were the one that started this. Can you at least tell me why you were so rude?"

Paul looked down, a hint of annoyance flickering across his face but then vanished. He looked back up at Renner, his charm back from the first day they met. "I think sometimes people take my sarcasm and humour the wrong way, that's all. You got so defensive, my fur went up. I can be a bit of a hothead sometimes. I hope you understand." He looked genuine enough. Thrusting out his hand, he waited for Renner to shake it. "Friends?"

Renner hesitated, still uncertain. Friends? Hardly. But, polite acquaintances, that much he could handle. Finally, he reached out and grabbed Paul's hand. He didn't want the extra dissension to get in the way of his studies. They smiled, on friendlier terms again. Renner wasn't sure how long the truce would last but accepted it for the moment.

Paul handed Renner a beer, but he declined. "I have my meeting tonight with Milena. I better keep my mind clear."

"Is that the psychic? I thought you might want to come out with the boys again."

"Honestly, Paul, I'm not much of a drinker or a partier."

"No problem, man. I get it. Are you free tomorrow morning?" Paul asked. "Maybe the bar isn't your thing but would you be up for a friendly game of soccer? Some of the boys are heading over to the playing field to kick the ball around. You should come."

"I am free. And I even brought my cleats just in case. I wasn't sure I'd get a chance to use them."

"If we get enough people out we can even have a real game."

Renner was shocked. Paul was being normal, dare he say, even nice.

"Great, I would love that. I'm going to take a shower and head out. I'll see you in the morning, then."

Renner was relieved to be on better terms with Paul. Their disagreement had been bothering him more than he realized. Awkward and uncomfortable in their dorm, now the tension felt cleared.

After his shower, Renner donned dark jeans, a white dress shirt and aftershave. He hoped the extra attention he gave his appearance wouldn't look too obvious that he was trying to impress Milena. Like Wendy's stench of desperation.

Taking the city bus to the address Milena had scribbled on his receipt, Renner disembarked near a deserted alleyway, at the end of which he found the office entrance. A sign was taped to the black door. "Milena Nowak. Psychic readings," Renner read aloud. He rapped lightly on the door but when no one answered he tested the doorknob and found it unlocked. A cool, poorly lit hallway with the scent of anise, myrrh and other incense guided him to a glass door with another sign taped to it, "Please enter quietly. Session in progress."

A bell jingled when he opened the glass door. On the right sat a doormat with cowboy boots resting on top. He shed his own boots and plunked on a couch in the waiting area. Hushed voices drifted through a mahogany door, a large aquarium burbled against the wall, teeming with tropical fish and plants.

Renner grabbed a magazine from a wooden side table, absently flipping through the glossy pages while he waited. He was eager to see her, again, marvelling at the strange effect she had on him. The voices in the other room grew louder, and the sound of chairs scraping against the floor indicated the session was over. As the couple exited the room, a smile spread across Milena's face as she saw him. Turning back to her customer, she thanked him with a warm handshake and exchange of payment. The tall gentleman pulled on his boots and exited the building. Milena returned her attention to Renner.

"You came," she exclaimed with a grin, blue eyes sparkling.

"I wouldn't miss this for the world. Not quite a circus tent, but I bet there's a crystal ball hiding around here somewhere."

She smirked. "Remember, you're strictly here to observe. I don't want to hear a peep out of you. Keep your thoughts and opinions to yourself until I'm finished. Do you understand?"

"Yes, ma'am. I'll be so quiet you'll forget I'm even here."

Satisfied with his answer, she led him into a room brimming with the smells of incense and her own subtle exotic scent of vanilla and orchids. Tapered candles were lit sporadically, casting an eerie glow over the sparse furnishings. A circular mahogany table on the left was surrounded by wooden chairs. Pictures of fairies and other fantastical flora and fauna decorated the lavender painted walls, some of the artwork swallowed by the shadows cast from the dim lighting. A tea kettle sat atop a credenza beside a glass jar of black tea leaves. Thick purple drapery blocked out all traces of light from outside. Tarot cards and old leather books were housed in a small bookcase. Milena grabbed one of the wooden chairs, sliding it into the far corner. With her eyes, she urged Renner to take a seat in the corner like a naughty school boy. Taking his orders, he swung the chair around and straddled it cockily, while the light tinkling of bells indicated the next customer had arrived.

Milena shot him a reproving look. "Remember, not a sound,"

Renner pantomimed zipping his mouth closed, locking his lips shut and throwing away the key. Nodding her approval, she slipped out of the room to greet her next customer. The sound waves from her sultry voice floated to him from the waiting room.

"Good evening, Patricia," she pronounced the name in her thick Polish accent as *Patritsia*.

"Nice to see you again, Milena. It's been too long, my dear," the woman responded in a raspy Polish accent of her own.

"Yes, time goes by quickly. How is your family?" Milena asked while guiding the old woman into the incense-filled room.

"They are doing well. That's why I'm here today."

"I see. Have a seat. Would you prefer the usual?"

The old woman nodded.

Milena sashayed over to the kettle. Carefully, she selected a tea-spoon of tea leaves from the glass jar, deposited them into a metal teapot and poured steaming water from the kettle over the leaves to steep. After several minutes had lapsed, she swirled the teapot and poured the tea into an antique china cup, and then placed the cup in front of the old woman, finally taking her own seat.

While Milena had been preparing the tea, the old woman, frame permanently doubled over in half, had taken a while to get settled into her chair. A crippled spine, probably a birth defect. She leaned her cane up against the wall, no longer in need of the support. She wore a long, knitted shawl, the ends tucked under her armpits. White hair was coiled into a loose bun at the base of her skull, and she had a skin tag that was stuck to her right eyelid, like a piece of crisped rice. Patricia glanced surreptitiously at Renner sitting in the corner.

Milena responded in her satiny smooth, calming voice, a voice that would put a small child to sleep at night speaking of fairy tales and castles and legends of old. "I hope you don't mind, we have an observer today. Renner will be watching over our session, if you permit. He's a bit of a skeptic."

"Oh, she's the real deal," Patricia directed towards Renner. "She knows things nobody else does."

Renner almost spoke up expressing his doubt, but a death glare from Milena reminded him of his promise to keep silent. He nodded respectfully. Milena acknowledged this appropriate response with her own nod.

"I don't mind if he watches," Patricia said.

"Then let's begin." Milena opened a leather-bound ledger she had grabbed from the adjacent shelf and jotted down what Renner assumed were the date and notes on her current client. She looked professional, lawyerly, her posture erect, and her attitude pure confidence. She wore a tight black turtleneck sweater, a long pleated flowing skirt and black, leather high heeled boots. Silken hair cascaded in loose waves over her shoulders. She glanced up at him with her dark, azure eyes framed by long black lashes and caught him staring, smiled enticingly, and then looked back down at her ledger.

A seductive heat crept over his body.

The old woman slowly drank her tea, oblivious to their quiet exchange. Almost finished with her tea, the woman swirled her cup and whispered a question out of Renner's earshot before sipping the last few drops of liquid. Finally, she flipped her cup upside down onto the saucer, waited seven seconds and righted the cup once more, placing it in front of Milena.

Milena picked up the pink flowered china cup with her long, delicate hands, slowly turned the cup, reading the arrangement of the leaves. Renner could smell a hint of tea in the air.

Focusing intently on the leaves, Milena gently spoke.

"Your grandson, Martin…he's getting married?"

"Yes, he is," Patricia responded excitedly.

"Your question was if Martin was making a mistake."

"Yes," the woman again replied.

"I see the image of a bird flying, which means there is good news." Milena closed her eyes, and waited a moment, as if searching from something internal. Eyes still shut, she responded, "The bride-to-be is with child. That is the reason they have decided to marry so quickly." Another pause. "She will have a baby boy. A very robust, healthy baby boy."

"Oh, my. That is wonderful news," Patricia rocked in her chair. "I was worried when he told me he was getting married so suddenly. I thought he was making a big mistake." Tears sprang into Patricia's eyes and she clumsily dabbed at them with a handkerchief.

The two women continued the session, while Renner observed. His curiosity kept him riveted but his skepticism grew. Milena could simply be reading nonverbal cues from the old woman or was drawing upon information Patricia had given her during prior conversations. He couldn't bring himself to believe that Milena had a psychic ability. It wasn't possible.

The reading ended, and the old woman was clearly happy as she retrieved her cane and hobbled out into the lobby. Renner wondered if all readings were positive, predicting things that one wanted to hear.

Milena followed Patricia, exiting the room without acknowledging Renner's presence. Through the doorway, he could see the woman hug Milena, pay her, and then leave the building. Melina re-entered the room, still ignoring Renner, jotted more information into her ledger, and then returned the book to the shelf.

Renner broke the silence, "So, you're telling me…" he froze mid-sentence as Milena held up her hand to stop him. The bell tinkled on cue, and Milena rose and left the room to greet her next patron.

"Come in, Jacob. We have a visitor today. Do you mind if he observes our session?"

"That's fine," the man replied in a rich baritone.

Entering the room, Milena introduced Renner to a young man with chiselled features and large straight teeth.

"Do you want me to use the tarot cards, as usual?" Milena asked.

He nodded, and she retrieved the tarot cards from the bookshelf, giving them a quick shuffle. "What can I help you with, Jacob?"

He scratched his thick head of hair. "I want to know what I should do with my relationship with Abigail."

Milena started laying the tarot cards on the table in front of her. When she finished, seven cards were displayed in front of her in a specific pattern.

The hanged man here," she pointed to a card out of Renner's vantage point, "shows that you're struggling, feeling powerless and thinking of giving up."

Milena closed her eyes, searching. "Your relationship has been difficult since the beginning, and you're not sure what to do. Are you thinking of proposing?"

"Yes, I was." Jacob acted surprised.

"Proposing will not help. Your relationship will continue to get worse." She moved to the right side of the cards. "The Devil Card. Your girlfriend has been dishonest, has betrayed you. Was she unfaithful?" Jacob nodded, lowering his eyes. Milena continued.

"She has little remorse and blames you. This relationship will cause you much pain, more than you've already experienced." Milena reached towards Jacob, raising his chin with her hand, so she could look deeply into his eyes.

Renner felt a glimmer of jealousy.

"I can't tell you to abandon this relationship, but the cards are clear. She's not the best one for you. But, don't worry. You're meant for another, someone you have already met. You will have much happiness with this other woman."

Jacob's brow furrowed in thought, but then he quickly realized who she was talking about. His attitude lifted, but he remained uncertain. "Julie? But we're just friends."

"I know this isn't what you wanted to hear, but I speak the truth."

"I know. You can't help what you see. Thank you, Milena. I'll consider what you've said."

They stood and left the room. The man paid and departed. Slipping the bills into her skirt pocket to join the others, Milena re-entered the room and sat at the table. After filling in her ledger and returning the book to the shelf, she startled Renner by addressing him, "That was my last client today. Now you can speak."

Renner flew over to the table and sat across from the raven-haired woman. "What if you're wrong? What if you told that man to leave his girlfriend, and in reality, she's the best thing that ever happened to him? You could be ruining his life. Is it really fair for you to be playing this game, telling people what to do with their lives based on a bunch of cards and leaves?"

"I never told him to break up with his girlfriend. I told him what would happen if he stayed with her, and that there was a better path for him to choose. I only told him what he asked of me. Besides, I'm never wrong," she looked at him with pure conviction.

"You're never wrong."

"Never."

"So, you can read anyone's future and you've never made a mistake?"

"Yes."

"I don't believe that," he said, shaking his head.

"To a point."

"I knew there would be catch." He slapped his leg.

"It's not what you think. I can read futures but not too far ahead, up to a year or so, maybe because there're too many variables that can change and alter someone's course. Or, maybe my gift isn't strong enough, but that's how it is. That's how it's always been for me."

"Are your predictions always based around marriage?" Renner asked, hinting at Milena's strange announcement at the bar on their first meeting, and the two sessions he had witnessed.

She blushed, but then her face grew sombre. "I wish all of my readings were happy."

That answered Renner's question about the content of the readings, whether they were all positive or not. He shuddered at the thought of someone being told they were going to die.

As if Milena could read his mind, she added, "If I see something too disturbing I tend to keep the visions to myself, as long as it's something that can't be changed or avoided."

"I see."

"Still a skeptic, I take it."

"As a scientist, my job is to make sense of the world. What you claim to be able to do can't be explained. So, if there's no scientific way to explain psychic abilities, they can't exist."

"Why does it bother you so much?"

"I've never believed in psychic abilities, and I'll be honest with you, the main reason I came initially was to get to know you better. But, now that I've watched you do several readings, I am a tad intrigued."

"I get it. You're the type of person who has to have an answer for everything. Does it scare you to think that supernatural abilities might actually exist because then you would have a giant unknown in your life, and to question one thing would lead to questioning others?"

"You might be on to something there. But, that doesn't make me wrong," Renner defended.

"I don't know what else to do to convince you. Perhaps, we should agree to disagree."

He wasn't about to be brushed off. "And here I thought you were the type of person that wouldn't give up so easily. Persuade me to believe. Do my reading."

"I don't know." Milena looked uncertain. "I already saw a glimpse into your future. The visions might be unsettling to see more if...you know...if I'm a part of that future."

"Now, you're making excuses. Are you afraid you can't and then I'll know for certain that there's no such thing as psychic abilities? That you're a fraud?"

"OK, buddy, the challenge is on. How can I resist doing the reading now? But, on one condition."

"Name it."

"You'll take this seriously; otherwise, the reading will be difficult to do."

"I promise."

"Pick your method, then," she urged.

"What do I have to choose from?" he asked, a true novice to the field of psychic readings.

"I can read tea leaves, tarot cards or your palms."

He chose a palm reading, any excuse for Milena to touch him.

"May I?" She gingerly grabbed his hands, and inverted them, cupping them from beneath, sending shivers all the way up his arms. With great intensity, she studied the lines and crevices in his palms. "You're right handed?"

Renner nodded.

She placed his left hand back down on his lap and concentrated more intently on his right.

"Let us begin."

Chapter 6

Milena slid her thumb up and down Renner's hand as she studied the various lines and grooves in his right palm. Although she was focused downward, he stared deep into her eyes as she worked. The blue of her irises had even deeper indigo flecks resembling an opal. Her lips were full and lush, a deep rose shade, her skin tone olive and flawless. Pleasant warmth spread across his chest and cheeks.

Her voice broke the trance.

"You're an intellectual and tend to be logical in your way of thinking."

"Clever. You saw me purchasing biology and genetics textbooks and put two and two together."

She shot him a disapproving glare. Then she looked back down at his well-proportioned hand.

"You're from a rich family?"

"Am I supposed to encourage you? Give you hints that you're on the right track?"

Milena was now clearly annoyed. "That's not necessary, skeptic." She continued. "You are wealthy now, but this wasn't always so. Your hands were once working hands, but now the calluses have healed. I sense you have come through troubled times."

Renner yanked his hand away, his face growing serious. His pompous confidence dissipated.

"I'm sorry, have I made you uncomfortable?" Milena asked Renner, unruffled.

"I'm not sure what you mean?" The chair squeaked as he uncomfortably shifted. Putting on a poker face, he added, "Can we stick to the present and future? Would that be alright?"

"As you wish. Should we continue then?"

Renner didn't want Milena to have the upper hand, know that her accurate vision had unnerved him. She could have guessed, the calluses giving him away. Returning his palm to the psychic woman, she again cupped it into her own hands. He braced himself for more.

"Your parents love you more than anything, even themselves. They miss you very much."

Renner knew this to be true, but this woman claiming to be psychic, again could be guessing. Most parents did feel this way about their kids, and she probably assumed he was from overseas studying here in America, so, of course, they would miss him. But, her next words stunned him once more.

"Your father, he is very ill." Her brow creased, but she remained silent, which closed Renner's throat, making the simple act of breathing difficult.

His skepticism was wavering. Although his father was well-known, few people knew of his illness.

Milena remained still, quiet. When she began to speak, Renner pulled his hand away once more, unsure he wanted to continue. The reading wasn't as superficial as he thought it would be. Not that he believed she was psychic. It wasn't possible. Still, she knew things she shouldn't. *How could that be?* His mind felt violated. Parts of his past were meant to be kept private, even he didn't want to revisit that part of his life anymore, let alone have someone else eavesdrop on those memories. His history was nobody's business. Similarly, he didn't want to know certain things in the future either, especially anything disturbing about his family or his father. The expression that flickered across Milena's features when she spoke of his father's illness was causing him distress because he didn't know what it meant, and his mind was jumping to the worst conclusion.

"Are you alright?" Milena asked gently. Any trace of defiance she had been exhibiting was now absent, looking genuinely concerned.

"Yeah, I'm fine. Just give me a minute."

"We can call it a night. I think maybe you've seen enough."

Renner was conflicted. The palm reading was proving to be more real than he had anticipated, and the discomfort from what she was telling him, coupled with the fact that maybe he was wrong, maybe psychic abilities did exist, was almost too unbearable. All the same, he didn't want the night to end. He wasn't ready to say goodbye to Milena.

"I'm OK," he smiled sheepishly. "I'm ready to go on." He placed his hand back on the table.

"Are you sure you want me to continue?"

"Yes, of course," he answered with false bravado. "Can we keep the focus on me, and not my family?"

"As you wish," Milena answered, grasping his warm hand and again studied the lines as Renner audibly gulped. She looked him in the eye and smiled, dissolving all of his apprehension. Suddenly, he felt as if he could trust her with anything.

"Ready?" she asked.

He nodded.

"You're a doctor...of medicine."

Although this was something she could have found out from others, he was starting to think that maybe she was able to see these parts of him with a special gift or ability. An unexplained, marvellous ability.

"You're here to study for another degree. You want to help people with your research."

Wow, she's dead on. This is uncanny, he thought. Still, he didn't want to give away that his skepticism was waning.

"You're having a conflict with someone close to you, a friend or maybe a co-worker." Again, the frown returned. She shook her head as if trying to make sense of what she saw. "I'm not sure why, but he's not to be trusted."

"You know, it's funny, but I know exactly who you're thinking of."

Paul. Their relationship was tumultuous from the beginning. Taking heed of her warning, he planned to keep him at arm's length, stay civil with him until the end of the year, and then find a new roommate or a new place to live.

A large flirtatious grin curled up the edges of Milena's luscious lips. "You'll meet an exotic woman who will sweep you off your feet."

"Now, I believe you must be psychic, because I've already met her," Renner flirted back.

Blushing again, she withdrew her hands. "That's the end of our reading."

"What, no prediction of our wedding?" Renner joked.

"What do you mean?"

"Did you see anything right now? Do you still see us getting married someday?"

"Maybe." She stood up and started blowing out the candles sending tiny strings of smoke coiling upward from their tips. The room grew darker.

"It's time to go," she announced.

"That's all?" he asked, disappointed. He suddenly knew how Wendy felt when he brushed her off. "How are you getting home?"

"I'm walking. I don't live far from here."

"May I walk you home?" Renner asked, not ready for the night to end. He realized this was not a date, which secretly he had been hoping. Maybe she thought of him as a potential client or wanted to prove she was a veritable psychic. Maybe she flirted with everyone.

"I'm not sure. I barely know you."

"What are you talking about? You know more about me than most of my friends," he chided, referring to the reading.

"All right. Sure. I'm not far, though."

"A beautiful woman shouldn't be walking alone on these streets at night."

"I said yes, already. Let me grab my coat." They retreated back into the lit lounge area, where Milena's onyx cape was draped over a coat rack. Renner wrapped the cape around her shoulders, inhaling her soft bouquet smelling of orchids, jasmine, and a hint of vanilla.

She extinguished the lights. Outside the building, she unhooked the sign, slipping it inside the doors before pulling them shut and locking them with a metal ring of keys. After leaving the alleyway, they walked down the street, their scuffling footsteps on the sidewalk the solitary sound. Traffic was non-existent.

"So, where are you from?" Renner asked to break the awkwardness. He offered her a cigarette from the pouch he extracted from his jacket pocket.

"No thanks. I can't stand the smell."

Renner placed the cigarette packet back in his pocket, unopened, ignoring the gnawing craving.

"I'm from Warsaw, Poland. I moved here three years ago when my parents passed away."

"I'm sorry, I didn't know."

"How would you know? It was sudden—a car crash. They were hit by a drunk driver."

"That's awful. You must have been devastated."

"It was very difficult. I loved them so much. There were too many memories in Poland. I couldn't stay there anymore. So, now I'm here."

"Your English is impeccable for only living here three years."

"Thank you. I studied English before I came to America. It was always my intention to move here."

"What brought you to Washington in particular?" Renner probed.

"I had a pen pal, Olivia, who came to Poland as an exchange student to study for six months. She stayed with her grandparents who lived right beside us. We became fast friends and kept in touch after she returned to America. She invited me to come after hearing of my parents' accident and offered for me to board with her until I got my feet on the ground. I have my own apartment now."

"Did you leave any other family behind? Any siblings?"

Milena shrugged indifferently. "One. A younger sister, Brigita. She's not well. At the age of seventeen she was diagnosed with schizophrenia and placed in an institution in Poland. After I came here and researched the different mental institutions in this area, I went back and brought her here to stay. That way I can still visit her. Not that it makes much of a difference."

"How come?" Renner asked.

"She's mostly in a catatonic state. She's not even aware that I'm present when I visit most of the time."

"Oh." Renner didn't know what else to say, didn't want to pry. She had the right to her own privacy as well.

"And you? Do you have any siblings?" she tucked an errant strand of hair behind her ear and then returned her hand to her cloak pocket.

"Miss Psychic, don't you already know?" he teased.

"I'm not always trying to read your mind, you know. I do have other things to think about. Randomly I'll have a flash, a vision, outside of a session. It's quite rare, signifying something profound."

"Like us getting married?"

Milena looked embarrassed. "Hey, I didn't want to freak you out or anything. The vision caught me by surprise. This has never happened to me before, where I saw into my own future."

"Do I look freaked out to you? Would I even be here right now?"

"I'm not sure."

Renner wanted to grab her hand, feel the soft warmth and tingling he had experienced during the session but thought the moment was too soon.

"In answer to your previous question, no, I don't have any siblings. I was adopted at the age of nine by my parents. My father owns the KS cigarette company."

She nodded in understanding, her vision now making sense.

"What happened to your biological parents?" she asked gently.

Renner's muscles instantly bunched into knots. "I'd rather not talk about them. They're not a part of me or my life. Best left in the past."

He wondered again what Milena had seen while reading his palm. Had she seen into his childhood? What ultimately happened to his parents? She gave no indication, no sign of horror or disgust flashed across her features, so he believed his past remained a secret. At least he hoped.

"Well, this is my place." Milena halted before a cobblestone staircase leading up to large black painted doors. The building was a modest-sized apartment complex, two stories tall.

Renner didn't want her to go.

"Seeing that we're going to be married someday, perhaps we should start with a date? A real date. Maybe tomorrow night, supper around six?"

"Sure, I suppose that will work." She rocked back and forth on her feet as she stared up at him. "So, are you still a skeptic?"

He smiled, exposing his irresistible dimples, "I'm not sure I'm a believer, but you've definitely captured my attention. Thanks for letting me watch you at your craft."

"You're welcome. Thanks for staying quiet during the sessions. And for walking me home."

There was an awkward pause.

"Well, good night, Renner Scholz." She turned to go up the staircase.

"Wait." Renner turned her gently and kissed the side of her cheek. Her warm skin tickled his lips. Again, he was washed over by her exotic scent, could almost taste the scent on his mouth. His olfactory senses exploded, luring him in, but he couldn't indulge yet. Hopefully, in time.

"Good night." Her voice husky, face flushed, she then retreated up the steps, disappearing into her apartment without a backward glance.

Renner floated on air all the way back to his dorm.

★ ★ ★

Barbora Playing Field was a huge expanse of perfectly manicured grass occupying a majority of the outdoor terrain on the BIT grounds. The field was the main hub for recreational activity at the university.

The grass was starting to brown in patches from the cooler temperatures that arrived over the past week. A baseball diamond was angled towards Brassard Street with weathered spectator benches bracing the outer wall. Sixteen men were gathered, warming up and stretching in the chill morning air, including Renner and Paul.

Renner was eager to dive into the game today, his break from soccer much too long for his liking. There were enough men gathered to have a real game, and from the looks of their athleticism, the game would be intense.

A few other familiar faces were spotted amongst the pack. Dennis and John were also present, wearing shorts, t-shirts covered in sports coats and long socks.

"Are you ready to get slaughtered?" Paul challenged Renner, puffs of white bursting from his mouth with each syllable as his warm breath collided with the cool air.

"Damn right. Bring it on."

Paul seemed to be the leader of the group. He divided the team in half, and Renner wasn't surprised to be assigned to Paul's opposing team.

The men took their spots on the field; Dennis draped a whistle about his neck, and then took to the midline of the field accepting the role of referee. Paul tossed Dennis the ball, and he caught it swiftly with one hand, poising it above the men positioned in centre field. Dropping the ball into play, the men attacked with a vengeance.

It was evident within seconds that these players were all exceptional and meant business. Renner exhaled in satisfaction—worthy opponents. He loved a challenge.

It was also evident within seconds that Paul was targeting Renner, always goading him, taunting him. There was a lot of unnecessary contact. Dennis failed to notice the slight altercations, and then their slightness escalated into more extreme, and then downright aggressive.

The ball travelled the length of the field, propelled forward by a short, stocky fellow with a buzz cut. Renner headed towards the goal net, wide open for a pass. Buzz Cut pummelled through two defensive players, spotted Renner next to the goal, and slowed enough to kick the ball toward him. The black and white Adidas soccer ball soared through the air. Renner lined himself up, ready to jump kick the ball sideways into the upper right corner of the net—a trick that always took the goalie by surprise and was impossible to block—when out of nowhere Paul came flying towards him, slamming his cleats into the side of Renner's knee joint. Renner collapsed onto the grass, howling in pain, clutching his injured leg.

Finally, Dennis tweeted the whistle, yelling at Paul for unnecessary hitting, directing him to the sidelines for a penalty. Paul extended his arms out to the sides as if the penalty was uncalled for. Dennis pointed to the sidelines, not letting the infraction go. Paul merely shook his head, smirked and stalked off the field.

Renner palpated the aching joint, fearful his leg was broken. The indent of Paul's cleats glared fiercely red, dotted in specks of blood. The pain was excruciating, but he was able to move his knee: bending and extending his leg repeatedly to test the mobility of the joint. He may have escaped a break, but a sprain was a serious possibility.

"Are you all right?" another player, a thin wisp of a man with a downy fluff of blond hair, asked, concerned.

"I think I'll survive."

The man extended his hand and assisted Renner into a standing position.

Paul had behaved so nice the day before, inviting him to play soccer with the boys. But, now Renner couldn't help but feel as if he had been set up.

As he limped off the field, the game over for him that day, he realized the competitive, somewhat volatile relationship he had with Paul would extend from their scholarly lives to the soccer field.

Milena's warning flashed through his thoughts. *I'm not sure why, but he's not to be trusted.*

Chapter 7

The Alameda was Barbora Bay's most enchanting park. Built along the Barbora River between Carlton Avenue and Lisbon Bridge, not far from campus, its walking and biking paths spanned nearly ten kilometres in total, dissecting the vast expanse of flat, green landscape. Renner Scholz walked one of the paths, arm linked with Milena's, a stupid grin spreading from ear to ear.

The park was especially crowded this evening, the locals attempting to salvage what little they had left of the milder temperatures before winter descended. The atmosphere was a people-watcher's dream. Mom's pushing baby carriages, kids dangling from playground equipment, a teenager throwing a stick for his Golden Retriever. Joggers, skateboarders, families with picnic baskets. Other couples strolled arm in arm, as Milena and Renner did, enjoying the romantic and tranquil ambience of the mystical park. Old relationships were being nurtured, new ones were blossoming.

Before coming to the pier, supper with Milena had gone as hoped. The conversation flowed easily and comfortably. There was a certain levity mixed with depth between the two of them. The physical attraction was present right from the start, but he was intrigued to find that he was becoming emotionally attached to this woman, something that had never happened to him before. Whether Milena returned his feelings, well, that was still unknown, but he had a plan for tonight that would reveal to him the true nature of their relationship, and where it was headed.

What the hell happened to the plan to stay single, uninvolved, and focused on your studies? Here, he was the one actively pursuing Milena, wanting more. The irony was not lost on him.

As they made small talk, a fluorescent orange rubber ball came bounding towards them, eventually docking against Milena's black boot. Renner bent over to retrieve the ball for an expectant three-year-old girl nearby. When he bent over, he tweaked his injured leg in the process, grunting loudly. He re-adjusted his weight to the healthy leg.

"Are you alright?" Milena asked, concerned.

"Ah, it's nothing."

Milena's eyebrows furrowed, "You can barely stand."

"I injured my leg this morning playing soccer," he confessed, tossing the ball back to the child. Up until then, Renner had been able to conceal his injury, despite the nagging pain that was ever present in his knee joint. But, when they continued to walk, he couldn't avoid limping now. His leg was killing him.

"Maybe we should sit for a while?" Milena suggested and assisted Renner over to a bench sheltered below a towering oak.

"Better?" Milena asked.

"Better." He welcomed the brief respite the bench provided, the throbbing intolerable.

Their bench afforded them the perfect view of the cherry trees lining the pier. Trading in their bright pink and white blossoms of spring for leaves tinged in deep bronze, orange, and light gold, their wide rounded canopies were ablaze in the waning sunlight. The temperature was cooling in proportion to the setting sun, and Milena shuddered from the chill. She pulled her cashmere sweater tighter around her body.

"It's a little colder than I expected. Here, let me warm you up." Draping his muscular arm around her shoulders, pulling her in closely to his form, Renner waited to see if she would slap him in the face, run away or laugh at his feeble attempts to come on to her.

Instead, she nestled against his torso, sharing his warmth. Sighing internally, he allowed his muscles to relax.

"So, how did you injure your leg?" Milena asked.

"It's a long story."

The way he accentuated the word "long" piqued Milena's interest. "We have all night. What happened?"

"Well, remember last night when you warned me about someone in my life I shouldn't trust?"

She nodded, remembering the palm reading session. Sweeping her raven hair over her left shoulder, she snuggled deeper into Renner's body. "Go on."

"Not that I'm convinced yet that you are psychic," he teased, "but when you said that prediction, I immediately thought of my roommate, Paul. He's, let's say, a tad unpredictable. One day he's your friend, the next day he's irritable and distant. Living with him is a bloody rollercoaster ride. He blames his bad temper, but I think it's more than that. Something's not right with that guy."

"He sounds a treat."

Renner coiled a strand of Milena's silken hair around his finger as he continued. "Anyway, he invites me to play soccer with him and some friends, and I think he's attempting to make amends for his dickish behaviour, but, now I think he planned to ambush me. Basically, he attacked me on the field, and then acted as if the aggression was all part of the game. My knee joint is buggered up as a result," Renner explained, his breath quickening, muscles bunching beneath his cream sweater.

"You poor baby," she said, rubbing the injured leg.

"He didn't even apologize. I don't know how I'm going to live with him for the whole year."

"Can you put in a request for a new roommate before then?"

"I doubt it. Apparently, I was lucky to even get a room in Leighton House. And I really want to stay there. The dorm is right on campus, has a great reputation, and I get to live with other grad students. Besides, I don't want Paul to chase me off. I need to stand my ground and not let him bully me."

"I guess that makes sense. How is your experience in America, other than that?"

Renner looked down at Milena's snuggling form, looked deeply into her azure eyes, their faces mere inches apart. "There have been some unexpected surprises," he whispered, giving Milena's shoulder a gentle squeeze.

Her cheeks pinked, and she sat up taller; this broke the connection she had with Renner's body. His side felt cold without her snuggled against him.

"What about your classes?" she changed the subject, much to Renner's displeasure, making him worry that she wasn't that into him.

"The classes are stimulating, and the professors knowledgeable, reminding me a lot of the campus back home where I earned my medical doctorate."

"So, what are you studying here, then?"

"I'm pursuing my graduate studies in biology, mainly conducting research using recombinant DNA technology."

Milena stared back at him blankly.

"It's the study of genetics and recombining the genetic code in order to investigate specific traits. I'm mainly trying to find a cure for cancer."

"Wow, that's amazing. Can you seriously change the genetic code?"

He nodded. "It's an amazing field, growing at an astonishing rate. We can do things now that scientists couldn't have even dreamed of doing, say, twenty or so years ago. Mind blowing things."

"But, isn't the concept a little scary? Who knows what can happen when you mess with nature?"

"It's not like that. We're attempting to create treatments for illnesses, cure diseases, and prolong the lifespan. Who wouldn't want that? For example, I'm attempting to create a rat model that will be able to grow human cancer inside of its body. That's never been done before at a genetic level. We're even using artificial insemination, a very new procedure, to impregnate rats with embryos containing human genetic information. Perhaps you don't understand the gravity of this model but if we are successful, it will be a profound discovery."

"Well, the goal sounds noble and all, but don't you wonder what the ramifications could be of messing with nature, changing something that is beautiful and natural into something unnatural? A man-made creation and a jumble of different living things?" Milena debated.

"Cancer is not beautiful."

"That's not what I meant."

A flock of bikers swept past their park bench, sending a flurry of autumn leaves spiralling uncontrollably across the ground.

A tense silence followed.

"Did I offend you?" Milena intuited.

"Sorry, I can't help getting defensive when my work is questioned."

"I don't mean to question your work, but this is all so new to me. I mean, have any of these methods been used on humans? Has anyone changed the human genetic code, combining it with animal traits?" she braced for the response.

"No, of course not. I can't see the validity in doing such research." He had a flicker of memory, Paul telling him about his thesis research, and the rumours that the government was working on building a super-soldier but forced the thought away.

"What about artificial insemination? Has that been done on humans yet?"

"Yes, but not very successfully. There's a new method being developed that's more promising, which is what we are using in our study with rats. The egg is fertilized with the male's sperm outside the body and then transplanted back into the female's uterus. The procedure will help people that previously were unable to have children finally have babies of their own. That's pretty amazing, don't you think?"

"I guess," Milena was pensive. "But, I can't help but wonder."

"Wonder what?"

"Do these children end up the same as other children? Do they have a soul, if they are made in a lab? Made by men?"

"Oh no. You're not getting all religious on me, are you?" he chided. "Who's to say if any of us has a soul?"

"Oh, we have souls. I see them every day."

"Do you?" Renner appeared amused, the concept of an afterlife as absurd as the possibility of psychic abilities, in his opinion. "So, are you religious then?"

Milena pondered the thought. "I wouldn't say that I'm religious, but I know there's something out there—something unexplainable. Something larger than us."

"I don't know what things you see, but it can't be anything spiritual. That's a bunch of horse crap. With some of the things I've witnessed in life, there can't be a higher being," he replied darkly.

"What have you seen?"

"Um," Renner cleared his throat, "I meant as a doctor. I spent one year as an intern at a hospital in Germany. Mainly stationed in the emergency room. I saw a lot of tragedy."

She nodded in understanding. "What do you believe in, then? Evolution?"

"I'm a scientist. What do you think?"

"I'll take that as a yes."

Renner noticed that the sun had nearly set, the park now bathed in violet shadows. With their passionate debate, he had almost forgotten about his plan. Grabbing the leather bag lying on the bench next to them, he stood up.

"How about we drop this topic for now. I have something else planned for us this evening."

Milena's eyebrows rose in anticipation. "But, what about your knee?"

"We don't have far to go. Besides, my knee's feeling better."

They manoeuvred through the remaining pedestrians and headed down to the pier. Several public docks sporadically dotted the shore line, and Renner led Milena to one of them—the couple's final destination.

"The view is breathtaking," Milena said in awe of their surroundings.

They had a panoramic view of the Seattle skyline and the sun laying shimmering orange rays in a long path across the surface of the Barbora River. Sailboats and kayaks slowly inched back to shore, coming inland after enjoying the calm waters of the autumn day.

Renner removed a red and black checkered blanket, spreading the material down on the dock. Cautiously lowering himself onto the blanket, injured leg held stiffly out, he took Milena's hand in his, and helped her ease down beside him. The water lapped gently against the base of the dock. Some geese nearby took flight, honking farewell as they receded into the distance.

From the leather bag, Renner plucked a bottle of champagne and a pair of plastic champagne flutes, handing them to Milena to hold as he struggled to release the bottle's cork. With a resounding pop that echoed across the river, suds exploded from the top of the champagne bottle and cascaded down Renner's fingers. He poured the remaining liquid into the flutes, and then licked the fluid now trickling down his wrist.

"May I?" he asked, as he took one of the filled flutes from Milena and held his cup up in the air. He placed the champagne bottle on the dock beside him.

"I'd like to propose a toast."

"I'm listening," Milena smiled, raising her glass to his.

"To new friendships."

"Friendships?" she questioned with raised eyebrows.

"And to where they might lead," Renner added.

"I'll cheers to that."

They clinked glasses, and each took a sip of the bubbly brew.

A dog barked in the distance. The sun continued to descend and as the last ray was about to disappear, Renner leaned over and kissed Milena softly. Surprised, she froze at first, and then responded with gentle passion. He could taste the champagne on her lips. At that moment, he felt as if they were levitating over the water, at one with the stars and the universe. After a few moments, they reluctantly parted, and descended back down to earth, back down to the dock.

Milena rested her head on Renner's shoulder as they watched the last ray of sunlight wink out on the horizon.

★ ★ ★

Three weeks later, the sweet kiss on the pier was summoned to Renner's mind in an attempt to soothe him from the rage he presently felt against his roommate. Unfortunately, the memory wasn't helping, the urge to charge across the room and rip Paul's face clean off of his skull still a possibility.

Renner normally slipped off into dreamland the second his head hit the pillow, but tonight sleep was beyond his reach because Paul was an inconsiderate prick. Oblivious to Renner's murderous thoughts, Paul was illuminated by a tiny orb of light on his side of the room, furiously clacking away at the typewriter keys. Typing up his assignment with ferocity, having just begun Dr. Shubally's essay on recombinant DNA two hours before. The paper was due later that morning.

Renner felt as if each key strike was physically embedding the letter into the soft matter of his brain. Click, click, clicking away.

I am going to kill him.

With forced effort, Renner suppressed the urge, instead pulling his pillow over his head, adding extra pressure against his ears. He stole a glance at his desk clock, which read 3:15 a.m. Exactly five minutes since the last time he checked. He audibly groaned. Paul kept clicking away.

Ready to pull out all of his hair, Renner flipped over in his bed loudly enough to send a passive aggressive message to his room-mate. Maybe Paul should have worked on his paper throughout the last month at decent hours during the day, as Renner had. No, instead Paul had partied more nights than not, staying up until the birds began to sing, drank enough liquor to pickle his liver, and slept with so many women he was afraid to imagine what types of STDs had taken up permanent residence in his roommate's body.

He didn't understand Paul's negligent behaviour. Renner allotted several hours per week to devote to this important assignment, hence completing the essay early. This gave him plenty of time to attend to the finer details, ensuring there weren't any typing errors and that all of his references were cited appropriately in the bibliography. In the end he felt good about the final result, a sound piece of work, worthy of a decent grade.

How did Paul think he was going to succeed at the graduate level by completing his assignments at the final hour? Perhaps he didn't care. Paul needed to get his head on straight, his priorities in order, or he would never survive the rigorous demands of the curriculum they had to endure.

A pause in the typing gave Renner a moment of hope. Was he finally finished? But then the clacking resumed: Renner's hopes annihilated.

"Are you frickin' kidding me right now?" Renner bellowed, bolting upright in his bed. "I have a test tomorrow, you inconsiderate dolt!"

Paul ignored him. Since the incident at the soccer field where Paul had nearly broken Renner's leg, they hadn't spoken a word.

"I've never met anyone with such a sense of entitlement before. But, you know what Paul? You're a dime a dozen. One day, you're going to have to go out into the real world, and you're going to be in for a rude awakening. People aren't going to fall all over you, or let you walk all over them."

Paul continued to give him the silent treatment, pressing return on the typewriter at the perfect time, while looking straight at Renner with a deadpan expression. *Ding.*

Paul was goading him. Well, Renner wasn't going to fall for his tricks. Was Paul hoping that Renner's anger would get out of control, ending in blows, and then he would get kicked out of school? *Sorry to disappoint you, Paul, but that isn't going to happen.* Time to simmer down, but with Paul, that was no easy feat.

Another glance at the clock told him four more minutes had passed. This was going to be a long night.

★ ★ ★

The following week, Renner sat in Dr. Shubally's class anxiously awaiting the return of his graded paper. The professor—looking unusually grey and wan, as if he'd aged a hundred years overnight—called the students up one by one to receive their papers.

Renner felt the familiar stirrings of self-doubt he always suffered before seeing his grades. When his name was called, he approached the professor with an arm stiffly extended to receive his paper. When he saw the large red numbers inked at the top of the first page, his body visibly relaxed and he heaved a sigh of relief.

Eighty-nine percent. Not bad.

Not his best grade but still sufficient. Worth thirty percent of his final mark for the class, he was off to a good start.

"Paul Barrington," Dr. Shubally bellowed, as Renner returned to his seat. Paul swaggered to the front of the classroom, head held so high his nose practically scraped the ceiling. Distinctly, he heard the professor's words as he handed Paul his paper.

"This was really impressive work, son. You surprised me." He patted him appreciatively on the back. Paul spun around to walk back to his seat, smug.

As he swept by, Renner couldn't help but see the giant red grade inked on Paul's paper, his roommate tipping his hand to afford him a better look.

Ninety-seven percent!

Renner nearly fell out of his chair. *How was that possible?* With his own sleep deprived eyes, he watched Paul struggling to finish his paper on time.

How could he get such a high grade? How could he beat Renner by almost ten percent, Renner, who had worked meticulously on his paper for weeks? Had he cheated, committed plagiarism? Or was he simply a closet genius?

The approval lavished upon Paul from Professor Shubally was a barbed wire stuck beneath his skin. The professor hadn't acted impressed by *his* paper, hadn't patted *him* on the back.

Renner suffered through the rest of class with the barbed wire digging ever deeper into his skin, gouging toward the soft tissue of his heart.

★ ★ ★

Several weeks later, Renner's mind was swirling as he got ready for school. Tossing his textbooks and writing utensils into his satchel, he simultaneously tried to organize his life in his mind. Make order of it all. He had a lot on his roster, and even though he was relieved to have the paper for Dr. Shubally's class completed, now midterms loomed on the horizon, his thesis proposal had been approved by the ethics board allowing the start of the experimental phase, and on top of all that, making his life even more chaotic, he juggled weekend soccer games and dates with Milena.

Pulling on his leather jacket, he headed out of the red brick residence building into the brisk autumn air. Wendy was the last person he wanted to see, but there she stood with coffee and doughnuts, ready to escort Renner to his morning class.

"I was starting to think I missed you."

Renner acknowledged her without enthusiasm.

Despite his cold indifference, Wendy started prattling incessantly about nothing of substance.   Remaining distant, he tried to discourage her crush. He strode at a swift pace leaving her gasping as she tried to keep up, white plumes of mist bursting from her mouth with each word.

His concentration remained internal, focusing on the unexpected shift that had happened in his life.

After being adopted and entering school for the first time, his eyes were opened to new opportunities that before had been beyond his grasp: to become someone important, to make a difference in the world, to be successful as opposed to being a nobody, a punching bag, a loser (his former destiny). Completely entrenched in his schoolwork, he vowed nothing would get in his way to achieving his goals. Especially not a relationship. He had no need of one, never desiring to settle down, get married or have children. He was a self-proclaimed loner and had no issue with this station in life. Had accepted it wholeheartedly. But, here he was, dating Milena for several weeks now, their relationship blossoming. A warm feeling was forming in his heart, a fondness beyond his comprehension, and intense passion was surging through his loins even though their physical interactions were still limited to hand holding and a nighttime kiss at the end of their dates. He wanted to see her more, feel her more intimately, but what he had feared would happen was indeed happening. His mind was distracted. His marks were not quite slipping yet, but the potential was there. And he felt he was falling behind.

Could he have both Milena and a career as a scientist? Or would one need to be sacrificed in order for the other to fully succeed?

And, Paul, with his partying ways, excessive drinking and hangovers, multitude of sexual liaisons, and ultimate lack of studying, was pulling ahead with his studies. He aced all his tests, received near perfect results on all of his essays and research papers, which he conveniently displayed throughout their dorm room for Renner to see. How could Paul effortlessly keep so many balls in the air and be doing exceptionally in all aspects? Perhaps he was a prodigy of some sort. Renner couldn't help but feel another tug of jealousy, while he himself felt he was losing control.

Remembering Wendy was trailing behind him, he muttered a hasty goodbye once he reached his class, leaving her looking flattened.

Inside the classroom, the clock read nine o'clock, but Professor Shubally was still absent. Students shifted impatiently in their seats, rustled papers, whispered spiritedly with their neighbours. Renner himself grew impatient but also concerned. Dr. Shubally was never late. Paul sauntered into the classroom behind schedule, lucky his tardiness wasn't caught this time, an air of supremacy about him, as if he had anticipated the professor being late today.

Ten minutes past nine, an older woman with a tightly coiled, grey bun, thick glasses perched above a pug nose, and plaid schoolmarm dress marched into the class, raising a hand to grab everyone's attention. Voices petered out.

"Good morning, class. I am Ms. Devereaux. I will be teaching the class today as Professor Shubally is home ill. Now, please open your text books to page ninety-six."

Renner obliged, opening his text, but his thoughts remained on his professor. They were supposed to be meeting after school, the crucial part of their experiment to begin. Now, the experiment would have to wait.

At the end of class, as Renner gathered up his belongings, Paul slipped up behind him.

"I wonder what's up with the Professor. Isn't he your thesis supervisor?"

Renner stared in shock at Paul. "So, you're speaking to me now?"

"I noticed he's been looking a little...peaked...lately," Paul ignored his remark. "I hope this won't delay your research at all. Falling behind would be a shame, especially with exams coming."

Renner's stomach knotted beneath his beige turtleneck. His face turned beet red, teeth clenching.

"Well, see you later." Paul swaggered out the door, leaving Renner behind with a bitter taste in his mouth, and the barbed wired now fully embedded in his heart, digging even deeper.

★ ★ ★

Unable to commence his experiment due to Dr. Shubally's absence, Renner decided to visit the library following his classes. The colossal library, one of several on campus was swarming with students preparing for their midterms and working on various projects and assignments, being one of the busiest times of the school year.

Renner planned on using the free time to do more research for his thesis. Not that he hadn't already combed through all of the existing literature, research papers and journal articles pertaining to his area of study. He had stacks of summarized notes to prove it. But, a little more research couldn't hurt.

The sea of books beckoned him, the library his haven: the aroma of printed ink on paper, the studied silence, the vast wealth of knowledge surrounding him. Gliding over to the genetics section, he snatched several journals off of the shelf. Lugging the heavy books, he reached a vacant table, and dumped the towering stack onto the desktop. Pulling out the wooden seat with a hearty scrape elicited a few annoyed glares as he settled in.

Rapidly he realized concentrating was futile. Cracking open the books, he would scan several lines but then his mind would wander, drifting back to the same thing, the same thought, the same person. *Milena.*

Her deep, red pout the colour of rose petals in the middle of summer. Her hair silken, smelling of orchids and vanilla. Her skin smooth as porcelain, effervescent, delicate. When she smiled, his body temperature skyrocketed.

He remembered the moment in her office when she touched his hands for the first time, could almost feel the sultry warmth of her fingers tracing across his skin. The pressure of her lips against his when they kissed.

Her gift.

Was it real?

She had only conducted the one palm reading, but the effect the session had on him still lingered. How could he deny the accuracy of her reading? She knew things, saw things. But, how was it possible?

Scanning the library, teaming with books on all aspects of existence, all subjects that a human could think of gave him sudden inspiration. Wandering around, he discovered a small section dedicated to research on psychic phenomena: telekinetic abilities, psychic practices, necromancy, and clairvoyance.

Scratching his head, he paused, not sure where to start. He hadn't considered that other realms of Psi abilities would even bother to be explored. Again, he thought the whole concept peculiar and implausible. But, Milena gave him questions that he needed to answer.

Snagging several books on each topic, he then hauled them back to his desk, swiping aside his thesis research to make room.

He delved into book after book on Psi abilities, absorbing and analyzing all of the information therein. The first few books lent very little credibility to the field of parapsychology, in his opinion, as researchers attempted (albeit feebly) to measure or quantify psychic abilities.

One study used cards with symbols on them, and subjects attempted to guess what symbol the card had before it was flipped over and revealed to them. People with self-proclaimed psychic abilities had a significantly greater probability of guessing the symbol on the card correctly, at above twenty percent.

Another interesting journal article tried to determine whether people could affect the roll of a die by using their mind in an attempt to measure telekinetic (TK) abilities. The findings suggested that people could make the die land on a specific side with their minds, but there were too many other variables that could have caused the results. Renner found the study's results trivial, probably due to chance or experimental error, not due to TK ability.

A trifle more interesting was a study trying to determine whether psychic abilities were more apt to present themselves while under hypnosis or other trance-like states. Again, the findings were minimal and still shed little light on how this phenomenon was even possible.

The bustle of students initially present in the library when Renner arrived slowly trickled out. A glance out the large plate glass window indicated the sun was setting, the time getting late. But, he wasn't satisfied. He continued to pore through the underwhelming research. Finally, after he was almost through all of the books and journal articles, he found one that was filled with case studies.

Individuals that had presented with significant, profound, and unexplainable psychic abilities were studied, observed, and causation was explored. Various contributing factors were considered. For instance, people who had psychic abilities such as TK abilities, clairvoyance, telepathy, and precognition all presented with some sort of condition involving the brain. A genetic link was also hinted at through the study of twins, especially twins that were separated at birth and raised apart, and Psi abilities tended to run in families, and could be passed down to children and grandchildren, in a similar vein as hair colour, eye colour and height. Family members with mental disorders, especially schizophrenia, were also common amongst case study subjects.

Hadn't Milena said her sister had schizophrenia? He brushed the thought aside for the moment, continuing his research.

He was so deeply entrenched in his newfound research that, so far, he had successfully ignored the tingling at the nape of his neck, the strange feeling that he was not alone anymore, that he was being observed.

Until the sensation became overwhelming.

A feeling of whispering so close, surrounding him, the words unclear. Was it his name? *Renner*, over and over again.

A quick scan of the floor showed him empty desks and cubicles. But, with the soaring rows of book shelves, someone could easily conceal themselves behind. Standing up, he walked the length of the library, peering down each aisle, finding them all to be empty. The front desk was the only area with movement, as the staff tidied up and prepared to close for the night.

Had ten o'clock already arrived? How had the time passed so quickly? But he wasn't quite finished, wanting to get through the last few articles. Returning to his table, he dismissed the feeling of being watched.

More case studies—these of individuals with various diseases of the brain or brain injuries—that were able to display profound psychic phenomena. Probably one of the most famous cases was that of Edgar Cayce. At the age of three, Edgar suffered a severe brain injury after which he experienced profound clairvoyant abilities. Able to communicate with deceased relatives and even the angels, and as an adult able to predict and cure illnesses by inducing an out-of-body experience through hypnosis. People came in droves from all over America to get a reading from him, earning him the title, "father of holistic medicine." Astonishingly, he also accurately predicted the rise and fall of Adolf Hitler, the assassination of two of the American presidents, the stock market crash, and the Great Depression.

Further research also suggested that some people with brain cancers exhibited supernatural abilities following tumour growth. Renner wondered if the area of the brain that was affected by the injuries resulting in Psi phenomenon was the same as the area where the tumours grew, which would hint at what part of the brain might be involved in psychic abilities but was difficult to determine from the studies alone. Similar areas of the brain appeared to be affected, but the information in the articles was not specific enough in describing location.

As he sifted through all of the resources, he questioned the epidemiology of psychic abilities, if—and that was a very big if—they truly did exist. Was there a part of the brain that could induce psychic abilities to appear? And with the indication of siblings and other family members having abilities, was this alluding to a genetic factor being involved? Could psychic abilities scientifically be possible? The area of heredity was his expertise, which piqued his interest further.

The library staff finally asked Renner outright to leave. Taking the book containing the case studies, along with a few others, he signed them out and left the library.

Chapter 8

The clouds were threatening, dark and robust. A storm warning was in effect for the evening, but the temperature was so blessedly mild, hovering below zero, that Renner couldn't pass the opportunity to spend time outdoors.

He invited Milena skating to the outdoor rink at Seattle's Salamander Park. The rink was well lit at night, had a fire pit in the centre for additional warmth and was the perfect romantic winter date for the most perfect, sensual woman. He had a great feeling about tonight, butterflies already causing a commotion in his stomach.

At a quarter past six, he rode the bus to Milena's apartment. After ringing her doorbell, she appeared at the entrance swathed in a textured wool scarf, hat, and mitts in vibrant hues of orange and pink. Her sweater was black, long, and belted at the waist. Black leggings and her signature black knee-high boots completed the ensemble. Breathtaking, as usual.

"Wow, it's so beautiful," she lifted her face to the sky, the softly falling snowflakes dissolving on her skin.

"Not as beautiful as you," Renner gushed.

She responded with a smile so warm it threatened to melt the surrounding snow. "Have you ever skated before?"

"A few times. I'm not a professional by any means, but I'm pretty sure I can stay upright. Most of the time."

"Well, you might need to show me a few tricks. I'm a complete novice, myself."

"You've never skated before?"

She shook her head in the negative.

"Are you sure you want to try?"

"Of course, as long as you promise to hold me the whole time."

"You can count on that," he replied with a mischievous wink.

They walked, arms linked, towards the skating rink. Tiny snow-flakes continued spiralling down from the opaque sky, drifting in slow motion. The air was a thick and comforting blanket, warming Renner on the inside as much as his extremities.

"You know, I've started doing a little research on psychic abilities. Some of the findings are truly fascinating."

"So, are you still a skeptic?" Milena questioned.

"That's still up for debate. Let me do a little more digging. Sometimes I feel like I'm chasing the wind."

"I'm not sure your science books are going to be able to explain such a phenomenon. Some things are supposed to remain a mystery."

"Everything real can be explained by science," Renner replied with certainty.

"OK, brainiac, what about near-death experiences? Some people who've almost died describe out-of-body-experiences as their soul leaves behind their physical body. They give detailed accounts of a supernatural realm, of sentient beings that glow white and know all. How do you explain that?"

"That's easily explained scientifically. When a person is dying, their body releases various neurotransmitters that aid in shutting down the brain. These endorphins and hormones act on the central nervous system, creating a sense of euphoria while simultaneously suppressing pain. They're responsible for the illusions and hallucinations you mentioned. The experience is similar to what someone has while using LSD or another type of hallucinogenic compound."

"But that doesn't explain how people have returned from their near-death experiences with new information, things they learned from the supernatural realm that are impossible for them to have learned any other way."

Renner shook his head. "They must have heard the information at some point, at a subconscious level."

"What about people who come back with supernatural abilities? That's been reported as well."

"Again, delusions and hallucinations, nothing more."

"Do you have an answer for everything?"

"Maybe."

They walked in companionable silence for a moment. The street was calm, now powdered white like a jelly doughnut, glittery in the streetlights.

"One of the interesting things I read was that psychic abilities may run in families. Did you have any other relatives that could predict the future?"

"Yes, my mother was a very intuitive psychic. Her gift was much stronger than mine. And my maternal grandmother was a gypsy. All over Europe, she travelled doing psychic readings to earn money for food and clothing. People sought her out to have their fortunes read."

"Do you remember your grandmother?"

"Yes, she was a remarkable woman, strict and harsh, but her main goal was to provide for her family. She taught me how to enhance my own gift. My mother, however, felt differently about being able to read futures. She believed her visions were a curse."

"What do you mean?"

"At times, she would have disturbing dreams so vivid she thought they were real. Once, she went to her friend's house to offer condolences over the death of their father, but they had no idea what she was talking about. Their father was fine. Then, that evening, the friend received a message that their father *had* passed away."

"Another time, she was outside hanging laundry on the line when a great, black cloud crept over the neighbour's house, contorting into the face of a hideous skull. Later she found out the neighbour's baby had died of pneumonia. Similar situations happened, often enough to disturb my mother, made her fear her gift. She didn't want to have any visions at all. But still, they came."

"I can see why she didn't want to have those kinds of visions. That would be extremely disturbing. Have you ever experienced anything similar to that?" he asked, remembering her forehead wrinkling when doing his reading, talking about his ill father.

"Where my mother's visions focused on death, mine are somewhat the opposite. I typically see more happy occasions, mostly weddings and births. I also have more control over my gift, limiting the visions to when I'm doing a reading. Well, most of the time, anyway."

They were nearing the rink, indicated by the sounds of skates scraping on ice, distant voices and laughter. The scent of coffee and fresh roasted chestnuts wafted over to them. A dim light shone ahead, a shimmering globe.

"And your sister?" Renner probed.

Milena looked downward, hesitated. "Let's just say my sister had visions of a different kind."

"What do you mean?" he encouraged, giving her arm a gentle squeeze.

"Before we knew about her illness, we thought she had the gift as well. Some of her predictions came true, but then she started talking about dark spirits. She could see them everywhere, and they would talk to her, call her name."

Despite the mild weather, Renner felt the blood chill in his veins.

"As her condition progressively got worse, she would go on rants for days, claiming that the spirits were demons trying to get inside of her, and that they would corrupt us too. She scratched herself until she bled. Pulled out most of her hair. Scars and unhealed scabs covered her body. At night, she would awaken screaming, and when we tried to calm her, she would sob uncontrollably, repeating over and over that they were trying to take over her mind."

"The demons?"

"Yes. My mother took her to the hospital to have her assessed, and that's when she was diagnosed with schizophrenia. Refusing to leave her at the hospital, my parents took her home with several medications meant to decrease Brigita's recurrent delusions and hallucinations. But, she eventually refused to take her meds, saying they made her weak against the demons. She was convinced that we were all doomed, that the world was going to end."

"That must have been hard on you," Renner sympathized.

She nodded. "Consequently, my parents realized Brigita was progressively getting worse, losing touch with reality. That's when they admitted her into an institution, so doctors and nurses could enforce her medication, and monitor her closely. The delusions stopped. Her scabs healed, and her hair grew back. But, then she started having catatonic episodes where she was unresponsive for days, even weeks. The doctors explained to us that the form of schizophrenia she had was the catatonic type."

Renner rubbed her back with a comforting hand. Something she had said stuck in his craw, making him uncomfortable, but he couldn't put his finger on it. Was it the mention of the voices calling her name? The demons? His thoughts were disrupted as Milena continued her story.

"When we visited, if she was alert, she would refuse to see us. We betrayed her, condemning her to the wiles of these evil spirits. But, she's barely ever alert anymore," Milena added.

"I'm sorry." Renner hugged her reassuringly.

"I miss her, how she used to be. But, I've come to accept her illness. And I don't want to ruin our date with my depressing stories. I think we're here."

The rink shone in the fluorescent lights, a sea of glass. Children and parents, couples, and groups of friends swirled around the rink, enjoying the warmth of the evening.

After asking Milena her foot size, Renner approached the rental booth, and grabbed them two pairs of skates from the brunette employee at the counter. Finding an empty bench, they donned their rental skates, Renner assisting Milena, tightening her laces for proper ankle support. As they stood up, Milena gave Renner a nervous look.

"You'll be fine. Here, take my arm."

Together they waddled towards the rink. Renner eased onto the ice first, and then offered his hand to Milena, who graciously accepted. He watched her tentatively climb onto the slippery surface, momentarily losing her footing. Renner caught her before she fell, and they both smiled into each other's eyes, him with comfort and her with relief over being saved from a broken ankle.

"Just take things slowly."

He kept her hand in his as they inched away from the edge of the rink. Sliding his feet side to side, Renner showed her how to move. She imitated his movement, appearing excited at her progress. Her movements were choppy at first but, within an hour, she was floating across the ice like a pro.

As they glided arm in arm around the rink, Renner spotted a familiar face approaching. Wendy—bundled in layers of warm clothing and a knitted scarf wrapped about her head, turban style. She was with a small group of friends. Looking up at him, her face instantly brightened, but when her focus shifted to his side where Milena clung tightly, her expression hardened. After saying something to her friends, she fled the skating area.

Should he go after her? Not willing to ruin the fun he was having with Milena, he dismissed his guilt, returning the focus to his date.

They continued floating in their fantasy world until the falling snow fell so thickly, they could barely see each other and the rink became difficult to skate on. Deciding they should leave the rink, although reluctantly, Milena and Renner removed their skates, and returned them to the rental booth.

"That was so much fun. Let's do this again some time," Milena exclaimed, eyes sparkling, cheeks rosy from the fresh air and their physical exertions.

"Does that mean the date's over?"

"It doesn't have to be. Do you want to come back to my place?" Milena nervously invited in a voice huskier than usual.

"Hmmmm. Can you read my mind?" Renner teased.

"I'm going to say yes?"

"Wow, you are good."

Together they sprinted the entire distance back to her apartment in the heavy snowfall, the blustering wind that had suddenly sprung up no obstacle to their desire. Reaching Milena's apartment, they clambered up the slippery steps, and entered the warm and cozy space.

"Nice place you have here," Renner complimented.

"Thank you. It is home now."

In the confines of her already toasty apartment, Milena ignited the fireplace, tossing logs and peeled tree bark into the pit. The flames danced over the wood, the shadows dancing across the walls. Her apartment was modern with army green upholstered couches, a grey and white brick fireplace, a brown, black and beige flecked rug, and sculptures of naked people on the mantel, end tables, and artwork. A zebra patterned rug sprawled on the floor in front of the fireplace.

Rummaging in the kitchen while Renner admired the fascinating artwork, Milena prepared warm buttered rum, pouring the amber liquid into tumblers, and then returned to the living room, drinks in hand. Offering Renner a tumbler, Milena lay down on the zebra skin rug, and invited him to join her. They sipped the intoxicating beverage while engaging in small talk.

Renner couldn't stop staring at Milena. Her beautiful skin was more radiant from being outside, soft and supple. Her long eyelashes accented her deep azure, almond-shaped eyes.

And her scent. Exotic orchids and vanilla swept over him. He couldn't control himself any longer. Taking the glass from her, he deposited both of their drinks on a nearby end table.

Pulling her in close, he gently pressed his body against hers. Kissing her tenderly at first, he felt the pent-up passion inside pushing to be released. She kissed him back, hands caressing his back, causing him to shiver.

Pulling her hair to the side, he kissed her neck, finding she tasted as sweet as she smelled. He whispered in her ear, "You continually amaze me."

"I could say the same about you, Renner Scholz," she responded with a seductive smile. She lay down on the rug and pulled him down on top of her, where they continued to kiss, more ardently now. Breathing heavily, Renner pulled away long enough to carefully untie the belt on Milena's sweater, and then slipped the sweater off of her shoulders, kissing the exposed skin with his lips. She moaned.

Tugging Renner's turtleneck over his head, she tossed the shirt to the side, and then slid off her black tights.

Renner followed the curves of her voluptuous body, his lips tracing each angle and curve, finally brushing the inside of her thigh. Milena moaned again, and then guided Renner's lips back up to hers, whispering between lustful kisses, "I'm all yours."

Tearing off the rest of their clothes, they made passionate love by the fireplace, their bodies entwined as one, as if they were perfectly formed for each other. The howls of the wind were coupled with the sounds of their ecstasy.

Afterwards, bodies spent, they lay together swathed in blankets and each other's arms. Renner had never felt so happy or so satisfied in his whole entire life.

"Milena, what are you doing to me?"

Sighing, she snuggled deeper into his embrace.

Overwhelmed by the moment, he couldn't help but ponder in his thoughts as he drifted towards sleep. *Is this how people feel when they fall in love?*

★ ★ ★

The next day, the young couple wrapped themselves in blankets, not bothering with clothes that would merely get in the way later when they made love again and again. Traipsing into the kitchen, Milena pulled a bag of coffee grinds from the cupboard.

"Holy crap, Renner, look!" Milena stood on tiptoe to look out the kitchen window.

Renner joined her, and the young lovers peered out of the snow encrusted glass. The storm had raged all night leaving behind a glorious white blanket over the world thick as a goose down comforter. Shapes hid beneath the snow, all but obscure. No more than the trees were distinguishable amongst the mysterious shapes, icicles dripping off branches like magnificent crystal chandeliers. The snow had blown into hard peaked drifts, giving the streets and buildings the appearance of a miniature mountain range. Some peaks reached six feet where the wind had been especially concentrated, one such drift creeping up the front of Milena's apartment building, completely snowing them in.

It would be days before the city would plow the streets, before they would be able to dig themselves out of their new snow fortress, so they decided to make the most of their solitude. Making love all weekend long, bingeing on the rapture they brought each other, stopping a few times to eat and sleep. After the weekend ended, and mobility in the external world was again possible, Renner prepared to return back to his own loft.

But, he didn't want to.

Not just because Paul was there, and he avoided his roommate's presence on a daily basis, but he knew at that moment that he wanted to spend the rest of his life with this exotic creature. He decided he could have both—a successful career as a scientist, and Milena by his side. He would have to make things work. And she had already predicted their marriage, so why delay the obvious?

He wasn't sure how or when he would propose, but he knew with a certainty that he would. And soon.

Chapter 9

On Monday morning, Milena glided through the sterile white hall-ways of McMillan Psychiatric Hospital, one of the more prominent psychiatric facilities in the Seattle area.

After signing in at the front desk, she secured a visitor badge to her silver blouse. Coming up to a hulking white door, she entered the solarium, a warmly decorated room with massive white framed windows, sea-foam green sofa and loveseat, and currently, an elderly patient with what she guessed was her adult son. They left as Milena took a seat on the couch.

They always met in the solarium. The room was filled with natural light and the pale brick walls and warm decor were excep-tionally soothing. Milena waited patiently until finally Brian, a handsome male nurse, wavy hair secured in a ponytail at the nape of his neck, wheeled Brigita into the sun-filled room.

"Has she improved at all?" Milena rose to greet them.

"I'm sorry, Milena. I wish I had more encouraging news, but this time Brigita's catatonic stupor is lasting longer than usual. She's had her standard round of treatments: Benzodiazepines coupled with Electroconvulsive Therapy. But, nothing is helping." To demonstrate her unresponsiveness, the male nurse lifted Brigita's thin pale arm to chest height, and then let go. The arm hovered there, staying exactly where he left it. She was exhibiting waxy flexibility, one of the symptoms of catatonic schizophrenia. You could move her into various positions and she would stay in that position, reminiscent of a marionette.

Brian took Brigita's arm and gently eased the appendage back onto her lap, to be reunited with the other. She did not react, did not flinch. Just continued staring into the ether. "Don't worry. She'll come around eventually. She always does," he smiled reassuringly.

"I hope so, Brian. Could you give us an hour?"

Nodding, he exited the room, pulling the door softly closed behind him.

Brigita continued to sit in the same position. If she had any awareness that Milena was beside her, she gave no indication. This catatonic stupor had already lasted more than a month, the average period usually limited to one to thirty days. The fact that Brigita's state had exceeded this range left Milena disturbed.

Was she thinner than usual in her pink-striped, flannel pyjamas and furry slippers? The PICC line, a soft, flexible tube inserted into her vein and taped to her forearm, reminded Milena that they had to feed her intravenously during her catatonic states. No wonder she had lost weight. Her auburn tresses were long, parted down the centre. The staff kept her well-groomed. Not a hair out of place.

Brigita's eyes continued to stare off in the same continuous direction. An occasional blink was her only movement. Milena peered deeply into her sister's hazel eyes looking for something, a flicker, an emotion, some sign that she was still somewhere in there.

Nothing.

"It's good to see you, Brigita. Your hair looks nice today." It was like talking to a statue. "I brought you something." Milena dug through lipstick, keys, wallet and tissues until she found what she was looking for in her purse, a new barrette made from brown leather, an intricate floral pattern etched deeply into the surface. She clipped the new barrette into her sister's hair.

"You look beautiful."

Still nothing.

Although speaking to Brigita while in a catatonic stupor felt awkward at first for Milena, the doctors assured that despite her sister's unresponsive nature, she presumably heard and understood everything. They encouraged Milena to speak to her while visiting but to keep the content of the one-sided conversation away from her condition or anything stressful or alarming.

"I have wonderful news." She paused, inhaled deeply, and then the words came rushing out. "I've met someone. His name is Renner Scholz. Oh, Brigita, he's so handsome and brilliant. He's a doctor, studying genetics at BIT. Sometimes, I feel too simple for him, but he treats me like a goddess. He makes me feel so happy."

Her sister stared ahead, frozen.

"I think I'm falling in love with him."

Gushing, all the details of their first meeting and subsequent courtship easily poured out of her. She had to tell someone, or she thought she might burst. With dating Renner and working two jobs, she hadn't had any extra time to spend with her friends lately. Putting them off, she could even feel them getting resentful. Talking with Brigita in this state, although awkward, was cathartic, similar to writing in a diary.

Milena often reflected on memories of her sister before she was this way, before she became ill at the age of seventeen. The relationship between the two sisters was intimate and loving. She was angry at her sister's illness for stealing Brigita away from her. The doctors had explained how schizophrenia was a brain disease that was still not very well understood. She wondered if Renner's research would one day focus on schizophrenia, look for a treatment that would cure *that* disease.

Brian returned after the hour was complete. "Did I come back too soon?" he asked, catching Milena mid-sentence.

"No, this is perfect timing. I have to get to work. I hope she wakes up soon. I'm starting to get worried."

"We'll contact you immediately when she does."

Bending over, she kissed her sister on the cheek. "Goodbye, Brigita. Maybe next time I'll bring Renner in to meet you. You'll totally love him."

★ ★ ★

Brian wheeled Brigita back to her room, leaving her chair positioned in front of a window overlooking a walking path covered in snow. Had Milena looked deeply into her sister's eyes at that moment, past her lifeless irises and pupils, she would have finally seen a flicker of emotion, fleeting but unmistakable. Fear.

Chapter 10

Early Saturday morning, Renner was on his way to meet Dr. Shubally at the lab. The professor had insisted on coming in today despite his habitual absences of late.

When Renner entered the lobby of the lab building and saw Dr. Shubally braced against the wall for support, face the colour of dust, skin folded over on itself like a Shar-Pei puppy, he wondered how the professor had made it in at all. His slacks and navy blue sweater drooped over his diminishing frame. His eyes still held a glimmer of his former self, but even that had dulled over the last two weeks, since the last time they met.

"Were you waiting long?" Renner asked, apologetic, having the shared key for the lab because he was the one primarily working on their project. He unlocked the glass doors and flipped a switch on the wall, the overhead lights flickering and pinging before bathing the room with their artificial yellow glow.

"No, I just arrived myself." Sweat droplets glistened on his forehead.

"I don't want to be disrespectful or prying," Renner cleared his throat, uncomfortably, "but...sir...you don't look so good. Are you sure you're up to microinjecting the embryos today? If not, I can do the procedure on my own."

"Don't be ridiculous. Of course, I'm up to it. I look worse than I feel," he wheezed, as he shuffled in slow motion to their cubicle.

"Besides, I'm in good form today," he added. "I'm out of the house, aren't I?"

At the cubicle, they put on lab coats, Renner not convinced but hopeful the professor was being honest. Working mostly alone on their experiment thus far, he had missed his supervisor's presence, vast knowledge and expertise.

From the desk drawer, Renner procured a pencil and log book to keep track of the methodology of their experiment. Every minute step had to be documented if the experiment were to be replicated someday, whether the outcome was successful or even if it were to yield insignificant results. Studies could always be improved upon, and sometimes the most profound discoveries presented themselves following a series of failed attempts.

Renner had already completed the preliminary preparations for the experiment, isolating and purifying the viral DNA, one commonly known to cause cancer, both in humans and animals. Then, three-week old rats had been injected with hormones, were mated with adult males, and the subsequent embryos that developed were flushed from the females' oviducts when they were two to four cells in their developmental stage and placed into Brinster's medium for forty-eight hours. This was the second day they were in the Brinster's medium, reaching the blastocyst stage, where the cells would now be divided into thirty-two to sixty-four cells. Today Renner and Dr. Shubally were going to microinject the embryos with the purified viral DNA, the most vital step in their experiment.

The animals for biomedical research were in an adjoining room kept locked, strictly available to the animal research personnel, the principal investigators with research grants and their subsequent employees.   As they plodded towards the animal research room, Dr. Shubally paused several times, gasping for air. The distance wasn't far for them to travel, but for the professor, it was too much.

"Let's sit for a moment," Renner suggested, sliding a chair over from a nearby workstation for the professor, who plunked heavily onto it in relief.

"What is wrong, sir? What's going on with you?" Renner asked.

"First of all, let's drop the sir business. You can call me David. It's the name my mother gave me and I'm quite fond of it." He coughed with a deep rattle in his lungs.

"I can't tell you what's wrong with me. The doctors can't find anything abnormal. I've had every test imaginable, been poked and prodded in places I'd rather not mention, and nada. Zilch. It's probably some bug I picked up and due to my age, it's kicked my ass a bit harder. I'll be back to normal in no time."

"I sure hope so. I hate to see you in this condition."

"Oh, I might be old, but I'm tough as leather. So, put your worries to rest." His breathing had steadied, a bit of colour returning to his cheeks. "And what have you been up to? There's a twinkle in your eyes, a new spring in your step," the professor hinted. "What's her name?"

Renner smiled, embarrassed. "Am I that obvious?"

"Yup. So, who's the lucky lady?"

"Her name is Milena." Just saying her name caused Renner's pulse to skyrocket. "She's absolutely amazing, completely different than anyone I've ever met. And get this, she's a psychic." Renner paused in thought, and then asked, "Now that we're on the topic, do you know anything about psychic abilities? As a scientist, I'm struggling with the concept."

"Oh, I wouldn't know much about that."

Renner wasn't surprised, didn't know what he expected, bringing the topic up. But then the professor continued.

"But, I have had an…episode…of sorts. I'm not sure what to make of the experience, whether it was imagined or not."

"What are you referring to?" Renner probed.

Shubally scratched his thinning white hair, a few strands liberated, lightly drifting to the floor. "A few weeks ago, I spiked a fever so high that I became delusional. The doctors thought I wasn't going to recover."

"I didn't know your health had gotten so bad. Why didn't you tell me?"

"I didn't want to worry you. Besides, I'm better now."

Renner knew that wasn't the case, far from being better but allowed the professor to finish his story.

"While I was lying there, my Mara appeared to me. I hadn't seen her since the breast cancer stole her away from me fifteen years ago."

Breast cancer. So, their experiment was personal for him as well.

The professor was lost in the moment, reliving the experience. "She looked so beautiful. Her hair had grown back, and her face was angelic, peaceful," he paused, taking a wheezy breath. "She took my hand and I felt her warmth, and she said, "You're not alone." He shook his head, coming back to the present. "I don't know if what I saw was a hallucination from the fever, but everything felt so real." Tears misted his sunken eyes. His body sagged in the chair, the emotional toll fully exhausting him again. "You know, I think I was being a bit optimistic. I'm not sure I'm up to doing the experiment today. Do you mind if leave?"

"No, of course not. You need to focus on your health. I'll be fine on my own."

Shubally patted him on the back. "You're a good man. Like the son I never had." He struggled to his feet with Renner's assistance.

"Can I help you get home?"

"That's quite alright. I can catch a cab." Renner knew he lived close to the university, well within walking distance, but in his current state a cab would definitely be necessary. "There's a phone in the lobby that I can use. Now, you get to work, young man."

"Yes sir. I mean, David." Renner replied sheepishly. "As long as you're sure you'll be all right."

"I'll be fine. Go on, now. Shoo."

Renner grinned as he watched the old man, still wearing his lab coat, hedge towards the lobby doors. Just as he was exiting, Paul and his thesis supervisor entered the lab. Paul gallantly held the door opened for Dr. Shubally, but once the professor was through, a strange smirk contorted his features.

Closing the door behind Shubally, Paul addressed Renner, insensitive as usual, "What's happened to your supervisor? He looks like death. Guess you're on your own again today. How awful to have to do your experiment without the assistance of your supervisor. The process is going to take much longer this way. That's a real bummer."

"What do you know about it?" Renner challenged.

With a sly smile, he shook his head, condescending, "I see you here, all by your lonesome, whenever I'm here working with *my* supervisor. It's heartbreaking, really."

"Well, save your tears for someone who needs them," Renner retaliated. "I'm right on schedule." Although Paul's comments irked Renner to the core, he didn't want his roommate to know. But the comments caused doubts to surface in his mind. Would he finish on time? Could he do this lofty project on his own?

Paul and his supervisor disappeared into their work station, and Renner stalked to the animal research facility, where he used an alternate key to unlock the door to the restricted area and flicked on the lights. The strong odour of animal musk, feces, and form-aldehyde assaulted his nose.

The doubts continued to percolate in his mind as he gathered his equipment. Why would Paul try to rankle him? Was he jealous? But, of what?

Did Paul's animosity have something to do with Dr. Shubally? Anytime the professor's name was mentioned, he became edgy and over-sensitive.

Locating his embryos, Renner then loaded them along with the other equipment he was using for the next stage of his experiment onto a metal cart and wheeled the cart to a clean work space. Then he snapped a pair of latex gloves over his thick hands where they clung like sausage casings.

Perching on a metal stool, he unloaded his paraphernalia, and then carefully immobilized one of the embryos using an "egg-holding" micropipette. He had already prepared a plastic Petri dish filled with the purified viral DNA, where he placed the embryo inside, covering it immediately with paraffin oil. Using a sharp pointed micropipette, he then took up some of the highly concentrated viral DNA-containing medium surrounding the embryo in the Petri dish and injected it directly into the blastocyst, his view of the process entirely through the lens of a microscope. The injected embryo was then placed inside a culture medium until it would be surgically transferred into a rat different than the egg donor rat. Renner proceeded to suction another embryo onto the end of the "egg-holding" micropipette, continuing with the same methodology he used on the previous blastocyst. He would be injecting the viral DNA into all of the embryos today, all one hundred of them, and then surgically implanting them into eight surrogate mothers. The monotony of the procedure caused his mind to roam.

His thoughts quickly latched on to Milena, his favourite daydream, as of late. The one love in his life, other than his studies. His plan to propose was formed, and now all he needed to do was orchestrate it, in the hope that she would accept. But, he was almost sure she would. Hadn't she already said so herself? She had foretold of their marriage even before they knew each other.

And they were made for each other. There was no question. No other woman had made him feel this way physically or emotionally, and she had told him that she felt the same. He couldn't picture his life without her.

The proposal had to be unique, something she would always remember. Thinking about the proposal for days, he had devised the most romantic plan he could possibly imagine. He was going to ask for another palm reading and have her "predict" the proposal. It was a risk, he knew because there were things he wanted to keep buried in his past. But, letting her know that he now had faith in her abilities would be the best gift he could ever give her, even more meaningful than the gorgeous, princess-cut diamond ring he had already purchased. If, for some reason, his plan failed, and she couldn't intuit the proposal, he would get down on one knee, in a physical sense, and ask for her hand in marriage the old-fashioned way.

Just then, something shifted in the lab, a shadow, snapping him out of his thoughts.   At first, he thought maybe one of the rats or other research animals had escaped and were running free, seen out of the corner of his eye. He could hear them shifting and skittering about their cages, and after a careful check he found all of them locked up securely. Yet, that strange uncomfortable feeling of being watched persisted, overwhelming his senses. He was not alone.

Renner.

The sighing sound of his name made the hairs rise on his arms and scalp.

Putting down the micropipette, he glanced around the lab. There were no obvious places to hide. He searched the cupboards even though he knew they were too small to conceal anyone. All he saw were empty beakers, solutions, microscopes, and cages upon cages of research animals.

Renner.

His name again, insistent, commanding, sounding male and inhuman at the same time.

It reminded him of something Milena had said about her sister that bothered him.

She started talking about dark spirits. She could see them every-where, and they would talk to her, call her name.

Renner jumped at the sharp rapping against the lab door. Had he been injecting an embryo, the organism would have been destroyed by the sudden jolt. His paranoid mind was getting the best of him.

It was only Paul.

"Soccer has been switched to tomorrow, in case you haven't heard. Too many players had prior commitments, so today's game is cancelled." His hair was messy, his lab coat yellow and wrinkled.

"We'll be playing at the indoor field in Seattle due to all the snow. We can walk up together half an hour before the game starts. Should give us enough time to get there, and the walk will be a good warm-up for us."

"Oh. Uh, OK." Renner was caught off guard. Did he want to walk to the indoor field with Paul tomorrow? Not particularly. However, changing his mind was not an option. Paul had already left.

Renner wondered if Paul had been there longer. Was the strange presence he felt just his roommate? Was Paul calling his name? But the door had been closed, and the feeling of being watched had come from within the room. Obviously, there was no one there, his overactive imagination playing tricks on him.

Why was Paul being friendly again all of a sudden? Renner found keeping track of his roommate's highs and lows was difficult. One moment, lighthearted and jovial, the next, sarcastic and irritable. Maybe he was bipolar. He certainly had all of the symptoms and personality traits. For the most part, Renner continued to avoid him as much as possible. The soccer games didn't count as they were with other men, whom Renner enjoyed being around.

After several hours of arduous concentration, precision, and effort, Renner completed implanting the embryos into all of the female rats. Returning the rats to their cages, he then locked the animal research door behind him, storing his notes in his lab cubicle. The day had grown short, but he thought he would visit the library again. After talking with Milena, his theory about psychic abilities having a genetic element was somewhat supported. He wanted to determine if anyone had taken a deeper look into this line of thought, discovered a particular DNA strand that differed between psychic and non-psychic individuals. He hadn't seen any such research during his first library search, but maybe the information had been missed.

When he arrived at the library, the atmosphere was chaotic, no vacant tables in sight. Instead of staying, Renner grabbed more research books on psychic phenomena and decided to bring them back to the dorm.

Approaching his dorm room, he shifted the armload of books he carried to open the door, but before he had a chance to touch the knob, the door flew open. And out popped Wendy. Dishevelled, shirt half-buttoned, shoes dangling from her fingertips. He had a momentary flash of déjà vu from his first day on campus. With eyes wide, she froze in surprise. Humiliation flashed across her features, and she rushed off down the hall with head held low.

Renner entered the apartment. Paul, clad in a thin pair of boxer shorts, was splayed on his bed. Long tendrils of smoke escaped his mouth as he puffed on a cigarette in post-coital satisfaction.

"What do we have here?" Renner asked bemused, unloading the library books on his desk and then closing the door to their room.

"Hope you don't mind, brother."

"Why would I mind?" Renner, in truth, was relieved that Wendy might have finally moved on. "Is she all right? She looked kind of upset."

"What's that supposed to mean? Of course, she's all right," he barked defensively, in a mood again. "Never better, I'm sure."

"Right." Renner dropped the subject.

★ ★ ★

A week later, after ironing out his plan for proposing to Milena, Renner escaped into the commons room of Leighton House, no longer able to delay the inevitable. Now that he had a plan in place, the time had come to make their relationship official.

Things were moving quickly, he was aware, but he was always the type of person to go after what he wanted. Obsessive to a point with his studies, he had pushed himself to the top of the class, through his medical training, and then to get the opportunity to come to America and work on breakthrough research with none other than Dr. Shubally. And now, with Milena, he felt the strongest need to secure her as his bride. Did it have something to do with his early upbringing, being deprived of opportunities and love, which drove him now so hard to get what he wanted? Probably, but he wasn't going to over think it. He just wanted to follow his heart.

His fingers trembled as he dialed the cherry red rotary telephone. She answered on the second ring with a breathless hello. Had she been anticipating his call?

"Hi, Milena. Are you free tonight?"

"Yes," she responded before he finished asking.

"I was wondering if you would mind doing another reading for me. Another palm reading?"

She hesitated, a little confused. "Oh. Of course. You want to take another swing at it?"

"Yes, I would. I have some important questions that need to be answered."

"Is everything OK?"

"Better than OK," Renner couldn't contain a smile.

"I have a few clients, but I'll be wrapping up around eight. You can come by my office then."

"I can't wait."

After hanging up the telephone, he extracted the one karat engagement ring from his pocket, tracing the delicate engraving on the gold band, stroking the angled surfaces of the diamond. His heart fluttered uncontrollably in his chest.

As if on cue, Paul came sauntering into the common room, and upon seeing the engagement ring in Renner's hand, froze.

"So, you caved in after all," he huffed. "You're going to strap on the old ball and chain. I knew from the second you told me about her crazy prediction that her plan was to pin you down, and you fell for her ruse, you stupid bastard." With face beet red, he was more agitated than usual. What was his problem? Was he also jealous of Milena?

"Paul, until you experience true love yourself—you know, I can't really explain it to you."

"What, you think you're in love with her? You hardly even know her."

"I know everything I need to know about her." He wasn't going to let Paul ruin this day for him. Everything had to go perfectly. Discreetly, he pocketed the ring.

Paul continued pushing. "What if she says no? You'll probably scare her off. It's too much, too soon."

"If you can't be happy for me, then maybe you should mind your own business," he advised Paul while exiting the lounge.

"Good luck! You're probably going to need it!" Paul hollered after him.

★ ★ ★

Although the wind was still, the air, icebox cold, bit into Renner's skin as he walked the last few steps from the bus stop to the now familiar building where Milena worked. He tried to ignore the strange sensation that he was being watched again, followed. His name being hissed in the wind. It had to be paranoia. Nothing else. There was never anybody there, only shadows. Nonetheless, he quickened his pace.

The familiar sign was posted outside the door of her building. That's when the first sliver of doubt crept into his mind. Paul's discouraging words echoed loudly in his head as if delivered through a megaphone. *You'll probably scare her off. It's too much, too soon.*

What if she did say no? Was he rushing things? They had only been dating since school started four months ago, not a long time. Yet, he felt as if he had known her forever.

The chimes announced his arrival. Sliding onto the lounge chair beside the aquarium, he placed his right hand in the pocket holding the ring, fingering the solidity for courage.

Milena's lilting voice floated to him from the adjoining room, along with the smell of incense. His palms grew moist, his breathing quickened. Could he go through with this?

But, didn't he have to? He had come this far and couldn't imagine another moment without securing Milena as his own, to be his wife, so they could be together forever, solidifying their bond so no one could tear them apart.

He would do it. No matter what fears tried to interfere.

The scraping of chairs and approaching footsteps told Renner the psychic reading in the adjoining room had concluded. A large man, black as night, left the room, thanking Milena as he passed a few crumpled bills into her hands. Tugging on dirt caked work boots and a fleece-lined jacket, he left the building.

It was time.

Milena turned to him, her blue eyes bright and brimming with love. Running to him, they hugged, and then kissed deeply. His fingers slipped through her silken hair.

"Are you ready, skeptic?" she teased with a captivating smile, not knowing what he was essentially preparing for.

"I'm ready." And he was. His nerves and stomach settled upon seeing his lover. She gave him courage, made him feel secure in their devotion and commitment to each other.

Grabbing his hand, she led him into her chamber. The scent of incense overwhelmed his senses, causing his head to swim. He had to stay focused for this to work.

They both sat, and Renner placed his hands, palms turned upward, into Milena's waiting hands.

She smiled warmly, causing his heart to melt.

"Ready?" she asked again.

"Ready." Focusing his mind, he started telepathically sending the message to her. *Will you marry me?* Simultaneously, he imagined the ring in his pocket, and going down on one knee to propose.

"What's your question?" she gently asked.

He opened one eye. "I want *you* to figure my question out." He grinned coyly, then closed his eye again.

"That's not usually how this works," she explained. "What do you have up your sleeve, Renner Scholz?"

It wasn't what he had up his sleeve, but rather what he had in his pocket that he wanted to relay to Milena. "I know this isn't how you usually do things but trust me for a minute. For this purpose, the reading has to be this way." He smiled cryptically.

Milena selected his right hand out of the two, cupped it in her own hands, and closed her eyes, her face peaceful, searching. Moments passed.

Renner kept sending her the same image over and over again. Him going down on one knee and asking for her to marry him. He kept repeating the words to himself, the biggest question he would ever ask anyone. He held his breath. Occasionally, he peeked at her through squinted eyelids.

Suddenly, a grim expression clouded Milena's features. Her eyes grew wide, and she threw Renner's hand away from her in revulsion, as if she realized she was holding a dead carp. "No!" she recoiled in horror.

Chapter 11

Renner, a young boy of nine, leans against his favourite, old apple tree in the front yard of his family's property. The hour is late, the darkness oppressive, the moon completely obscured. The grass is tall and damp, soaking into the one pair of pants he owns. He hears the commotion inside the house despite his constant attempts to block out the sounds, glass shattering, voices raised in anger. This is not an abnormal occurrence; fear is evident in the child. As the struggle inside grows increasingly violent, Renner retreats to his usual hiding place—the kitchen cabinet under the sink. Cautiously, he creeps into the house, careful to avoid the door banging shut behind him, the one with the busted hinges that need replacing. Stealthily, he crawls through the kitchen, slipping under the sink as he hears a loud bang.

"You think you're better than me?" Vater's voice bellows.

Another crash.

Something topples over, shattering into pieces. A loud moan escapes his mutti's mouth earning her another round of punches. Renner can hear the sound of his vater's fists strike her repeatedly.

"Pleeze, thstop," she pleads, words muffled, her jaw possibly broken again.

"That's the last time you talk back to me. Do you hear me? DO YOU HEAR ME?"

"I...can't take thish...anymore. Just let ush go."

Renner hopes his mother will stop talking, realize that this makes Vater angrier. Doesn't she know he will never let them go?

Another slam, bodies crashing into furniture.

"You think I'm gonna let you take away MY son? MY flesh and blood? You stupid Schlampe. Just for saying that, I'm gonna teach you a lesson you'll never forget!"

A struggle ensues, indicated by more crashing, and then, unexpectedly, his father yelps out in pain. His mother comes scrambling through the kitchen door, eyes filled with terror like a hunted animal. A nasty gash on her forehead spills blood down her cheek.

She almost reaches the back door. Almost.

Renner watches from the cabinet, the door cracked open a sliver, to view the horror beyond. He's frozen in his spot, unable to move. Unable to help. Unable to look away as his father slams into her from behind, sending her sprawling across the kitchen tiles, her head connecting with the partially open back door that had almost granted her freedom. She claws the ground, trying to inch away from him, fingernails splintering, but he drags her towards him as if she weighs no more than a young child. Viciously, he flips her over onto her back. Mutti stiffens.

Heavy fists rain down on her, wave after wave, her face instantly swelling and ballooning until she is unrecognizable. Her head cocks to the side, seeing Renner behind the cabinet door. Bruised, swollen eyes search his, pleading, begging him to do something. But he's frozen in his spot, fearful his vater will notice where her attention is focused.

His mutti's body spasms and then becomes still. Face muscles slackening, eyes now glazed marbles, unseeing.

Even after she is long dead, Vater keeps pummelling until her skull caves in, and blood leaks out of her ears and mouth. Dark, red blood, so much blood.

Renner watches as Vater finally stops, his anger spent. His expression is flat, devoid of emotion. Gathering cleaning supplies, he rolls his wife's body up in the flat-weave rug with the yellow flowers from the kitchen floor, and sterilizes the kitchen, until every last drop of blood is gone. He leaves with the rolled-up rug casually slung over his shoulder as he would a sack of potatoes.

★ ★ ★

When the vision came, Milena didn't know what she was seeing. At first, there was a rug with bright, yellow flowers rolled up into a lumpy tube. Then a red spot appeared in the fibres, spreading until the entire rug was saturated in vibrant blood.

The scene shifted, and she was there, watching through Renner's eyes as a young child. His father brutally beating his mother. The blood, the smell of iron in the air, her grunts as she was hit over and over again. And Renner's emotions flooded through her as if they were her own: her stomach clenched, bile rose in the back of her throat, and an intense fear of being next froze her insides.

Why hadn't he told her what had happened in his past? A bit of a warning would have been appreciated. Instead, she felt traumatized by the violence she had witnessed first-hand. The air felt sucked out of her lungs. Now, paralyzed with shock, she sat there in her office, unable to respond.

Renner looked confused, brows furrowed, holding his discarded hand as if injured. "What's wrong? I thought you'd be happy," he asked, shaking his head.

"Happy? How could that make me happy?"

Renner's face fell, and Milena wondered what he thought she had seen. For clarity, she asked, "Why didn't you tell me your mother was murdered?"

"Oh. I see." He sat back in his chair with a look of resignation. "You weren't meant to see that. I'm sorry, Milena. I had other plans for our reading."

"Oh, Renner. What you went through." She reached out to console him, but he flinched. "You don't have to hold back from me. I would never judge you for your father's crime. I know how you felt in that moment, the fear. I felt as if I was in your body, watching the whole thing happen. The experience was absolutely horrifying. Have you ever talked about this to anyone?"

"No, never."

"Would you feel comfortable enough talking to me? I can't imagine how hard it would be to keep that type of trauma bottled up for so many years."

"Honestly, I don't want to talk about that night, never planned to, but what difference does it make now that you know the worst part?"

"I'm here for you. You can tell me anything" Milena reassured him.

With head held low, reluctantly he spoke about the secret from his past.

"It was an arranged marriage. Ulrich Reinhardt, my biological father, convinced Berta's parents to give him their daughter in marriage before he went off to fight in the war, even though he was fifteen years her senior. During the war, he stood right by Hitler's side, enforcing his rules, doling out whatever heinous punishments he was ordered. When the war was finally lost; somehow, he escaped arrest, and returned home."

"My mother didn't say much. She wasn't a very talkative woman, but I remember her telling me once, after I had endured a heavy beating from my father that he had been a different man before the war. Not kind or gentle or anything. But, confident, cocky almost. Sociable. People enjoyed his company. But, the war changed him, ruined him. He became an alcoholic after, trying to forget what he saw or maybe what he did. He was a disgusting man. That's the way I remember him."

"So, you were beaten too?"

"It was as if he was looking for excuses to release his rage on someone. If I so much as breathed the wrong way, I paid the price. And my mother, she was afraid to interfere. I often hoped she would stop him, you know?" He glanced up at Milena, then down again. "And that she would take us away, somewhere safe, where he'd never find us." He fidgeted with the seam of his shirt.

Licking his lips, he swallowed hard. "The day...it...happened, she finally stood up to him. And then I was watching her get beaten, her last beating. And I didn't interfere. I could have spoken up. Maybe I could have saved her life or given her that extra moment to reach the door...get through it."

"Or it could have been you who was beaten to death. And what good would that have been? You can't blame yourself for what happened, Renner. You were a little boy."

"It might have made a difference." Tears slid down his cheeks, his voice choked up.

"My mother was timid, had no friends, and wasn't allowed to socialize. Nobody would have noticed her missing. If the neighbour hadn't heard her screams and called the police, my father probably would have gotten away with murder."

"What happened afterwards?"

"My father was arrested, and I was taken straight to the orphanage where shortly after I was adopted. That's when my real life began. I was enrolled in school for the first time, and my adoptive parents gave me everything I could ever ask for."

"I can't believe all that you went through. I'm glad you shared this with me, even though you had different intentions. What was your plan for today's reading if you weren't intending to show me your past?" As soon as the question fell off of her lips, realization dawned on her as she caught wind of his thoughts.

A proposal. He had wanted the moment to be perfect.

"I'm sorry, Renner. Were you going to propose?"

He nodded, eyes filled with remorse.

"And I ruined it," she stated.

"No, this isn't your fault. The idea was stupid to begin with. Somehow, I thought I could control what you would see with your gift, but I couldn't have been more wrong. I'm sorry I wasted your time."

Abruptly, he stood up to leave, the sound of the chair scraping the ground, jarring.

"Yes."

He paused. "Do you mean what I think you mean?"

"Yes, I will marry you," she said more clearly. Standing, she moved around the table and engulfed him in her arms.

"What happened in your past, that's not who you are, and has nothing to do with the wonderful, warm, compassionate man you've become. The man I have totally fallen head over heels in love with. This does nothing to change how I feel about you. So, if the offer is still on the table, my answer is yes."

Renner gripped Milena's shoulders tightly, kissed her with a new ferocity. "I thought I would lose you if you knew the truth." Wiping the tears from his eyes, he withdrew a velvet box from his pocket, and got down on one knee. The box sprang open in front of Milena, displaying the gorgeous jewel within.

"I've been planning this moment for a while, and although the proposal didn't go according to my plans, I still want this to be a special moment for you."

"The fact that you're able to trust me with your past is special to me, Renner. I wish you had told me sooner."

He smiled, "We still need to make this official. Milena, will you marry me?"

She pulled him up, tearful. "Yes. Yes, of course I will marry you, Renner." They kissed passionately. When they pulled apart, Renner slipped the sparkly bauble onto her slender finger, and softly kissed the top of her head.

"I love you, Milena," he whispered. "Now we'll be joined forever."

★ ★ ★

When Renner returned to the apartment, Wendy and Paul were parked on the mustard chairs as if awaiting his return. Wendy had become a permanent fixture around their place in the last week, and Renner thought perhaps they were a couple. Paul denied any relationship, claiming she was an easy lay, but Renner thought there was more to the situation. Perhaps, the real purpose of having

Wendy around was intended to aggravate him. And her presence did aggravate him, since most of the time she would stare at him, accusingly, pouty. Their relationship confused Renner. Why would Wendy even want to hang around with Paul? She clearly didn't have any warm and fuzzy feelings for his roommate. They had zero chemistry; she was distant around him, and he treated her like crap.

Secretly, he felt that maybe the real reason she hung around was in case things didn't work out between him and Milena or to be in his company however she could.

"So, did you do it? Did you pop the question?" Paul grilled as if he suddenly cared. Apparently experiencing a high in his mood swings.

"Yes, I did."

"And what did she say?" Paul continued acting his best friend, excited to hear the details.

"She said yes."

Wendy looked as if she had been stabbed in the heart.

"So, when's the big day?"

Suddenly Renner felt emotionally wrung out, like an old wash cloth. The reading hadn't gone according to plan, and even though he was glad Milena now knew of his past, he had enough emotional excitement for one day. He wasn't in the mood for Paul's annoying nature.

"I'm not sure yet." Renner went into the cooler on his side of the room and grabbed a soda. Popping the top, he drank deeply.

"So, are you going to have a big wedding or a small one?"

"I haven't had a chance to think about the details. We don't have any family here, so we'll probably elope. Get married at city hall by the justice of the peace. Milena's a legal citizen so I don't think we'll have a problem."

"Well, you're going to need witnesses, right? What about me and Wendy?"

Renner almost choked while swallowing another sip of soda. "Why would you want to?"

"I'll try not to take offense to that. Of course, we would be honoured to be your witnesses, right, Wendy?"

Looking at him tight-lipped, daggers shooting out of her eyes, she nodded her assent.

"It's settled then. We'll stand up for you at your wedding. Congratulations, man!" Paul stood up and hugged Renner, patting him several times on the back.

Renner didn't know what just happened.

Chapter 12

Renner Scholz strode off the bustling campus grounds of BIT and onto the more tranquil street of O'Hara Crescent. A semi-circle of slumbering bungalows greeted him. The warm spring wind whirled about him in gusts and gales, resembling the inner turbulence of emotions he was battling—frustration, guilt, nervousness, and elation—a strange combination, confusing and constant.

His first year in America had been the opposite of what he had envisioned. He'd predicted he'd be entrenched in academia, not romance. At this point, he assumed his dissertation would be well underway, the experiment successfully progressing as hypothesized, the Nobel Prize within his grasp. Instead, he was behind in his progress as Professor Shubally became permanently absent due to his worsening mysterious illness. Of course, the old man wasn't to blame, his last intention would be to hold Renner back from their research, but that's exactly what was happening. Renner had continued to forge ahead with as much as he could, but now the professor's assistance was necessary.

Glitches in the cancer rat model were slowly cropping up, hinting at flaws in their hypothesis and procedure. Firstly, the rat embryos injected with the viral DNA had a higher mortality rate than expected. Seventy percent of their specimens perished within the first month of birth. Of the thirty percent survivors, a mere portion contained the modified gene in their genetic code. Secondly, tumour growth amongst the surviving specimens containing the modified gene had failed to occur. How could their model serve as a tumour model to test cancer treatments and medications if there weren't any tumours? Renner was trying to remain hopeful, but there should have been malignant growths by now.

One year remained to complete his thesis experiment. The clock was ticking, and he was starting to fear he wouldn't finish in time to graduate.

Now that summer was a few weeks away, and Renner was planning on taking Milena out of the country for the holidays, the professor had promised to step up to the plate. Hence, the guilt.

Renner selected Professor Shubally's brown, brick bungalow from the cluster of homes, marched across the unkempt lawn and up the cracked and crumbling steps to his door. Giving a loud knock, a full minute passed by the time the door eased open. The professor wore a weak smile on his sunken face, along with slippers, a royal blue robe, and a tattered old blanket draped around his withered shoulders.

Renner almost keeled over. Having solely conversed with the professor by telephone the past few weeks, he was shocked at seeing how much more he had deteriorated in such a short time. His complexion, formerly the colour of dust, now looked jaundiced and most of his downy, white hair had fallen out. He had lost an alarming amount of weight, and his eyes had completely lost their lustre.

"Come in, come in," the professor stood to the side allowing Renner to enter. "Sorry about the mess." Clutter and unwashed dishes were strewn about the living room.

A strong, sour smell assaulted Renner as he entered. He shed his black trench coat and shoes. Smoothing out his windblown tresses, he replied, "Please don't apologize."

"Being an old bachelor and in poor shape, keeping up with the housekeeping has been difficult. Please, have a seat."

The old man shuffled over to an orange loveseat, Renner following, pushing aside a knitted mauve blanket, so he could join him on the couch. He then placed the briefcase on the floor in front of them, the one containing all of their research and experimental data.

"Look, Professor, if you're not up to looking through all this material, we can wait until another time. You should continue focusing on your health right now."

"Nonsense, lad. I'm bored cooped up in here week after week. High time I got up to speed with where we are in the experiment."

Renner hesitated. "Are you sure?"

"I insist."

Renner acquiesced, unlocking the briefcase, fishing out research documents and findings, and handed them to the professor who accepted them with a feeble hand. He riffled through the paperwork, giving a quick glance at the results.

"Still no tumour growth," Renner provided.

The professor nodded, disappointed.

"Are you sure you're strong enough to go to the lab and check on the rats while I'm away?" Renner asked the professor, doubtful.

"I'll manage. Somebody needs to monitor the little critters while you're on holidays, check for tumours and subsequent metastases, if we're lucky. Fingers crossed. Worst case scenario, I can have one of the lab assistants check on them for me. They can monitor any changes in the rats' conditions as good as I can, maybe even better. So, where are you heading for your holidays, if you don't mind my asking?"

Renner couldn't suppress his smile if he tried. The nervous excitement and jubilation rekindled as he shared his happy news with the professor.

"I'm happy to say, sir, that I'll be going on my honeymoon."

"Congratulations, Renner!" The professor struggled to his feet and shook Renner's hand, patted him gently on the back. "Are you marrying the young woman you were telling me about before? The psychic?"

Renner nodded, with a wide smile.

"When's the big day?"

"Today," Renner responded, stomach somersaulting as the reality struck home.

"Well, I'm so happy for you both, and I wish you the best!" the professor again patted him on the back. "That's wonderful news. Marriage isn't easy, by any means, but if you find the right one, it will be the best thing you've ever done." The old man erupted into a coughing fit so intense, Renner had to assist him back onto the couch, and then rushed to the kitchen, searching through endless sullied dishes, finally settling on the cleanest looking glass to fill up with water. He delivered the drink to the professor, who was still hacking uncontrollably.

Graciously accepting the glass, the old man chugged down the contents, which brought instant relief.

"Thank you, my boy."

Renner looked deeply concerned. "You're much worse. I'm sorry to be so direct, but I'm worried about you. Are the doctor's still unsure about the nature of your condition?"

"They're stumped. They keep running their tests but nothing conclusive. And none of the treatments are helping. I feel a little stronger today but other days...I'm sorry if I'm holding you back," he said with sincerity.

"We'll get through this, sir."

Professor Shubally coughed again, the rattle in his chest indicative of infection or fluid in the lungs. He wiped his mouth with a sodden handkerchief.

"Now tell me more about this honeymoon."

"I'm surprising Milena with a trip to Germany to meet my family as my wedding present to her. She has no idea."

"I'm sure she'll love the gesture." The old man's eyes were growing heavy and his voice sounded thin. Getting the feeling that the professor needed rest, Renner wrapped up their visit.

"Just hold on to the research until I get back into town. Take your time going through everything. There's no rush."

"I'll take good care of our research, no worries there. I'll guard it with my life. Just have a great time."

Renner waved goodbye, genuinely concerned for the old man. However, as heavy as the professor's mysterious illness weighed on his mind, today was not the day to ruminate over sad matters.

After all, today was his wedding day.

He strolled with determination back to Leighton House, where his suit was pressed, ready for the big day. He had decided upon a white, ruffled blouse and wide lapelled baby blue suit, a surefire hit. As Renner had anticipated, they chose to get married at city hall and had already completed the pre-requisite applications, paper work, and blood tests.

Paul and Wendy would be their witnesses. Milena suggested inviting some friends—Olivia (the foreign exchange student who invited her to America) and a few other girls Renner hadn't even met. But, after careful consideration Renner persuaded her to keep the wedding a private affair. They didn't have any family to include, and friends would expect a fancy reception, which they hadn't planned and couldn't afford. Milena still didn't know that Renner had invested most of his spending money on her engagement ring and wedding present.

Instead of a big wedding reception, they would celebrate together in Germany with Renner's parents. He hoped Milena would be surprised and pleased with his wedding gift.

When they returned from their holiday, Renner would be moving in to Milena's apartment. No more Paul to deal with or the discomfort of Wendy's constant presence.

Renner continued to sail down the familiar streets, eager to return to his dorm room to get ready for the big day. As Dr. Shubally said, getting married would be the best thing he ever did, because he knew without a doubt that Milena was the one love for him. Now and forever.

★ ★ ★

One by one, Milena unravelled curlers from her hair, until her mane cascaded over her soft shoulders in flawless black ringlets.

Once her hair was perfected, she delicately peeled back the plastic protector covering her wedding dress. They had decided to keep their wedding simple, but she couldn't resist when she saw the elaborate gown at the bridal shop, even though the price put a large dent in her savings.

The gown was made of flowing material in alabaster white, with a fitted bodice, delicate lace and silk embroidery, a modest train and off-the-shoulder straps. White satin pumps and a lace veil covering for her face completed the ensemble.

She couldn't believe the day had finally arrived.

Pulling up the heavy bridal gown, she had to shimmy her hips past the tight bodice. With a contortionist's flexibility, she twisted and reached behind her, zipping up the dress, so the bodice fit snugly against her slim frame. She tried not to think of how glaringly absent her mother and sister were in the moment, as next, she nestled the veil amongst the raven curls on the crown of her hair, and finally slid satiny shoes on her perfectly manicured feet. The mirror reflected her image once all of her ministrations were complete. The woman looking back at her resembled a princess from the fairytales she used to read as a young girl.

Renner will be pleased.

They agreed to follow tradition and resist seeing each other until the wedding. Renner, wanting the best for his new bride, had hired a limousine to escort her to Barbora Bay City Hall, where she would meet up with him, Paul, and Wendy for the ceremony.

She wasn't fond of Paul, from the stories Renner had confided in her. He was described as moody, impolite, abrasive and at times downright mean, and Wendy—she didn't know her whatsoever. Still not sure why Renner wanted them serving as witnesses at their wedding, she would have much rather had her friends there. But, Renner had been insistent, and besides, what could she do now. That ship had sailed.

An hour later, the limo pulled up in front of city hall, a large beige, brick building with Richardsonian Romanesque architecture, a tall central tower with peaked roof and a tower clock, and a grassy landscape in front dotted with trees and pink spring flowers.

What am I doing?

With the ceremony mere moments away, Milena was suddenly overcome by a wave of nervousness. Her heart pounded in her chest, and a light perspiration dampened her forehead and palms. Calming down took several moments. Inhaling deeply and exhaling fully, she pushed away the jitters threatening to ruin her day.

Come on Milena, get a grip.

A number of deep breaths later, she felt sufficiently composed to enter the city hall and marry the man she loved more than life itself.

Thanking the limo driver, she gathered the heavy lace train of her gown into her arms and waddled up the concrete steps. Entering the city hall lobby, an elderly receptionist welcomed her and then guided her to where the wedding ceremony was to be held.

As soon as she saw Renner standing at the front of the main hall, all dapper in his suit, and a goofy love-sick grin on his cleanly shaven face, all of her nervous energy dissipated. This man was going to be her husband, this wonderful, brilliant, gorgeous man, and she couldn't be happier.

Upon seeing her framed in the doorway, Renner immediately rushed over, scooping her into his arms. Breathily, he whispered in her ear, "You look amazing."

"You're looking pretty handsome yourself." The blue shade of the suit transformed his eyes into a tropical aqua that drew her in and gave her sea legs.

Paul and Wendy shuffled over to the young couple and stood awkwardly behind them.

"Oh, Milena, this is Paul, my roommate." They clumsily hugged, and he kissed both of her cheeks in a lingering unpleasant way.

"It's funny we're meeting for the first time, seeing that you and Renner have been dating for months," Paul commented.

Milena knew the reason why. Renner had purposefully met with Milena everywhere other than the dorm to avoid his roommate. She still wondered why Paul had to be a part of their big day, the gesture completely at odds with their relationship.

"I've heard so much about you," Paul leered.

"Me too."

"Nothing bad, I hope," Paul said jokingly.

Milena shot Renner a conspiratorial look. "No, not at all."

"And this is Wendy, Paul's, um, friend."

"I used to think we were friends, too," Wendy responded, hurt.

Renner cleared his throat uncomfortably. "Let's commence, shall we?"

Milena gave him a questioning look. "What did she mean by that?" she whispered underneath her breath as they walked towards the front of the hall. "She *used* to think you were friends?"

"She was never a friend. I'd say she was more of a stalker." Milena giggled.

Renner grabbed Milena's hand and guided her to where the magistrate had just entered.

The magistrate was a bald, pasty gentleman wearing a formal black suit and tie. Introducing himself, he briefly explained how the process was to unfold, then swiftly began with the ceremony.

"On this special occasion of your marriage, two lives, two hearts, two souls are joined to become one. You remain unique in your individuality, still fulfilling your own destinies, but now with the love and support from each other, you have a commitment that transcends all circumstances."

Renner's turquoise eyes were lit from within, sparkling, and Milena felt that she had never seen anything so beautiful.

The magistrate continued in a rehearsed monotone, "We use rings to represent the commitment you now make to each other. Renner, I now ask you to place this ring upon Milena's finger and repeat the marriage vows after me."

Renner and Milena turned their bodies to face each other. Grasping each other's hands, Milena could feel the warm and sweaty palms of her husband-to-be. She smiled supportively.

"Do you, Renner Scholz, take this woman, Milena Nowak, to be your lawful wedded wife, to love, honour and cherish her through sickness and in health, through the good times and the bad, until death do you part?"

Renner agreed in a shaky voice, "I do."

"Place the ring upon her finger and repeat after me," the magistrate instructed.

As Renner slipped the wedding band onto Milena's left ring finger she had a sudden flashing glimpse into their future.

Her blood ran cold. Her entire body went rigid.

"With this ring I thee wed," she could hear Renner's voice from a great distance, like she was at the end of a long winding tunnel and he was at the opposite side.

All the warmth and happiness drained from her face. The ability to breathe or swallow became impossibly difficult, and her heart pounded in her head, threatening to burst her eardrums. Surely the vision was false or a remnant of the story Renner had told her about his biological parents. Masking her feelings, she attempted to act as if nothing was wrong. She pushed the horrifying image down deep into the farthest recesses of her mind.

Despite her attempts to hide her emotions, Renner noticed the look of despair on her face. Bending over, he whispered in her ear, concerned, "Are you OK?"

She nodded yes, reassuring him that everything was fine, but, inside, she was in turmoil. *This isn't real, the vision is wrong. It's just confusion over the images from the day Renner proposed mixed with my nerves. It has to be. Everything really is OK. This vision must be a mistake. So, why do I feel so terrified?*

Somehow, she got through the rest of the ceremony.

After repeating the vows back to Renner, bathed in a cold sweat, she, too, placed the wedding band upon his ring finger, and the magistrate directed the couple to again join hands.

"By the act of reciting your vows you are now bound by your love and the law. Therefore, in accordance with the law of Washington and by virtue of the authority vested in me by the law of Washington, I do pronounce you husband and wife."

Renner beamed with elation. Milena attempted to match his feelings, but the effort was forced. Her smile wavered, her eyes nervously flicking about.

"From this day forward, you are one. You must share all your experiences with each other—your happiness and sorrow, your successes and failures, your goals and transitions. I wish you both a life brimming with your love. You may now kiss the bride."

Milena cringed, concerned she would have more visions upon their lips connecting. Thankfully, the opposite occurred. Renner lifted the lacy veil away from Milena's face, leaned over, and kissed her so fervently that the disturbing images dissolved like an ice cube on a hot, sunny deck.

The ceremony complete, the young couple proceeded to sign the appropriate marriage documents. The disturbing images were gone, as if they had never existed, and when Milena tried to see them again with her psychic gift, they were no longer within her grasp. Relieved, she felt even more certain that the visions were nothing concerning, and she was able to fully immerse herself back into the moment. Paul and Wendy remained stoic throughout, apparently not as elated as the newly married couple, but their reactions didn't matter. Milena and Renner barely noticed them.

Swept away in the moment, they only saw each other. Finally, their union was complete.

★ ★ ★

Milena's face was strained as the cab pulled up to Renner's parents' elegant two-story residence in Erfurt, Germany, Renner's hometown. Anxiety cramped her insides despite Renner's constant attempts to placate his wife.

"I can't believe I'm finally part of a family again. But, what if they hate me?"

"Relax. They're going to love you."

With furrowed brow, she replied, "Maybe we should have told them we were coming. Maybe we should have told them we got married. This might be too much excitement for them all at once. What if they're angry that we didn't invite them to the wedding?"

Renner kissed the top of her head. "You worry too much. Everything will be fine."

The young couple exited the cab and unloaded their matching pewter luggage onto the concrete driveway. Renner paid the driver, adding a hefty tip, and they crept up the front steps to the door.

"Here goes," he said, winking as he gave the brass door knocker three brisk raps. Milena cowered behind Renner.

After what felt an eternity, Renner's unsuspecting mother opened the door, froze, and dropped the dishtowel she had been clutching.

"Renner, is that really you?" she exclaimed, touching his face to make sure he was real. "Oh, my baby, my baby! Konstantin, he's here! I can't believe this is happening, he's here! Our son!" she bellowed back into the house with joy. Reaching up, she engulfed Renner in a fierce hug. During their emotional embrace, Renner's mother noticed Milena nervously hiding behind him.

"Mutti, let me introduce you to Milena...your new daughter-in-law."

"My what? Oh my, oh my!" She engulfed Milena in an even stronger bone-popping hug, and then hugged Renner again in what was now a group affair.

"Why didn't you tell us? You should've gotten married here." His mother looked disappointed, although still brimming with joy.

Milena shot Renner an "*I told you so*" look.

Renner's father slowly hobbled out of the hallway towing an oxygen canister behind him. A massive smile lit up the older man's face, temporarily masking his sickly state. "What's this I hear about a wedding?"

Renner translated from German to English as his parents welcomed Milena into the family.

The enticing aroma of freshly baked bread and potato soup filled the cozy home. Renner's mutti ushered the young wedded couple into the kitchen for a meal and demanded details of their courtship and wedding. Renner had been keeping his parents abreast of his relationship with Milena via letters, but the engagement and marriage were a complete surprise.

"Ah, I'm happy to be home," Renner sighed. "I missed you both so much." He turned to face his father, concern in his eyes. Touched the tube connecting his father to the oxygen tank. "This is new."

"You know the doctors. Always over exaggerating every little thing. No need to worry. I'm fine. Just happy you're home."

"How long can you stay?" Mona, Renner's mother, asked.

"A few weeks. I want to show Milena as much of Germany as I can before we have to return to America."

"You're welcome to stay as long as you wish. If the choice were up to me, I would have you stay permanently. What about when you have kids, how will we see our grandbabies? You are going to have children, right?" Renner's mother addressed Milena, eyes filled with hope and longing. Milena was about to respond when Renner abruptly interjected.

"Mutti, we just got married. That's the furthest thing from our minds." Standing up from the kitchen table, he grabbed the suitcases they had left at the front entrance.

Milena and Mona exchanged slighted expressions.

"I'm assuming we'll stay in my old room. Is that all right?"

"Of course, Renner. You don't have to ask, it's your room. I'll grab an extra pillow and towels." Mona left the kitchen to fetch the promised items, while Renner led Milena up the olive carpeted stairs to his old bedroom.

Placing the luggage on the floor, he gathered Milena into his arms and kissed the tip of her nose. "So, what do you think?"

"Your parents are amazing. They're so warm and loving. I already feel part of the family, and we've barely been here a few hours."

"I have so many plans for us while we're here."

"I can't...," a giant yawn the size of a lion's interrupted her sentence, "...wait."

"You're exhausted."

"A little."

"My plans can hold off until we take a nap. The sights will have to wait."

They climbed into bed, and their warm bodies in such close proximity naturally migrated towards each other. Within seconds, they were kissing and groping each other, their fatigue forgotten, until a gentle knock on the door interrupted them. Before they could react, Mona poked her head into the room catching the young couple making out, thankfully before any clothing had been removed.

"Oh, I'm so sorry!" She covered her eyes and thrust the pillow and fresh towels through the doorway. Renner leaned over and grabbed them. "It's fine, Mutti. We're not doing anything."

She removed her hand from in front of her face, clearly embarrassed.

"We're going to take a nap."

"You poor dears. You must be tired after such a long trip. I'll make sure you don't get disturbed...again." Rapidly, she left.

"Now, where were we?" Renner reached over to Milena, attempting to resume their kissing session, his lips searching hers, but she stopped him.

"Maybe we should wait until we get home. You know, out of respect for your parents?"

"We're married, Milena. We didn't just meet. I'm sure my parents assume we're sleeping together."

"Still, I would feel better."

"All right." Exasperated, he rolled away from her, back to his side of the bed. "But I don't know how I'll be able to keep my hands off you. How am I going to survive that long?"

"I'll make it up to you when we get back home. I promise."

"I'm going to hold you to that." He kissed her once more, this time a chaste peck on the cheek, before they fell fast asleep.

★ ★ ★

After a hearty breakfast of warm baked rolls, sausage and vegetable omelettes, hash browns, and hot coffee, the young married couple started visiting all of the sites that Renner treasured.

First, they travelled northeast to Leipzig where they toured Renner's old university and Milena was introduced to the colleagues and professors he'd worked with for years in the Faculty of Medicine. They welcomed him with polite professionalism, and Milena could tell the depth of the relationships were no more than work-deep. But, the respect and admiration they held for Renner was clearly evident.

For the subsequent days, they travelled around Germany by train, hand-in-hand they hiked through the infamous Black Forest, dined in the romantic city of Heidelberg, and enjoyed several spas containing hot springs boasting of healing properties. They sampled all the local cuisine: Wiener schnitzel with green sauce, sauerkraut and bratwurst, apple wine, spaetzle and, of course, lots and lots of Pilsner beer.

In the evenings, reminiscing with Renner's parents and neighbours, they roasted bratwurst over a fire pit in the backyard of Renner's childhood home. Milena especially loved this part of their day, hearing stories about Renner as a teenager and young man, the burgeoning feeling in her heart that she was becoming more a part of this family with each passing moment she shared with them.

One particular story was Milena's favourite. And she asked many times for the neighbour, Alena, to repeat the tale, even though she spoke in German, and Renner begrudgingly had to translate each time.

"When Renner was thirteen, my daughter, Monika, had a huge crush on him," Alena would start. "But he was always too interested in his experiments to pay her any heed. Still, day after day, she would march over to the Scholz's home vying for his attention."

"Well, one day she didn't come back home right away but was gone for many hours. When she finally arrived, she was acting strangely, her eyes wide, pupils dilated. She said she felt like Alice, from the story *Alice in Wonderland* after she drank the shrinking potion. She felt so small, as if everything towered above her. She truly believed she had shrunk from something Renner had given her. Well, I grabbed her hand and we marched next door, and demanded Renner to explain what happened."

"And?" Milena asked. The embers in the fire pit shifted, releasing a burst of sparks that rose heavenward.

"He'd ground raw immature poppy seed capsules and concocted a tincture. The poppies grow freely in the fields, and Renner figured out how to harvest the seeds for his own purposes. He always was good with the sciences."

"That sounds harmless. We eat poppy seeds all the time," Milena said, confused.

"In that state, it's more like pure opium," Mona provided.

"Oh," Milena stifled a giggle, while the gathered crowd erupted into raucous laughter.

Still laughing, Alena continued, "It took her until the next day to feel normal again. She truly believed that Renner had created a magical potion which had shrunk her to the size of a mouse. She didn't bother him again. I think that was secretly his plan."

"I feel a little bad about that now," Renner apologized.

Alena continued, "I was mad at first. But, there was no harm done. She was fine after that. But you…we all thought you would never get married. And look at you now."

Milena and Renner sat cuddled together on a wooden bench made of oak, hands clasped together, as the others looked at them approvingly.

"I even surprised myself. But, how could I resist Milena?"

As the trip came to an end, Renner spent as much time in quiet conversations with his parents as he could. Milena allowed them their privacy, knowing they sorely needed the time to catch up. Renner's mother wept often, not ready for her baby to leave again.

Even Milena felt the urge to keep blinking back the tears. Why did they have to live so far away? Her new in-laws had welcomed her with open arms, and she wished they could stay here forever, could even imagine them living in Erfurt, Renner attending the university there, her opening up an office to do her psychic readings.

On the morning of their departure, Renner pulled his father aside. "Is she going to be all right?" His mother was a basket case. Worse than the day he initially left for school.

"She'll be fine. I'll take good care of her. Just keep in touch, and don't be a stranger. We want to see your lovely faces as often as we can." They warmly embraced.

Next, Renner turned towards his mother, and swept her up in his arms. More tears were shed. Renner kissed her head and whispered in her ear, "I love you, Mutti. We'll see you again soon. You'll see."

"It would be so much easier if you stayed here. Promise me, Renner, after you finish school, you move back here, be with your family where you belong. Work in Germany," his mother pleaded.

From the look on Renner's face, Milena thought for a second that there was a chance that they would, an alternate path for their lives to take. She could picture easily in her mind, a future of family gatherings, happiness, and so much love. The picture was erased by a flash of foreboding in her gut. Another path would be taken instead, one that would end much differently.

Chapter 13

After returning from his honeymoon overseas, Renner returned to Leighton House for the last time. It was a transition period for him in many respects. Completing his first year at BIT with grades in the upper percentile despite the constant distractions, he was now anticipating the start of his second and final year. Regarding his marriage to Milena, their relationship was blossoming into the next stage for them—moving in together. Finally, Renner would be free of Paul, and instead have Milena by his side, in his bed. No more emotional roller coaster rides to endure. No more needless diversions from his studies and research.

Renner entered the dorm room, arms loaded with empty boxes for packing his school books, personal effects, and other belongings he had acquired over the year.

Paul was lying on his bed, brooding. Why was he upset over the move? His reaction didn't make any sense. Showing mostly contempt and jealousy towards him, Paul was mainly pleasant when it served his own needs and devices. He would never figure Paul out, and now he didn't have to.

"Let me help you with that," Paul rushed over and grabbed half of the boxes, sliding them into the corner.

"That's not necessary."

"No, I insist," he demanded, snagging and toting one of the empty boxes over to Renner's side of the room. He grabbed several text books and tucked them inside the box.

"How's your family? What did they think of Milena?"

"Everyone's fine. And they loved Milena. She fit in perfectly, as if she was always meant to be part of our family."

Paul looked to be fighting an eye roll. "Not much of a honeymoon, though. Did you even get any privacy? I bet Milena's a wild ride." He gyrated his pelvis offensively.

Renner glared, "That's my wife you're talking about! You're never to talk about her like that again! Do you understand? Ever!"

"Hey, calm down. You should know me by now. I'm just teasing." Paul shrugged his shoulders at Renner's overreaction.

Renner picked up the pace, more eager than ever to be rid of his roommate.

"I think this one's overdue." Paul handed a heavy worn tome to Renner—the case study book on psychic abilities Renner had checked out from the library back at midterms. There were other library books mixed in with the pile.

"Crap, I forgot about those." He rubbed his forehead.

"Doing some research into your wife's abilities?"

"Something like that. Leave those out. I'll have to return them to the library." Renner slid the library books Paul handed him off to the side.

"You know, the library here in Leighton House is better than the libraries on campus. It has books on psychic abilities, ones that are...different."

Renner remembered the school secretary's words when he first arrived at BIT.

There's even a library that has a reputation for its unique selection of books. Originals, not found anywhere else in the world.

"I kind of forgot there was a library here. I figured, due to the limited size, the selection wouldn't have anything that would strike my fancy or help in my research," Renner responded, sealing the box he was working on with a zip of packing tape, and then selecting another empty one from the corner of the room.

"On the contrary. The library has special books. They're one of a kind, no other copies in existence. You should check it out."

"I don't know. I'm not going to be living here anymore. I probably won't bother."

"I can check it out for you."

"That's really not necessary."

"I don't mind."

"Suit yourself. But, if you don't have time, don't bother." Renner didn't want to have any connection to Paul after he left.

They packed in silence for several moments.

"So, what are you going to do about your thesis now?" Paul inquired.

"What do you mean?" Renner stopped packing and looked up at Paul. "I'm eager to get back to work. I only took a short break."

"You don't know?" Paul's eyes widened in disbelief. "I thought you would have heard."

"Heard what?" Renner asked, stomach clenching.

"Professor Shubally. He died two weeks ago."

Renner sat heavily on his bed. "What happened?"

"His ticker gave out while he was sleeping. The fact that he lived as long as he did was a miracle. You saw him. The guy was a walking corpse," Paul stated flippantly.

"But, the doctors couldn't find anything wrong with him. Have they done an autopsy?"

"An old fart like that? Why bother? He died of old age. We're all going to die someday."

"At least he won't suffer anymore."

"How do you know that? Who knows what awaits him?"

"Don't be stupid. He's at rest now." Renner, grief stricken, was in no mood to argue with his almost former roommate, trying to get under his skin.

"So, what *are* you going to do about your thesis?" Paul asked again.

"I'll continue my research. I can always get a research assistant to help. I'm sure the school will let me continue under the extenuating circumstances. We've done so much already."

"Well, good luck with that." The note of sarcasm was difficult to ignore. "And don't worry, we'll still be seeing a lot of each other."

Renner choked back his growing anger, gathered up the rest of his belongings into a pile at the door and called a cab from the lounge.

★ ★ ★

The sky was overcast, sombre and bleak. The wind was still, the air heavy and muggy. A large mass of students, faculty, friends and acquaintances in black attire were assembled at Pinewood Hill cemetery. A fresh rectangular gap in the earth awaited the body of Renner's professor, his thesis adviser, and friend.

The priest zealously prayed over Professor Shubally's spiritless body, about life after death and other nonsense Renner didn't believe in. Milena stood by his side, their arms entwined. She hadn't met the professor, but that didn't stop her from sniffling into a tissue at regular intervals.

The funeral had been postponed until now—a distant relative was to fly in from Ireland for the funeral but at the last minute cancelled due to lack of finances for the trip. The postponement meant Renner could pay his final respects to Dr. Shubally.

The priest's voice rose, his sermon increasingly passionate in delivery, but Renner's attention was pulled elsewhere, his neck prickling, followed by the familiar feeling of being watched. Stronger this time.

Renner.

The word, his name, echoed so loudly that he thought the other mourners could hear the voice too. But, not one person reacted. All eyes remained focused mainly on the priest or looking down at their laps in reverence. All except for Paul. His ex-roommate was openly glaring at Renner, Wendy sullen at his side. When Paul noticed Renner looking back at him, he gave a military salute, a nod of the head, and then looked away.

Was Paul the one he felt watching him? The uncomfortable feeling lingered even after Paul looked away. Why did this keep happening to him?

Renner, come.

Was he was losing his mind? Milena must have sensed his discomfort, squeezing his arm reassuringly.

After the beautiful, mahogany casket was lowered underground and covered in dirt, the crowd dispersed. Milena went home, while Renner joined other students at a reception in the university cafeteria, where he sat quietly, sipping a hot cup of chamomile tea with honey. As soon as the reception concluded, he strode over to the faculty director's office to inquire about Professor Shubally's personal effects. Were they still in his house or had they been packed up and placed in storage? His entire thesis, data, and research had been left behind with the professor. In order to continue his thesis, which he wanted to do immediately, he required his materials.

He also needed to check in on his rats, see how they fared while he was away, especially because the professor obviously hadn't been tending to them as planned.

The faculty adviser contacted the biology department where Dr. Branson, Dr. Shubally's closest friend, worked. He had a spare key to the professor's home and had been the unlucky one to find the professor after he died. Following a brief explanation of Renner's predicament, Dr. Branson promised he would let Renner in to grab his thesis paper and research.

He arrived at the professor's home first, pacing back and forth through the unkempt lawn. Dr. Branson appeared shortly after Renner, his large swell of red hair marching up the street difficult to miss. With faces grave, they exchanged greetings, and condolences, and then the doctor unlocked the front door. They were immediately assaulted by the stench of spoiled meat. Renner wondered how long Dr. Shubally's body had lain unnoticed before being discovered by Dr. Branson.

"Thank you for meeting me here. I know this must be difficult for you." Renner patted the professor on the back.

"Yes, the past two weeks have been tough. He was such a wonderful man. So, you said he had your thesis materials here?"

Renner nodded.

"Let me help you look."

Inch by inch they scoured the home, combing through all of the professor's belongings, even digging through the foul-smelling garbage cans.

No research, no thesis, no data was found. Renner felt the first glimmer of panic.

"Are you sure there weren't any items removed from the premises? Anything put into storage, perhaps?"

"As far as I know, nobody's been to the place since I found him, besides the paramedics," the doctor replied.

The panic swelled. Without his research, his project was doomed. He would have to start from scratch, but he didn't have that sort of time. Why hadn't he made a backup set of research documents?

"If you do find anything has been removed, can you contact me immediately?"

The man nodded. Renner wrote down Milena's phone number on a slip of paper and handed the slip over to the doctor.

"Thank you for your help."

Renner left, his hopes deflated. Next stop was the lab. Was there a chance that before the professor died he left the research there, maybe with the secretary, to await Renner's return? A long shot but worth checking out.

He entered the long, familiar halls of the lab building. Making his way into the office at the far end of the hallway he approached the tall, brunette secretary, glasses perched on her sharp beak of a nose, a large mole camped out on her lip like a fat beetle. Her face lit up with a smile when she saw him.

"Renner, you're back. I'm sorry about Professor Shubally. I know you were close."

"It was a complete shock hearing about his passing. I'm going to miss him." Abruptly, he switched topics, "Francis, did the professor by any chance leave any of my research with you before he died?"

"No, sorry. I haven't seen him in months."

Renner's face blanched. *Months! What about the rats!* If Shubally hadn't visited the lab, then who was looking after the vermin?

"Did he, by any chance, have an assistant tending to our research specimens while we were away?"

"Yes, a woman by the name of Jignasa."

Hopeful, Renner dashed to the animal research room, unlocked the door and approached the rat cages. Or, rather the cages where the rats used to be. The cages now sat empty.

Flying back over to the secretary, he asked if she had any contact information for the assistant. Jotting the number on a scrap piece of paper, she handed it to Renner who was now sweating and flushed.

"Can I use your phone?"

"Of course," she spun the phone to face him.

Jignasa answered on the second ring, and when Renner inquired about the rats, she stammered, "One day the rats were fine, the next they were all dead. I did everything I was told to do. I don't understand what happened. I bagged them and placed them in the freezer, so you could still analyze them when you returned. Maybe determine the cause of death, salvage some samples. I'm so sorry."

With tight lips, he thanked her and slammed down the phone. When he returned to the animal lab to check the freezer for the frozen rodents, they weren't there, either.

What the hell is happening here?

Storming back to his lab cubicle, he paced a few steps, and then grabbed a beaker, whipping it at the wall, where the glass receptacle exploded into a thousand fragments.

Renner buried his face in his hands, too frustrated to clean up the mess.

"You'll probably have to pay for that," Paul materialized out of thin air in front of Renner's work station. Under Paul's white lab coat, he still wore his black dress pants from the funeral.

Renner ignored him.

"What's all the commotion?"

"I'm not in the mood right now, Paul. I need a minute to myself."

"I get it, rough day. Can I help you in any way?"

"Not unless you can find all of my research and data or my experimental rats, no you can't!" Renner barked.

"They've gone missing?"

"Yes, somehow all of my research has vanished into thin air. Shubally borrowed the paperwork while I was away, and now it's gone. Do you know how much work was in there? And the rats, how much effort it took to implant them with the viral DNA? We haven't even had the chance to mate them, to determine if the oncogene would be inherited by the offspring."

"Wow, that's a bummer. Have you checked everywhere?"

"Yes, I have. It's gone!" He couldn't help but be short.

"What're you going to do?" Paul asked, genuinely sympathetic.

"Without the rats and my paperwork, I have no choice but to start over, I guess." He pounded the table with his fist.

"But that'll take an extra year or more. And that's if you can even find another professor able to supervise you on this type of project, qualified to do that research. You won't graduate next spring like you're supposed to."

"I realize that. But, I don't have any other options."

There was a pregnant pause.

"What if you join us? Work with us?" Paul finally asked.

Renner's brow furrowed, "I can't do that. I barely even know what you're working on. Top secret, remember?"

"As long as we get approval from the department and the government, I'm sure you can work with us. We already completed most of the experimental procedures, compiled most of the data. We could use an extra hand to complete all of the work on time."

Renner hesitated. Did he want to abandon his own research and start something else, maybe outside of his expertise? Did he want to work with Paul?

No, not really.

"I don't know. I appreciate the offer, but I was passionate about our research, the project Dr. Shubally and I were working on."

"So, after you graduate you can pursue the same project, redo the experiment from scratch and even get paid for all your work. But, for now, this may be your best alternative."

"I would have to know what you're working on before I commit to anything."

"I'm sorry, but that's not possible. Once you're approved and guaranteed to be on board, then you'll be briefed. We're mainly focusing on increasing growth size in animals. That's all you need to know for now."

"Well, I'll have to decline, then."

"Do me a favour and think about joining us. Maybe after some thought, you'll see the opportunity is your best option," Paul pressed.

"Sure, I'll think about it. Look, I don't want to appear ungrateful or anything. I appreciate the offer."

"Anytime." Paul left the cubicle.

Renner's frustration and anger now dwindled to a dull simmer, he gathered a broom and dust pan to sweep up the shattered remains of the beaker—a metaphor for his ruined project. Now, he had to gather up the pieces but how?

He could start over from scratch. Find a new supervisor. Paul was right; that wouldn't be easy this late in the game. Another problem—he had been approached by two companies to work for them upon graduation next spring, one government run, one private. If he started his research over, he could lose both of those job offers, because he wouldn't be graduating on time. The companies might not wait an extra year for him. Probably hire somebody else.

Or, he could join Paul and his professor, and still graduate on time. But, he didn't know what their research was really about, would be going into the project almost blind. And from what little he knew of the project, he wasn't sure he was even interested. Where Renner's research was focused on helping mankind, Paul's was geared more towards self-enhancement.

And then there was the university. Would they even approve? Starting a thesis mid-way was unorthodox, especially at the PhD level of study.

Even if they did, could he bear to be stuck with Paul for another year, forced to tolerate his scathing remarks and volatile temperament? But, this time Paul acted genuinely concerned about Renner's predicament and had graciously offered for him to join them, even after they had already completed most of the work. Paul was usually so competitive, so it surprised Renner that he would want to be on the same team. Even during their soccer games, Paul always put Renner on the opposing side.

He would have to think about the decision some more.

Dumping the glass shards into the waste basket, he switched off the lights in his work station.

★ ★ ★

Renner had craved Milena's comfort all day, and as the night clouds rolled in, he cuddled with her, secure in her embrace by the warm fireplace, swaddled in knitted blankets, sipping red wine.

He told her everything. Primarily, he complained about his lost research and Paul's surprising proposal. He was waiting for Milena's response, for some practical advice.

"What's in it for Paul?" Milena asked.

"That's a good question. I don't know."

"I don't get why he's being so nice all of a sudden. I don't trust him."

"Me neither."

"Do you think you'd be able to stomach working with Paul?"

"That's what I keep asking myself. He's such an ass. But, I'd also be working with Dr. Kirby, his thesis supervisor. He's an excellent professor, remarkable and brilliant. Maybe not as suited to my needs and personality as Professor Shubally was but still amazing."

"What about your other research? What will happen with that?"

"It can wait. There are other researchers who're attempting the same feat, but we were ahead of the pack. I don't think anyone else could possibly publish before me, even if I'm delayed a few years. We already completed all of the research, and the proposal was approved so it's basically a matter of redoing the actual experiment. I would be repeating what I had already done, so the process should go smoother and faster compared to someone trying for the first time. I could even make some improvements to the model. The experiment wasn't exactly going as planned."

"What do you think they're working on, Paul and his professor?" Milena asked, referring to the "hush hush" government project.

"I have an inkling. I'm a bit curious to know more. Part of me wants to join them in order to find out."

"What if they are working on something you don't agree with?" Renner had told Milena about Paul's coy remarks at the bar the first day they met. The research was top secret and military in nature—possibly a quest for creating a super-soldier in the long run.

"I've thought about that. They still had to go through the ethics board, so if they were approved, then the research can't be that bad, right?"

"I guess not. The ethics board is fairly stringent, from what I gather."

"Yes, definitely."

"So, what are you going to do? School begins in a few more weeks."

"I think I'll accept the offer. I'll join Paul and Professor Kirby in their illicit government research." he said with a cocky grin.

Suddenly, he felt a sense of relief, felt he was making the best decision. He would save himself an extra year of university, still be eligible to accept one of the jobs he was offered. Eventually, he would finish the research he was doing with Dr. Shubally, as homage to his old professor.

And, finally he would discover what Paul's top-secret research was all about.

Chapter 14

Renner paced in front of the laboratory entrance, each step heavy and anxious, echoing down the corridor. He was early. His anticipation, too difficult to ignore, had kept him up all night. The moment his alarm chimed in the morning he had hastily showered, brushed his teeth, scarfed down a bowl of cereal, and sped over to the lab.

Now, with half an hour until the big reveal, Renner was experiencing an overwhelming combination of excitement, nervousness, and even a mild case of nausea.

Once Paul and Dr. Kirby arrived, he would know everything.

Renner glanced up, detecting voices approaching from the stairwell. Paul and Dr. Kirby materialized at the end of the hall where the stairwell reached the lab floor, and when they saw Renner, enthusiastically welcomed him to their team.

"I knew you'd be here early," Paul announced. "See, Dr. Kirby, he's eager to get going. He'll be a great asset to our project."

They heartily shook hands, and then turned towards the glass doors that led into the lab.

"Shall we?" Paul gestured to the entrance, and the researchers filed into the room, and headed towards the new cubicle they shared. The lab was otherwise empty.

"It's fortunate the university accepted your request to work with us," Paul said as he dragged an extra stool into their work station and they all took a seat. "They must have felt responsible for the awkward predicament you were placed in, as they should. Who

161

else, but the university would be responsible for your thesis and lab rats disappearing. It's the least they can do."

"I am relieved the university agreed to us working together. Dr. Kirby, thank you for agreeing to this arrangement, as well. I appreciate the opportunity."

"No problem. We can use another researcher on our team. Especially one with your credentials."

Paul's jaw visibly clenched.

"I'm anxious to learn more about this research," Renner responded, ignoring Paul's jealous gaze. "I must say, I'm very curious."

"Now that you're officially on board, we can give you all of the details."

Paul rudely interjected, "Before we continue, you have to promise not to divulge the contents of this research to anyone, not even Milena. Especially not Milena."

"I understand. Of course, I promise."

"I mean legally. We have documents that you're required to sign before we can go any further."

Renner was uncomfortable keeping any secrets from his wife. They had reached a pivotal point in their relationship, where she literally knew everything about him, from his past up to his present. He didn't want to start having any new secrets from her now. Unsettled by the request, he understood that if he was to be included in the government funded project, he was forced to comply with their terms.

Dr. Kirby extracted a sheaf of documents and a fountain pen from his briefcase, laying them out on the steel counter in front of Renner.

"Take a moment to read through the paperwork and then sign each agreement, here and here." he said, pointing with a hairy finger.

The first set of papers was a summary of the sensitive nature of the experiment and his agreement to abstain from disclosing the information to any outsiders. The second set of papers was in regard to officially joining their team and research, ensuring all findings would remain the sole property of the government. Renner scribbled his autograph across the bottom of the appropriate documents and handed them back to Dr. Kirby.

"It's official," Dr. Kirby exclaimed with a smile. He returned the signed forms to his leather briefcase and extracted a fresh set of papers. "You're also going to have to read through this." He plunked the thick stack on the counter. "It's our proposal for the experiment, outlining our hypothesis, procedure, etcetera. You'll have to submit your own, but I can't imagine the approval taking too long to come through. Our study is already approved and has commenced, so it's just a formality. In the meantime, you can start working with us as an assistant."

The last set of papers was placed before Renner.

"Here are our results thus far. You'll want to go through them on your own; but for now, we'll give you a brief synopsis of our research to date," Dr. Kirby said, handing the floor to Paul.

Finally. The big reveal.

Paul shifted in his chair to face Renner. "With the ability to recombine DNA and promote favourable characteristics in organisms, it was simply a matter of time before the government would see the advantages of this discovery. The ability to develop characteristics to promote strength, size, fighting ability, and regenerative healing could lead to an army of undefeatable soldiers. Resistance from the ethics board prevents such genetic manipulations on humans, until we know the specific implications and side effects of this type of research, so we're currently working with rats and dogs."

Renner had been told all of this by Paul the first day they met. What he didn't know was how they proposed to create their desired effects.

Paul continued, "This experiment focuses on increasing the size in rats and we've created a working model that has produced significant results. The modified rats developed faster and much larger compared to a control group of rats, ones that weren't genetically manipulated."

Two pictures were placed in front of Renner, side by side. "The rat on the left was genetically altered by inserting human growth hormone, responsible for promoting protein anabolism and inhibiting protein degradation, into its genome. The one on the right is the control rat." The rat on the left was three times the size of the control rat, able to swallow the control rat for dinner. A definite super-rat.

"This finding supports our hypothesis that inserting human growth hormone into rat DNA will increase overall growth of the rat, and because the manipulation is done at the genetic level we hypothesize the trait will be passed down to its progeny. Another predicted effect is a delay in the aging process. So, hypothetically, future applications to humans could help older soldiers be capable of fighting longer by increasing their endurance levels and their ability to maintain muscle mass."

"Ah, a potential elixir of life," Renner added.

"Exactly."

Renner's skin tingled in excitement. Although his research was geared more towards the health and well-being of mankind, the research Paul and Dr. Kirby were working on was quite similar in the manipulation of the genetic code to induce a desirable effect. He would still be knee-deep in his field.

"Our implications are such that we could one day manipulate human DNA by inserting both specific human and animal DNA into its genome to create a super-soldier, magnifying certain desirable traits. I believe the ethics board may never let this pass due to ethical and social concerns, but it would be remarkable to try."

The talk of creating a superhuman reminded Renner of eugenics, which then segued into thoughts of racial hygiene and Hitler's determination to preserve the Aryan bloodline to remain "pure," believing they were the superior human race. It reminded him of his biological father and the war, strangely out of context, or was it? He shrugged the discomfort aside.

"Yes, that would be very interesting indeed."

"In the future, we'd be aiming to expand by manipulating other positive traits such as intelligence, speed, aggression and fighting ability, healing properties. The possibilities are endless."

"Our soldiers would have a dramatic advantage over their adversaries. Think of the Vietnam War. Our soldiers would have ended the war by now, would have had a greater chance of survival and success with their heightened capabilities. Instead, they are being withdrawn as we speak due to Nixon's orders. But, there will be other wars, I guarantee you, and we best be prepared," Dr. Kirby added.

"What if human clinical trials are never approved? The research will all be for naught."

"It's the government. If they see value in the research, they'll make sure the project gets passed by the ethics board. As far as finding human research subjects, there are always ways to get people to agree to experimentation. Offering a large payout for participating or reducing prison sentences for convicts willing to participate."

"Superhuman convicts? There's a great idea," Renner replied sarcastically.

Paul ignored him, "And, so far, our research has shown minimal negative effects on its targets."

Kirby shot Paul a look, who responded with a headshake.

"What am I missing?" Renner intercepted the exchange.

"Tell him," Dr. Kirby advised.

"Some of the subjects have developed some…minor symptoms. Pain, enlargement of the internal organs, heightened incidence of cancer and tumour growth."

Renner couldn't help but note the irony that Paul and Dr. Kirby were able to grow tumours in their research subjects without even trying, unlike his own research in which that was the goal. "The symptoms sound pretty major to me."

"The larger organisms are responding the worst. Initially there was rapid muscle growth, but once they reached full growth the muscles began wasting, degenerating. They can barely walk or even move without experiencing intense pain."

"Several animals were euthanized because of this side effect. Mostly the dogs. Here, follow me." They led Renner through the animal research lab, where he had formerly worked with his rats, to a second door at the back of the room leading to the area designated for larger animals used in research. Manoeuvering through cages of mostly primates, birds, and swine, they stopped in front of what appeared to be a peacefully sleeping dog. The greyhound, however, was no ordinary canine but looked pumped full of steroids. Its dimensions were well over that of an average greyhound and it was exceptionally lean, with definition in its musculature. It continued sleeping as Paul and Dr. Kirby explained the limitation in their research.

"His name is Samson. He's six-months-old but has developed more rapidly than dogs without the human growth hormone incorporated into their genomes. We have to keep him heavily sedated to minimize his chronic pain," said Paul. "He's the last surviving canine from our specimens."

Dr. Kirby picked up from there, "He suffers from severe arthritis, a lack of co-ordination and extreme muscle weakness. Ultrasounds are suggestive of stomach lesions and gastric ulcers. He's kind of a mess."

A sudden clattering interrupted them. The three researchers spun around to see a surprised young woman wearing a white lab coat, eyes wide as if she had been caught with her hand in the cookie jar. She was young and striking, with long, brown hair plaited into a side braid, a dimpled chin, no makeup, and a body that was slender and athletic. She attempted to straighten up the pile of boxes she knocked over, the source of the clattering.

"Can we help you?" Dr. Kirby demanded.

"Sorry to interrupt. I was trying to get acquainted with the animal research lab. I was hired as an attendant last week."

Paul stalked over to the young woman and pressed his face an inch from hers. "Just to give you a little constructive advice, your job is to care for the animals, not to eavesdrop on our conversation."

"I wasn't, I was just , just..." she stammered, face reddening.

"Your orientation can wait until the lab is no longer occupied," Dr. Kirby ordered.

Nodding, she excused herself from the room, but Renner saw a hint of another emotion in her eyes. Contempt?

"Now, where were we?" Dr. Kirby brought Renner back to the point at hand.

"You were explaining to me the side-effects of the dog model."

"Yes, they are unfortunate. He'll need to be destroyed, but we still need to do more tests before that happens. We'll attempt to keep him as comfortable as possible in the meantime."

"What about the rat models?" Renner asked.

"They've been more successful, with only a few mortalities with similar side-effects," Paul explained.

"Do you have any theories as to why the animals start to deteriorate?"

"A few. The skeletal frame doesn't appear to mature at the same rate as the organs and musculature. If we could figure a way to correct for the immature skeletons, the success rate should improve."

"The main question then becomes how to accomplish that?"

"That's what we're working on. We're proposing ideas to correct our model for future study. We're open to any suggestions you may have as well. That's part of the reason we're happy to have you on board. We know you're a bit of a genius in this area."

"Thank you," Renner replied, flattered. He felt his adrenaline kick up a notch. He loved a challenge. Already, ideas were percolating in his cranium. "I'm eager to get started."

And he was. This was exhilarating research; perhaps not life-saving like the research he'd been pursuing with Dr. Shubally, but life-changing in a different way. Groundbreaking. And still in his area of expertise. Maybe even a path to a Nobel Prize.

The group of men returned to their cubicle, gathered their jackets, and headed their separate ways. Renner escaped to the library where he avidly read over the proposal and data he had been handed by Paul and Dr. Kirby, and already saw some areas for improvement. He gathered books and journals he would need for further study, now that he knew the nature of the research he'd be participating in and signed them out at the front desk.

How receptive would Paul be to his input? Working with Paul so far had been virtually free of confrontation, almost easy. Perhaps, now that they were on even ground, on the same team, Paul would be more pleasant.

He hoped things would stay that way.

★ ★ ★

At home, amidst the succulent aromas of home-made beef stew and freshly baked biscuits, Renner divulged what he could to Milena about his day.

"I was surprised at how civil Paul was. Perhaps I was wrong about him after all," Renner surmised.

"I wouldn't be too hasty jumping to that conclusion," Milena contested, the voice of reason as she ladled piping hot stew into a ceramic bowl for Renner and added a wedge of biscuit to the side. She poured red wine into a glass, handed the glass to her husband and then poured some for herself. She joined him at the table. "He still makes my skin crawl."

"Look, if it weren't for him, I'd be totally screwed. Besides, the research is very interesting."

"So, what are you going to be researching then?"

He paused.

"Well?" she queried, the biscuit she was about to bite poised in front of her mouth, awaiting his answer.

"They made me promise not to tell. I even had to sign documents to ensure my secrecy."

She looked wounded.

"Hey, don't worry. You'll know everything as soon as we're finished, and the research is published."

"What they are doing isn't unethical?"

"Of course not."

"I don't want us to have any secrets."

"You know I'd tell you if I could."

He found her hand, gently squeezing in a reassuring gesture. She smiled without conviction.

They finished their meal in uncomfortable silence.

Renner helped Milena clear the table and wash the dishes before retreating into his office to immerse himself in the new research.

They had transformed a storage area in Milena's apartment for him to use as an office. The space was quaint but would do for now. A large bookshelf housed his textbooks, and a glass cabinet was stocked with a variety of hard alcohol and liqueurs. A teakwood desk rested under a window overlooking the alleyway, and the hardwood floors were covered with a beige rug. A sturdy floor lamp cast a cordon of light over his paperwork.

He couldn't wait until he was officially working at a real job and could afford to get Milena a place she deserved: a magnificent house with exquisite architecture, stuffed full of furnishings from the finest shops. He wanted the best for his wife.

Although Renner's parents were wealthy, they had allowed Renner to learn about the importance of earning his own way in the world, to respect money and the necessity for hard work. He wasn't a privileged child, despite his father's vast wealth and empire. They provided him with a modest sum of cash to live on while he pursued his studies and paid for his education. But, that was it. And that's how Renner insisted things should be, as well. He saw how life was on the other side, entrenched in poverty, living that

existence for the first nine years of his life. He never wanted to
return to that way of life. Was driven to avoid it.

Renner had a lot of catching up to do. So absorbed in his
research, he missed the click of the front door opening and closing
as Milena left the apartment.

★ ★ ★

Milena selected a fresh ledger from the shelf for her final client of
the evening, a new client. Calling that morning, he claimed he
urgently needed to see her.

It wasn't the first time someone demanded an emergency
appointment; but, usually, they would give her some information
ahead of time. This man had provided none.

She was still reflecting on her earlier conversation with Renner
and the new secret that lay between them and the sense of foreboding that surrounded the situation, when the door tinkled
announcing her new client's arrival. She met him in the lobby.

The man was tall, mid to late forties, sand-coloured hair greying
at the temples, rugged tanned face, with stubble two days old.
Grabbing her hand, he shook firmly. She could feel rough calluses
on his palms.

"Thank you for seeing me on such short notice. I'm Grant
Armstrong," he introduced.

"I'm Milena Nowak...I mean Scholz. Sorry, I recently got
married, and I'm not used to my new last name yet. Anyhow,
welcome. I'm happy to accommodate you. It sounded important."

"It is."

"Shall we?" she ushered him in.

Ducking to avoid hitting his head on the doorframe, he then
settled into a chair at the wooden table where Milena did her
psychic readings.

"So, how can I help you?" she asked, joining him at the table,
leaning towards him, elbows on her knees.

Grant scratched his stubbly chin, not sure where to begin. "I'm assuming people usually come here to have their futures read."

"Yes. And you? Why are you here, Grant?" Milena encouraged.

"First, I should give you a little background on myself."

The handsome gentleman was warm and pleasant, with a rugged voice and callused hands, yet his demeanour was well refined. Although mysterious, Milena felt safe in his presence. "Go on."

"I'm what you'd call a treasure hunter. Do you know what that is?"

Milena nodded.

"I have a regular job. I'm a mathematician. But, I've always been interested in ancient artifacts, missing treasures. Whenever I get the opportunity, I go on digs with colleagues in the archeology department where I teach. We've found many fascinating, priceless artifacts. My collection has grown over the years—worth well over a million dollars, some of which I've donated to museums. But, some I can't help but keep for myself."

"The other night, I had a dream. But, perhaps the experience was more akin to a vision than a dream. I'm still not certain. A being—a spirit or an angel—visited me, giving me an errand. The moment was surreal and bizarre. Both beautiful and terrifying. Shook me to my very core, which is why I'm here."

"What was your vision about?"

"You," he answered.

Bewildered, she sat taller in her chair, backing away slightly from the stranger.

"About me?"

The man reached inside the pocket of his green, corduroy jacket and withdrew an ancient pendant. Made entirely of tarnished metal, the engraving was of two cherubs facing each other, foreheads bowed and touching, wings outstretched behind and around them so that the wings comprised the circular shape of the pendant. The relic reminded Milena of a flat, round coin. Grant placed the pendant down on the table and slid the artifact over to Milena, who merely gawked.

"The apparition was beyond beauty, bringing tears to my eyes, and I haven't cried in ages. But, it also frightened me. I could sense the power. The figure spoke to me with urgency, telling me to bring this to you immediately, that you would need the pendant more than me. I know this sounds crazy, believe me, that's the first thing I thought was happening to me—that I was losing my mind. But, the vision felt so real," his voice trailed off.

"What is it?" she asked with a slight tremour in her voice.

"I found the pendant in a water cave in Western Iran. There with one of my colleagues, we unearthed several different artifacts, and split them up between the two of us. This particular one I personally found myself and knew immediately that the pendant was extraordinary. I brought the relic back to the university, cleaned and restored the surface the best I could and searched the archives to see if there was something written about the history, the value, the origins of the relic. I tried to determine the age, and if the engravings were symbolic in some way."

"And?"

"I couldn't find anything exactly the same, but I found similar pendants."

Digging back in the same pocket, he extracted a bundle of folded papers. Unfolding them, he then smoothed them flat on the table's surface in front of Milena, and pointed to the picture on top, which displayed a circular pendant also of angels posing with wings stretched around them in a protective circle.

"These pendants bear a striking resemblance to the one I found." He flipped through the rest of the pages and indeed there were profound similarities between them all. "They're meant to ward off evil spirits. They're supposed to be extremely powerful."

"Do you believe in such things?"

"Up until I had the vision, I've always had my doubts. But, now I have trouble denying the possibility. Will you please take the pendant?"

"I can't accept something so valuable. And you went through so much trouble obtaining it."

"Please, if only to make me happy."

She hesitated.

"Please," he implored as he slid the pendant closer to Milena.

Tentatively, she touched the metal, and then lifted the pendant up to look more closely at the etchings. The handiwork was exquisite, so detailed on such a small working space. The metal was cool to her touch and grew colder in her hands instead of getting warmer with the transference of her body heat to its surface.

"I must go now. Always keep the pendant close."

The man hastened out of the room and abruptly left.

Milena was left with the cool pendant in her palm and a colder feeling of dread in her soul.

Chapter 15

The following morning, Paul and Renner met at the university laboratory to take samples from the genetically modified specimens. Making another early start, they were both surprised to find the exterior doors were already unlocked, the main room flooded in light. The surprise visitor was located in the animal research lab section.

"What the hell are you doing here again?" Paul barked at the young brunette who had been eavesdropping on them the day before.

"I was monitoring the animals." She fidgeted anxiously, guilt written all over her face.

"You're supposed to be out of here during lab hours. Did they forget to teach you that during orientation or are you just an idiot?" he paused, but the young woman didn't respond. "We have work to do, now scat!"

"I'm sorry, it won't happen again," she mumbled through gritted teeth, scurried past Renner and Paul, and hastily exited the animal research lab. Renner caught the name on her ID tag—Sandra Peters.

"You didn't have to be so harsh. She's just doing her job," Renner defended the new lab attendant as he dragged a stool over to the lab counter, and then propped his form on top.

"There's a reason they have a schedule. The rules strictly state that they are to stay out of the lab during research hours." He paused, glanced around the room at the agitated, chittering animals. "Hey, does the temperature feel warm in here?"

"You're right, it does."

"Great! What did that bitch do?" Paul growled as he sped to the thermostat. "Eighty-eight degrees F! That's 20 degrees above the usual setting! That's warm enough to harm the animals! No wonder they're acting restless." He adjusted the thermostat back down to the ideal temperature for the lab animals to thrive. "That moron should be fired," Paul seethed, checking the animals to make sure they weren't affected by the sudden tropical conditions in the room. "If even one of our specimens becomes ill or dies because of that twit's negligence, I'm going make sure she pays!"

"Relax. Most of the animals in here are rats and mice—they can adjust to the worst possible conditions. Nothing's going to happen to them if the temperature is a little warmer in here."

"Can you stop defending that idiot and help me check the animals?"

Just then Dr. Kirby entered the lab, noting the researchers' heated exchange. He rubbed his bushy, black moustache.

"What's going on here, fellows? I could hear you all the way down the hall? And why is it so gosh darn hot in here?" He pulled at his collar to let some of his own body heat escape.

"One of the lab assistants, that new girl that was eavesdropping on us the other day, jacked up the heat in here."

"It's definitely too warm in here. Are you sure she's to blame?" Paul nodded vigorously.

"All right, I'll place a complaint against her with the human resources department. Did you happen to get her name?"

"Sandra Peters," Renner provided. "I saw her name tag as she fled the room." He didn't want her to get fired but if she was to blame, she needed to be aware of the lab rules and the importance of sticking to them. Those rules were to ensure that the animals and research specimens were stored in the most favourable environment. Something as seemingly mundane as turning the heat up a few degrees could ruin their experiments. Or, did she already know that? Could she be sabotaging their research on purpose? He thought of his own experiment, the one he was working on with Dr. Shubally, and their missing specimens.

Checking on their rats, Paul, Dr. Kirby and Renner made sure they weren't in distress. Samson the dog slept soundly in his pen, hopped up on pain killers, oblivious to any change in the environment.

The three researchers suited up in lab coats, latex gloves, and retrieved the necessary equipment for the day's work: syringes, test tubes, microscopes and slides. They would be taking blood and tissue samples from their specimens and testing the DNA as part of the ongoing data collection vital to their research.

It took two hours. Once the delicate task was completed, Dr. Kirby excused himself. "Would you mind cleaning up on your own today? I have a lecture in one hour and I have to go home and shower beforehand."

Working with chemicals and animal subjects made them all want to scald their bodies in boiling water afterwards, so they understood. After exchanging farewells, the two former roommates cleaned their work station, first labelling and storing the samples in the refrigerator, then disinfecting the equipment they used and returning the paraphernalia to the appropriate cupboards and shelves. The animals were returned to their cages.

"How're you feeling about the research so far?" Paul asked Renner as he wiped down the chrome table. He'd continued surprising Renner with his polite demeanour, although the tantrum over the temperature change in the room was a reminder of his volatile temper. At least the antagonism wasn't aimed at Renner this time.

"The research is interesting. I can see the huge impact this will have on the scientific community and the massive implications for future research. I'm proud to be a part of this project."

"Well, I'm glad to hear that. You were hesitant at first. I thought you might not join us."

"You made the experiment sound more suspicious with your secrecy, but I guess now I understand why. Thanks again for including me."

"No problem. You would have done the same for me, right?"

Renner highly doubted he would but nodded in agreement. No sense ruffling any feathers at this point

"So, how's your other research going?" Paul asked with eyebrows raised.

Renner looked back at him questioningly.

"You know, into Milena's psychic abilities?"

"Oh yeah, that. I've been so involved in this new project that I haven't had any extra time to focus on it."

"Well, if you're ever interested, I have a way for you to learn more about the Psi phenomenon firsthand. Not from a book, but from physically witnessing a psychic event."

Renner stopped drying the beaker he held and looked at Paul, puzzled. "What're you talking about?"

Paul appeared uncomfortable for a moment, shuffling his feet, scratching his greasy head, like someone was forcing his hand. "Have you ever wondered how I get great grades even though I'm not the scholarly type, never study, never do any homework?"

Renner had always wondered that. Thought possibly he was a genius, the type of which you hear about but never meet in person. Even Renner, although brilliant, still had to study and work hard for his grades.

"How then?" Renner asked, curious.

"My parents wanted me to be a doctor. But, I always sucked at school, got terrible grades. I couldn't stand studying. They were unrelenting, always on my ass. I was a complete disappointment to them, but then I heard about a woman that knew special...spells."

"Spells? What is she, a witch?" Renner asked, incredulous.

Lanie Mores

"I know this sounds crazy. I wasn't a believer myself until I went to see with my own eyes, mostly out of curiosity. But, after I saw her, what she could do—it blew my mind. My experience was completely life changing. I mean, look at me now. I'm almost a Doctor of Biology, working on groundbreaking research for the government of all people. I've had some of the highest marks in school. The one person to ever come close to me is you. You kept me on my toes this past year. Of course, you don't need a spell to do well," a flashing glare of resentment was shot at Renner but quickly dissipated.

"I don't understand. How did a spell help you get all that you've accomplished? Maybe she hypnotized you to believe that you could succeed, and then you accomplished your goals on your own."

"I know this sounds hard to believe, but, didn't you think psychic abilities were ludicrous before you met Milena? And now...now what do you think?"

"I don't know yet."

"Come with me, tomorrow evening. Watch the psychic in action and then make up your own mind, as a form of research. You can go in, make observations while witnessing a psychic experience firsthand. Bring your notebook and pen if you want, take notes. Perhaps you can even write a paper on the topic. You won't be disappointed, I assure you."

Renner wondered why Paul was pushing so hard for him to go. But, the concept was intriguing. "Explain how this psychic woman helped you get into the doctorate for biology."

"She's more than a psychic. She's a medium. She can communicate with the spiritual realm and draw upon the powers there."

"Right," Renner said sarcastically.

"The angels can grant any wish you desire. Drawing upon the power of your guardian spirit, she helps you to achieve your goals. And, get this: afterwards, some people even report having psychic abilities as a result of the experience—ESP or telekinesis. As if, somehow, they've borrowed powers from the supernatural realm."

"It sounds like black magic or voodoo to me. You probably shouldn't mess around with someone like that."

"It's perfectly harmless. Would I draw you into something that's dangerous?"

Hmmm. Good question.

"Look, I'm living proof that the spell works. Isn't there something you would wish for? Any questions you want answered? Any goals you want to reach?"

Renner's mind flicked to his ever-present desire to be successful. After his tumultuous upbringing by his birth parents, he vowed never to go through that again. Of course, his adoptive father had provided for them beyond their means, but Renner always felt the need to prove himself. Maybe due to his birth father always calling him "a useless piece of crap" when he was a child. Constantly drilling into his head, over and over again that he would never amount to anything. Renner fought the insecurities brought on by his father's words. He knew he was better than that. Didn't he? He deserved to be a successful researcher and discover something that would change the course of human history, such as Einstein had, or Watson and Crick. But, he wasn't about to admit his desires or insecurities to Paul.

"I already have everything I could ever want," Renner finally stated, earning an envious look from Paul.

"Well, suit yourself. Let me know if you ever change your mind. You can bring Milena with you. I'm sure she'd find the ceremony interesting as well, with her background and all." They returned to the cubicle they now shared in the main artery of the lab department. Paul rummaged through his backpack, withdrawing an old tattered book and handed the book to Renner.

"Here, take this. I found this in the library at Leighton House. Remember, the one I was telling you about? The book will shed light on what I was saying about the Guardian Angel Spell. Maybe you'll change your mind after reading about how harmless the spell is."

Renner hesitantly took the book and placed it in his own bag.

After replacing their lab coats with their regular jackets, the men went their separate ways, Renner's mind whirling with the strange information Paul had given him.

A medium channelling the spirit world? The idea was a little too far-fetched to believe. Renner always thought that once a person died, that was the end. There was no spirit that floated off into another realm. No forgiveness for our sins. No life after death. So, Paul's idea of channelling a guardian angel and harnessing its powers for his own good sounded preposterous. Yet, Paul was convinced that this medium was legitimate, that the Guardian Angel Spell was real, and he even attributed all of his scholarly success to this strange spell.

It must be the result of a placebo effect or perhaps an element of hypnosis.

As Renner continued to think about the medium and the Guardian Angel Spell, his curiosity grew to the point where he actually pulled out the book from Leighton House Paul had given him. Sequestering himself in his office at home after kissing Milena on the forehead, he plunked the thick, weighty book on his desk, ready to dig into the water-stained pages.

The title, "Magic, Spells, and the Occult," was deeply etched in the cover of the tome in metallic gold, and he traced the letters with his finger, feeling exceptionally cool to his touch.

Opening the hard cover, the smell of must puffed out. A few pages in, he located the table of contents, and scanned the chapter headings.

Intrigued, Renner flipped the book open to a chapter on spells. Reading the titles of the spells, Renner couldn't help but snicker. There were spells for protection, love spells, curses and hexes. More bizarre was the list of ingredients used for each spell such as chicken bones, dead flowers, graveyard dirt, cat hair, and butterfly wings. There was even a spell to induce sickness of the mind, a curse that would cause mental illness in the unfortunate recipient of the spell. A similar spell was meant to cause physical maladies.

Who would cast such heinous spells?

A warning was written in bold beneath the harmful curses and hexes: *Use with extreme caution! Use only against those who have already hurt you or in defence, as any negative energy unleashed into the universe will eventually return back on those who unleashed it.* Macabre drawings accompanied the words on the pages.

Finally, Renner found what he was looking for—the Guardian Angel Spell.

The book described the origins of the spell and explained the incantation as "an invitation to your angel to keep you safe from misfortune and guide you in the direction of success and prosperity, and aid in the accomplishment of personal goals." Seemed harmless enough.

Reading on, the book described how drawing on the powers of the angels could often manifest in psychic abilities, help you discover your own inner powers such as enhanced intuition, telepathy, clairvoyance, astral projection, and in rare instances, telekinesis.

Renner's main interest was the ability to achieve specific goals. This is what Paul had been referring to, what he claimed was responsible for his scholarly success. The spell itself was written in an ancient language and meant little to Renner.

The last chapter of the tome also piqued Renner's interest. Well-known individuals in history—political leaders, scholars, famous literary and artistic luminaries, philosophers, and scientists—rumoured to be influenced by or involved in the occult.

Names such as Plato, W.B. Yeats, King Arthur, Nicolas Flamel, and Sir Isaac Newton, a fellow scientist, flew off the pages. Why, even the Fuhrer himself, Adolf Hitler, was documented as consulting with psychics and even claimed to have clairvoyant abilities himself, predicting a near-fatal assassination attempt on his life that he escaped because of his premonition. Renner couldn't believe his eyes. Did these famous and iconic historical figures achieve their successes through the occult? Through mere spells, incantations, astronomy, and horoscopes?

Or were these dubious stories of legends, hearsay, unable to be proven or disproven?

The following section focused on well-known psychics and occultists to influence history such as Aleister Crowley, Grigori Rasputin, Merlin and Morgan Le Fay, and Rosallen Norton, the infamous "Witch of King's Cross." Heavy usage of hallucinogenic drugs by these mystics was implied.

Interesting.

Renner tried to compare and connect this new information with the scientific studies he researched at the library. Although he felt there was a connection, a common thread, he wasn't able to tie them together.

At the back of the book in small lettering, another word of caution was inscribed, so minuscule that Renner almost missed the warning. *When working with the spirit world, always shield yourself from psychic vampires, people who drain you of your own psychic energy and use you for their own purposes.*

Again, he snickered. The notion that many famous people had been influenced by the occult was noteworthy, but he wasn't sure how much of the information was credible. There was no author written on the cover of the tome, no publisher, no one to take credit for this work.

Renner still thought the book of spells and Paul's claims were unfounded, but his interest was beyond piqued and was getting the best of him. Maybe he would go and watch the medium deceive her followers. What harm was there in attending the ritual? He had even thought of a question he wanted answered, a goal he wanted to reach. The question he'd been asking himself ever since he met Milena. How do psychic abilities manifest in individuals, and can these abilities be produced at a genetic level? Is there a genetic basis after all?

Perhaps, visiting the psychic woman would help subconsciously nudge him in the right direction to figuring out the problem through the hypnotic process or whatever tactic the medium used to manipulate her subjects. He was glad Paul reminded him of his interest in Psi abilities, for he had temporarily forgotten with Dr. Shubally dying, his cancer research disappearing, and then getting caught up on his new thesis experiment with Paul and Dr. Kirby. Maybe, this could even spiral into new research down the road, working with DNA to identify the chromosomes or DNA sequences responsible for Psi abilities. Wouldn't the government be excited about that finding?

A super-soldier indeed.

It was decided then. The following evening, he would go with Paul to see the medium.

★ ★ ★

Leaving Renner at home, locked away in his private office, Milena had ducked out of the apartment and headed to her office, several psychic readings booked for the night.

Her gift was always at the forefront, waiting to be called upon. But, by her third and final client that evening, she was starting to get worried.

Attempt after attempt to tap into her gift, whether she was trying to read the arrangement of the tea leaves, the delicate lines in the palms of her clients or the pictures displayed on the tarot cards, was unsuccessful. Nothing came to her. No images, no premonitions.

Dismissing her last failed client for the evening, her pockets empty—no fee for services not rendered—she closed the door and engaged the lock.

What was happening to her?

Although, she already knew the answer to the question, didn't she? But to face the answer also forced her to have to face the disturbing visions she was having.

The first vision, the day of her wedding when Renner slipped the wedding band onto her finger, she saw a glimpse of something she wasn't willing to accept. The horrors she saw couldn't possibly come to pass, so she had pushed the images down, ignoring them.

For a time, all was well. Until the treasure seeker came to visit, giving her the ancient pendant. That's when the dreams began.

Renner charging at her, attacking her, beating her to a bloody pulp. She would plead for him to stop, but he would continue, relentless, apathetic. She would awaken bathed in a cold sweat, consumed by fear and revulsion. Afterwards, she would stare at Renner sleeping soundly beside her, appearing peaceful, harmless, and eventually the terror would subside.

How could her husband ever hurt her? The possibility didn't exist. He loved her and cherished her with all of his being.

Still, the visions persisted. And Milena continued to repress them, push them down deep into the farthest recesses in her mind. And, by constantly pushing the visions away from her conscious thoughts, she was inadvertently pushing away her gift, denying her psychic ability. If she acknowledged her gift, the visions would return.

And she wasn't the only one having visions that she was in danger. The treasure seeker's vision was clear: she needed protection by a relic that warded off evil. But, what evil? Renner? A shiver crept up her spine. She pulled the pendant out of her skirt pocket, fingering the cold metal.

Giving the situation considerable thought, she came to an unavoidable conclusion: she would temporarily close her business until she figured out a way to get rid of the visions so that she could use her gift again without being paralyzed by fear.

★ ★ ★

Later that evening, snuggled into Renner's warm embrace, she struggled with the desire to tell him her predicament. She didn't want to have secrets and had made such a big deal over Renner's secrecy regarding his new research. But, wasn't she holding back from him? She never mentioned the visions or even the strange pendant she kept with her ever since the treasure seeker had entrusted the relic to her. And now, her decision to close her business, and her trouble with using her gift. If she told him she was blocking her abilities, she would have to tell him why, tell him about her visions. And she couldn't. He'd be livid that she could even think such things. She would offend him, hurt him. And he didn't deserve that. He'd been nothing but loving and kind. So, after considerable thought, she came up with an excuse as to why she was temporarily closing her psychic business. Not only an excuse, but a true desire she'd been nurturing since their wedding vows.

"So, I've been thinking a lot about us, and our future. And, I've decided to close my psychic business for a while."

Renner propped himself up on one elbow, surprised. "What? You love your business! What happened?"

"The landlord contacted me the other day and told me he was hiking up the rent. The price is too steep for me to afford for the few clients I see each week." She hesitated, trying to find the right words. "And I was thinking about the next step in our relationship. The natural progression of things would be to start a family, and I don't want the extra hassle of a business. I'll probably re-open one day. Just not now."

"I can help you pay for the rent with the money my father gave me for living expenses. You have to keep doing what you love. And the thought of kids is so far from my mind. I'm starting new research, and I haven't even graduated from the university. I don't have a steady source of income to support a family. So, you have lots of time to continue to do your passion. Besides, I'm not even sure I ever want kids."

Milena mimicked Renner's posture, pushing up on one elbow and twisting her body around to face him, accusingly.

"What do you mean? I assumed you'd want a family one day. Especially after what you went through. Your parents adopted you and showed you unconditional love. Don't you want that for yourself, with your own children?"

"My past is precisely why I don't want kids. Look at what I went through with my biological parents, how I was treated."

"You can't compare yourself to your biological parents."

"How do you know what kind of parent I would be? Some part of them must have rubbed off on me. But, that's irrelevant. The timing is all wrong. I'll be so busy with my work; I won't have the time or the patience."

"And what about me? Am I supposed to be alone, then, while you do all of your work? I all but gave away my friends for you, sacrificing every free moment to be with you. Now when I call on them, they're too busy."

"That's even more reason for you to keep your business. Seeing clients will keep you occupied. And I never told you not to see your friends. That was your choice, so don't blame me."

This wasn't going at all how Milena had planned. She felt on the defensive and was heartsick over the realization they may never have children.

"I'm not enjoying my work as much as I used to, so I'm taking a break and that's final."

"But, doing readings is such a big part of who you are. It's in you. How can you stop?"

"I just can, OK? Now let's drop it." She felt her voice rising. Could he tell she was lying? Getting emotional and defensive wasn't helping matters.

"I have an idea. Maybe this will change your mind," Renner proposed. "I'm going with Paul to see a woman who's a medium. She only sees people by invitation. I know it sounds weird, but I'm curious to see what she does. Paul says she can channel the spirit world."

"That sounds ominous. And since when do you listen to Paul?"

Renner sat all the way up now, pulling away from Milena.

"Hey, if Paul hadn't come to my rescue, I'd be totally screwed with my thesis. He single-handedly helped me out. Our work relationship is great, and frankly I'm getting a little tired of defending him to you all the time. Maybe Paul and I weren't suited to be roommates, but now I think he's OK. He saw I was interested in psychic abilities and offered to take me to see this woman to learn more about the phenomenon. I want to learn more because of you—because being psychic is such a big part of you and your life. Don't you get that?"

"Well, it's not going to be a big part of me anymore, so don't bother."

Their voices were continually elevating with every sentence in both pitch and volume. Milena couldn't believe they were having their first argument. And all because she couldn't be honest with him. And, her timing with bringing up children couldn't have been worse. What had she done?

"Well, I'm going. And Paul invited you, too, so you're welcome to join us. But, I'm going regardless."

"Fine. Go. But I'm not going to let you go there by yourself."

"Fine. Then you'll come with me." He took a deep breath, and huffed. "Look, I don't want to fight anymore, Milena. I love you."

All of Milena's anger evaporated with those three words.

"I love you, too," she sighed in resignation.

Renner nestled back into Milena's body, pulling her in close, and kissed her gently on the shoulder. "I'm sorry I raised my voice."

"Me too."

"Our first fight. I guess we had to get the first one out of the way, eventually. There's one good thing about this."

"Oh yeah? What's that?" Milena asked confused.

"Now, we get to make up," his green eyes sparkled mischievously.

Again, he kissed her shoulder, then her neck and earlobe, pressing his body against hers as they lay spooning each other.

She rolled over to face him and gave in to his advances.

Their passion melted away all of her apprehension. This was the man she loved. The man she married. The man she trusted. Renner Scholz.

The visions had to be wrong.

Chapter 16

The rain poured heavily all day. Finally, the deluge relented as dusk settled over Alsacar, one of the older sections of Seattle. The worms had been summoned along with the sweet scent of moist earth, lying hidden below the writhing fog.

The street was deserted. Cold, moist wind lashed Milena's face. The warmth, passionate intimacy, and safety she had shared with Renner the night before—after they reconciled their differences—those feelings and memories were becoming like the mist that surrounded her, dispersing in the air, no longer tangible.

"Are you sure we're in the right place?" Milena asked, her Polish accent more pronounced as a result of the fear and anxiety that clenched her gut. "There isn't a single person in sight, and probably for good reason."

Renner ran a hand through his dampened hair. Milena couldn't help but notice him, standing tall, so handsome and virile, gazing back at her with adulation and subconsciously fingering the newly placed gold ring on his left hand. The ring represented their commitment to each other, and she realized perhaps not for the first time that this was a moment to test its strength.

"Paul says so," Renner responded.

Milena didn't want to appear weak in front of Renner and his alleged friends, Paul and Wendy, struggling to keep up the facade that she was strong and independent. And, she was, wasn't she?

Then why did she feel so vulnerable and afraid?

Something was off. The area reeked of danger and unrest, stirring some inner instinct that she should be cautious. She knew of certain psychics and mediums that were not to be trusted, who used dark magic, and often the people they were claiming to help were left unaware of the danger, making them vulnerable. The fact that the spell was to harness a guardian angel's powers made her feel more nervous, not more at ease. She had never heard of such a spell.

"Aren't you excited, Milena? This woman is extraordinarily talented. She might even teach you a thing or two," Paul mocked.

"I don't know what kind of woman this is. What you describe is considered dark magic, drawing on spiritual energy to do her bidding. That's not right."

"Look who's the hypocrite. Isn't that what you make your living on? Who do you think gives you all the images you see, but spirits themselves?"

"I don't know how I get the images, I just do. But, this woman conjures up spirits on purpose, trying to get angels to do favours for you. Some things are meant to be left an enigma—unrestrained, unprovoked."

Renner tried to encourage his wife to continue his quest. "I'll be with you the whole time. We'll observe the spell, and then go home."

Standing on the rain-darkened cobblestones of the deserted street, he looked at her pleadingly. Why did this mean so much to him? Although she didn't understand, she couldn't let him down.

"Fine. But, I'm only staying a little while. And for the record, this medium of yours is probably a witch. I'm not sure how you heard of her."

"She's the best," Paul replied. "Maybe you're jealous that you can't harness that kind of power."

"I would never want to."

"Aw, come on Milena. Isn't there anything you want, anything the clairvoyant could grant you? Isn't there something you desire, that would make you happy, make you feel complete?"

Looking down at her feet, she averted his gaze, the thought of having a baby instantly springing to mind.

"Of course, there is. I can tell by the look on your face."

"Why am I here again?" inquired Wendy, unusually quiet, looking weary and uncomfortable.

"Shut up, Wendy. Nobody's talking to you," Paul rebuked.

"Wow, Paul, it takes a special kind of asshole to treat his girlfriend like that," Milena came to Wendy's defence.

"Who says she's my girlfriend."

"I can't believe you let him talk to you like that," Milena directed her question to Wendy, incredulous.

"Nobody asked you for your opinion. I can talk to her however I please. Besides, I don't know why you'd want to defend her, when she's really in love with your husband."

Milena's jaw dropped, and she twirled to face Wendy, who's drooped posture told her what Paul said was true.

"I might be jealous of Milena and Renner's relationship, but you were jealous of his relationship with Dr. Shubally," Wendy divulged in a mousy voice.

The blood drained from Paul's face. "Put a sock in it, you stupid twat, before you say something you'll regret."

With more assertion, she glared at Paul accusingly. "You wanted to work with Dr. Shubally, and you hated Renner for taking your spot. Admit it!"

"She's insane," Paul shook his head in dismissal, addressing Milena and Renner. Then, back to Wendy, he added, "He'll never want you, so you might as well quit trying. He has Milena now, and she's ten times the woman you'll ever be."

Wendy, gutted, dropped her gaze back to the road, and again became silent.

"Guys, enough! No wonder we're taking so long to get there, with you fighting the whole way. Let's focus on getting to the chapel, and then we can go home. OK?" Renner intervened.

They all agreed. Milena wrapped her mink coat tighter around her torso to ward off the chill, not from the damp weather, but from whatever lay beyond.

"One day, you might even feel the need to thank this woman for the gifts she will bestow," Paul added.

"Honestly, Paul, enough," Renner urged.

Milena wanted no such gifts from this woman. Even being a witness to such dark magic made her flesh crawl. Adamantly refusing to participate in the ritual, she was mainly going along to ensure Renner remained safe. But, could she protect him?

They had taken the subway to Alsacar station and then proceeded on foot. The streets were at first familiar, but then dramatically changed, the buildings transforming before her eyes, the shadows transitioning, piling atop the existing structures until they grew into towering gothic monsters. The architecture, initially quaint and modern, now loomed over them, dark and menacing. Windows were smashed in several of the buildings, shards of glass attached to the edges reminiscent of shark teeth, threatening to disembowel anyone foolhardy enough to enter.

"We're getting close. The entrance is behind one of these buildings, but they all look so similar."

They walked slowly past each dilapidated structure, Milena and Renner's arms linked, looking for the building that would lead them to the secret entrance of the psychic's lair, signified by a marker—graffiti of a serpent devouring a lamb.

"Here, this is the one," Paul announced, stopping in front of a particularly decrepit house, the door hanging on by one hinge. "It's in the alleyway behind this building."

"But, is the alleyway safe?" asked Milena, tightening her hold on Renner's arm. "It's so dark."

"There's no other way, my *Liebling*. Don't worry, I'll protect you," Renner reassured his trembling wife.

Paul pantomimed a gagging gesture. "Let's just go. We're already late for our appointment."

Renner extracted a metal flashlight from the pocket of his black raincoat, turned the power on, and trained the light down the darkened alleyway. Rats scurried from its path as if they would incinerate under the rays, even though the beam was faint, as if the batteries were dying. Renner tapped the flashlight briskly on his opened palm, and for moments the light intensified, then faded once more.

★ ★ ★

A flurry of excitement danced within Renner's chest. This adventure was more stimulating than he had predicted. Could this mysterious woman possibly answer his questions about the genetic basis of psychic abilities? Help him to achieve his goals of being a pioneer in his field, discovering something so profound that the knowledge would alter our view of humanity? Driven forward by his thirst for knowledge, understanding, and inspiration for future research, he also knew part of this drive came from his upbringing, his past experiences. He wanted so much more for Milena, not only to provide for her but to lavish her in luxury. To make her and his parents proud.

Suddenly, Milena shrieked. "What the hell was that?" A rat scurried over her boot and retreated into the distance. She clung to Renner's coat, hiding behind the lapel. "What was that in his mouth, a finger?"

Paul chuckled. "You're right, Milena. I saw it too."

"Stop teasing her, Paul. I'm sure the rat was carrying something else. Maybe a hotdog wiener," Renner tried to de-escalate the situation, although it really had looked like a human finger clamped between the rat's jaws.

"Why is the street so deserted? Did something bad happen here?" Milena asked, trembling.

"The area is said to be haunted. Even the building where the psychic does her readings," Paul stated matter-of-factly without a break in stride.

Milena's face blanched.

"It's a rumour, dear Minka, nothing more," Renner consoled.

"This place is enchanted," Paul continued. "This street only exists for those formally invited, similar to a sponsorship. Someone has to make a formal request to the medium via mail; all guests have to be vouched for by a prior client. I vouched for you guys, otherwise you wouldn't be allowed to attend the Guardian Angel Ceremony."

Paul plucked a cigarette from his jacket pocket and lit up. Exhaling a plume of smoke, he added, "The entrance we're looking for leads into The Alsacar Asylum for the Insane, which was closed down in the early 1960s and has since been demolished. But, part of the underground portion of the building remains intact. The graffiti marks the secret entrance to allow us inside. Few people know a part of the building is still in use."

"I don't feel good about this," Milena whispered.

Paul ignored her, playing on her fears. "Seattle has always been known for having a dense population of specters, ghosts, and spirits that wander between the realm of heaven and earth, and for some reason this area is particularly densely populated, as if the spirits were drawn here by some supernatural magnetic force, accumulating here over the centuries, rather than roaming blindly around the earth alone. Soldiers, movie stars, homicidal mothers, and victims of murder or suicide—their spirits trapped here, a purgatory for their sins. The psychic specifically chose this area to practice her craft, drawing on the closeness of the spirits, able to contact them more easily, control them more effectively."

★ ★ ★

Spirits. That's what Milena felt was off about the area: a strong sense of something out there in the fog, watching them, and waiting. Her skin erupted in goose pimples. Remembering the talisman given to her by the treasure seeker, she reached into her felt-lined pocket, searching with her hand, feeling a tremour of relief as she grasped the icy metal. The pendant was too cold to hold for long, numbness quickly spreading through her hand, but she refused to let go. Is this what the adventurer foreshadowed, what the talisman was supposed to protect her or Renner from?

"It's not too late to turn around and go home," Milena begged.

"Milena, I know you don't understand this now, but I'm doing this for both of us. This'll help me to understand your gift, and answer questions I didn't realize how much I need answering. But, I do. Can we continue?"

She resigned once more to their search, with head hung low, eyes on the lookout for whatever lay beyond the shadows.

They scanned the darkest corners of the alleyway. Finally, the beam of light locked on the image they were searching—the graffiti of a serpent consuming a lamb, its faded green reptilian mouth grotesquely stretched around the lamb's corpulent body, the lamb's eyes petrified, mouth bleating in protest. The artwork appeared alive. Almost animated.

"This is the place," Paul exclaimed. "I knew we were close."

A dark staircase, shrouded by shadows, sat immediately below the disturbing artwork. Milena hesitantly followed her husband down the stairs into the inky, crypt-like walkway beneath the abandoned building, aware of the distant, unnatural sounds emanating from within. Chains clinking and scraping, a high-pitched wailing that Milena desperately hoped was the wind whistling through the windows and cracks in the walls, but she feared may be something else entirely, refusing to think about what was truthfully creating the sinister sounds.

Paul and Wendy followed the young, married couple inside. As the group walked almost blindly through the derelict archway, and subsequent tunnel, which twisted and turned multiple times, Milena was certain they wouldn't be able to find their way out, forever buried in this dungeon. Often, a smell of rotting meat permeated her nose, sometimes the acrid smell of something burning, causing her to gag. Her boot heels clicked loudly, echoing down the halls, announcing their presence.

At times a shadow was caught in the thin beam of the flashlight, slithering ahead, showing them the way, the movement so fleeting Milena wasn't sure she saw anything at all, her mind simply running wild in the dreary, dank dungeon. Then she'd hear whispering sounds, coaxing.

Renner, come.

Never had she been anywhere so utterly frightening and alive with death. Her heart raced, certain that danger awaited them.

A dim light seeped menacingly from beneath a large, wooden door up ahead. Rapping on the door, they were beckoned inside by a deep, raspy voice, genderless, with a guttural quality. The foursome entered the candlelit room, the air crackling with static electricity. The stench of rotting meat was more concentrated in the room, and Milena wavered on her feet, not sure if she was going to pass out or throw up.

A series of broad oak pews stood in two distinct rows leading to an altar. Upon the altar, a table stood with one matching chair, dust thickly coating the rough surfaces of the wood.

The pews were occupied by cloaked figures, hoods pulled over their heads, hiding their shadowed faces as they turned to gaze upon the new guests. As one, they returned their stares back to the altar. Milena couldn't help but feel unwelcome. Resisting the urge to flee, she forced herself to follow Renner and the others to sit in one of the unoccupied pews.

The room must have been a chapel in the hospital, probably once a sanctuary where people would go to pray for loved ones when they were sick or recovering from illness or psychological turmoil. There was such a room in the psychiatric facility her sister lived in.

Milena had visited the chapel many times, always feeling a sense of peace. Now, in this dimly lit chapel, she felt anything but peace.

The sounds of chains clinking and scraping was heard again in the distance. And again, clinking, scraping even louder now, followed by a sudden, remote moaning echoing in the twisted walkways they had previously travelled, and Milena had a flash, a vision of a young child whose life was extinguished but whose pain and suffering infinitely carried on.

An elderly woman hobbled into the chapel and sat in the lone chair by the table on the altar. The clairvoyant. Clothed in tattered rags, a moth-eaten lace veil obscuring her face, Milena was reminded of the old spinster, Miss Havisham, from the movie *Great Expectations*. The decrepit bride, once jilted at the altar, now rotting in her bridal gown, refusing to let go of the past. She sat waiting, expectant.

More chains clinked, scraped.

One of the cloaked figures stood and approached the altar. The old woman withdrew a pipe from the desk before her, filled the bowl with an unknown substance, and lit the top portion, drawing in deeply through her veil the smoky drug. It left behind a yellowed stain on the lacy fabric. She held it out to the cloaked figure and he also inhaled deeply from the end. He then walked over to the nearest pew, and passed the pipe to the next cloaked figure, who kept the ritual going. The pipe continued to be passed throughout the small congregation.

Paul leaned over and whispered into Renner's ear. "They're smoking ayahuasca, a hallucinogenic compound that'll greatly enhance your experience. Some people believe the drug connects you to the spirit realm. The experiences are intense, and utterly amazing. I strongly encourage you to partake if you want to have the full experience. I promise you, the drug is safe, made entirely from natural compounds. The effects will wear off quickly."

Milena shot Renner a warning glance, forbidding him to even consider smoking the pipe. Who knew what could really be inside?

"I have to try, right? It's not the first time I've ever experimented with drugs. This is the '70s."

"Renner, think about what you're doing. You can't trust these people. You don't even know them," Milena urgently whispered.

"Relax, everything will be fine," Renner gave her a reassuring smile, which failed. But, his mind was made up, she could tell.

When the pipe reached their pew, Paul took the initial drag from the tip and then passed the drug to Renner. Confidently, Renner also drew deeply on the pipe. The old woman watched, a statue, unmoving, unperturbed.

Coughing, Renner passed the pipe to the next hooded figure. Milena and Wendy abstained. Once the attendants had finished smoking the drug, the pipe was passed back up to the front of the chapel, where the old woman placed it on her desk.

"You are all here by select invitation to join in the ritual of evoking your guardian angels for certain reasons, all of them different, and very personal. Focus on those dreams, those goals, those questions. Focus your mind on what you want most."

Milena flinched. Here was the moment they were waiting for, the purpose of their visit. Nothing good could come of this. Why hadn't she tried harder to talk Renner out of this plan?

"Think deeply about what you wish to gain from harnessing control over your angel," the psychic's voice crackled. The lace covering should have fluttered with each syllable she spoke, but the material remained inert, flat.

Everyone was concentrating deeply. Looking at Renner, Milena could see his eyes were closed, focused internally on whatever he sought from this evil woman.

"Now ask yourselves, are you positive you want to unleash the strong powers from the angels?" She waited expectantly.

Was she warning them, testing them, Melina wondered?

"Yes," Renner and the collective group responded in unison, reminding Milena of a responsorial psalm in church.

The psychic looked pleased with their reply.

"Then you will get what you wish," the feral woman hissed. With stilted jerky movements of her gnarled, arthritic hands, she removed her veil. Her eyes were large black orbs, with no whites or irises showing, in a sea of wrinkled flesh. Patches of eczema, red and flaky, were splotched on her cheeks and neck.

All was silent for a moment, nothing stirred.

Then the gravelly voice issued forward from the mystic's mouth, chanting now in another language, spells that spewed forth from a dark, ancient place. The black orbs grew darker still, two black holes threatening to suck Milena into their depths should she stare at them for any great length of time. An unnatural coldness filled the room, yet Milena felt an intense heat creeping up her spine. Tearing her eyes away, she tried to shake free of this predator or she believed she would die. Attempting to keep her mind blank, her deepest desire hidden, she clutched the ice-cold pendant in her pocket with such force that her entire hand was now completely numb.

Renner's eyes opened when the chanting commenced, and now remained transfixed on the evil woman's black orbs. Gently, he swayed as if in a trance. His eyes rolled back in his skull. The other individuals also swayed, save for Wendy who looked as petrified as Milena felt.

The chanting became louder, stronger, more insistent and demanding—and Milena thought she detected a second voice beneath this superior one, that of a low guttural growl and heavy breathing.

Milena wanted to escape but felt pinned to her seat, paralyzed, unable to move anything but her eyes, and continue her body's basic parasympathetic functions—breathing, heartbeat, swallowing. Everything else was beyond her control.

Instinctually, she felt she should act unaffected by the evil psychic, believing she had to give the woman permission to be able to influence her. She did not. She fought against the sensation with all her will.

A blue ellipsoid light began to emanate from Renner's body, intensifying as the chanting continued. Simultaneously, a white light grew above his head, the light gradually intensifying as well, as if the chanting breathed into it life and strength.

Within a few minutes, the chanting and sinister guttural sounds reached a climax, the air feeling more statically charged like before a lightning strike. Unexpectedly, the growing white light above Renner's head transformed into a dark menacing shadow, with a distinct head, torso and arms, and the shadow looked at Milena, eyes consumed with evil and hatred. The apparition hovered there above her husband's body, growing, expanding, until Renner was completely enveloped in darkness. And as she watched, frozen, the shadow was absorbed inside of his form, the darkness sucked into him like a vacuum. The beautiful blue aura that had originally surrounded Renner abated.

Startled out of his trance, he looked around as if awakening while sleepwalking, unsure of his whereabouts. Then a large, frightening grin spread across his face.

★ ★ ★

"It worked. I can feel it!" Renner exclaimed.

"Let's get out of here," Milena whispered in a tremulous voice. Hastily, she stood up, knocking over an old hymnal that had been left in the pew. The book crashed loudly to the floor, echoing in the sudden deathly silence that ensued the hysterical chanting that thickly permeated every inch of the room moments before.

Renner picked up the book, and started towards the door, still dazed, when Paul seized his arm with inhuman strength.

"Are you forgetting about payment?"

For the first time during this process, Renner looked unsure of himself. Paul told him there was a price, something he would be asked to trade with the psychic for the spell to work. An absurd arrangement, but he was too curious to be dissuaded from attending the ceremony. Now his face fell. What was the psychic's price?

"Yes, yes, of course. How do we arrange this?" he asked Paul, stroking his chin impatiently, wanting to get this part over with.

"Follow me," Paul insisted, walking to the front of the room with the other parishioners where they formed a line before the old woman. Milena and Wendy waited impatiently by the exit.

The old woman produced paperwork from the top drawer in the oak desk and laid the sheaf on the surface of the table. Renner almost expected they would need to sign with their own blood, but a pen materialized in the ancient's other hand. The attendants started signing the papers, one at a time, and then moved on, back up the aisles and out the door.

On his turn, Renner grabbed the pen, and perused the paper handed to him by the old psychic. She was even more hideous up front, so he averted his gaze as much as possible.

The contents of the paperwork made his mouth run dry. The pages were professionally typed, but the contents were absurd. The first thing that made him uneasy was that his wish, his desire, was written in black ink in front of him on the page. How did the psychic know what he was going to ask?

The method of payment was even stranger.

Renner was to promise the souls of his unborn children to the spirit they had conjured. The request made the ritual feel more cultish, was in all probability part of the show, an attempt to enhance the delusion that this was a real spell.

There's no way this is for real, he told himself.

After a few moments consideration, he signed the documents, never planning to have any children with Milena, anyhow, so there wouldn't be an issue. He also didn't believe in promising "souls for service," more convinced than ever that this was just a part of the sinister experience, a part of the occult-like atmosphere. Like a joke. Milena didn't need to know of this arrangement, of course, still clinging to the hopes that they would someday have a traditional family, and already labelling the psychic as a witch.

Hoping the contents would never be exposed to Milena, he returned to his wife, trembling by the door. Her fear now rendered her mute. If she were to ask about the paperwork's contents at a later time, he would lie. He planned never to tell Milena the truth about the psychic's price.

Chapter 17

Milena stands on the deserted street, the one they occupied two days before in reality. Framed by a cone of lamplight, she looks fearful, out of place. In this lighting, her olive skin looks darker. The image shifts as past memories surface in Renner's mind, a direct reflection from his childhood. A buried memory.

A fishing trip, one of the few he was invited to with his biological father. They hit turbulent waters, and there, in the middle of the lake was a hummingbird, its wings too saturated with lake water to take flight. The bird fluttered frantically, eyes wide with surety it was going to drown. Renner paddled the boat near and scooped the tiny creature into his hands. Energy completely spent, the hummingbird lay unmoving on his palm. Grabbing an orange, he brought on the voyage, he squeezed a drop of sugary liquid into the bird's beak. Within moments, its head perked up and it began fluttering its tiny wings again. He was a hero in that moment, saving the helpless little bird.

His vater delicately plucked the bird from Renner's hands. Vater never spoke much, unless he was berating Renner or his mutti or yelling about something they did wrong, but now he spoke in a calm voice filled with conviction, causing Renner to listen and remember his words, verbatim.

"Have you ever heard of the Eugenics Movement?" he asked Renner.

Renner, not having attended school, even though he was already eight-years-old, had no idea what his father was talking about. He shrugged his shoulders.

"Of course not. You're a stupid boy." Shifting his heavy frame on the boat seat, he turned to face Renner head on. Renner shrank under his gaze.

"There's a hierarchy among all living things. We are given certain genetics to allow us to survive in our environments. Some of us are stronger than others and it's in our best interest to snuff out the weaker individuals, the weaker races, and promote our clean genetic lineage. If we allow the weak to survive, to pollute our gene lines, then we as a human race will eventually die out. Do you understand that?"

Renner nodded his head in assent, because he knew he would be slapped if he said no. In truth, he wasn't sure what his father was getting at.

"See this creature? He's injured, disabled now." He pointed to the fracture in the right wing. "He's not the fittest of his kind, and should be prevented from procreating, having children of his own." Tightening his fist around the frightened animal, Renner could hear the bones popping, could see the blood spurt out between his fingers, and then he threw the carcass into the lake, washing his hands in the lake water as if he swatted a fly. Grabbing his fishing rod, he then cast the minnow into the lake's murky depths and continued to fish despite the unstable weather.

Horrified, Renner sat frozen in place.

"Promise me that you'll never marry anyone of an inferior race. That is, if anyone will want to marry your sorry ass."

Renner nodded again but was too disturbed to truly grasp the meaning of that promise.

The image wavered and there stood Milena again. To Renner, she was a strong and independent woman, but in his father's eyes, she was as useless as that tiny injured hummingbird based solely on her Romani lineage. Evident in her olive-coloured skin and black hair worn long and wavy, not to mention her psychic gift, Milena was a gypsy, through and through.

To his vater, Ulrich, she was nothing, an inferior race, like all the victims of the holocaust.

The dream transformed again, another memory, one of the few times his father talked with him, man to boy, in hopes of teaching him something, passing on the wisdom he had garnered from fighting in the Second World War under Hitler's regime.

"You have to see that you're of pure blood. Your duty is to keep your lineage clean. Look at you, with your blond hair and blue eyes." Renner's eyes were green and his hair was golden brown, of course, a fact his father chose to ignore. "You're a superior being. We are the superior race, and we can rule the world."

Those words resounded in Renner's mind as he startled out of his restless dreams. Milena wasn't in bed with him. As his mind cleared, he remembered she was working at the university bookstore this morning.

All those images and memories had been deeply buried, he thought. He had made a point of forgetting them. But, here, they had popped into his mind as clear as a shallow pond on a windless day. Was it the visit to the chapel that stirred them up?

As a young child, Renner didn't know the brutality of the Second World War, specifically Hitler's reign. When he became an adult, he had finally learned of the abominable acts performed during that dark period in history. People actually believed that Hitler must have been possessed by the devil himself to have orchestrated such a horrific movement.

And yet, Hitler wasn't the first to think along these lines. Further back in history, the philosopher, Plato, explained the benefits of rulers overseeing marriages and reproduction: to strengthen the human race, unknowingly planting the first seeds of racism.

Later, Francis Galton suggested that genes could be carefully selected in humans to strengthen the human race, weeding out illnesses and weaker genes—like pulling dandelions out of the garden—coining the term eugenics to describe this concept. In 1904 he launched the Eugenics Movement, where people with illness, disabilities, and mental health issues were sterilized—by law—so they could no longer procreate and weaken the human race. Strangely, this movement was backed up by political leaders, royalty, the elite, and scientists, and was orchestrated around the world

When Hitler came into power, again backed by the credibility of scientists, he took the Eugenics Movement to a whole other level. By the time his regime had fallen, the Nazi's had slaughtered millions of Jews, mentally and physically handicapped individuals, homosexuals, blacks, and gypsies, using the concept of eugenics as an excuse for their abhorrent acts of cruelty.

Being a scientist, Renner understood that eugenics, in theory, did indeed strengthen the population to which it was applied. But, he saw the value only as applied to plants and animals, such as a farmer attempting to breed cattle that produces more milk, more lean meat, survive diseases better, and so forth. The resultant offspring would be stronger, more attractive, and healthier. But, to apply this concept to the human race was, well, insane.

The war drove his father insane—there was no doubt about that. The ideas based on Darwin's and Galton's teachings regarding survival of the fittest and eugenics had been taken too far during Hitler's rule. Hitler and his followers strongly believed in the Aryan race, a race that was superior to others, and that gave them the right to sacrifice those they accused to be of a lesser race or inferior beings.

Renner's biological father was a mad man, completely sadistic, ruthless, and incapable of love. His father's teachings were despicable. There could be no value in them whatsoever. Renner obviously hadn't been influenced by his father's racist, fascist ideas. He didn't believe one race was superior over another in any way, shape or form. He never viewed gay people or handicapped people as being less important or less strong than others. He even married Milena, a gypsy woman, for goodness sake, an act that surely made his biological father roll over disgruntled in his grave. But, he was having difficulty shaking off his dreams. Did they hold a hidden message for him that he wasn't grasping, some relevant morsel of importance?

Had his dreams been stirred up and raised to the surface of his mind stimulated by his experience with Paul in the old chapel? Like walking through a pool of water, disturbing the debris settled at the bottom, so the wet leaves and fractured twigs float up to the top, becoming visible to the eye?

After leaving the abandoned chapel buried deep beneath the earth, Renner didn't have a profound revelation of how psychic abilities worked and how to produce them in humans. But, what he did have was a certain clarity and understanding that he would know. He needed to be patient, do more research.

Firstly, he wanted to learn more about the drug he had smoked, ayahuasca. What psychoactive ingredients were used in the drug, and what area of the brain was affected in particular? His experience with the spiritual world while under ayahuasca's influence was profound. A world beyond ours that he never believed in, he finally could see with his very own mind that it was real. He wondered if the others present in the chapel had seen what he saw or felt what he felt. A current of energy still pulsed through him, as if he was never fully alive until that moment when the woman's chanting reached its climax. His strength was visibly increased. He saw things differently, more clearly. Colours were more vibrant. Objects more profound, even the most insignificant held major purpose. His thoughts appeared to be more organized, and focused. Paul wasn't kidding after all.

He reflected on the moment he smoked the pipe, taking a drag from the tip, releasing the drug into his system. Surprised at how quickly he was transported into an altered state of consciousness, his surroundings dissolved away. He felt coldness, sharp and intense, coursing through his body, through his veins, his heart rate accelerated, and the back of his neck felt hot, on fire. A distant humming grew louder, closer, as the pressure in his head and sinuses increased, and he felt as if his head would burst as his mind extended into another universe.

He left his body.

Looking down at his rocking form on the pew below, he saw Milena sitting stiffly beside him. An out-of-body experience. Time as a concept shifted, no longer linear, with no past, present or future.

The image of the chapel completely peeled away, and he was walking towards blinding white light, feeling wholly engulfed in a state of utter bliss, euphoria, as if he was a part of all creation, joined through his cells, his very DNA. There were entities there, in the light, made of a cornucopia of colours, and he could feel a glowing rainbow of love radiating outwards from them to him. A divine realm. An immense power exuded from these beings. Would he ever want to leave this wonderful place of light and love? This was what life and the spirit was all about, and he knew that he could be happy here for eternity. That he was already a part of eternity.

But, as these thoughts swarmed his mind, the effects of the drug diminished. He became more aware of his physical self, sitting in the pew below him, and his spiritual self drifted down to reunite with his body. As the two parts of him again became one, he felt a sudden rush and surge of power as if something aided him in slipping back inside his body. As if something accompanied him, staying with him.

How long had he been gone, he wondered? Feeling as if decades, even centuries had passed, when he checked his Rolex, the actual duration of the spell had lasted a mere twenty minutes. He felt shaken, but exhilarated. How limited the human mind was in perceiving the real universe, he now realized. We saw but a minute fraction of what was out there, and the drug had somehow been able to connect him to this hidden reality.

Afterwards, Milena refused to talk to him. She was upset by the whole ordeal, especially the fact that he had taken the drug.

Forcing him to promise never to return to the old woman or the chapel ever again, sheepishly he agreed. But, he wanted to return. To feel that psychic energy course through him once more.

There's plenty of ayahuasca in the research labs.

Where had that voice come from, so clear in his mind? Not his own, different somehow. Was this another side effect from the psychic experience, a closer connection to his subconscious thoughts?

The voice was right. There was ayahuasca in the chemical storage locker, and also the more purified form, dimethyltryptamine (DMT), probably used for experiments on narcotics and hallucinogens back before the law had been established forbidding such research. At the time he saw the psychedelic in the storage locker, he barely noticed, having no relevance to him or his work. But now he wondered how accessible the drug was. Could he acquire the drug and experiment with it on his own? Then he wouldn't be breaking his promise to Milena, and still be able to study the drug, experiencing the amazing powers over his mind once more.

Slipping out of bed, he quickly showered and changed, grabbed his leather jacket, and decided to head to the library first to research the drug. Milena started working more hours at the campus bookstore to replace her lost hours doing psychic readings. She would be at work until six o'clock, giving him plenty of time.

Thinking of Milena working at the bookstore reminded him of the subsequent dissension in their relationship since the chapel visit. Having her upset with him was torture. Hopefully, she wouldn't take long to let go of her anger and disappointment.

He took city transit to the BIT campus, one disadvantage of not living in the dorms anymore. Walking into the library, he located the floor and aisle that housed the books on psychedelic compounds. Scanning the spines of the books lining the shelves, four books fit the bill for his research interests, containing information on ayahuasca and DMT. Piling them in his arms, he carried the careworn books to an empty desk, removed his leather jacket and slung it on the back of the wooden chair before sitting down to read. Starting with the older references, he flipped the pages to the chapter on DMT and dove in.

"Dimethyltryptamine (DMT)—a highly psychedelic chemical that will greatly enhance mystical experiences. Commonly used in ancient rituals, the drug is usually smoked or ingested as a brew but tends to exert the strongest effects when injected directly into the vein."

Interesting.

How could the effects be even more profound than he experienced in the chapel?

"Originally used in healing rituals, a brew is made from extractions from the Banisteriopsis caapi vine and leaves of the Psychotria viridis plant to make ayahuasca. These plants are prevalent in the Latin American regions. The psychedelic experience after ingesting ayahuasca is comparable to Peyote, San Pedro cactus, Iboga, and Psilocybe mushrooms, other psychedelics commonly used in healing ceremonies by aboriginals, and still used today."

"DMT was first synthetically made in the lab by a Canadian chemist in 1931."

Since then, several studies had been conducted on the drug to determine how the psychedelic compounds worked on the brain to produce such profound spiritual effects. The studies attempted to link both science and the spirit world together—same as Renner was attempting. His pulse quickened.

Reading on, he studied the many theories postulated as to what produced the drug's effects, and why the experiences were so spiritual and intense. A word suddenly jumped out at him.

Witchcraft.

The word acted as a trigger, immediately transporting him to the ceremony at the abandoned chapel. In his mind's eye, he could see the room with graphic precision, see the old desiccated-looking woman who conducted the Guardian Angel Spell as if he were there again. Milena feared the woman was a witch, that black magic could be involved. Was she right?

Clearing his mind of the memory, he focused more intently on the passage containing that word—witchcraft. According to the article, there was an extensive use of mind altering compounds such as ayahuasca or DMT, Psilocybin and mescaline in black magic rituals in order to link to the spirit realm and push beyond normal perception to draw on the power and forces there.

But, as soon as Renner pushed the idea away, moving on to other research, he was met with similar theories posed by actual researchers, reputable scientists and anthropologists. They, too, believed DMT could potentially be a link through which people could contact another realm—the spiritual landscape. The driving support for their theories rested in the feelings of enlightenment and the spiritual visions that users achieved after DMT use.

The last book, a journal on psychedelics and research, was the most informative and thought compelling of them all. A group of scientists had discovered and isolated DMT in the brains of mice and rats, and then in the human body. The actual human body. What a profound discovery! DMT became the first known naturally occurring psychedelic to be made within the human body. The pineal gland was hypothesized as a possible primary source of this endogenously manufactured DMT. But the purpose for the DMT was unclear.

What was DMT doing in our bodies?

Being a doctor, Renner was familiar with the pineal gland, the tiny pinecone-shaped organ located in the centre of the brain. An odd little gland, it was unique for being an unpaired organ, as opposed to the rest of the brain, and was comparable to the eye, containing a lens and being sensitive to light. The oddities surrounding the pineal gland coupled with its location, being central in the brain, had inspired many theories regarding pineal involvement, touting the organ as the meeting point between the spiritual and physical self, often referred to as the "seat of the soul", "third eye" or "inner eye."

Based on these theories, the DMT produced by the pineal gland acted as a tether to the spirit realm. During profoundly intense or stressful periods, a burst of DMT is emitted: like at birth, a burst of DMT facilitates the transfer of the spirit into the human form, and at death it allows the spirit to exit the body and find its way back to the spirit realm. In near death experiences (NDEs), a burst of DMT allows the spirit to see the other realm, but when the person is revived, the spirit returns to the body, still retaining the memories of the spirit realm after awakening. Milena mentioned this phenomenon during one of their discussions. At the time he had thought she was naive, but now he saw a glimmer of possibility.

While the body and mind were not in duress, the DMT levels were theorized to be kept stable by some internal mechanism. But, in cases of schizophrenia and other diseases involving psychosis, the thought was that the mechanism keeping the DMT stable was broken, resulting in uncontrollable bursts of elevated DMT causing hallucinations and delusions. Could the consciousness of these individuals be floating in and out of the spirit realm, and they are just attempting to make sense of the things they witness there? Renner had worked with patients with varying levels of psychosis, and many of the delusions were based around religious beliefs and iconic spiritual figures. Coincidence, or were they truly seeing something beyond our fabric of reality?

The pineal gland. Something about this part of the brain reminded Renner of his previous research.

And then the idea hit him. The case studies. They had indicated certain brain trauma, defects or tumours in similar areas as to where the pineal gland was located that were hypothesized as the possible causes of psychic abilities manifesting. Perhaps the pineal gland in these individuals was stimulated to produce more naturally occurring DMT in the body, linking them more easily to the spiritual world and somehow allowing them to harness the powers within, to use in the physical world. Abilities such as predicting the future, teleporting things through space, and reading minds, suddenly at their disposal.

It all was absurd, when he thought too much about the possibility. A story from a science fiction book or movie where portals miraculously opened up allowing us to enter other dimensions. But, perhaps the portal was not an external entity but rather came from within us. Maybe DMT was our connection, our portal to this other realm. There was no real known reason why organisms produce DMT, according to all the research he devoured—only theories. Was the purpose of DMT to act as a genetic link to all living things connecting us to a different realm? A chemical neurotransmitter that acts externally, with other sentient beings, tying us all together?

He thought about other neurotransmitters, ones commonly made within the body, such as serotonin, epinephrine and norepinephrine, dopamine. These chemicals were messengers, communicators, allowing the body to act and react in certain ways. The communications occurred within the body. Pheromones, also chemicals made in the body, were meant to communicate with the outside world, helping us to attract an appropriate mate, claim a territory, alarm others to possible dangers being present or to warn off an enemy. So, could this internally produced DMT help us communicate with another realm, with spiritual entities?

Of course, it was just a theory.

And theories were meant to be tested. But how?

Was this a possible area of research? Could the pineal gland be manipulated to produce more naturally occurring DMT? Would this extra DMT result in the individual exhibiting psychic abilities? Or lead to psychosis?

He was on to something. The concept was not so far removed from the research he was working on conjointly with Paul and Dr. Kirby, attempting to create a super-soldier. Their research was funded by DARPA, the Defense Advanced Research Projects

Agency, which was a faction of the government specifically interested in researching technology that could be used by the military. Would they be interested in such research as he was contemplating, or was he teasing the ethical boundaries?

In order to test his hypothesis, the experiment would need to be done on a cellular level once he figured out a way to get the pineal gland to increase DMT production, which would require working on fetuses. Starting with animals if the concept ever got passed by the ethics board, he would be faced with the challenge of how to measure psychic abilities in rodents, swine or canines. Could animals even exhibit psychic abilities? He recalled a few stories of animal Extrasensory Perception (ESP), mixed in amongst the research, but how could that be quantified?

As he explored the issue, rolling his thoughts around his brain like a potter softening the clay, a solution eventually took shape. Maybe he could measure DMT production in animals. He could determine a baseline for DMT production by the pineal gland and then after gene manipulation he could test to verify if DMT levels had increased. That would tell him if he was moving in the right direction. Once he could prove that DMT could be increased safely, the next stage would be to use human clinical trials. That would be difficult to get approved, but he would cross that bridge when he got there. If he ever decided to follow this course of study, that is. The concept was intriguing, could prove valuable research for the government in their quest to develop a super-soldier. If there was a way to enhance the human form, the mind, and its abilities, DARPA would be very excited to get their hands on such a prototype—a superior being that could fight with weapons unforeseen by, and definitely not present, in its adversaries. Paul would be jealous.

Maybe this is what his dream was trying to tell him. Hinting at the development of a superior being. Again, he reaffirmed in his mind that he wasn't racist or discriminatory to any group of individuals. His concept was to improve upon what we were born with, no matter what race, sexual orientation, religion or social status, to be used to fight against enemies that threatened our safety. There was nothing wrong with that.

His research proved fruitful. He would allow his thoughts and theories to simmer together in his mind, like his mutti's meat and potato stew that required cooking for hours to reach full potential. But, he knew he was on to something. And his breakthrough had everything to do with the visit to the abandoned chapel a few days before.

The next step in his plan was to get his hands on the DMT in the lab and experience the profound effects again.

His heart leaped with anticipation. Clearly, he could see that his destiny had changed, and he was headed for greater and bigger things.

Chapter 18

A sliver of light glowed beneath the door to the animal research lab. Renner wasn't sure who was present and wasn't about to find out. He had one thing on his mind—to get the DMT.

It was in the storage closet, a vast space that housed chemicals, beakers and other laboratory equipment. An inventory sheet dangled from a hook attached to the wall, where students and faculty were required to list any equipment borrowed, the date and time taken out and when returned. In this fashion, the school would know when to order new equipment or when something would go missing as was often the case.

Renner searched the contents on the chemical shelf. A locked glass door kept most of the researchers from accessing their contents, but Renner had a key, being one of the students cleared to work on this floor. He unlocked the cabinet and shifted the bottles around until he found one labelled DMT. Deciding he would try injecting the DMT after reading that the effects would be more intense, he bypassed the ayahuasca for now, knowing he could try that form next time if he didn't enjoy the injected pure DMT experience. There was a large supply of DMT, so he siphoned off enough for one treatment—he didn't want to be greedy—placing the drug in a bottle he brought along for such a purpose, and then concealed the bottle inside his jacket pocket, along with a sterile syringe.

Suddenly, he felt someone breathing down his neck. Without turning, he instinctively knew that someone was Paul. How long had he been standing there?

"What're you doing here? You're supposed to be coming in tomorrow," Paul asked, suspicious.

"Well...I...isn't it my day to give Samson his narcotic injection?"

"No, it's Dr. Kirby's turn. You're scheduled for tomorrow," Paul answered.

"Really? I could have sworn it was my day today. Thank goodness you stopped me in time. That could have been a catastrophe."

Paul cocked an eyebrow. "You OK, man? You look nervous."

"I don't know what you're talking about." Renner sidled past Paul, locking the storage room behind him. "Well, I guess I can take off, then."

"Sure. Oh, by the way, what did you think of the medium and the Guardian Angel Spell?" Paul asked as they walked back to the lab cubicle they shared.

"It blew my mind. I still don't understand what I saw, but the experience was intense."

"Have you noticed anything...different?"

"Different? Not really. What do you mean?" Renner lied.

"You will. In time. Anyhow, I'm heading home now, too. Walk you out?"

They left the building in silence, Renner pondering Paul's strange words.

★ ★ ★

Renner rushed into the apartment he shared with Milena, grateful she was still at work. He needed to try the DMT before she returned. Not sure what he was looking for, he mainly wanted to feel the experience again, the sensation of soaring and connecting to a world that a few days ago he didn't believe existed. Boy, was he wrong. This other world did exist and was full of life.

And power.

He couldn't deny the strong pull of this other world any longer.

From his research, he learned that taking DMT in needle form magnified the effects, and also had a longer duration in the body's system. Carefully, he filled the needle, releasing any air that may have been trapped inside with the flick of his finger, and then plunged the contents into the vein on his left arm.

The effects were immediate. His mind became clearer, objects in the room that looked flat before were now more defined, more vibrant in colour. The whole world was bursting alive around him. His existence before had been so limited, he could see that now.

A surge of power coursed through him, more salient than before.

He recalled what Paul had said—some people experience psychic abilities with the Guardian Angel Spell. Not a believer at first, Renner now did believe the transference of power was possible, was feeling that power inside of him, and knew the DMT was responsible, by connecting his human mind to the spiritual realm.

He had lied to Paul, for there were definitely changes. For one, he was stronger in a physical sense. Testing out his newfound strength, he had successfully crushed a pop can with his fingertip, ripped a textbook in half, and lifted the refrigerator in their kitchen without any effort. But, also mentally he felt more powerful, able to stretch his mind outward, and tap into other people's thoughts. He knew Paul was standing behind him at the lab by reaching out his mind and seeing him before he even turned around. He saw a perfect image of him in his mind's eye. Now that was remarkable.

The fluid travelled through his veins and continued to work on his mind, which was opening up like a blossoming flower.

You can be even more powerful, possess even greater abilities.

Renner agreed, although this thought had come from elsewhere. His mind stretched outward like a balloon, travelling, exploring, reaching over the land, over the city. He transported his consciousness wherever he wanted, there was no limitation.

And then he saw Milena—on her way home! A clear vision in his mind. Fast approaching, a few steps away. Renner remained rooted to the spot, body still paralyzed by the drug's effects, not able to react before she reached the door, turned her key in the lock and entered their apartment.

She can't see me in this state!

Struggling for control both mentally and physically, he finally found the ability to move again. He stumbled into the bathroom, locking the door behind him.

"Renner, are you home?" Milena called out.

Renner could hear her removing her coat and hanging it up in the closet. Then, he could see her—in his mind's eye—walking into the kitchen, grabbing a glass from the cupboard, turning on the sink and filling the glass up with water.

Renner waited. How long would the effects of the DMT last? Using the injected liquid form of DMT *was* lasting longer than the smoked form, as he had read during his research.

Milena walked into their bedroom, rifled through one of the drawers. There was a pregnant pause. Silence. And within that silence Renner remembered he had left the syringe lying on the end table beside the bed. Had she found the spent needle?

A second later, loud thumping shook the bathroom door.

"Renner, are you in there?" Milena howled through the plywood. Again, thumping, louder and angrier this time.

"Renner, open up!"

Scheisse!

Exposed, he finally unlocked and opened the door.

"What the hell is this?" Milena asked, holding the spent syringe in her hand.

"It's nothing. That's for work tomorrow. I got it from the lab."

"Why are you lying to me? It's already been used." She thrust the empty needle in his face, her other hand perched on her hip, which jutted out to the side. "And you look weird. Your pupils look like saucers. Is this the same drug you used the other day?"

"I don't know what you're talking about?"

"Stop lying!" She threw the needle at the bathroom floor, shattering the glass into a thousand pieces. "I can tell!"

Storming out of the bathroom, she went to the hall closet and yanked her jacket out, sending the hangar flying. Hastily, she threw on her jacket and tore open the door to leave, tearing up.

Renner ran after her, simultaneously feeling anger and guilt. Waves of the mixed emotions flew off of him and before he knew what was happening, the front door slammed shut in front of Milena entirely of its own accord.

Milena recoiled, almost struck by the door and from the repercussive force. She froze, standing in shock, trying to comprehend what had happened.

Renner was equally stunned. Did he do that? Instinctively, he knew he had. But, how?

Milena whirled on her heels to face him.

"How did you do that?"

"I didn't! It must've been the wind!" Renner ran his hands through his hair, giving a sharp tug. "Milena, I'm sorry. I didn't think you'd be so upset."

"Then why did you lie to me? You promised you'd stay away from this drug."

"No, I promised you I would stay away from the psychic woman and I will."

Milena started sobbing.

Renner cautiously approached her, slowly bringing his arms around her, and after a few tense moments, finally felt her body sink into his. Her shoulders shuddered with each sob beneath his embrace.

"I'm sorry. Please, forgive me. I don't ever want to hurt you."

Milena clearly flinched again, even more pronounced than when the door slammed in front of her face. Unwrapping his arms from her body, she pushed him away.

"I'm fine. I need some space right now. Time to think." Re-opening the door, her face registered fear and trepidation, as if she were worried it would slam shut by itself again. But, this time the door remained opened and she fled the apartment.

Renner was concerned by her reaction but knew she would forgive him. She loved him with all of her heart and she was a merciful, kind woman. He would give her a little time. Let her cool off. Then, regain her trust.

In the meantime, he would have to be more careful not to get caught.

Chapter 19

She's holding you back.

The voice, unbidden, crept into Renner's mind. Pushing the thought away, he tried focusing back on his current research—part of his thesis he needed to write up before meeting with Paul and Dr. Kirby later that day. Despite his attempts to stay on task, his mind kept floating back to the DMT.

He had tried the drug six times now, easily pilfered from the lab storage room. Keeping better tabs on Milena's work schedule, he ensured that he would have time to sample the hallucinogenic compound, the effects wearing off long before she returned home.

After several days of silent treatment, Milena had come around, as he had predicted. They made up with another passionate night and his senses now alive with a new vigour, he had responded more powerfully than ever before. The moment was magical.

The special side effects of the drug—heightened strength, clarity of mind, and a clairvoyant ability—lasted longer each time he administered a dose. Did that mean that if he kept trying the drug, eventually the effects would become permanent? It was a distinct possibility.

The pineal gland must be involved in creating the psychic aura and spiritual experiences, he concluded. Possibly, people with innate psychic abilities were born with the pineal gland secreting more naturally produced DMT into the system than the average person. And why not? If diabetics produced insufficient levels of insulin in their body, and depressed individuals had less serotonin, why not a disruption in DMT production? Further on this line of thinking, if the nervous system was heightened—through trauma, injury or illness—perhaps the pineal gland was stimulated enough to cause psychic phenomena for some individuals.

The theory was plausible, but how could he get proof? If he could find the marker on the genetic strand responsible for heightened DMT production, he might be able to create this ability in human subjects. But, first he would need to study the DNA of a psychic individual, to determine any anomalies in their genetic code that set them apart from non-psychic individuals.

What about Milena?

It hit him like a thunderbolt, a jolt of electricity shooting down the length of his spine. Why hadn't he thought of this before? *Milena!* She had psychic abilities, and she could easily provide a sample of her DNA. Not willingly, of course. The subject was touchy, as of late. No, he would find another way to get the DNA.

Abandoning his hopeless efforts at focusing on his thesis research, he stood up and glided into the bathroom he shared with his wife. Had he glanced up at the mirror, he might have noticed a dim shadow draped over his back like a cape, but he did not. Pulling open the top drawer in the vanity, he scooped up Milena's paddle brush, the dark strands of her hair still coiled around the prongs. Grabbing tweezers from Milena's makeup bag on the counter, he used them to tease free several strands of hair for later analysis at the lab. Placing the hairs on a piece of tissue, he then folded the tissue several times, and tucked the bundle inside the pocket of his leather jacket, which was hanging in the closet by the front door. Afterwards, he returned the tweezers and comb back into their appropriate places, so Milena would be none the wiser.

★ ★ ★

What was happening to Renner? Not only was he acting strange, but he had a haggard sunken look, his eyes unexplainably growing darker by the day, no longer the lively burned turquoise shade they used to be. And he had started lying to her. That was the part that disturbed her the most. Since visiting the psychic woman, he had changed, and she was unsure if he could change back.

She still loved him. How could she ever stop? But, she wasn't sure how to handle this situation. Defensive whenever she mentioned his mood or his new obsession with psychic abilities, she ceased bringing the topic up. But, how could she ignore these changes? How could she forget the door slamming shut in her face? It was not the wind.

She was walking home from the bus stop after finishing a late shift at the campus bookstore. The hours were long and boring but gave her somewhere to go during the day while Renner was at his classes or working in the lab. Getting lonelier by the day, she had attempted to reach out to her friends several times but was met with excuses. They were busy, and she was guilty of neglecting them over the year while she and Renner had been absorbed in getting to know each other.

The night was cold and crisp as she followed her normal route home. Autumn had fully descended, and desiccated leaves littered the sidewalk, crunching beneath her boots. A crescent moon dangled in the onyx sky, mixed amongst sparkling stars. Normally she would have been entranced by the sight, but tonight her thoughts were turned inward. She was so completely self-absorbed that when she heard faint singing in the distance, she assumed the sound was the wind sighing. But, after a few more steps she realized that what she heard was a chorus of voices, and the beautiful harmony drew her attention outward.

After walking another block, she met the large, marble staircase of St. Anthony's Church, which led upward into a warm, radiant, inviting space. The source of the uplifting melody. Milena passed this way a thousand times and not once noticed the building, how stunning the structure was up close, rising prominently amid the surrounding buildings, with intricate statuary of angels guarding the entrance. Stained-glass windows depicting stories from the Bible, and one larger window of St. Anthony caressing the baby Jesus' tiny little face, were illuminated from the lights within the church.

St. Anthony. The patron saint of lost things. She was definitely feeling lost at the moment.

Lured by the music, Milena found herself automatically walking up the stairs and into the cathedral.

The hymn concluded as she reached the top stair, signifying mass had ended. Parishioners began filing past her, shaking hands with a young priest before exiting the church.

Milena waited patiently. After the last few stragglers were gone, she approached the priest, who looked the same age as she was, with thick, black hair oiled, and parted to the side, warm brown eyes, and a welcoming smile.

"Excuse me, Father, do you have a moment?"

"Of course," he answered, ushering her into a pew at the rear of the church.

"I feel silly asking you this." She looked down at her hands, fidgeting with the hem of her sweater. "Do you think a person can become possessed?"

The priest looked thrown. "Possessed? By a demon?"

She nodded.

"There are many documented cases, but I've never witnessed such an event myself."

"So, you believe possession is possible?"

"I suppose. But, the chance of occurrence is extremely rare. Why do you ask?"

She stalled, not sure how much to divulge to the priest. Weren't they bound by some law to protect the confidentiality of those they counselled? She had heard that somewhere, but unsure, she answered, "It's for a paper I'm writing for school."

The priest nodded his head. "I see. Well, what are you interested to know?"

"I guess I'm curious as to why and how such a thing can occur."

The priest leaned his slender figure back against the unyielding wood of the pew. "I guess, ever since God created man in his image, loving him above all his other creations, the devil has been jealous of the human race. His revenge started with Adam and Eve but still happens every day in our lives. Looking for any way to slip past our defences and convince us to sin, put us out of favour with God. Cunning, deceptive, and corrupt, he tries to persuade at a subconscious level, to cheat on your spouse, steal, lie, overindulge in riches and unhealthy pleasures, and even kill." He paused. "A healthy person uses their free will to decide their behaviour and can ignore his voice, turn away from sin. Choose between right and wrong. But, with possession, the person becomes overwhelmed by the evil spirit. The demon controls them and free will is no longer a factor."

"Why some people and not others?"

"Usually, the person affected is either severely ill, suffering from addictions or a mental health disorder that leaves them vulnerable. Or they may have gone through a great tragedy and never fully recovered, their mind as a result, splintered."

"What about a spell?" Milena interrupted.

The priest raised his brows. "What kind of spell?"

"Have you ever heard of a Guardian Angel Spell? Asking the angels to grant you wishes?" Milena remembered the chapel, as if she were there again, seeing Renner swaying in a trance. A dark shadow had enveloped his form, looked at her with eyes of pure evil, and then disappeared inside of him.

"I've never heard of that before. But, anything to do with witch-craft is considered evil. The angels are not at our bidding but rather are restricted to doing God's will. That type of spell is tapping into something darker. Where did you hear about it?"

"In a book I read." Milena felt guilty lying to the priest. "How would you help someone in such a situation?"

"Are you worried about someone?" the priest asked, concerned.

"No, no, of course not. That would be absurd. The information is for a paper. Honestly."

"Well, you could pray for them yourself, but usually a priest needs to be called on to do an exorcism, to free the person from the demon's control."

"I see."

Milena suddenly felt ridiculous. What was she thinking? She was totally overreacting, jumping to conclusions, imagining things. There must be a more logical explanation for Renner's altered behaviour.

"Like I said," the priest continued, "it's extremely rare." He dug beneath the pew in front of him and extracted a copy of the Bible. Handing the book to Milena, he added, "There are several cases of possession in the Bible you can read about. Here, this might help you with your project."

She glanced down at the book clutched in his hand. Navy blue leather with gold letters and gilt-edged pages.

She graciously accepted, tucking the book under her arm.

"Good luck with your project."

As she left the church, she felt relieved. The priest said possession was rare, and hearing him talk about the phenomenon made her realize she had been overreacting. Something else was almost certainly to blame for the changes in her husband. She felt lighter, a glimmer of hope guiding her home.

★ ★ ★

Renner slipped inside the lab, hoping to go unnoticed. Paul had an eerie way of showing up, and he hoped today wouldn't be one of those days. He needed privacy, his task one to be kept secret. At least, until he figured out what he was looking for, and proved his theory correct. Only then would he let others in on his findings.

Setting up one of the microscopes, he plugged the chord into an electrical socket, powering up the light. Cutting the hair into small sections, he attached one piece to a microscope slide, and then added fluid for better viewing. A cover slip was carefully placed on top of the slide. Next, he fixed the slide under clasps on the microscope, securing the slide in place. Leaning forward, he pressed his eye against the ocular lens.

The microscope was not the type found in elementary schools and minor labs, feebly magnifying up to sixty percent. No, this high-powered beauty was able to magnify six hundred percent and enabled the naked human eye to see right down to the cellular level, to analyze DNA as he was about to attempt with Milena's hair segment.

Observing the structure of the double helix, he noted the various protein patterns, recorded some notes. Nothing immediately popped out at him. Nothing appeared different or abnormal. But, after twenty minutes of observation and recording values, he noticed a balanced translocation involving chromosomes number nine and eleven.

Well, what do we have here? Could this be what I was looking for? The factor that causes the pineal gland to secrete more DMT than average? There were no other discernible abnormalities on Milena's hair strand. But, how could he know for certain that this was the anomaly that he was looking for? The best way to determine this conclusively would be to perform experiments on live organisms and see if the result was enhanced DMT production. Would the procedure be possible to do on animals? Recombine the DNA with a balanced translocation on the ninth and eleventh chromosome? He wasn't sure, still wondering if the project would ever even be approved.

Yet, he had countless animals at his disposal. Trying the trans-location on one of the mice or rats in the animal research lab, no one would be the wiser, although experimenting on animals without getting formal approval would be a huge breach of ethics. But, only if he got caught. Until he was certain he was on the right path, he wanted to keep his ideas to himself. This was his baby, his profoundly exciting theory. His alone.

What about your own DNA?

An interesting thought. He took out another slide and a finger prick. After swiping the site with alcohol, he stabbed the point of the finger prick into the tip of his ring finger, and then squeezed a drop of blood onto a fresh slide, again adding liquid with a pipette for better viewing.

Milena's hair sample was removed, replaced with the slide of his own blood. The dials were cranked, enhancing the image.

As part of their studies in genetics, the students were required within the first year to study their own genetic code. Renner had studied his own double helix countless times and knew his code well.

His genetic code had changed.

There were distinct alterations in the sequences. Immediately, he focused on the ninth and eleventh chromosome and found what he was looking for. The beginnings of a translocation, similar to what Milena showed on her ninth and eleventh chromosomes but somehow incomplete. Fuzzy.

But how? Could experimenting with the drug, DMT, or the Guardian Angel Spell have altered his genetic code? The idea was preposterous, with no logical, scientific explanation. Yet, something had altered his code and was still in the process of doing so. Once complete, the end result would resemble Milena's strand. He knew this instinctively.

Looking again at the slide, he noticed other changes in his DNA sample, other protein patterns that had been altered. Could these changes explain the sudden onset of psychic abilities he was displaying? He noticed they were getting stronger each time he used the drug and were more within his control. And, he couldn't deny that his eyes were changing. The irises were darkening, turning a deep brown, the shade of coffee beans.

He was a mutating being, adapting, transforming, developing, able to move objects with his mind, read other people's thoughts. Milena wouldn't approve. He, however, felt the discovery opened up a wealth of opportunity for improving upon the human race. Who else could say they had created a new race, besides God himself. Exhilaration surged through his veins. What he had achieved so far was phenomenal.

And this was only the beginning.

Chapter 20

"Animal killers!"

A sea of angry bodies flooded the lab building's exterior entrance. Signs boldly lettered in black and red paint swayed in rhythm to the chanting.

Boots caked in muck, and arm glued to his forehead, Renner shielded his eyes from the falling sheet of rain. "What the hell is going on here?"

The chanting mob shifted their attention to Renner. Now that they had an audience, the protests escalated.

"Stop the suffering!" a petite blond bellowed, thrusting a damp wooden sign depicting the same message in his face.

"No more torture, no more lies!" a bearded fellow encased in a banana yellow rain slicker joined in.

"Unseen cruelty, suffering and death. Leave the animals alone!" This voice Renner recognized from the lab.

"You! I know you! You were spying on us in the lab!" he jabbed an accusing finger at the pretty brunette, Sandra Peters.

She stepped towards him, unabashed. "Yeah, I saw what you were doing. You and your associates. You robbed those animals of their dignity. You deserve what you get!"

"What's that supposed to mean?"

Sandra crossed her soaked arms, jutted out her chin, "Have you no shame? Those are living creatures that you're torturing! And for what?"

He couldn't believe this.

"We're doing our jobs. And what about you? Do you even work here, or were you trying to get some ammo for your silly little protest?"

Before she could respond, Paul squeezed out from the middle of the crowd, rushing over to Renner.

"Do you know what the hell is going on here?" Renner lashed at Paul.

"What do you think, genius?" Paul swiped the rain from his eyes. "This band of idiots blocked off the lab. They chained the doors shut. We can't get in."

The brunette interjected, "You guys aren't gonna get away with this! What you're doing should be illegal. Somebody had to stand up for those poor, helpless animals and stop you. You're too late! You're research here is over!"

Sandra's words sent a bolt of fear through Renner's body. What did she mean, they were too late? What had the protesters done?

"Ignore the stupid twit. I called the police from the building next door, and they'll be here any minute. These dickheads will be charged with trespassing. Then we can get back to work. Protests usually lead to nothing but a headache."

"That's what you think," Sandra Peters mumbled under her breath.

Renner seized her by the shoulders, shaking her violently. "What did you say?"

Her eyes widened. Blood drained from her face. "Let go of me!" she hissed.

A flash of lightning unzipped the sky, releasing another torrential downpour of rain.

Suddenly, sirens wailed, fast approaching. Renner released his grip, shaking his head. "You're lucky."

Sandra attempted to smooth out her rumpled jacket, face taut. Then conveniently, she was reabsorbed by the crowd.

Several police cars came barreling down the street, screeching to a halt in front of the horde. Red lights flashed on the protesters suddenly wary faces. Armed with tear gas and wooden truncheons, the policemen filed out of their vehicles and surrounded them. Although the protesters hadn't exhibited any violent behaviour so far, who was to say what would happen when the police tried to disband them. Forced compliance could be a necessity.

"All right, let's break this up," one of the cops announced, raising the truncheon as he approached. Paul shoved his way over to the cop.

"Paul Barrington. I was the one that called. These boneheads padlocked the lab doors and are refusing to let us in. As far as I know, doing this on private property is against the law. We politely asked them to leave, but, as you can see, they refused."

"He's right, people. If you don't get moving, you'll be charged. Who's heading up this protest?"

Nobody stepped forward. They looked around at each other, feigning confusion.

"I think they might've done something to the lab," Renner provided, still worried about Sandra's threats.

"Is this true?" he addressed the protesters, but again they remained silent. "Let's check the place out. Lyle, get the bolt cutter."

Renner glanced down at his watch, which indicated the time was 10:30 a.m. What should have been a routine day at the lab—collecting samples with Paul and Dr. Kirby, graduation lurking around the corner—had turned into a fiasco. A wasted morning. They didn't have time for this kind of drama.

Lyle, his physique clearly inspired by Arnold Schwarzenegger, Mr. Olympia himself, hefted a red handled bolt cutter to the entrance and snipped off the lock like he was pruning a twig. At the snap of the metal, the group instantly dispersed, washed away by the heavy rains, scattering in all directions.

Why the sudden exit?

Sandra Peters' words rang in Renner's ears. *"You're too late! You're research here is over!"*

★ ★ ★

On the second floor, the double glass doors leading into the lab space were smashed. Two policemen led the way through the rabble, Paul and Renner close on their heels. Renner's breath caught in his throat. The entire lab was trashed, each cubicle raped of its possessions. Costly equipment littered the tile in pieces, paperwork strewn from one end to the other like confetti, smeared in red paint. Every drawer from the lab had been upended onto the floor.

Picking up a sheet of paper, he glanced at the writing. The careful script he recognized as his own, the sheet a part of their ongoing research. The paper fluttered back down to the ground.

"Oh shit! The animals!" Paul's face blanched.

"You don't think..."

Together they sped to the animal research section. From the gouged wooden frame, the door had clearly been forced open. Renner followed Paul into the room, back stiff, full of dread. He felt stuck in a nightmare, the moment surreal.

The animal lab was thoroughly violated.

Several cage doors hung open, animals missing. Other less fortunate specimens had been euthanized, lying stiff and lifeless. Renner and Paul raced towards Samson's cage. Samson, too, laid still, the stench of expelled urine and feces saturating his muscular carcass.

"Mother fricker!" Paul punched the wall. "Hypocrites! They call this protecting the animals?" He paced back and forth in a rage. "They're gonna pay for this!"

Renner pulled his jacket up over his nose to block the smell of waste. "No wonder they ran so fast."

"They're getting away!" Paul shrieked at the officers that followed them into the room.

Lyle radioed his colleagues still stationed outside the building, "There's extensive damage in here. They must have been here all night. See if you can apprehend anyone."

The other officer, short and balding, with a thick neck, approached Paul and Renner for their statements.

Telling the officer everything they knew, Renner added, "That woman, the brunette, had a name tag on the second time we saw her in the lab...it said her name was Sandra Peters. Who knows if that's even her name? Claimed she was hired as a lab employee. We caught her eavesdropping on us, and another time tampering with the temperature controls. I have a feeling she orchestrated this attack."

"We'll check employee records, see if we can get an address. Thank you, men. This information helps. Hopefully we can find who's responsible for this mess. Now, I recommend you call the insurance company."

How could this happen? Again!

Their experiment had almost been complete. Key word...almost. All their paperwork, all their specimens destroyed. Faced again with the real threat of not graduating on time, Renner had a disturbing feeling of déjà vu.

★ ★ ★

Renner, age seven, plays in the front yard of his dilapidated home. Kicking around a perfectly circular rock he discovered by the pond, he pretends it's a soccer ball. He has been practicing the few moves he knows for several days, travelling with the rock down the stretch of their yard and then aiming at a gap between two trees that serve as goal posts. As he practices, his form improves, speed and precision sharpening each day. But, the burgeoning pride in his skills gets the best of him. Kicking the rock much harder, much further each time, he ends up kicking it right through the basement window of his house. The glass pane shatters.

"Renner, you stupid idiot!" his father roars from inside. Renner's insides turn to ice. Desperately seeking a hiding spot, he's too late. His father comes crashing through the front door, charges over to Renner like a bee stung rhino, and painfully yanks his arm. "Look what you did! You think money grows on trees? That we can replace that window? Why are you such a stupid idiot? You're a loser and you always will be! You'll never amount to anything!"

Next thing he knows his father is shaking him, whipping his head forward and back. Then he's punching and punching, his ribs, his stomach, his face. Renner folds his arms over his head, but they do little to protect him from the powerful blows.

"You'll never be anything!! You're nothing but a loser! A stupid loser!"

★ ★ ★

Renner's eyelids flickered open.

It took a moment for his mind to register that he was at home, in bed. Several days had passed since the animal protest. Ever since discovering the vandalized laboratory, he felt lost, in a haze. His brain not able to wrap around the situation. Here he was with graduation a flea's breath away and he was stuck at square one. No research specimens, no data.

Briefly, he had wondered if the two situations could be connected—the disappearance of his and Dr. Shubally's cancer model research, and now this. But, after further consideration, he dismissed the thought. Who would want to sabotage both of his experiments, and why? There was no reasonable connection. Just a devastating coincidence.

Rolling to the side, he gazed upon Milena slumbering peacefully, unaware of his inner turmoil. So lovely. The one constant in his life right now.

Should he awaken her? Share with her all of his feelings the way he used to, Milena always there to support him? Share all of his insecurities, his fears over not graduating, and his shame at letting her down? Vent his anger at the protesters? If he were to see Sandra Peters in person right now, he would tear her smug little head right off of her shoulders.

Nah, better not let Milena into his thoughts right now. They were too dark, even for her to lighten. Better not to burden her. Or show her how weak he had become.

Settling back onto his pillow, his mind reflected on the dream that had pervaded his sleep, another memory of his father. So many memories surfacing as of late, ones he hoped would stay buried in his past. Renner's recent failings were starting to sink in and affect his confidence. All the old insecurities resurfacing. Was his father, right? Maybe he was a loser. A failure. Never to amount to anything.

The threat of not graduating on time was crushing him. Not to mention the disappointment of having nothing to publish, no chance of winning any science awards. And an absolute miracle would have to happen for the university to even allow them to finish their research with what little data they had left.

Gazing back over at his gorgeous wife, her face angelic in sleep, hair fanned out around her in a halo. She deserved better than this. Someone who was strong, confident, successful, and rich, with an established career and a beautiful home.

Nothing was going his way.

Damn it! What am I going to do?

Pull yourself together.

Out of nowhere, the voice popped into his cranium.

It snapped him out of his sulking. He was letting his insecurities get the best of him. Wasn't he past all the self-hatred? But, with these constant obstacles blocking his success, and the dreams reminding him...

Use the dreams, use these obstacles to inspire you, drive you forward, not break you down.

Yes, that was a good way to look at this. Time to change perspective. Think positive. But, how? What was he going to do?

You always have your other research.

The other research...

At this point, the other research wasn't even considered a legitimate project. But, was there potential? If he could manage to create psychic abilities in humans, he would be successful indeed. At last, he would be the man Milena deserved.

But, how could he get the project going? He still didn't have a good enough handle on the theory or how to test his hypothesis, and knew the experiment would never be passed by the ethics board. Still trying to connect all of the information he had gathered so far, he hadn't even bothered to construct a valid thesis proposal for the experiment.

That's the easy part. What you need to focus on is a venue. Where the experiment will take place. What about Geneticode Laboratories?

His subconscious was relentless, pushing the issue but had an interesting point.

If he could manage to graduate on time, he had been offered a position at a new, privately owned research company, Geneticode Laboratories. They invested capital into cutting edge research, mainly in the development of innovative recombinant DNA technologies, and then sold their patented inventions to the highest bidder, government or other.

Being privately owned, they may have fewer restrictions than a government lab. Would they invest in the type of edgy research he was contemplating? Or was the concept too edgy, even for them?

But, wasn't he getting ahead of himself? The real issue at hand was if he would even graduate on time. The job offer hung in the balance. No degree, no job.

Right now, his priority was to figure a way out of the current mess. Fortunately, he was a persuasive man, getting out of difficult binds before. He would get out of this one. He just needed to figure out how to negotiate his way into getting his degree and then he could move on to the next step. Focusing on his other research.

The pressure around his chest loosened. The insecurities reburied, back down where they belonged.

Nothing could get in his way.

Chapter 21

Milena rolled the sticky dough out on the counter. Flour covered most of the kitchen, even coating her brow. She was attempting to make Renner's favourite German meal, spaetzle, to celebrate the completion of his final exam of the semester, the year and his degree. Although his grades weren't in yet, she knew he would ace them. He always did.

She jumped at the sound of the doorbell chiming. *Who could that be?* Not Renner, as he had his own key. Wiping her doughy fingers on a damp cloth, she rushed to open the door, where she was greeted by a slim man in postal uniform.

"Urgent telegram for Renner Scholz."

"I can accept the telegram for him. I'm his wife." Signing the clipboard, she then closed the door, and retreated back into the kitchen, taking a seat at the table.

Nervously, she tore open the telegram, scanning the letter, her heart dropping. She slumped over the table, tears flowing. At some point, she grabbed a tissue, mopping at her eyes enough to re-read the letter, with the hopes that she was wrong. That she misunderstood. But, the message read the same as the first time.

The front door clicked open. Moments later Renner appeared in the kitchen.

"What's going on?"

"This came in the mail today. I hope you don't mind that I opened the letter. The envelope was stamped urgent." She handed the tear dampened paper over to Renner. "Oh, Renner, I'm so sorry." She silently sobbed again.

Body stiff, he sat heavily beside her.

Renner unfolded the paper.

"It's a telegram from Germany, sent from your parents' neighbour, Alena," Milena informed her husband. "Your parents were killed in a car accident after your father suffered a heart attack while driving to a medical appointment. They swerved into the opposite lane and were hit by a passing transport."

Watching Renner as he read the letter himself, Milena thought she saw something inside of him snap, the final tether holding him to his former self. Stoic, Renner refolded the paper, and stood up from the table. As if cursed by Medusa's glare, he transformed into stone.

Tucking the folded telegram into his pocket, he said in a flat voice, "I'll be in my study." With granite strides, he exited the kitchen.

Milena was dumbfounded. Completely bereft over the loss of her new parents-in-law, she had been bracing herself to tell Renner the devastating news, ready to help him through the grieving process. But, he had handled the news without emotion. No reaction whatsoever. As if she told him the neighbour's cat had died. The Renner of old would have mourned openly for them, weeping, overwhelmed by their loss. She saw first-hand how close they were, how much he loved them. But not the new Renner. The new Renner was devoid of emotion—except for anger. That emotion now came too readily.

The singular display of intimacy he appeared capable of lately was when they had sex. She could no longer call the act making love as love had little to do with it. Rough and painful, she always felt used and abused afterwards. At times, she asked herself if she should leave. But, what if there was still a tiny portion of the man she fell in love with hiding somewhere inside? If she didn't help him find his way out, would he be forever lost? Besides, they were married, a sanction she took seriously. She had taken a solemn vow to support him through the good times and the bad. This moment was one of the worst.

She dabbed her eyes and blew her nose into the tissue she had balled in her fist. Cautiously she approached the study door, listened through the rough wood, and then gently tapped on the surface.

"Renner, can I get you anything? Are you OK?"

Startling her, he opened the door. Eyes dry, face flat, unaffected.

"I'm fine." His voice was robotic. "What's for dinner?"

★ ★ ★

"Olivia, I'm so glad you're here." Milena gave her first friend in America a warm embrace and ushered her into the apartment. Olivia shucked her navy pea coat and folded the garment over the loveseat in the living room.

"It's been ages since we've had a girl's night," said Milena, thrilled to be in a woman's company. She needed this desperately.

"It sure has. I guess other priorities have come up."

Olivia's words stung, mostly because they were true. Milena had neglected her friendships. Hurt her friends' feelings by not inviting them to the wedding. She deserved Olivia's remark.

"I'm sorry, Olivia. I haven't been the best friend lately. Stuck in my own world. Hopefully I can make it up to you." Milena grasped her friend's hand.

"Of course. Water under the bridge," Olivia reassured, patting her hand.

"Can I get you a glass of red wine?"

"Sure, that sounds fabulous. So, how's married life?" Olivia asked, accepting the merlot, and taking a small sip.

"It's…fine," Milena faltered.

"Well, that's not very convincing. What's up? Trouble in paradise?"

"No, no. Everything's fine," she led Olivia to the couch, "really." She sat delicately beside her friend. "I'd rather hear about what's new with you," she shifted topics, taking a hefty swig from her own glass of wine.

"Oh, OK." Olivia deposited her wine glass on the coffee table. "Remember I was telling you about one day opening my own clothing boutique?"

Milena nodded, taking another gulp of merlot.

"Well, I'm doing it! I've already rented a space, and purchased the clothing. I'm planning the grand opening in a few weeks. I hope you can come. I'll be serving champagne and, of course, you'll get all the best deals."

"Olivia, that's wonderful! I'm so proud of you. Of course, I'll be there." Milena gave her friend a tight hug.

"Thanks." Olivia's smile dissolved. She gave Milena an odd look. "Are you sure you're all right? Something's off with you today. Is there a problem with you and Renner?"

"It's nothing. I don't want to burden you." Milena's hands fidgeted in her lap.

"Milena, I'm your friend."

Milena picked the lint off her jeans, and then finally looked up at Olivia. "Renner's parents died."

"Oh no, that's awful!"

"We got a telegram from Germany three weeks ago. Renner... isn't taking it well."

That wasn't exactly a lie. He wasn't reacting as expected, not that mourning needed to follow a certain schedule. But, he wasn't mourning at all, which was disturbing.

"I'm so sorry. He must be devastated. Did he go back for the funeral?"

"No, he chose not to." She didn't explain any further, didn't allude to his unusual behaviour, still somewhat protective of him.

Keys rattled in the door, causing Milena's back to stiffen. She wasn't expecting Renner home so early. Whipping her head to look at the door, she watched him blow into the apartment on a strong gust of wind, a scowl etched deeply in his features.

Milena rushed over and gave him an obligatory kiss on the cheek. "You're home early," she whispered.

"Well, last I checked this was my house too. I didn't realize I had to be home at a certain time," he snapped. "You didn't tell me we were having company."

"Renner, I heard about your parents. I'm so sorry," Olivia said compassionately.

"It's none of your business."

"Excuse me?" Olivia balked. "I was simply expressing my condolences."

"Don't bother." Staring at Milena with contempt, he addressed her apparel. "And where are you headed? Down Simpson Lane?"

Simpson Lane was a derelict side street in Seattle where prostitutes were found in droves.

Milena opened her mouth to respond but no words immediately came, jaw opening and closing, a guppy out of water. Finally finding her words, she uttered, "Olivia and I were just heading out. Sorry Olivia that you had to hear that. Let's go."

"Don't apologize on my behalf. If you want to go whoring around town dressed like a slut, be my guest." Storming into the kitchen, he sloshed wine into a glass and downed the liquid in one slug.

Milena looked down at her flared jeans and fitted lavender turtleneck. Perhaps her shirt was a bit too tight. She hadn't thought so before, but maybe she should change.

By now, Olivia was standing and heading for her coat. "This is a bad time. I think you two have some things to work out." She pulled her coat over her tiny frame and opened the front door.

"Olivia, please don't leave," Milena pleaded, grabbing her arm.

"No offense, Milena, but I'm feeling awkward being here right now. We'll talk soon, all right?" The friends embraced once more, and Olivia walked down the exterior apartment steps, and climbed into her vehicle.

Slamming the door shut behind her, Milena spun around to confront her husband. "Could you be any more rude?"

"I don't appreciate people sticking their nose into my business."

"She's my friend. She was concerned."

"You clearly care more about her feelings than mine."

"What are you talking about? Look, I've been patient with you, and I know you're going through a difficult time, but that's no excuse to be mean."

Renner was already working on his second glass of wine. "You're just mad you can't go out now. Trying to find a replacement, is that it? Am I no longer good enough for you?"

"What's that supposed to mean? All I wanted was to spend some time with my friend, and now our night's ruined. She'll probably never talk to me again."

"It's always about you, isn't it?" he spat into her face, and stormed to his study, newly filled glass of wine in hand, slamming the door behind him. The lock engaged.

Frustrated, angry and embarrassed, Milena drooped into the cushions by the fireplace with her own glass of wine to spend the evening alone.

★ ★ ★

"Damn it!" Renner cursed, gulping the contents of his wine glass. Why was she being such a bitch? Always harping at him about this and that. First, upset about the drug use, pestering him about the way he was changing, and then pissed at not attending his parents' funeral. That was his choice to make, not hers.

He stomped over to the cabinet in his office where the strong spirits were kept, needing to calm his nerves, the wine not up to the challenge. When he stood in front of the mirrored glass of the cabinet doors, he saw his image reflected back at him, giving him a start. There was a dark shadow draped over his back in the shape of a man. The shadow's edges were soft, as if made out of smoke, and moved along with his body to the right and to the left or whichever way he shifted. He rubbed at his eyes, certain he must be seeing things. But, the shadow was still there, its face hovering above his own, with deep set eyes, dark and filled with wrath. The image repulsed him, and he quickly glanced away terrified. A few seconds later, tentatively, he looked back at the glass.

The image was gone.

Sudden intense emotion overwhelmed him, doubling him over. A thousand memories flashed before his eyes: his parents in various points in his life, always there for him, now lost forever. Gasping for air, he collapsed to the floor.

They're gone! Killed! I'll never see them again! Tears coursed down his cheeks, sobs convulsing his body.

Why hadn't he gone to the funeral? He couldn't remember now but regretted not going so deeply that he felt his brain was being pulled apart in two directions as if by sharpened meat hooks. He lost the chance to pay his final respects, to say goodbye, and he would never get that opportunity back.

What would he do without them?

The pain was intolerable, every cell aching in his body. The depth of despair literally killing him.

Come back to me, Renner. I'll make all the pain go away.

The voice gave him pause. Lulled by its promises, he acquiesced.

Yes, I beg you. Make it all go away! I can't take it!

Immediately, the tears ceased flowing. Renner swiped at his eyes, wondering why they were damp, why he lay crumpled on the floor. Confused, he stood up, grabbing a double shot of whisky from the liquor cabinet, oblivious now to the shadowy figure again draped over his shoulders. Bringing the whisky to his desk, he settled in the chair.

Now, what was I thinking about? he wondered. Nothing came to mind. *Oh well, it couldn't have been that important.*

Chapter 22

Traffic was a bitch. Renner drove like a hyena chasing an injured calf, determined to cut through the congested highway. Laying heavily on the horn, he finally managed to bully his way to the off ramp, submerging onto a calmer street. Fewer obstacles to hinder his travel.

It was his first day at Geneticode Laboratories and he refused to be late. A light rain pattered the windshield, immediately swiped clean by the wiper blades of his new cerulean blue BMW.

Finally, he was achieving something again, working in the right direction towards his goal: passing his final exams with flying colours; the university accommodating Paul and Renner, granting them permission to graduate despite the destruction of most of their thesis materials, happily acquiescing to his well-rehearsed pleas; and with his PhD in his back pocket, he was finally able to commence his position as assistant researcher at Geneticode Laboratories. He had made it to the big leagues. So, all was on the up and up. Now, he could start focusing on what truly mattered.

The passing of his parents was a bit of a snafu. A blip. A detour. At times, he was surprised at how distant his feelings were regarding their deaths. He could see the pain and grief in the distance but out of reach. Perhaps it was a good thing, for he knew that people who grieved also wasted precious time. And right now, he didn't have time to waste. His parent's passing was a tragedy, but now that was a part of his past.

An interesting development, however, as a result of his father's death, was Renner's inheritance. The vast wealth and assets his father had accumulated over his life span, a direct product of the success of his nicotine company, was dissolved into equity and deposited into Renner's accounts. He was now a billionaire.

This new station in life gave him many possibilities. Yes, he had wanted to make his own way in life...and he would...but there was no reason not to take advantage of his new financial situation. The money came at the most opportune moment.

Milena was getting restless. To amend this problem, he was procuring a new house for himself and Milena, one she deserved, one she could be proud of. Also, he would need his own lab for various parts of the clandestine new research he decided to proceed with, planning for the project to remain secret, for the time being. Now, he had the funds to purchase most of the equipment he required. And perhaps equipment more difficult to obtain by normal means could be "borrowed" from his new place of employment. His spirit soared whenever he thought of the potential of this new research, finally able to come to fruition.

That voice in his subconscious spurred him on, spurred him forward. Encouraged him that this was the path he must take.

The massive research facility materialized before his eyes. The white and grey brick building had prominent concrete pillars flanking the entranceway and silvery, reflective windows that reeked of status, authority, distinction, and power. Bursting forth from the ground, the structure stood proudly amongst the bland Seattle backdrop, a misplaced fortress.

Paul was waiting for him on the tenth floor, as planned. His ex-roommate had also been accepted at Geneticode Laboratories. He couldn't get away from the chump.

Paul was looking greasy and unkempt, as usual, shamelessly flirting with the secretary. "Well, it's about time. I was starting to think you weren't going to show. Nothing like waiting for the last minute," Paul sassed Renner.

"That's ironic, coming from you."

"You must be slipping if I beat you here. Any first day jitters?"

"Of course not. I can't wait to get started. I've been waiting for this my whole life."

A golden-haired gentleman in a lab coat approached the two new employees.

Dr. Westbourne shook hands with both of them. They already met Dr. Westbourne during the interview stage.

"We're very excited to have you both on board. You were the highest scoring students overall in your classes. And your thesis, even though you had setbacks, was still impressive in its purpose, and was what inspired us to approach you with job offers in the first place. It's in tandem with the nature of research you'll be involved in here at Geneticode Laboratories. Welcome aboard."

"I feel privileged to be working here with you, sir," Renner added. Paul, in true Paul fashion, delivered an exaggerated eye roll.

Renner's muscles tensed. "Could you excuse us, sir?" Renner flashed an engaging smile towards Dr. Westbourne, and then pulled Paul out of earshot, turning his own back to the doctor.

"I have to make one thing clear, do you understand? No more disrespecting me. Or else," he hissed.

"Or else, what?" Paul smirked.

"You don't want to find out."

Paul backed down, noticing something different in Renner's eyes. This was not an idle threat. The alpha established, the two scientists returned to Dr. Westbourne, and began the tour of the facility.

★ ★ ★

"Close your eyes," Renner demanded of Milena. When she didn't cover them fast enough, he clamped his own palms over her face.

What was he up to? He'd been acting strange all day. Not necessarily in a bad way, on the contrary behaving more excited than usual. Perkier than he'd been in a long while. Asking her to accompany him on a road trip, Renner had driven them through the countryside for over an hour, past green rolling hills and farmlands full of ripening crops almost ready to be plucked. The day was sunny and clear, full of optimism and hope. Milena forced herself to enjoy the moment while it lasted; they were few and far between.

After parking on the side of the road, they had proceeded on foot.

"Where are we going?" Milena questioned nervously. The visions she had on her wedding day and in her dreams ever since flickered around her brain causing her to become increasingly uneasy as she blindly hiked down an overgrown path into the forest.

"Just trust me." Renner kept his hands pressed over Milena's eyes. She could smell the aftershave lotion on his fingers, feel the rough, dry skin of calluses. "Just a few more steps."

They walked for an eternity. She wondered what she would see when Renner removed his hands. More forest? Trees and grass? A steep cliff? A freshly dug, empty grave awaiting her corpse?

Once they reached their destination, Renner lifted his hands. "OK. You can look."

"What...?" A large mansion towered over her, composed of brick and stucco, with broad, cream siding, and massive tinted, glass windows. A soaring, white fence circled the property, and was electrically wired.

Milena gasped, gawking at Renner. "What is this?"

"It's our new home. We move in tomorrow."

"We what?" Milena, paralyzed with shock, was momentarily speechless. Surveying the premises, one fit for a king or a superstar, she shook her head in disbelief. The property was stunning, but she was bothered that Renner would buy the house without her consent.

"Don't you think you should have consulted with me first? If this is to be our new home, don't I have a say as well?" She crossed her arms over her chest in defiance.

"This is my gift to you. I wanted to surprise you. Besides, what's not to love about this place? There's a pool in the back, lots of privacy. Nobody will bother us out here."

This was precisely one of the issues Milena had about the place. The mansion was completely secluded and the amount of security absurd.

"Who exactly bothered us in town? And how am I going to get to work? We have one vehicle, plus I don't have my driver's licence, and I'm sure the buses don't come out this far. Even by car, it would take over an hour both ways to get to work."

"Milena, don't you see? You don't have to work anymore. We have enough money for three lifetimes. This is my gift to you."

"We should have discussed this first. Buying a house is a huge decision and we're a couple. We should have made the decision together." Milena's voice was rising.

Instead of yelling back, Renner met her growing anger with a steel gaze.

"I see you don't appreciate my gift. But, it's too late. The house has been purchased and we move in tomorrow. You'd better pack quickly."

Stomping back down the long, grassy driveway to his BMW parked at the side of the highway, Milena remained glued to the spot, again rendered speechless. Renner's steeliness and deep seething anger proclaimed the discussion was over. She realized they hadn't even gone inside the property. Didn't even know how the interior looked, and tomorrow this would be her new home. Hurt that he hadn't considered her opinion in purchasing the mansion, she also felt the control over her life slipping away. She would be moving out into the middle of nowhere against her wishes, and also forced to quit her job. She would be completely isolated out here. What would she do while Renner was at work all day, every day? The whole situation made her exceedingly uncomfortable.

Skulking back down the overgrown path to the car, she met up with Renner, and slipped inside the BMW. They drove home in silence.

Chapter 23

The silence between Milena and Renner persisted. All through the evening, the next morning, through the hustled packing of belongings, and the onerous moving of overloaded boxes and bulky furniture. Only Paul's arrival broke the quiet, slimy remarks tumbling off his lips as he helped Renner carry the heavier furniture and items to the moving van parked outside, rented for the day.

Milena struggled to keep up, tossing her beloved possessions willy-nilly into boxes. Dishes with towels, figurines with books, clothes in with the candles. No time to even label what each box contained or to properly wrap the breakables in tissue.

When Renner was absent from the room, she would catch Paul leering at her, stripping off her clothing with licentious eyes. Milena would turn away, repulsed, and Paul would carry on with whatever he was doing, but then she would catch him staring again.

"What's wrong, Milena?" he finally piped up. "You couldn't look sadder. Here you are, moving into your first house with the love of your life. You should be thrilled."

"Should I?"

"Yes, but obviously something's tearing you up inside." Paul slithered over to Milena's side. "Tell me what's wrong. I know we haven't always seen eye to eye, but I can be a friend to you. Renner doesn't need to know," he said, fingers coiling through Milena's wavy hair.

"Paul, could you give me a hand with this table?"

253

Paul sprang a foot in the air, hand ejecting from Milena's hair so fast, the movement a blur. "Yeah, man. Of course." Paul flew over to Renner, grabbing the edge of the dining room table.

Renner's glower was murderous, upper lip curled in a feral snarl. How much had he heard, Milena wondered? Still, he managed to remain calm. Eerily calm.

Milena returned to packing her figurines, acting as if nothing had happened. Trinkets and knick-knacks again tossed half-assed into the box she cradled against her hip. Breath held.

Grateful for the interruption, Milena was still concerned about Renner's perception of the exchange. Paul was a slime ball. Surely, Renner knew she had no impure notions where his ex-roommate was concerned. But, she was pretty sure she caught her husband's hostile glare shot her way when he thought she wasn't looking. As if she was partially to blame.

Together, Paul and Renner lugged the dense, oak table out the door. Renner still containing his anger. Something had clearly shifted in his relationship with Paul. Renner might be holding back the anger now but not forever. She felt he was stalking, crouching, ready to strike but waiting. Patient.

Milena pulled at a sweat dampened strand of hair and tucked it behind her ear. Packing at an accelerated pace to keep up with her husband was leaving her breathless and sweaty. He was on a mission, overly eager to get into their new home. Milena wished she felt the same, but her heart was deflated. As much as she hated Paul, he was right. She was torn up inside.

She would miss her apartment, her first home in America. And the new mansion was completely secluded, making her lonely even thinking about it. The move would be more palatable if she could imagine the house would one day be filled with the laughter and voices of children. Their children. But she knew that was never going to happen. An automaton, she went through the motions of packing until every last item, every last article that was a part of their lives, was boxed up and placed inside the moving truck.

As the packed vehicle moved away from her apartment, a tear slipped down her face. She swiped the tear away, bottling up her emotions. She would release them later, in private.

Even Paul was silent during the lengthy journey out to the mansion. The sun flitted in and out between the trees along the road. A cargo train raced against them for several moments. Then, farmland after farmland after farmland. When they reached the neglected grassy driveway leading up to their new home, Milena's gut clenched.

Tree roots and thick vegetation made the jaunt bumpy, and their boxes and furniture shifted and banged in the back compartment of the moving van. Something cracked—a plate, probably, with the less than stellar packing job Milena was forced to make. A little further up the driveway, and the estate suddenly appeared, looming over the tops of the trees, growing larger and larger as they approached. The estate was as intimidating as the day before, if not even more, because she knew she was being forced to live there against her will.

Renner pressed a button on a remote device clipped to his key ring, and the steel gate swung opened, allowing them entry. This was as far as she got the previous day. Now, entering the grand premises, she realized the property was larger than she predicted.

The moving van carefully inched down the circular cobblestone driveway that curved upward to a massive door—the entrance to their fortress. Renner switched the van to park, and hopped down from the driver's seat. Unlocking the back of the van, he then walked over to Milena's side, opened the door for her, and helped her out of the vehicle. He kept her hand in his, walking her up to the doorway, where he unlocked the front entrance. Without warning, he swept her up into his arms and carried her over the threshold. The act was anything but romantic, and Milena wondered what was going on in Renner's head. They hadn't spoken since the day before, aside from his bossy orders as they packed their belongings. Finally, Renner spoke, restoring the lines of communication.

"Would you prefer a tour before we move everything inside?" Not waiting for an answer, he grabbed her hand again and pulled her about the exquisitely decorated space.

"Here we have the spacious living room and dining room," his hand gave a flourish.

Milena continued to be blown away. The house was somehow even more enormous on the inside. Everything made from the richest of materials. The floors were marble tile, and rich, thick fabric was draped over the windows, gathered together with silk sashes. The walls were painted in bright vivid hues: peaches, yellows and greens. He pointed to the creamy white grand piano standing central in the room. "I talked the previous owner into throwing the piano in with the house. Perhaps you can learn to play?" Again, he neglected to wait for an answer, continuing into the next room.

Milena was surprised to see that the room, a kitchen, was not empty.

"This is Franc. He'll be our personal chef. I hired him a few days ago after trying his many specialties. He used to work for the previous owner."

Milena shuddered. Based on his appearance, she presumed he was more an ex-convict than a chef. He was tall and heavy set with short stubbly hair made of salt and pepper quills, and a large meaty face. His eyes were small, his lips thin as paper. Grunting a hello, he then returned to organizing the kitchen space.

"What's wrong with my cooking?" Milena asked.

"Come now, Milena. Don't be silly. Why would you need to cook when we can afford our own chef?"

Outside the kitchen, they ascended a spiralling staircase, carpeted in plush cream that led to a hallway overlooking the first floor. Several doors lined the right side of the hall, the left side hemmed in by a maple banister. Renner swung the upstairs doors opened for Milena to take a look.

"This one is a sitting room, with a balcony overlooking the backyard and pool." They walked a few steps further. "This is a closet for storage." The closet was as big as a bedroom. "Here's the bathroom, and on the end is the master bedroom." This room they entered. The space was enormous, with a bed already situated against the far wall—a king size with a duvet made of purple silk and mounds of soft, fluffy pillows piled against the headboard. An ensuite bathroom held a Jacuzzi, shower, and double sinks. A bidet rested beside the toilet. Milena had heard of such places but never seen in person. This house was fit for royalty.

"Whose house *was* this?" Milena fingered the velvet curtains framing a window that also overlooked the backyard.

"Have you ever heard of Emiliano Spinelli?"

Had she ever heard of Emiliano Spinelli? He was supposedly one of the meanest and notoriously violent members of the mafia from the Seattle area. His nickname was The Magician because as soon as the police got a warrant for his arrest he vanished into thin air. He had been missing for seven years, and finally, after being on the most wanted list for ages, was spotted at a remote gas station buying toilet paper of all things.

"Of course I know who he is. He was arrested on nine counts of man slaughter, as well as other drug and weapons related charges."

"He was doing apparently well for himself until he got arrested. Very unfortunate for him. But, not so for us. His father sold me the house at a reduced price."

"I guess that explains the exorbitant amount of security. But, don't you think it's a little too much for us?"

"It's going to keep you safe, Milena." He cupped her elbows in his palms, drawing her in close.

"Safe from what?"

"Don't you worry about a thing," he said, kissing the top of her head. "Let's go get Paul and start moving everything in. I can't wait to see how our new home looks with our belongings inside."

"And where exactly will our belongings go? You kept most of Emiliano's furnishings."

"Milena, you can be so difficult sometimes. Don't ruin the moment." Renner sighed, and left the room.

What moment?

Milena ignored the slight. Taking in her surroundings, she glided her fingers over the luxurious bedspread, opened the drawers to the wardrobe. As impressive as the decor was, she cringed at the thought of a drug lord owning the mansion, these possessions. As if she didn't have enough reservations about their new home.

Retracing her steps back to the kitchen, she noticed their tour had been incomplete. Tucked behind the opposite side of the kitchen was another hallway expanding into a living room, adjacent hall with a bathroom, another bedroom, more closet space and a door that exited into an attached garage. A stairwell led downward into the basement. Milena crept down the plush, beige carpeting blanketing the stairs, clutching the maple banister secured to the wall. When she reached the bottom of the stairs she saw the basement was completely finished, housing a spacious game room with pool table and bar, and a fully stocked wine cellar, complements of Emiliano Spinelli. A steel door sat flush against the far wall behind the bar, complete with security locks.

"I was wondering where you wandered off to."

Milena jumped. Whipped her eyes over to Renner descending the stairs.

"Just finishing the tour." Her eyes roved across the game room, gaze finally settling on the rows and rows of aged wines.

"I'm sure these will come in handy," she plucked a dusty bottle of red off of the shelf.

"You might want to be careful with that. The vintage is quite old...and valuable."

Milena twirled the bottle in her hands, focusing in on the label.

"1836!" She almost dropped the Bordeaux in surprise, and then carefully transferred the bottle back to the shelf with the delicacy of placing a newborn in a cradle.

"Are you finished snooping around down here? I have to get back to unpacking," Renner asked.

"I would hardly call it snooping if this is supposed to be my new home. I'm trying to get used to the place. Acquaint myself with the drug dealer's possessions. What's behind that door?" she referred to the locked steel door.

"That will be my lab. For any work I do at home, so I can stay on track at the research facility. There will be dangerous chemicals stored inside, so I'll keep the door locked at all times."

"You don't have to lock the door on my account. I have no interest in your lab. Although, why would Geneticode expect you to work from home? Don't you have all of your equipment at work?"

"You sure are nosy. I'm just letting you know the lab will always be locked, and you are to stay out. Got it?" She nodded. "Let's go back up and finish unpacking. This is taking too long. I have other things to do rather than babysitting you."

Rebuffed, resentment rising, Milena followed Renner back up the stairs.

Later, in the evening—all of their furnishings, clothing, and decorations properly stowed within their new home—Renner retreated to his private lab, locking himself behind the heavy, steel door, remaining there long after Milena went to bed.

All night, she tossed and turned. The spaghetti with marinara sauce Chef Franc had prepared for their supper sat heavily in Milena's stomach, undigested. The meal was surprisingly tasty—the chef had skills—however, her present isolation left her with an unsettling feeling. Something was very wrong. She couldn't shake the dark sense of foreboding, the anxiety that welled in her gut. How should she handle this situation?

Again the thought came to her...should she leave Renner? Or was that even a possibility anymore? Something told her that leaving would be very difficult, if not impossible. He would not allow it.

And she still loved him, didn't she?

The truth was, she wasn't sure anymore. With every passing day, he changed more and more. Where had her lover gone? Was it too late to bring him back?

PART II

Interlude

From the beginning of earth, of man,
I planted my seed in his fertile heart,
And that seed grew.
For centuries it grew, it flourished and spread,
Like a Crown of Thorns.
Choking out the blossoming crops so their fruit would never ripen.
Or, turning their fruit, so it would spoil and rot,
Causing others to rot along with them.

Through the gentle power of persuasion, deception,
Empty promises from poisoned lips,
They become my pawns.
Their actions, my will.
Senseless acts of violence and cruelty,
No mercy, no compassion.
But, one limitation, one deficiency I have had.
Until now.

The act of creation.
The young scientist bends over his microscope,
Golden brown hair dishevelled, dark crescents below his eyes,
His eyes growing darker each day.
A vein pulses in his forehead,
His concentration so intense.

Hands splice and attach, splice and attach
With perfect precision.
He is not a pawn like the others,
But something more.
A perfect host.

Not since the Anakim has this been possible,
His body accommodating,
Adapting physically to my spiritual presence.
Changes at a genetic level,
Permanent mutations,
Along with a transference of my power and control.
The transformation not quite complete,
But almost.

Through Renner's hands, we shall do great works.
A new line of human—greater, stronger, more powerful—
Genetically mine.
They will be my children, I their father.
Renner, not aware of what we do,
Must continue the DMT use,
For each visit to the spirit realm,
The more my genes fuse to his,
The stronger my hold on him.
Only one thing stands in our way.

Milena.
Constantly meddling, whining about the drug use,
How Renner is changing.
As if that is a bad thing.
My hold is strong but his love for her,
For his beloved Milena, could it pull him away?
Stop the transformation, interfere with my plans?
The man so moved by the woman,

A story told a thousand times.
An obstacle...but does she have to be?

Or could she become part of the solution?

—The Prince of the Power of the Air

Chapter 24

Three months, three weeks, and three days. One hundred and fourteen days in total—the gestation period for swine. That's how long Renner had to wait on pins and needles to get his results.

In his hands he held a potential blueprint to alter mankind—enhance mankind—created within the walls of Geneticode Laboratories unbeknownst to the rest of the research facility.

Since his first day on the job he had been plotting the entire process, how the experiment would unfold—assessing the premises, the equipment, the research animals at his disposal—ensuring everything was in place. Then, the careful genetic manipulation of the swine cells, swine chosen for their similarity to the human genome and short gestation period.

The waiting had been hell. Going about his daily routine experiments kept him busy, but this...this was his baby, his passion, the research he really cared about.

The timer binged.

This is it!

This final test had taken forty minutes, but each second felt an eternity. Now, Renner could finally determine if the genetic manipulations on the pig embryos was successful, meaning their DMT production was increased compared to a non-manipulated control group of piglets.

Staggering on his feet, mouth falling open, he gawped at the results. He tugged the reading glasses off the bridge of his nose and dropped heavily onto the stool behind him.

It worked! The sample showed a clearly significant result. Support for his theory that manipulating changes in chromosomes nine and eleven enhances pineal gland secretion of DMT, the notion originally inspired by Milena's hair sample.

As exciting as this discovery was, what was the next step? The futility of this research again crashed down on him. The Research Advisory Committee (RAC) at the National Institute of Health was primarily the governing Federal Agency in genetic engineering. They had to consider social and religious repercussions if attempting to enhance human capabilities. People would accuse him of pretending to be God by manipulating his creations. And the main issue that would be balked—using human embryos, little unborn babies to experiment with—the project would be shut down before he got through introductions. He would be harshly reprimanded for the clandestine research he had already done so far, perhaps even fired, maybe even criminally charged.

In his hand he held the key to creating supernatural abilities in humans...and it wasn't supposed to exist.

The government would spend billions to get their hands on this type of biotechnology. Rumours abounded that they were already attempting to create their own form of superhuman via intensive training regimens, enhancing medications, minor surgeries, and initial attempts at genetic modifications, such as Paul's research had entailed. Even Geneticode had research underway similar to that effect, but all experiments were centered on animals. What Renner could potentially give them—a super-soldier with such advanced capabilities that their enemies would be decimated—they would never know about. Not unless he took matters into his own hands again and got some proof. Proof that the technology would be successful and safe. That was the main thing he needed to prove—its efficacy at creating powers in humans at no harm to the fetus. Only then could he show the government his profound discovery.

Frustrated, he tugged at his hair. Destroying the significant test result, he stood up and paced the floor. He was stuck, no matter which way he turned. How could he ever prove that elevated, naturally occurring DMT in the body resulted in psychic abilities, if he couldn't test this theory on humans?

A tiny pink piglet was plucked from his cage. Renner trailed fingertips across the soft, white fur on the squealing animal's back. The other piglets, still in their cages, squealed back in response.

All of the manipulated piglets had survived, were healthy, strong, and vital. Not one of them perished and all contained the vital elevation in DMT production. Even the control group had some casualties, as was the norm. But somehow this genetically enhanced bunch was heartier, more resilient. Ignoring the glaring severe physical deformities that the mutated pigs manifested, Renner felt this still proved to him that the manipulation was perfectly safe.

If he could get proof, irrefutable proof that the experiment was safe on humans, the RAC might overlook his rule-breaking and approve further testing on human fetuses, understanding the value of the discovery.

Returning the squiggly piglet to his cage (this one missing his right eye and ear), Renner cleaned up the lab table, ensuring to properly dispose of the destroyed DNA sample, evidence of his misconduct. He then wheeled the cages on a cart, returning them to animal storage. These little piggies were part of an ongoing experiment studying IQ that Renner was primarily running, of which he had restricted access. No one would be the wiser to his orchestrations.

Not an hour later, driving through suppertime traffic, bleeping horns, and disgruntled drivers, Renner had loads of time to contemplate his next move.

Proof. How could he possibly get proof?

Geneticode was a wealthy, resourceful company, but they doubt-fully had human fetuses kicking around in storage.

Abortion centres? With the recent legalization of abortions in the U.S., would women choosing to end their pregnancies agree to have their aborted fetuses experimented on? Probably not. Even though participation would give their unborn children a chance of survival, maybe even become some of the most profound creatures to walk the face of the earth.

When Renner arrived home, Milena was already seated at the dining room table for dinner. Renner sat across from her in his usual spot at the head of the grand table. They had settled into a routine over the past eight months while living together in the mansion. They shared morning and evening meals together but nothing more. Speaking only when necessary. He knew they had drifted apart, but this observation was with emotional detachment, same as how he viewed his parents' accident. He felt as if he was looking at somebody else's relationship, not his own.

"What did you do today?" he formally asked her.

"What am I supposed to do out here in the middle of nowhere?" she answered brusquely.

Agitated again. She's moody as of late.

"Do you want to go into town tomorrow? I could arrange for Franc to drive you to Olivia's Fashions. Is that what your friend's store is called? Maybe shopping will cheer you up?" Without waiting for a response, he hollered into the kitchen, "Franc, tomorrow, bring Milena to town after breakfast."

"Yes, boss," Franc's rough voice responded from the kitchen.

"Don't bother," Milena interjected. "I'm not in the mood." Despondent, she pushed a pork chop around on her plate, creating a trench in her simmered apples.

She wasn't eating much anymore, her face becoming gaunt, shoulders bony, clothing sagging over her once curvaceous figure.

"She's pregnant, you know," she mumbled, eyes remain-ing downcast.

"She?"

"Olivia. She's due in a few weeks."

"I didn't even know she was married."

"She's not. She lives with her boyfriend. He's super happy. They both are."

"Good for them," Renner replied sarcastically.

Milena's azure eyes flicked up at him, filled with resentment. Then back to playing with her pork chop.

She's depressed.

The voice erupted in his subconscious.

Is that what's happening here? The life had drained out of her— all her former vitality left at the front door when he valiantly carried her over the threshold.

But why?

He had given her everything she could ever possibly ask for... the beautiful mansion now their home, all the clothing, jewellery, purses and shoes she desired. She didn't even have to work anymore. And his passion, his research would bring even more riches if he could figure a way to continue. They would want for nothing.

She wants a baby. A family.

A family? He didn't want any children. Not after what he went through as a young boy. And his focus was on his research, barely having a moment to spare. He was at such a critical part in his findings—on the brink of true genius. About to change the future of mankind. How could he possibly have time or even patience for a family? Even trying to picture him and Milena having children, the image defied him.

Unless...

Unless what? What was his mind getting at? He could almost sense his subconscious sighing in exasperation.

Olivia's pregnancy has re-awakened her desire for a child, a baby.

Olivia. Renner had no use for her. Her baby, well, he could have a use for the baby while still in the embryonic phase...in his experiment. He chuckled internally.

270

The revelation dawned on him. His eyes locked on Milena, so broken down, so melancholic.

A baby.

Adrenaline shot through his veins at the thought. But, no, no, he couldn't. Milena was his wife. His love.

A baby would give her a sense of purpose.

She would never agree. Not this way.

Then think of another way.

What his mind was hinting at...could he follow through? Kill two birds with one stone? Eyes still frozen on Milena, he took in her hunched shoulders, defeated posture. No sense of purpose, just existing. A baby would reignite her flame, her passion for life. A small flicker of remembrance of her former vivacious self surfaced in his thoughts. And along with the memory, a stirring of something within himself. Love?

This could be the answer he was looking for to his stalled research. Much planning would be involved, strategizing, but the result would be worth the effort. In the end, they both would get what they wanted most.

★ ★ ★

The following night at suppertime, Renner was in unusually high spirits. Even pulling out Milena's chair for her when she came to the dining room table, earning him a suspicious look. A large turkey rested prominently in the centre of the table, crisp and golden, surrounded by all the trimmings: maple glazed carrots topped with slivered almonds, a tossed green salad, mashed potatoes and gravy, cranberry sauce and even dessert—a Black Forest cheese-cake—her favourite. Her stomach rumbled in anticipation despite her chronic lack of appetite as of late. The combined aroma of the food was intoxicating.

"What's the occasion?" Today wasn't a holiday, and the feast before them bespoke of a celebration of some sort. She noticed on the fireplace mantle a vase filled with red and pink roses. Something was definitely going on.

"Do we need a special occasion to dine like kings? We're like royalty now, Milena. High time you accept the fact. Look at these walls? This is all yours."

Looking around at the now too familiar walls, the walls she stared at every day, walls she felt imprisoned by, she had no sense of pride or emotional attachment.

Indifferent, she shrugged her shoulders, and fondled the cutlery, observing the table had been set with their best silverware, along with the expensive china and crystal.

"I've been worried about you, my Liebchen. You've become so thin. I'm concerned about your health."

Milena had ceased believing Renner thought about her at all, let alone worried about her. She was merely one of his possessions, a decoration in the house, mostly ignored.

"Eat, my love, eat. You need to take care of yourself."

"Why are you so interested all of a sudden?"

"I'm always interested in you, Milena."

Was she pushing too far? His fur was starting to stand on end, she could tell. If she kept pushing, she would suffer the consequences, for his outbursts were more intense now, scary, a balled-up fury festering inside his soul screaming to get out, one vestige of his former self still managing to hold it intact. For now.

Renner prepared a heaping plate of decadent food for his wife, far more than her shrunken stomach could accommodate. But, she accepted obligingly, popping a forkful of steaming turkey into her mouth.

It was the most scrumptious turkey she had ever tasted. Sampling everything on her plate, she found the trimmings were every bit as decadent as the turkey. And did she not almost finish everything Renner had dished out for her? He sat watching her, a contented smile on his lips.

After the meal, still trying to cram a bite more of cheesecake into her fully distended stomach, she noticed Renner hadn't touched his plate.

"What about you? Aren't you going to eat? Your food is growing cold. The meal truly is delicious."

"I'm enjoying watching you. I'll get Franc to reheat the food after. So, you approve?"

"Can't you tell? I'm completely stuffed."

Renner slid around the table, wiped a fleck of cheesecake from Milena's lip, then bent down and kissed her fully on the mouth. So much time had passed since they had been intimate that she reflexively flinched from his contact.

He noticed, withdrawing immediately.

"I still love you, you know," he spoke through tight lips. "Things are going to change, I promise." Leaving the room, he headed towards his private laboratory where he spent the majority of his time locked behind the door, his eyes growing ever blacker.

★ ★ ★

As Renner's BMW pulled away from the mansion the following week, Milena retreated to her flower garden, which framed the pool in the backyard of their lavish estate. The flowers blossomed early this spring, the temperature milder than usual. Tulips of purple, pink, and white poked their petals out of the earth from firm bulbs, another reminder of the previous owners of the mansion. Despite their origin, they made Milena smile. Last fall she had planted her own perennials, and they too burst forth from the fertile soil growing in tandem with the tulips. A vision of new life, colourful and bright.

Had almost a year passed since they moved in? She shook her head in disbelief.

Pulling on flowered, pink gardening gloves, she knelt in the moist soil and proceeded to pluck the weeds from the flower bed.

She kept busy in this way. Tending the garden each morning, followed by swimming laps in the pool for one hour, and then cleaning the vast house. Her regular routine. On occasion, if bored, she would sketch, a talent she wasn't sure she possessed but was attempting nonetheless. She even plunked the keys on the grand piano, mostly without success. Anything to pass the time in her solitude. But, the outdoors is what she loved most. The fresh air and fictional sense of freedom.

Attempts to contact her old friends had met with resistance. They were always busy. Once in a while she saw Olivia at her store, but their relationship was strained ever since Renner drove her out of their apartment. Plus, with her new business and a baby on the way, Olivia didn't have time to sit with an old friend. During these times, Milena ached for her family, and in need of filling the empty space in her heart, she turned to mindless daily routines. Still, although mindless, engaging in her daily chores was better than being idle and letting her mind go wild...go mad.

She reflected on Renner's behaviour the previous week, spending time with her, talking with her much more than usual. As if she mattered again. Was this a glimmer of his old self trying to return? Should she let her hopes grow or merely accept this as a passing phase that wouldn't last? If she grew accustomed to his newfound interest in her, if she re-awoke her feelings of love for Renner— re-awoke herself—then if she were to lose the connection again, the loss would crush her more than initially, would possibly break her this time. The numbness was what allowed her to survive in this glacial, love-deprived environment.

But, who was she kidding? She already felt a part of her was broken. That something had changed within herself, changing her permanently. Like a part of her had died.

At times she thought she might be going crazy.

How far removed was her condition from her sister's? A few degrees, probably but not by much.

She thought of her poor sister, alone in her own prison. Living so far from town had made visiting her difficult, barely a handful of times was she able to get to the psychiatric facility. The last time she visited, Brigita was out of her catatonic stupor and had been cognizant of her presence, alert but in distress. Horror filled her eyes, and she had grabbed onto Milena's blouse as if her life depended on it.

"They're here!" she screamed in her face. "We have to get away! Please, Milena, we don't have time! It's not safe anymore!" The nurses were forced to inject her with Haloperidol, a tranquilizing medication, to cease her tormented delusions. But, Milena felt uneasy after she left. Was Brigita warning her of a real threat?

★ ★ ★

Finished with the gardening, Milena tossed the soiled gloves onto the grass, yanked her sundress over her head, and draped the fabric over a plastic deck chair. She gathered her hair into a ponytail, twisted the ponytail into a doughnut shape, and then secured the bun atop her head with an elastic band she had worn around her wrist for this purpose.

A black knit bathing suit was already on beneath her sundress, looser around her bust and hips than usual. Never one to be self-conscious about her body, she knew she had grown too thin.

Standing at the edge of the pool, toes curled over the pool's concrete lip ready to dive in, her vision suddenly blurred. A rushing sound filled her head, like a swarm of bees disturbed from their hive, and she swayed on her feet, dizzy, disoriented. Her body flushed hot, followed by a cold pinging on her face and scalp. Darkness filled her eyes, threatening to pitch her forward unconscious into the pool water below. Adrenaline hiked up in her system, causing her heart to race.

But, as quickly as the moment came, it passed. Her heart rate slowed back to normal, the hot flush passed, her vision cleared with a cooling sensation.

What was that?

Taking a deep breath, certain the dizziness had passed, she dove into the cool, refreshing water and immediately went into the front crawl, doing laps the length of the pool. Back and forth, back and forth. She continued, switching forms, from the back crawl, into the side stroke and finally the breast stroke, swimming for an hour total.

Once her body was spent, her mind in turn calmed down, and she was able to release her fears: over her sister's frantic warning, Renner's change in heart not lasting, and of being alone. The calming effect would last until the morning, as she had come to know. And then the mindless routine would start again.

Chapter 25

"I had Franc prepare the eggs over easy, just how you prefer."

Milena yawned, struggling into a seated position, and then watched as Renner placed a breakfast tray on her lap. Surprised with breakfast in bed—Renner was chock full of surprises lately—she eyed the tray hungrily: eggs, cinnamon toast, maple pork breakfast sausages and orange juice, hand squeezed. She wasn't sure why, but her appetite had picked up nicely, almost too nicely, now feeling ravenous most of the time. In a little over a week, the sharp bony angles of her body had already smoothed out.

In contrast to eating more, however, her energy levels had plummeted dramatically. Even the simple task of getting dressed was a chore. But, today she wouldn't have the luxury of staying in her pyjamas for the majority of the day. Renner had arranged an outing.

Renner's renewed interest in her was again present as he flitted around her, a momma bird taking care of its hatchling, ensuring she was always happy, well fed and comfortable.

"Can I get you anything else?" Renner inquired when she finished her meal.

"I am a little thirsty. Maybe a glass of water?"

"Yes, right away, my *Schätzchen*." Slipping out the door, seconds later he returned with a sparkling glass of ice water.

Milena guzzled the water, still thirsty despite the entire glass of orange juice she already drank. Why was she so thirsty all of a sudden? She tried to ignore the strange sensation, her bladder unable to take in one more drop of fluid at the moment, even though her body craved water like a drug. She crawled out from under the purple mound of covers. Scratched her tousled hair.

"Where are we going?"

"It's a surprise," Renner responded, cryptically.

Milena remembered the last time Renner had taken her on a surprise trip, how her life had been permanently changed. The excursion to the very house they now lived in.

What does Renner have up his sleeve for today?

Attempting to pull more information out of him, she asked, "How do I know what to wear?" She gazed into her closet at the inordinate number of outfits she possessed. How did she accumulate all of these things?

"Something light and casual will do."

Milena pulled out a white lace baby doll dress, and flat white sandals. She retreated into the washroom to take a shower and change, each movement difficult, almost a little painful, she was so fatigued.

After her ministrations were complete, she returned to the bedroom where Renner waited patiently in khaki pants and a collared yellow and green striped golf shirt. His hair was feathered softly back, his newly worn goatee trimmed to perfection.

He looked handsome.

Milena felt the familiar fluttering of affection and love blossom in her stomach. Then tried to suppress them, still not ready to accept or believe her Renner was back.

"Let's go. You're going to love what I have planned for today," Renner gushed. He grabbed Milena's hand and walked with her hand-in-hand all the way through the house, down the stairs, through the living room, out into the courtyard and up to the car where he chivalrously held the door opened for her. He ushered her into the BMW, slamming the door closed behind her.

Nervousness filled her in anticipation of where they were going. But, the ride was long and peaceful, and before long she drifted to sleep, the hum of the BMW and the scenery racing by calming her like a sedative.

She awoke when the car finally pulled to a stop. Opening her eyes, her breath stopped short. They were in front of the genetic research facility where Renner was employed. Renner drove up to the security gate, flashed his identification card, and the fluorescent orange arm that barricaded their entry, raised.

Renner parked in the underground garage, and then led her into the elevator.

"You always ask about my work, so I thought I would show you where I go every day. You can meet some of my co-workers," he explained as the floors passed by, indicated by the numbered lights pinging above the elevator door.

"Thank you, Renner. This means a lot to me." Truthfully, she was shocked. His work had been a non-topic of discussion, ever since he started working on his thesis with Paul, which continued when he accepted his position at Geneticode Laboratories. He had been secretive, often moody if she even mentioned his research, so she finally ceased mentioning his work at all.

The elevator deposited them on the tenth floor, into a lobby complete with a secretary's desk, windows overlooking Seattle, and a hallway with several steel doors on each side receding into the background, creating an infinity illusion. Renner walked up to the secretary, and she followed close behind.

"Cindy, this is my wife, Milena."

"Hi Milena, nice to finally meet you." She offered her hand, and Milena graciously accepted. The perky blond secretary continued, "I've heard so much about you. It's nice to put a face to the stories now."

Milena wished she could say the same about this young, friendly woman, but she had never heard about her before. She wondered what stories Renner had told her. Was he a different person at work than he was at home?

"Cindy, could you please page Dr. Westbourne for me?" Renner asked, honey in his voice.

"Of course." With fuchsia painted nails, she dialed a number into the rotary phone. "Dr. Westbourne?" she paused. "Dr. Scholz is waiting for you in the lobby. Yes, sir, I'll tell him." She turned back to Renner. "Dr. Westbourne will be right out."

Moments later, a tall, handsome, silver-haired man emerged from one of the steel doors and sauntered towards them with a smile on his broad face.

"Renner, good morning. And who do we have here?" He turned his smile in Milena's direction, and she couldn't help but immediately be fond of this man.

Renner beamed with pride, giving her the feeling that she was his trophy on display. "This is my wife, Milena. Milena, this is my boss, Dr. Jeffrey Westbourne." They shook hands.

"Renner has told me a lot about you," Dr. Westbourne said, again surprising Milena.

"He has?"

"He has. And you are much lovelier than he could have ever described." Again, Renner beamed with pride. "Can I give you a tour of the facility?"

"Yes, I would love that," she exclaimed.

They followed Dr. Westbourne through the many halls and laboratory rooms of the facility, Dr. Westbourne providing commentary on the different types of research and state of the art equipment that were found on each floor. Some areas remained off limits, these rooms they bypassed without comment, the stencilling on the doors providing enough explanation as to why they weren't part of the tour.

Classified. Restricted Access. Authorized Personnel Only.

It was out of one of these rooms that Paul popped out. He was thrilled to see Milena and gave her one of his leering grins that made Milena feel as if she had been molested by his thoughts. Repulsed, she nodded, mumbled a hello to him, and averted her attention back to the doctor. They continued on with the tour, Paul leering after her as they walked away.

Milena was fascinated by the facility and asked many questions of Dr. Westbourne during the tour. He insisted she call him Jeffrey. She obliged. She felt excited to be learning about what Renner did each day and meet the coworkers with which he spent so much of his time. She could imagine him now bustling through the halls, doing experiments in the labs.

But, somewhere around the third floor, her mind had difficulty following what the doctor was saying. She kept trying to keep on track but staying focused was getting harder and harder. Not that she couldn't follow the terminology, although the words were quite new to her, and complicated. But the doctor tried to put everything into layman's terms, so she could follow. This helped at the onset, but now she was distracted by a growing feeling of numbness in her hands and feet. At first, she thought maybe they were falling asleep, the familiar tingle and burning felt in her extremities. But then she lost feeling completely. She wiggled her fingers and toes in an attempt to improve circulation.

Nothing. No tingling, no feeling, as if they were no longer attached to her body.

She nodded her head and faked a smile in response to whatever the doctor had said, feigning everything was hunky dory. But, internally she was completely panicking.

What was happening to her body? She stepped gingerly on her numb feet, the lack of feeling now extending to her ankles and calves.

A hot flush swamped her body. Her vision blurred, blackness threatening behind her eyes, and her throat became so dry she couldn't swallow. The experience was reminiscent of the pool scene, except considerably more intense. Looping her arm through Renner's, she sagged against his form. She felt his arms tighten around her as her body went limp, the floor rushing towards her.

★ ★ ★

Milena's eyes opened, bleary, not sure where she was. As her vision cleared, she saw Cindy leaning over her, holding smelling salts under her nose.

Attempting to sit up, she felt dizziness swarm over her again like a cluster of bees and lay back down. She felt better lying against the cool tiling.

Renner, Dr. Westbourne, Cindy, Paul and a few other gawkers she hadn't even met yet, were circled around her, looking on in concern.

"How are you feeling?" Renner asked. He was kneeling beside her on the floor.

"What...what happened?" Milena cupped her forehead with a sweaty palm.

"You passed out," Cindy exclaimed. "Can I get you a glass of water?"

Milena nodded. Throat parched, she was still having difficulty swallowing. Her excessive thirst had returned with a vengeance, and she graciously accepted the paper cup of water Cindy handed her. Renner helped prop Milena up so that she could drink the water without choking. She felt shaky and out of sorts, but the water helped dramatically and soon she was well enough to sit up on her own.

"Can you explain what happened before you passed out?" Renner probed.

"I don't know, I...I felt weird. My hands and feet were growing numb. Then my vision blurred, and I don't know what happened after that. I guess that's when I fainted."

"She has been feeling strange for a while," Renner informed the onlookers.

That's odd. She didn't remember telling Renner about her other symptoms. "How did you know?" Milena questioned.

"Oh, well, you've lost so much weight, and you haven't looked yourself in a while," Renner stammered. "Have there been other symptoms? Other things that haven't felt normal?"

"Well, not really, not like this."

Renner waited patiently.

"Well, I guess I felt a little dizzy the other day, when I went swimming. But the feeling passed quickly."

"Anything else abnormal?" he continued to probe.

"I'm so tired, always so tired." She sagged back against Renner.

"Should I call an ambulance?" Cindy asked with genuine concern. "She looks as if she's going to black out again."

"No, please don't. I'm fine," Milena lied. She was already uncomfortable with all of this attention and wanted, for the first time, to go home.

"Are you sure?" Renner asked.

"Yes, I feel much better. Can we go back to the house? I'm sorry Dr. Westbourne, for interrupting your tour. I had such a wonderful time."

"Well, I'm glad. I wouldn't be surprised though if you pretended to faint as a means of escape. I do have a tendency to prattle on," he joked, attempting to make light of the situation. His staff nodded and snickered in agreement.

"I'll take her home and monitor her from there. Thank you, everyone, for your help," Renner said.

Milena couldn't help but feel as if she was a part of some staged performance.

Renner assisted Milena to her feet, which thankfully had returned to normal, all feeling restored. After saying their goodbyes, they rode the elevator back down to the garage.

As they sat in the car, Milena felt tears welling, from a combination of worry over her health and embarrassment over fainting in front of Renner's boss and coworkers. On top of everything, she had ruined Renner's surprise, knowing how much bringing her to the laboratory had meant to him, and to her.

"I'm so sorry, Renner." A tear trickled down her cheek. He looked at her, intently, and she noticed the colour of his turquoise eyes were no longer evident, their shine obliterated by inky blackness. She quickly looked away, startled.

He mistook her repulsion as another sign of her embarrassment over the situation.

"Don't worry, my Liebchen. I have a hunch I know what's going on."

That makes one of us.

"Just relax. We'll be home soon."

At their mansion, Renner carried Milena—despite her protests that she was fine to walk—up to their bedroom and lay her down on the bed. Retreating down the stairs, he returned ten minutes later with a syringe and several empty tubes.

"What's that for?" Milena blanched. "You know I have a phobia of needles!"

"Based on the symptoms you've described, I think I know what's going on."

"You keep saying that. Do you mind filling me in on your theory? We're talking about my body, after all."

"I'll need to take a blood sample to be certain. Then we can go from there."

She kept her arms stubbornly out of reach.

Renner gave an exasperated sigh, patience wearing thin. "Milena, I'm a medical doctor, first and foremost, remember? I know what I'm doing. You can trust me. Now, let me take a sample. I can analyze the blood work in my lab downstairs. Or would you rather go to the hospital and have a total stranger do it?" he added, defensively.

"If you're sure this is the only way to see what's wrong with me." Tentatively, she surrendered her arm. Renner tied a rubber band around the top of her bicep. He tapped the crease in her arm above her elbow encouraging the vein to bulge, and then slipped the needle inside, extracting three tubes of blood. Milena couldn't even watch. She looked away, wishing the ordeal to be over, a sheen of sweat laminating her skin. After gathering his samples, he pressed a cotton ball over the insertion point, applying pressure to stop the bleeding. Finally, he placed a bandage over the cotton ball.

"Keep that on for an hour, and don't lift anything heavy."

All Milena could think about was sleeping, now that the terror of the needle had passed. She was completely exhausted.

"See how simple that was?" He helped her lie back down on the bed, drawing the covers up to her chin. Her shoes were still on, but she didn't have any energy left to ask Renner to remove them.

"Rest easy, my Liebchen." His lips softly brushed against hers. Turning off the lights, he left the room.

Chapter 26

Milena shuffled into the dining room for breakfast. Her head pounded, and the grit refused to leave her eyes, but the time was already noon, and she had to get up sometime.

Renner was home, she was surprised to see, reading the paper at the dining room table.

"Good morning," Renner proclaimed, folding the paper and placing it beside his coffee mug. "How did you sleep?"

"I slept fine. Waking up is the problem." Milena slumped into a chair. "Aren't you supposed to be at work?"

"After what happened yesterday, I couldn't leave you alone, now could I? And," he tapped a sheet on the table, "I have the results. I tested your blood work last night in my lab, and my hunch was right."

"You know what's wrong with me?"

"Yes, the result is what I feared but it's definitely something that can be treated and monitored."

"Well, tell me," Milena demanded, sitting up taller.

"You're diabetic."

Milena reeled at the sudden diagnosis. How would her life change because of this illness?

"Did you have any relatives with the disease? Your mother or father?"

Milena reflected on her family history, taking a few moments to respond. "My grandmother on my mother's side."

He nodded, as if this made all the sense in the world. "It doesn't surprise me. Diabetes tends to be genetic, runs in families. There are two types of diabetes, and you have type 1, which requires insulin shots daily."

Milena groaned—her pulse quickening. *More needles!*

"Don't worry, my Liebchen, this is good news. We finally know why you've been feeling so awful lately. The dizziness and the numbness in your extremities now make sense since diabetes affects circulation. The dramatic weight loss and excessive thirst are also symptoms."

She didn't remember telling him about her thirst. Had he noticed she was drinking more?

"Now that we know what's causing your symptoms, we can start treating you immediately. You'll notice the nasty symptoms abate quickly."

"You know how much I hate needles."

"I'll administer the shots. You'll get used to them."

"I highly doubt it."

Renner stood up, "I'll get Franc to whip you up some lunch. In your condition, you can't afford to skip any meals. You need to keep your blood sugar stable."

He left the dining room and headed to the kitchen to speak with the cook.

Milena was stunned. Was this possible? She had felt fine up until a few weeks ago. Was the onset of her grandmother's illness so sudden? She couldn't remember. Plus, her grandmother had type 2 diabetes, needing to take oral medication instead of insulin injections, so the two situations may not even be comparable. She tried to pull from her brain all of her knowledge, what little there was, on diabetes. Wasn't type 1 diabetes usually diagnosed during childhood? She thought she had heard that somewhere. But, Renner should know what he was talking about...he was a doctor, after all. Who was she to question his diagnosis?

She had to accept her new illness. There would be difficult days, no doubt, and her life would dramatically change in many ways, starting with her diet, but there was no sense going into denial.

When Renner returned twenty minutes later, Franc followed closely behind carrying her well balanced meal. Warm spiced oatmeal, cranberry juice and bacon were unloaded on to the table in front of Milena. Stomach already in knots, she wasn't sure if she could eat. But, she must. Franc, creepy as usual, retreated back into the kitchen without a word.

Renner sat next to Milena, placing her first insulin shot on the table.

"Whenever you're ready," he said gently.

Strange, she thought, that he would happen to have insulin in his lab. However, he probably had many chemicals and medicines down there, locked away behind the big steel door.

"Let's get this over with," she feigned bravado.

He prepared the needle, squeezing out any excess air and then plunged the contents into her arm.

"We'll change the insertion site daily, so you don't develop patches of callused skin tissue. Medicine has come a long way. You may have some mild side-effects from the insulin at first, but they'll be much more bearable than what you were experiencing before. There's no need to worry when these become present. They are entirely normal. You'll feel better in the long run."

She suddenly felt silly for her suspicions. Here, Renner was trying to take care of her, trying to make the adjustment to her condition easier. He was only trying to help.

"Thank you," she said sincerely.

"Anything for you, my Minka."

★ ★ ★

The following morning, Renner returned to work. He hadn't needed the previous day off, knowing Milena was perfectly fine, staying home mainly to enhance the believability of his story—that he was concerned about his wife's condition.

Once at work, he again thanked Cindy and his boss for their help, acting worried about his wife, while trying to remain strong and optimistic. They fell for his act, of course. Really, he deserved an award after his performance.

Everything was going as planned.

"How is she doing?" Cindy asked. "Do you know what caused her to faint? And the numbness she was feeling?"

"I'm afraid she's been different lately—mainly her behaviour and some strange physical symptoms. I'm not sure what's wrong. She'll need some more tests before we know anything concrete. I'd rather not talk about this now, if you don't mind."

Dr. Westbourne and Cindy looked embarrassed.

"Of course. Sorry to be so intrusive. We're simply concerned. Do you need any more time off of work?" his boss offered.

"No, I'm better off keeping occupied. She's at home resting and will probably be doing so for most of the day. I would worry myself silly if I were to stay at home. Probably pace a hole right through our floor."

"Well, if you change your mind, let me know."

Renner escaped into his lab. Miss more work? No way, not for Milena who was completely fine at home. And, he had a lot of work to do.

No sooner had he donned his lab coat when Paul plunged his head through the door. "How's Milena?"

"She's resting." Renner thought as he snapped on a pair of latex gloves and started pulling a beaker out of the cabinet. *Don't think I don't see you lusting over her whenever you see her.*

"What are you working on today?" Paul asked. They had some research projects they were doing conjointly and some independently. Renner's private research on psychic abilities was, of course, secret and Paul had no knowledge of its existence, nor ever would.

"I was going to run the pigs through the series of IQ tests again today."

"Then what's the beaker for?"

Shit, Renner. You can't afford to be sloppy right now. You can't let Paul get suspicious. Renner pretended to ignore him, assuming he would drop the subject and leave. He didn't.

"Hey, have you noticed any equipment missing? I was looking for the micropipette I was using the other day, and now I can't find the damn thing anywhere," Paul inquired.

"Sorry, I haven't seen it." He had, of course. It was in his lab at home. Renner returned the beaker he was planning on using for his own project, not the IQ testing, to the cabinet. He would have to be more careful not to look suspicious around Paul, who was always snooping nearby. He would retrieve the beaker as soon as Paul left. "Is that all?" Renner added, icily.

Realizing he was being dismissed, Paul uttered, "Just let me know if you find the micropipette. Tell Milena I hope she feels better."

Paul pulled his head out of the doorway and left.

As he thought about Paul's little visit, Renner was left with an unsettled feeling. Why did Paul come directly to him to see if he knew about the missing equipment? Hundreds of employees worked at the research lab, any one of them could have taken the micropipette.

Did Paul already suspect something? Was he trying to let Renner know about his suspicions, perhaps as a warning? Or to make him sweat?

Renner didn't appreciate Paul's questions or his incessant nosiness.

The unsettled feeling intensified, grew inflamed like a provoked ulcer, and began to fester.

★ ★ ★

Another mild day with a cobalt sky iridescent like a butterfly's wing, Milena found herself escaping to her garden again. Dandelion puffs drifted past her on soft gusts of warm wind, along with the subtle scent of her garden, welcoming her with fragrant arms.

It had been one day since her unexpected diagnosis, and miraculously she already noticed an improvement in her symptoms. Heightened energy, and the thirst, although still present, was not as pronounced. Deciding to forego her swim, she chose to pass the time in the tranquility of her garden, a tonic for her mind. Besides the therapeutic effect, today, her venture to the garden had further purpose. The tulips were in full bloom, and she planned to collect the stately flowers and arrange them in a vase to place on the dining room table.

She was lucky to have Renner as a husband. Helping her in a time of need. Diagnosing and treating her, so she could feel better immediately. How many wives could say that? Had she gone to the hospital, she would be waiting weeks for the results, and then waiting again before she received treatment. Instead, here she stood a day later feeling as if everything was going to be all right. She was already responding well to her treatment, and with Renner's continued help and support she could learn to live with her condition. She would just have to be diligent with her insulin shots, as much as she detested needles, and also pay better attention to her diet.

Renner had returned to work today. For the first time in a long while, she missed his presence.

Before Renner's recent improvement in behaviour she had started feeling a sense of relief when he would head off for work each day or retreat to his lab in the basement. Of course, she wouldn't admit this to anybody but herself. How sad to admit that you have grown fearful of the one you married, the one you promised to spend eternity with, but she couldn't help her feelings.

But now, was there a glimmer of hope?

For so long she had felt lonely, craving attention, not from the bizarre Renner that had transpired from their visit to the abandoned chapel but from the Renner she had married. The one that made her feel protected, loved, cherished. And now he seemed to be back.

Still, something kept niggling at her in the back of her mind. A feeling of unease, that she couldn't fully trust him. Perhaps the feeling was her psychic ability continuing to nudge below her subconscious, along with the memory of Brigita's incessant pleas to get away, warning her that she wasn't safe.

Milena had suppressed her gift for so long, ever since having the visions of Renner's beatings, but there were times when she wanted to heed its message and found she could not. The visions were beyond her grasp, slumbering, and any attempts to awaken her abilities went unsuccessful. So, the feelings sat there below the surface, like a lake filled with life, stuck below an impenetrable layer of ice.

Finding a cluster of robust scarlet tulips, she snipped the verdant green stems at an angle, and then tucked the blossoms into a wicker basket she had placed on the grass.

Why couldn't she accept that Renner had changed back into his old self? Why was she trying to ruin this fortuitous transformation of events? Isn't this what she wanted, what she prayed for every night? Why couldn't she let herself be happy?

She wasn't naive. Realized he had continued to use the drug the old witch had given him at the abandoned hospital chapel despite his promise to her. Did his eyes not betray him, the fact they were blacker every time she looked into their depths? But, lately, with his mood changing—improving—had he cut back usage or was he abstaining altogether? Was he trying to come back to her? She supposed she could ask him. Or, should she let it be?

Maybe one day she would find enough courage to ask.

Basket loaded with freshly cut blossoms, she retired to the house in search of a large vase that could accommodate and support their stark beauty.

Chapter 27

Renner arrived at Geneticode Laboratories before the facility's scheduled time to open. So early, in fact, that he was forced to use the front entrance of the building rather than enter through the underground parking lot that was still locked up tight. Gerald, the fat tub of lard that manned the security gate, wouldn't be in for another hour.

Walking below the steel cubic awning of the front entrance, Renner slipped his key card through the electronic entry system eliciting a welcoming beep. Once inside, he punched in a code to deactivate the alarm, and then locked the doors behind him. Immediately, he could see that the place was empty, save for an older, bearded janitor swirling his mop along the tiles.

Renner ignored him, travelling down the smoothly polished lobby to the elevators, the low hum detectable in the funereal silence. He plucked at the "up" button, colouring the circle green. Within moments, the elevator pinged, and the doors parted.

As the elevator rose to the tenth floor, Renner considered the two reasons that motivated this premature start to his day. The first reason was to further his secret experiment, requiring uninterrupted, unobserved time in the lab to complete the task—determining if the genetically modified elevation in DMT levels in his piglet specimens was an inheritable trait, able to be passed down to its progeny. And his second reason was that he needed more materials for his home lab, materials that were complicated to procure in the outside world without raising suspicion but easily attainable in the Geneticode storage department.

The pressure for him to progress in his research was high. Milena had been undergoing treatment for a month now. Her body primed for the next stage.

The elevator deposited him on the tenth floor with another loud ping. Cindy's desk was empty. She wouldn't be arriving for another two hours, her shift starting at 8 a.m. The lights were still dimmed from the nighttime settings, and the floor was vacant and still.

Perfect.

He sauntered towards his personal lab, the hub of his existence at Geneticode, where he performed most of his experiments (both personal and for the company), and where his results were securely stored. Fumbling with his keys in front of the lab door, Renner paused. Something had moved on the other side of the door. He craned his ear, listening, and heard again the sound of movement, of shuffling. Tapping into his newfound sixth sense, the one that had continued to develop and strengthen with each use of DMT, he searched beyond the door and into the lab room. The familiar angles and colours were blurred at first but then cleared, giving him an unimpeded view of the source of the noise. Anger flared instant and hot. There was no need to plunge the key into the lock, for the door blew opened from his thoughts alone.

Paul froze in surprise. His hand was buried within one of the cabinets where Renner stored his notes and research data, which was normally locked. Somehow, his old roommate had broken in without the keys.

"Renner, wow, you're in early," Paul stammered. "If I knew you'd be here I would have waited," he paused, trying to collect himself. A bead of perspiration trickled down his face, which he swiped away with haste. "I, um, needed some of the data that you were working on the other day. The assignment Dr. Westbourne gave you. The results are necessary for something I'm researching, and I thought I'd help myself. I hope you don't mind."

Renner knew he was lying. Not because of the guilty, red flush that crept up his neck, although that was a dead giveaway but rather by the thoughts that percolated in Paul's stupid skull. Renner could read what he was thinking, like he had cracked open the cover of a novel, the words plain to see.

I hope he doesn't know what I was really doing.

But, what was he really doing? What was he looking for? The stolen lab equipment? If so, why was he looking through paperwork? No, he was looking for something else. But, no matter how hard Renner attempted to read what the real motive was for breaking into his office, he could not. The information was beyond his reach, that specific chapter ripped out of the novel, leaving behind frayed edges. Paul was blocking him out.

"Get out!" Renner whispered with a venomous hiss.

"Cool, man. I'll get the research later." Shakily, Paul dropped the sheaf of papers he had been clutching back into the filing cabinet and disappeared down the hallway.

Renner's head felt ready to burst. A vein throbbed on his forehead like an engorged worm. His fists were clenched into tight balls at his side, his fingernails digging into the skin on his palms.

How dare Paul come into his office and rummage through his private papers! Renner wasn't daft enough to leave anything incriminating lying around. But, still. What was he looking for?

Careful to cover his tracks, Renner had all data, research, and confiscated materials for his private research safe and sound, locked up in his lab at home. Behind the secure steel door. Any genetically modified experiments he had conducted while at Geneticode were cleverly disguised as his IQ pigs and nobody would ever figure out that the DNA within some of the tubes, frozen in storage, were human instead of swine, since the labels indicated otherwise, and he was the only one in charge of that specific division of research.

But, after Paul's unexpected visit and molestation of his office contents, he would need to be even more careful.

Deciding to postpone the next stage of his experiment until a later date when Paul would be absent, instead, Renner checked the shuffled papers that had been violated. After assuring himself that nothing was missing, he relocked the cabinet door.

You're on my radar, Paul.

By ten o'clock, the facility was lively with the staff attending to their daily routines, projects, and paperwork. Renner remained in his lab, oblivious to their presence. The vein still pulsed in his temple, in suppressed rage. Delving into a research assignment Dr. Westbourne had given him the day before, Renner channelled his rage into analyzing various tissue samples for potential disease markers. Slowly, the vein flattened out, and then finally disappeared.

So entrenched in the task, he almost missed a light rapping at the door.

"Yes, come in," he made sure the annoyance at being disturbed was relayed by the edge in his voice.

Cindy popped her blond head into the lab. "Dr. Westbourne needs to see you immediately." She glanced several times behind her, skittish.

"I'm a little busy right now. Can it wait?"

"Sorry, Dr. Scholz, but he said it was urgent."

Cindy was brushed aside and Dr. Westbourne himself stood framed in the door, fringed by two uniformed officers.

"Renner, you need to come with us immediately. Information has come to our attention this morning. We have questions you need to answer."

Chapter 28

Renner returned the sample he was analyzing to a beaker of form-aldehyde, sealed the opening with a cork, and snapped off his soiled latex gloves, disposing them in the trash. Anxiety ripped through his gut as Dr. Westbourne and the two officers waited for him.

Putting on an air of nonchalance like donning a cashmere sweater, he glided behind them into the hall, into the lobby of the tenth floor, past gaping staff and researchers, and finally into Dr. Westbourne's office.

A rustic, mahogany desk braced the far wall, framed by a massive window overlooking the smoggy cityscape. Bookcases packed with tomes on science, genetics, and other associated research lined the walls. A plastic replica of a DNA strand stood three feet tall beside a picture of Dr. Westbourne shaking hands with the famous geneticist, Maurice Wilkins. The remaining decor was sterile and orderly.

They all took a seat around the mahogany desk.

"I wanted to talk somewhere private because we have delicate issues to cover," Dr. Westbourne began, leaning forward in his chair, fingers steepled in front of him. "It's come to our attention that several pieces of equipment and lab materials have been stolen." He slid a piece of paper across his desk over to Renner, who picked it up with sweaty hands. "Here is a list so far of what we have documented as missing."

Renner's throat constricted. The list was very familiar, detailing all of the materials he had confiscated over the months and that now sat locked in the lab in his home basement.

"Stolen?" Renner feigned confusion.

"We are questioning all of the staff, not just you, of course, to see if anyone can provide us with information about these disappearances."

Renner's heart rested slightly. He was not caught, but somebody had informed them about the missing lab materials.

Paul.

He was certain. As certain as he was that Paul had been messing with him since the first day they met. Was Paul trying to get him in trouble? Get him fired? Did he know anything? Have any concrete evidence? Renner had taken great pains to cover his tracks so that was doubtful. But, until he knew for certain, he would play it dumb.

"Sorry, sir, I have no idea." He shook his head.

"Are you sure? Because, the equipment that's missing includes many items that you're using on a daily basis. You haven't noticed anything out of place, absent or any materials running lower than they should?" his boss probed.

The officers waited with pens poised over their notepads ready to record any new information for the investigation.

"Well, I guess I noticed certain equipment missing, but if a piece of equipment wasn't there, I assumed one of the other staff members was using it. Are you sure that's not the case? Is this investigation, perhaps, a little hasty?"

"I assure you it's not. This is a serious offence and we'll find who is responsible. And they will be dealt with. We're talking prison time here."

Renner felt like he was swallowing a cotton ball.

"So, one more time, are you sure you don't know anything about the missing equipment? Mainly you and Paul are using those materials on a regular basis, and we've already questioned Paul."

Renner's lips tightened. Of course, they had already talked to Paul. Wasn't he the one who had started this whole investigation? Again, Renner shook his head in the negative.

"Well, if you do hear anything or find anything, can you report back to us immediately? I need to resolve this issue as quickly as possible. In the meantime, we'll be forced to order new equipment, a huge expense we weren't prepared to make. We're not happy about this."

"I'm sure you're not. I hope you find the culprit, sir. Officers." He nodded at them respectfully as he dismissed himself. "If you'll excuse me, I have to get back to work."

They nodded in return, faces stoic.

Renner hurried back into the hall, in time to catch Paul scuttling away from the door, reminding him of a cockroach exposed to light, the back of his neck reddening.

Was Paul eavesdropping? Hoping to hear something more incriminating? *He's so frigging guilty of trying to get me caught*, Renner thought. *He can't even look me in the eye.*

Renner returned to his lab room, and as the door slammed shut behind him of its own volition, a beaker sailed through the air, again on its own, hitting the door and smashing with great impact.

Renner, get a hold of yourself. You don't want to appear guiltier, do you?

But he was so furious, he didn't feel capable of calming himself down.

Paul, that rotten snake! This investigation was all his doing. Renner had endured all that he could put up with. Time to deal with the situation.

★ ★ ★

While Renner was being interrogated in Dr. Westbourne's office, Milena tended to her luxuriant garden—plucking weeds, weaning out crowded sections, so healthy blossoms wouldn't need to compete for space and nutrients, and then hydrating them with a hearty burst of water from the hose.

Admiring her gardening handiwork, she took great pleasure and pride in its beauty. Asters, stretching their bright pink petals towards the sun, a patch of lavender and white freesia mingling with the small pompom flowers of the Chrysanthemum, resplendent in shades of white, purple, and red. She had even cultivated a flowering Hydrangea shrub, bunches of flowers now blossoming pale cream in clusters at the end of their stems. The garden gave her a sense of purpose. She needed them as much as they needed her.

Physically speaking today was a good day. The side effects from the new medication were minimal, barely there. Her treatments had been going on for a month now. Each day, Renner would administer her insulin shots and take blood samples, and although she no longer felt the symptoms from the diabetes, a new set of symptoms had cropped up as Renner had warned.

The nausea came and went, although the symptom was easy enough to control with the anti-nausea medication Renner provided. But the weight gain, mood swings, and tender breasts took some getting used to. Strange symptoms for insulin, she thought. But, she remembered Renner telling her the symptoms were perfectly normal, and nothing to be concerned about. The symptoms weren't life threatening, how the diabetes could progress if left untreated. Taking her orders without complaint, she suffered through the discomfort in silence.

Emotionally speaking, however, today was not the best. She had been retreating to her garden for solace more regularly, for longer periods than before. Her blossoms her only companions.

Renner had drifted away from her again.

His attention was waning, the hours he spent at work and in his private lab lengthening, and even surpassing his previous logged hours. What could he be doing in his home lab for so long? Of course, the genetic research he was working on was top secret. She would probably never know.

A car door suddenly slammed shut in the distance, startling her from her thoughts. Was Renner home? He wasn't expected back until evening, yet here he was, barely midday. Sliding the glass patio door open, she tugged off her gardening gloves, and hustled into the house to see what had brought Renner home from work so early.

The moment she saw him, rage contorting his features in a macabre, ghoulish way, she knew something was dreadfully wrong. Should she slip back into the backyard? Let his anger have a chance to subside? He hadn't noticed her; his attention was elsewhere.

But, he had helped her so much with her illness. Taken the liberty to treat her as if she was his own patient. She should push herself to be supportive in return.

She closed the glass door loud enough to get Renner's attention, as he stood rigidly in the foyer.

Brows furrowed deeply, hair in disarray as if he had been tugging at in frustration, his lips set in a thin line, he gave Milena a warning glance, and then looked away. Shucking his coat, he tossed it on the couch.

"Are you all right, Renner? What's wrong?" she asked, worried but still fearful of his temper.

"It's none of your concern," he spat, slamming his keys on the side table, denting the wood. Renner stomped past Milena to the glass cabinet holding the strong spirits. He poured himself a hefty snifter of scotch, the amber liquid quickly disappearing down his gullet in one swig. Grimacing, he poured himself another.

"Something is clearly wrong. You can still talk to me, you know. I'm your wife."

"It has to do with work, not with you, so leave me alone," he snapped. Turning towards the mirror, which sat on the wall behind him, he looked at his reflection. Milena could see the reflection as well, the furrowing in his brows softening for a moment, transitioning from anger to confusion, as if unsure of what he was seeing or who he was looking at, the reflection unfamiliar. Milena saw a sliver of vulnerability expressed in his eyes, his posture.

She edged up behind him, draping her arms around him. Abruptly, he spun around and shrugged her arms away. "Just leave me alone!" He stalked away from her, out of her reach.

She wasn't sure why she pressed, perhaps, due to the feeling of rejection resurfacing with so much pain or finally reaching the limit of her tolerance. She had put up with so much in their marriage, far more than most women would have endured. Finally, she had enough.

"Look Renner. I'm trying to help, and you keep pushing me away. Rather rudely, I might add. I've had enough of what I can take. I'm stuck here alone most of the time, and even when you're here, I still feel alone."

"It's all about you, then, I see. Have I not been taking care of you, giving you all that you ask for? Making sure you're healthy? But, it's never enough for you, is it Milena?" he spat vehemently.

A flicker, a flash of warning from her subconscious. But she couldn't stop now. Finally able to vent her feelings, they came rushing out in a torrent before she could take them back. A dam of emotions bursting.

"Ever since you went into that chapel and started messing around with those drugs, you've changed. You're a different person."

"Here we go again. I thought we were past all of that. And now is definitely not the time," Renner warned with a voice suddenly icy, threatening.

But, Milena had been stuffing her feelings in for so long, she knew if she stopped now she would never get the courage again. The deluge of emotions took over her common sense.

"I can't take this anymore! You call this a life? You go on and on about how lucky I am to have this beautiful house, but to me this place is nothing but a prison. Stuck day in and day out in this frigging house! I hate it here!"

Flying across the room, he pushed his face within an inch of hers, so she could smell the scotch on his breath. "You ungrateful bitch," he spat. "What're you going to do, you weak piece of shit?"

Shocked by his hurtful words, she pursed her lips, and squared her shoulders in defiance. "Maybe I'll leave."

Without warning his hand lashed out, slapping her so hard across the side of her face that she went sprawling onto the ground. Her cheek stung where his hand had connected with her skin, and she protectively cupped it with her palm.

Immediately, she saw the regret in his eyes. An internal struggle was taking place, a battle only he could control. She wasn't about to wait around to see which side of him would triumph. With a clarity that had been evading her for a while, she realized she had to get out.

Now!

This moment was familiar. With an instant rush of memory, the vision she had on their wedding day—the one she had been repressing ever since then—returned with full lucidity.

This is how it began.

And she knew what came next.

Sliding backwards on the ground, she inched towards the door away from Renner. He reached out his hand, eyes apologetic, offering to assist her to her feet.

"Come on, Milena. I'm sorry," he pleaded. "I've had a bad day. You kept pressing me and pressing me. I didn't mean to."

Milena kept inching slowly backwards, until she felt she was far enough out of his reach to be able to flip over and make a run for the door.

Finally close enough, she flipped over like a beached fish angling towards water and darted for the exit. Renner charged after her and slammed the door shut before she was able to get it fully opened. He trapped her against the door with his full body weight, wrenching and pinning her hands out to the sides.

She struggled to free herself but was cemented to the door. Panic surged through her as she twisted and writhed, attempting to escape his grasp but to no avail. His strength was inhuman.

"You can't leave me," he whispered in her ear. "You're my wife. For better or for worse, remember? Until we die," he growled, grinding her against the door.

"Please, Renner, let me go," she sobbed, face squished into the door, making her mouth spray spittle. "I never married this person you've become. I can't be your wife any more. Just let me go. Please!"

Flipping her around, he again pinned her with his weight, but now so her front was facing him. Their bodies so close, almost intimate.

His features contorted again. Confusion as he fought something from within? "Come on, Milena. You still love me. I know you do. These past few weeks have been wonderful, like old times. You still care about me." Breath quickening, he kissed her neck, then her lips, until the force of his mouth on hers grew painful.

Those familiar lips.

That's when she bit him. The taste of iron flooded her mouth. Reeling backwards, Renner touched his mouth where her teeth punctured his skin. He looked stunned, swiping the blood off of his lip, now glistening red on his fingertips.

"You stupid bitch!"

That's when he punched her square in the jaw.

The force from the blow sent her head flying backwards where her skull then ricocheted off the door behind her with a sickening thud. She slid to the floor, landing in a seated position, legs splayed out in front of her, barely conscious. The edges of her vision wavered in and out, clear then blurred. Stunned, she couldn't move away as he came at her again, grabbing her by the shoulders and shaking her over and over.

"Why, Milena, why are you doing this?"

Her shoulder blades bruised with each thrust of her body against the hard wood of the door. Finally, he stopped shaking her. His face within inches of hers, he repeatedly asked "why" like a scratched record. She mustered up enough energy to spit in his face, a foolish move, provoking him to more violence but was all she could manage.

With each punch, her body slowly slid down the bottom of the door until she lay supine on the floor. She saw his knuckles had cracked, the skin split, spraying ruby droplets all over the marble tile with each punch. Body now completely immobile, Milena endured the punches and kicks with ever lessening feeling. The pain drifted away as her mind wrapped around the reality of her plight. The vision had come to pass. Her husband, her Renner, a few blows away from killing her.

Slowly the light, the pain, the fear slipped away, transporting Milena into a welcoming place of nothing.

Chapter 29

Renner was wracked with an emotion he hadn't experienced in a while—guilt. The sensation was pushing past a barrier, fighting for him to notice.

How could he have done that to Milena? He loved her. She was his wife. His beloved. He hadn't meant to explode, lose control of himself, and even now was having trouble remembering all that had happened, parts of his memory missing. But he knew he had hurt her. Her blood had stained his knuckles.

Of course, his day had already been going badly. There was that.

First, catching Paul rummaging through his lab files. Problem number one.

The second problem—the catalyst to his fury—was the interrogation by his boss and the policemen. Renner felt he handled himself well, shirking suspicion from his shoulders. But, the meeting rattled him.

Renner couldn't manage to calm down after that, unable to focus on his work, his mind completely distracted by Paul's betrayal and the pending investigation. He ducked out early, wanting to go home and plan a way to get Paul off of his back. Just needing a drink to settle his nerves. A few minutes to himself. But, Milena just wouldn't leave him alone.

She provoked you. It's all her fault.

What the voice said was true. Stuck her nose in where it didn't belong. Pressing and pressing. Problem number three. And hadn't he asked her nicely to give him some space? If she had just listened, none of this would have happened. But, had she deserved what he had done to her?

Yes, she did deserve it. You did what you had to do. She was going to leave you.

But, he had reacted as his biological father would have. Where had that anger, that violence, come from? Never in a million years would he have thought he was capable of that depth of aggression. Milena was helpless against his fury.

I love her, he thought. *I honestly do. How could I do that to her?*

Would it have been better if you let her go? You need her, remember? She can't leave. Not now, not ever.

It was true. He could never live without her. And he also needed her for his research. She was essential to his plans, and even though up until now he had gained her compliance through his elaborate ruse to fake her illness, he would not have to trick her any more. Everything was much easier this way.

Slowly, his guilt—assuaged by the voice in his mind—abated, and his focus on the prize returned. The timing was actually opportune; did Milena's last set of blood tests not tell him so? All of his preparations were leading to this point. She was finally ready.

It is time.

★ ★ ★

No light. No pain. No feelings. Just nothing. And then…

Milena parted her left eyelid with great difficulty. The right eye was crusted completely shut. A sledge hammer worked away at the top of her skull. Her good eye roved the ceiling, then sideways towards the walls and floor where she still lay. Where was she? Nothing looked familiar. Attempting to sit up, she quickly turned to the side and painfully retched onto cold concrete. A wave of dizziness washed over her, and then slowly dissipated. Her head continued throbbing, slightly more tolerable, but her body felt wrecked. Her lip was swollen, and with her finger, she felt a crust of dried blood that had accumulated at the corner of her eye—the reason her eyelid couldn't open. She also felt bruised in her stomach, her ribs, and her right leg. The ring finger on her left hand was bent at an odd angle, surrounded by puffy mottled skin. Carefully examining the rest of her body, she found her skin was dappled in purple bruises. An especially sharp pain cut into her lower abdomen. Lifting up the blood spattered maxi dress she was wearing revealed a three-inch sutured incision directly below her bellybutton.

What the hell is that!

Horrified, she struggled to her knees, attempting to put all of the pieces together. What had happened? And, most importantly, where was she?

The area was dim, and the meagre light made navigating the small space she was confined in difficult. Cautiously, she inched along the circumference of the room, hugging the walls as she walked, still unsteady on her legs. Her eyes slowly adjusted to the darkness, the fuzzy edges surrounding her more defined. The walls were cold concrete, one side holding black, metal shelves filled with an assortment of canned foods, other non-perishables and emergency supplies. A small door led to a simple bathroom housing a toilet, sink and small shower. Several rolls of toilet paper were stacked in the corner.

Returning to the main room, she eventually reached a large, steel door that lacked a doorknob. She was locked in some sort of room, a cage or prison. A lone vent was fixed high up on the wall close to the ceiling, her source of fresh air, otherwise there would be the risk of running out of oxygen. A thin beam of light crept though the vent—the only source of lighting.

There's got to be a light switch somewhere. Another painful tour around the room paid off. Close to the bathroom, something brushed against her forehead. A string dangling from the ceiling. Milena pulled the string, eliciting a popping sound, and the room was bathed in light.

Slowly, the events that led to her current imprisoned state crept back into awareness.

Renner had attacked her. Viciously. The vision she had seen so long before on their wedding day had finally been realized. She had ignored its warning, and now it was too late.

Re-examining the incision, sudden fury replaced her fear.

What did he do to me? Violating her while she was unconscious. Had he stabbed her, and then tried to repair the damage? The incision didn't appear to be from a regular knife but was most likely from a scalpel. The line was perfectly straight.

Drunkenly, she staggered on her feet. Whatever Renner had given her, the effects had not fully worn off. Loping to the door, she hammered the surface with her fists, tears springing to her eyes.

"Renner! Where are you? Let me out! What did you do to me, you sick bastard! Show yourself, you son of a bitch!" she pounded with her one good hand.

She continued pounding and screaming until her voice grew hoarse, her fist bruised.

But, nobody came.

She slid back down onto the floor. Her exertions had caused her abdomen great pain, and now she could barely breathe or move.

More sobs wracked her damaged body. What had she gotten herself into? More importantly, what did Renner want with her? Was the cut in her abdomen evidence that she had become a part of one of his research experiments?

Was she even diabetic? What had he been injecting her with for all these weeks?

"You're sick, you know that? I hate you!" she cried at the walls, voice cracking, hoping somewhere Renner could hear her. The pain doubled her over.

What was he going to do with her?

★ ★ ★

Renner left her locked up for a week.

She figured a sleeping gas was being pumped into the room each night, knocking her out deeply enough, so he could come in without her waking up. She always felt groggy and disoriented when she awoke and would find fresh food and water at her side.

While she slept, he was obviously treating her injuries; the abdominal incision was regularly stained brown with iodine, her broken finger had been set and splinted, the gash above her eye was stitched, and the blood had been cleaned off of her face and lip. A toothbrush and her favourite face cream had appeared in the bathroom.

Her stomach clenched at the thought of him near her.

All of her dignity had been stripped away.

She spent her days lying listless on the floor, her muscles slowly atrophying, along with her resolve. Remembering her visit with the priest, she prayed for Renner, for the evil that was most likely controlling him to release its hold so he could then set her free. Throughout her imprisonment, she continued to pray to be released, for God to give her the strength to survive, and it gave her great comfort, the only sense of control she had over her situation, her only source of hope.

After a week had passed, the door was suddenly flung open letting in so much light that Milena was temporarily blinded. As her vision gradually returned, she squinted at Renner standing there. He stared back at her for several seconds, face blank, as if she were a stranger, and then he slowly walked away leaving the door open behind him.

She wanted to charge after him, pummel him with her fists, get some kind of vengeance, but her former bravado had dissipated, the recollection of the beating he had administered a week before still fresh in her memory. She would hold herself together for now, and the first possible moment she could escape, she would.

Walking out of the unfamiliar room—her holding cell—found her in a grey stone hallway, still unfamiliar. Renner stalked up to the wall, a solid looking structure, but after he poked a button on a remote control he held in his hands, the wall rotated one hundred and eighty degrees revealing the basement living room beyond.

How clever. A secret room that the former owner had built. A bunker of sorts. She never even knew the room had existed. As she followed Renner through the new opening, he again pressed the button, and the wall returned back to its former position, concealing the secret passageway and room beyond.

She wasn't sure what to expect from Renner. He kept walking, leading her slowly, proceeding up the stairs. Didn't he feel any remorse? He offered no apology, no explanation. His quiet demeanour was unsettling.

He continued towards the living room. Milena followed cautiously, keeping her distance in case he decided to turn on her in violence again. She had always thought she could still see a glimmer of the old Renner, the real Renner behind his eyes, even though they had grown so dark. But, now that glimmer was gone. Completely extinguished. Something within him had changed.

Once they reached the living room, Renner simply stood at the entrance, allowing Milena to walk past him and enter the spacious room.

There were some new additions, she could immediately see. A large screen was attached to the wall directly to the top right of the front door. Renner still held the remote control, tapping the device against his palm. He continued to stand there as if waiting for Milena to do something. Was he letting her go? Did he feel remorse after all? Did he realize he couldn't keep her here against her will? Come to accept that she wanted to leave?

Tentatively, she inched towards the front door, glancing in his direction to determine his reaction. Wasn't he going to try to stop her? Trying the doorknob, she met with resistance. More aggressively, she tugged and yanked on the handle, but the damn thing still wouldn't budge.

A sinister smile crossed over Renner's mouth. Milena raced to the window. It too was securely locked. Same with the glass patio doors leading to the backyard—to the pool, and her garden of sanctuary. Her heart plummeted. How could she be so idiotic as to even entertain the idea that he would let her go easily? He would never let her go. She still was a prisoner, except now her prison was slightly larger.

Raising the remote, he waved the only means of escape back and forth, then slid the device into his pocket and left the room.

He had made his point.

She was locked in, and he held the only key to get out, the device that was now in his shirt pocket. She assumed he had activated the security system used by the previous owner but had reversed the mechanism so that she couldn't leave. Keeping her locked inside instead of keeping predators out.

She slunk up to their bedroom, took a proper shower, and put on slacks and a white t-shirt. Gathering all of her personal items—as much clothing, shoes, and sundries as she could carry in one haul—she permanently moved into the spare bedroom on the main floor, as far away from their matrimonial bed as possible. She would have preferred to be much further from Renner, perhaps another planet, but she didn't have a choice. For now, moving to another room would have to suffice.

What is his plan? Why go through all of this trouble? She knew something diabolical was going through his mind but didn't know what part she played in all of this. The one thing she was certain of was that she had the lead role in his twisted play.

Chapter 30

Renner, outfitted entirely in black, polyester balaclava obscuring his face, lurked in the dark night shadows. Though he had been crouched in the same position for two hours, and his muscles and joints cramped painfully, he did not stir. Patiently, he watched, waited.

Overhearing a conversation between Paul and a co-worker at Geneticode Laboratories, he discovered that Paul would be going out tonight, back to the research lab to work on a time sensitive experiment. Now that Milena was securely locked away, no longer capable of leaving Renner as she had threatened, he could refocus his attention on Paul. The ever-present thorn in his side. The painful blister that wouldn't pop. The speck of dirt in his eye. He fit all the clichés of a nuisance. Paul's presence was aggravating and impossible to ignore. He had to be dealt with.

Renner had devised a strategy to take him down once and for all. The plan was inventive, clever and crafty. His ex-roommate would be taken out by his own devices. Trying to get Renner in trouble—Paul should have known who he was messing with.

Yet, hadn't he been messing with Renner since the beginning? First, with the soccer incident, then the constant scathing remarks, his obvious impure thoughts and desires for Milena, and now the suspicions he had inspired in Dr. Westbourne's mind, leading to the investigation that could harm Renner's career if anyone ever found out what he was up to. He could even end up in jail.

Yes, this would be sweet vengeance, a long time coming.

Renner adjusted the canvas bag he had slung over his left shoulder. The first movement he had made in hours, his stiff shoulder joint popped in protest.

Why wasn't Paul leaving?

Renner's hiding spot remained inconspicuous. River Street was thankfully quiet at this hour, the odd car passing by. After graduation, Paul had moved off campus, finding himself a small house near the genetics laboratory where they worked together.

Together.

That was a farce. Paul had been working against him, his every move. And a house divided cannot stand. Where had he heard that phrase before?

It was easy to find Paul's new domicile. Cautiously, from a distance, he had followed Paul home from work the day before. As Paul pulled his battered second-hand Zephyr into the parking lot of a simple core-floor house, Renner couldn't resist the swelling pride that consumed his heart—compared to Renner's home, a home fit for a king, Paul's was more apt for a pauper, a loser such as he was. A deceptive, sneaky loser.

Renner continued to wait behind the hedge concealing his position—exactly two houses away from Paul's bungalow—affording him the perfect vantage point. After twenty more minutes, finally he saw his old roommate's familiar cocky swagger as he exited the tiny home, opened the creaky door of his crappy, rusting Zephyr, and folded his body inside. The engine revved and black smoke blew out of the exhaust pipe. Loud rock music from an 8-track tape player pumped out of the gaping windows. The Zephyr sputtered out of the driveway, and once the tires hit the main road, he sped away with a screech.

Renner waited exactly ten more minutes before he left his hiding spot to ensure Paul wasn't going to return.

After the tenth minute expired, he slunk out of the shadows and around to the back window of Paul's now vacant home, where he was planning to make his entry. The unfenced backyard was overgrown with towering grasses and weeds, uncut probably for the entire summer. One thing hadn't changed: Paul was still lazy. However, Renner was grateful for the extra coverage.

He hauled a garbage can that had been hidden in the dense foliage over to the back window. Standing on top, the lid crunched loudly beneath his boots. Darting his gaze around the yard and from side to side he concluded that no neighbours had been alerted to his trespassing, his heartbeat decelerating back to normal. Popping out the window's bug screen and removing the lock on the glass pane using his newfound telekinetic ability, he then slid the unlocked pane to the left and pushed the canvas bag through the opening first, before following through. He ended up in Paul's kitchen. The place was a mess, exactly as Renner had imagined. Dirty dishes littered the kitchen counter, spills were left unclean, a full garbage bag sat untied on the floor, reeking of spoiled eggs.

Renner navigated carefully through the diminutive house, refraining from turning on any lights and alerting the neighbours to his presence. Removing a flashlight from the canvas bag he had again slung over his shoulder, he swept the beam around the room, illuminating a clear path for him to follow.

He was looking for a hiding spot—a place where Paul would hide stolen equipment, had he actually pilfered any in the first place. Of course, he hadn't. But, Renner would alert the authorities, anonymously, and when the authorities found the stolen equipment in Paul's house, Paul would be incriminated, removing him from the equation while relieving Renner from being suspected. *Two could play at this game*. The rotten, lying weasel would finally get what he deserved.

Renner continued to search the clutter for the perfect hiding spot, a place that was large enough to conceal the equipment, as if that was Paul's intention all along.

Check his bedroom.

Renner slunk through the unfamiliar home, trying to locate the bedroom. He stumbled upon a bathroom, a spare bedroom that was completely empty, save a layer of chipped yellow paint on the walls, and eventually Paul's bedroom.

The room was depressing; sombre grey walls, a single bed situated in the middle of the far wall covered in a white comforter—familiar from being at the university flat they once shared—one end table supporting a dusty lamp, and a closet against the left wall.

If anything, Paul was not materialistic.

Check the closet.

Renner let the inner voice lead him to the closet. He trained the light on the closet door that was cracked open an inch. Sliding the wooden accordion-style door to the side with a loud squeal, he detected piles of clothes strewn on the ground, a bare few still dangling from hangars.

At first he didn't see it.

Move the clothes around.

Renner tentatively shifted the clothes, relieved he was wearing gloves and his skin wouldn't have to touch the soiled, musty smelling items. Underneath the clothes, formerly hidden, was a safety deposit box. A large, black chrome square with a padlock sealing the opening.

Renner was in too much of a rush to find the key, so he summoned his telekinetic powers, concentrating on the lock. Even with a lot of power and concentration, the metal lock stayed stubborn and resistant. At last, a loud snick. Renner tested the lock, which now easily lifted off.

Reaching his hand into the canvas bag, he retrieved the missing micropipette and various other chemicals he had pilfered from Geneticode Laboratories but would not be requiring any longer. Only a few items would be necessary to deflect suspicion from himself onto Paul. The rest of the equipment—items he was still using—were safely hidden in his lab at home.

Swinging open the safety deposit box, he noticed the space was already full of papers and files. They would have to be removed to make room for the stolen lab materials.

He extracted a sheaf of papers, the top page looking oddly familiar. As Renner read the title, his jaw dropped. Rage filled his head like a balloon.

Of course, the paper looked familiar to him. The sheaf he held was his thesis paper, the first one he was working on with Dr. Shubally. The one that had disappeared. He rummaged through the rest of the papers. All of his data that he had so futilely searched for after his professor died were there in labelled files. Paul must have gone to Dr. Shubally's house and stolen the papers.

But, why would Paul steal his thesis? Was he that threatened by Renner's success…was he that competitive? Or had he wanted Renner to work with him and Dr. Kirby all along? If so, why? This didn't make any sense.

And what of his professor's death? Was Paul responsible for that as well, or was the professor already dead when Paul raided the old man's home? Renner knew his mind was running away with him, but could Paul be responsible for the old man's illness? He thought of Milena's illness, and how he had faked her symptoms. Could Paul have done the same? The thought was absurd.

Or, was it?

He recalled from his memory images of Paul consistently commenting on the professor's absence, his illness. And then he remembered the curse from the occult book Paul had lent him, the one that could inflict disease on another person. Did Paul cast some sort of curse on the professor, making him ill?

His head now pounding, Renner quickly slipped the papers into his rucksack. A manila file folder was extracted next. He flipped open the cover, and inside staring back at him was a picture of Sandra Peters, the woman who had led the animal rights protest and destroyed their experiment. The dossier was a job application, revealing that she was an actress.

Did Paul hire her to orchestrate the rally and then ruin their research? His mind reeled at the thought, but the situation didn't make any sense to him. Why would Paul destroy his own research?

There would be time to decipher the anomalies later. For now, he had a job to do, and the faster the better. He couldn't afford to get caught. Taking the Geneticode equipment he had brought, he filled the now empty security box with the stolen lab materials. Relocking the safe, he recovered the box with the dirty clothing and returned to the kitchen. Slipping out the window, he then replaced the pane, and the screen. Again, he summoned his telekinetic ability to relock the window from the inside, so Paul would never know he had been there. Until it was too late. He crouched into the tall grass, happy again for the cover the overgrowth provided.

Slinking several blocks down River Street, he ducked into an alleyway where his BMW waited, and sped home in a blind rage.

Chapter 31

Several weeks had passed since Renner brutally attacked Milena and imprisoned her in their home. Left alone today, she was greatly surprised to hear a knock at the front door. Milena had begun frequenting the wine cellar as of late to cope with her predicament and believed at first that her senses were playing tricks on her. She had already downed a bottle of Chardonnay worth three hundred dollars. Pretty expensive, but she found she didn't give a damn anymore. Next, she planned on opening one of the pricier Bordeaux, dating from the 1800s. See what Renner thought of that.

A bit tipsy, she stumbled to the window that displayed her beautiful garden, now reduced to rotten brown sludge, the flowers bowed down and stuck in the mire. The darkness did little to hide the neglect, breaking her heart. She missed walking amidst their beauty, smelling their sweet perfume, nurturing the colourful blossoms.

The rapping came again, louder, more insistent, causing her to jump. Perhaps her mind wasn't playing tricks on her after all. But, who could be there? Renner wouldn't bother to knock at the door, and the gates were locked to prevent anyone from entering. Even the electricity had been turned on the fences surrounding their property.

She staggered to the front door, confused and hesitant. Trying the doorknob, she was shocked as the handle moved beneath her grip. Was the door unlocked the whole time? Could she have escaped? Or was this some sort of twisted test? She wouldn't put it past Renner, his new personality sick enough to do just that.

But, when she threw open the door, Paul stood there, hair wind-blown, eyes sunken from lack of sleep, face drawn, and determined.

He barged inside with a curt greeting, closing the door behind him. Was he a part of Renner's plans? She had never trusted Paul, so the possibility was real.

"Is Renner here?"

Milena shook her head in the negative.

"Good."

"How did you get in here?" Milena cried.

"Oh yeah, I forgot. The old man has you under lock and key now," Paul said with a smirk. "How are you feeling?"

"What are you talking about?" Milena responded, more confused than ever. "You know?"

"Of course, I know. Everybody does. How bad is it?"

"How bad is it? What the hell are you talking about? How could you let him do this to me?"

"Did he have a choice? Renner told us you were having mental issues as a result of your growing brain tumour. If he didn't keep you confined, you might hurt yourself or wander off."

"He said that?" *That bastard!* "It's not true!" Deciding she would have to place some trust in Paul, she continued, "Paul, you have to help me. That's a lie. I don't have a brain tumour. Renner has gone crazy. He's done...something...to me. And he's locked me up and won't let me go. You have to get me out of here!" she pleaded.

"Renner said you would try anything to escape. If you ask me, you probably went crazy living with that fool, not because you have a brain tumour."

Realizing Paul wasn't being any help, she shifted to the left and attempted to flee, but Paul firmly grabbed Milena's arms, pinning her in place.

"Paul, I'm not lying. Please, you have to help me!"

"I don't have time for this right now. I was wondering if Renner has some place in the house that he uses as an office. I can see by your reaction that he does."

"He has a lab."

Paul's eyes widened, and then he nodded in understanding.

"Milena, sweetheart, I need to see Renner's lab. Um, there's some research he took home that I need for my experiment. You know how we work together? He was supposed to leave the research in the office and must have brought it home. Can you show me to his lab?"

"It's locked."

"Do you have a key to this lab?" he coaxed, in a soothing tone reserved for small children.

Milena could tell immediately that Paul was lying about his excuse to get into the lab. But, this could be her one chance to escape, and she wasn't about to waste the opportunity.

"Paul, you have to help me get out of here," she tried to pull him towards the door, his hands still gripping her arms. "He's locked me in against my will. I don't have a tumour, he's crazy and he's using me for something."

"Show me to his lab, and *then* I will help you escape."

"It's locked, remember?"

"Let me worry about that."

Realizing he wouldn't help her until he saw Renner's lab, she led Paul into the hall and down the stairs to the basement. Not risking her escape, he kept his hands fastened on her shoulders from behind as she led the way through the vast home. She shuddered when they passed the wall hiding the secret room, and then stopped in front of the locked steel door.

"The lab is behind this door."

Paul placed her to the side of the door to wait while he broke into Renner's lab. "Don't even think about running," he threatened, still blocking her way in case she got any funny ideas.

Paul pulled out a credit card and started sliding the plastic rect-angle into the crack between the door and the doorjamb. After several attempts, the lock clicked open.

"Piece of cake."

He slipped inside the room, and Milena couldn't help but follow him in as he dragged her by the arm. The mysterious room where Renner disappeared every night was finally revealed to her.

It was more advanced and well-stocked than she had imag-ined. Where had all of this stuff come from? Paul looked equally blown away.

"I knew it!" he exclaimed. He withdrew a camera from his bag and took several Polaroid pictures.

"Knew what?" Milena asked, now getting more anxious to get out of the house. She wasn't sure where Renner had gone or when he would return.

"Your sweet little husband is a thief."

"Well, if you got what you came for, maybe we should go?" she urged. Pulling on his arm, she swerved him towards the door.

As she tussled with him, urging him to leave, his face suddenly changed, and he focused in on her for the first time, fully taking in her rainbow-coloured turtleneck stretched tight over her chest, her luscious red lips. Stroking her silken black hair, he shifted his body in closer to hers. "What's the big rush?"

"I know you don't believe me, but Renner is holding me here against my will. We have to go now! He's dangerous! He almost killed me!"

Paul pulled in close to her, smelled her breath, and purposely, as if accidentally, brushed his lips up to hers. "Have you been drinking?"

Milena recoiled, completely repulsed. Paul's presence, and her possibility of escape had sobered her up instantly, but Paul obviously smelled the alcohol still lacing her breath. His eyes filled up with lust and his voice grew husky.

"I wouldn't blame him, you know, for locking you up. You are stunning," he whispered breathily. "No man could be trusted around you." He kicked the lab door shut.

"Are you deaf? You have to help me!"

"Of course, Milena. I'll help you." He reached his hand up to caress her face. She flinched under his touch. "I'll take great care of you." He firmly pressed his lips against hers, kissing urgently, and then pushed Milena down onto the developing Polaroid pictures resting on the lab's steel counter. Lying down upon her, she struggled beneath his weight, trapped.

"Paul, stop!" Milena yelled.

Suddenly the door flew open with a deafening bang as it struck the wall. Renner stood in the entrance, his face purple with rage.

Paul sprang off of Milena, adjusting his shirt, stammering unconvincingly, "This isn't what you think."

If looks could kill, they would both be dead. But, Renner's voice remained disturbingly calm. "What should I be thinking?" he spat.

"Um, Milena was trying to show me what she thought was stolen material, and then she said she was going to escape, and I, um, pinned her, so she w-wouldn't get out," Paul stammered.

"How did you get in here?" Renner demanded.

"Milena let me in."

She wiped the remnants of Paul's kiss off of her mouth, shaking her head emphatically in the negative.

"I see." Renner paused, regrouped. "I believe you should leave." He moved over, so the door was free for Paul to exit. Renner shot another murderous glare at Paul, the contempt evident below his externally calm demeanour.

Paul dashed out of the lab, up the stairs, and out the front door. In his haste, he forgot the camera and now developed Polaroid pictures of the stolen lab materials. Renner closed the steel door behind him. He marched over to the pictures splayed on the lab countertop, picking several up, scrutinizing them and then tossed them back down with pent-up hostility. Milena sped to the door, tested the handle, but found it had automatically locked.

Her chance to escape was lost.

Renner took a seat on the metal lab stool. "I didn't realize you and Paul were so close?" he hissed.

"You know I detest Paul! He forced himself on me, and he was the one that wanted to get into your lab."

"I know, Milena. You would never betray me, would you?" The question was thick with threats.

"Paul said some strange things. He said you told everyone I had a brain tumour and that you had to lock me up, so I wouldn't hurt myself. Is that true?"

"Paul was simply messing with your head, but you can forget about him. He won't be a problem anymore."

Renner got up from the stool, still stiff with anger, somehow unlocked the door without touching the knob or any type of remote and allowed Milena to leave the room and head back upstairs.

Milena hurried straight to the spare bedroom, the one she had been using since Renner went completely mad, and the one place she felt moderately safe. Renner had warned her, what felt a million years ago, that his biological father might have rubbed off on him, even using it as an excuse not to have any children of his own. Well, he was right, and at that moment, Milena's single solace was that they didn't have any children that would have to endure his brutality.

Sitting heavily on the bed, she was glad to be out of Renner's sight, but was still filled with troubling questions.

How did Paul get into the premises in the first place? Did Renner forget to arm the security system, or had he left it off on purpose? What was Paul looking for, where had the stolen equipment come from and what was Renner using it for? Where did she fit into the picture? Why did he lie about her condition to Paul? Did everyone now think that she had a brain tumour—that she needed to be locked up for her own safety?

And how had Renner opened the lab door without moving a muscle?

Chapter 32

Renner lost track of time. Fingers aching, he absentmindedly rubbed the bruises on his knuckles, flinching from the sudden sharp pain—a reminder.

He hadn't iced his hand, rushed as he was; the purple marbled skin now stretched taught over swollen fingers. How did Vater do it? And so often? His bones must have been forged from steel.

Renner lured his mind back to task. Sequestered in his lab at Geneticode Laboratories, he was working diligently on what culminated into the most critical stage of his experiment. With the heightened suspicions at the facility that an employee was pilfering equipment, he couldn't risk taking any more materials off the premises. With all of the events that had transpired over the past week, he felt time was running out.

So, he pressed forward, logging in more hours than his mind was accustomed to, his body also starting to complain after being cramped in the same position for hours, perched atop a metal stool, hands transforming the building blocks of life itself. All his hard work and preparation came down to this moment. The process was tricky, intricate work, and although he had great faith in himself, in his abilities, there was always a margin of error in any experiment. Look at his experiment with Dr. Shubally, the one Paul had stolen. Their results were hinting at a fault in their hypothesis or procedure. The rat-cancer model that was supposed to help researchers study cancer and cancer treatments was flawed.

Most of the rats they had genetically altered had perished, not able to withstand the genetic alterations, and the surviving ones failed to produce cancerous tumours.

Still fuming over the discovery that Paul had been responsible for his lost thesis research, more salt was added to his wounds when he read in *Proceedings of the National Academy of Sciences*—a prominent science journal that covered breaking scientific discoveries—that another research team had successful accomplished what himself and Dr. Shubally were attempting. Jaenisch, Mintz, and colleagues had developed an animal-cancer model using mice, cleverly labelled as "oncomice". Tumours had appeared in the genetically manipulated mice, and he concluded that the method they used was more efficient, using Simian Virus 40 as the vector for altering the genetic code. They had also corrected for other errors now glaringly obvious from Renner's experiment.

Reading the experiment over and over, he finally realized that although he was incensed at Paul's interference, his ex-roommate had inadvertently saved Renner embarrassment in trying to publish a substandard experiment.

Even the experiment he had joined in with Paul and Dr. Kirby, the one attempting to increase size in animals by using human growth hormone, had not been successful. The animal subjects failing in health, suffering. The project again destroyed, presumably at Paul's bidding. Would some other research team attempt the same feat, and be more successful? Highly likely. He never truly cared for that experiment. Initially, the research had held his interest, but was never a passion of his. Not like the one he was presently working on. Destiny had intervened, his path changed, leading him to where he was right now.

But, what if this didn't work? Would there be other attempts, should this one fail? He couldn't be sure. He had several viable specimens preserved, much more than he would require, but the host—that was the tricky part. The procedure had to work the first time.

His pig IQ research had continued to be the perfect cover for his private research. The frozen samples, supposedly from his pig specimens, were instead human samples from himself, and now Milena. Samples that were modified. Enhanced. Next came the creation of the embryos, again disguised as pig embryos, these were mostly human but with more modifications, ones he was currently working on. The intended end result, a human with profound enhancements and abilities. The first real superhuman. Not just a myth or a rumour. If all went well.

Contrary to the research he was supposed to be working on at the research facility, he would have a hell of a time explaining his actions had anyone tested his specimens. But, there was no reason for anyone to examine his embryos. He was working independently on the pig intelligence experiment. He was the only one monitoring and handling these samples. And now, there was no need for the Geneticode Laboratories staff or police to be suspicious of him since Paul was going to be implicated as the lab equipment thief. Free from suspicion, Renner could now continue with his plans.

As he completed his final genetic insertion, he felt an immense sense of gratification, almost rivalling how he felt after graduating from medical school. The complicated component was complete. Now he could test his specimens, finding out once and for all if his theory was correct. If his embryos survived the initial manipulations and the cells successfully replicated, a feat requiring just a few days, he could implant them into the host. From there, he would be forced to wait, be patient until the gestation period was complete, but then he would finally see if psychic abilities could be created in humans. He had invested so much of himself into this experiment, it had to work. It had to be worth all of the sacrifices.

Thinking of sacrifices, his thoughts turned to Paul.

It infuriated him that Paul was at his house, in his private lab. Milena confessed to Renner that Paul was hell-bent on gaining access to Renner's home lab because he suspected he stole equipment from Geneticode Laboratories. He was right, of course, but how had he known, and what else did he know? That was the biggest question.

What was Paul really up to?

Was he trying to find the stolen items from the facility, to get proof, so he could turn him in to the authorities? Possibly. But, Renner suspected there was more.

Why had he stolen Renner's old research paper and data? Did he want to publish the paper himself, or was he trying to manipulate Renner into working with him and Dr. Kirby on their research? Why had he sabotaged that experiment as well?

Was he trying to steal Renner's new research, the one he now laboured over, the one that would bring him unlimited respect, fame and fortune? Did he somehow know what Renner was creating? Paul was the one constantly bragging about building a superhuman, a super-soldier to fight for the country in times of war. Maybe he wanted to take credit for Renner's ingenious breakthrough and painstaking labours.

And how had Paul gotten past the security system at Renner's mansion? Renner was fairly certain he had engaged the security system, although chunks of his memory were missing—remained dark.

There was something more, just beyond his grasp, a subliminal thought that danced in his brain. The key to all this nonsense.

Intuitively, Renner's mind travelled back to the night they visited the abandoned chapel, and Paul's revelation that he had achieved his scholarly success from the old witch's Guardian Angel Spell. Paul had obviously been to the chapel a few times. Did he also possess an element of power? Hadn't Paul asked him, right after the night they visited the witch, if he noticed any changes, any special abilities? Paul wouldn't have asked that unless he had experienced new abilities of his own, besides the escalated intelligence that he was seeking. Maybe he did know what Renner was up to, if he was capable of reading his mind. And getting into Renner's locked lab and filing cabinet at Geneticode Laboratories, and past his advanced home security hinted at a possible telekinetic ability similar to what Renner possessed.

If Paul did have Psi abilities, that would have been very dangerous for Renner, indeed. For if Paul knew what Renner had discovered, what he was creating, and his future goals for that research, he could have destroyed those plans in one fell swoop, simply by ratting him out.

Besides the threat of exposure, Renner was enjoying the feeling of being superior to others due to his supernatural capabilities. Now that superiority was threatened.

And what of the others? There were many people present during the spell in the chapel. Were they also gifted now? An angry flush suffused his skin and he gnashed his teeth.

It couldn't be! *He* had to be the only one! *He* was to be the father of a new generation. And nobody could get in his way.

At least he knew Paul would no longer be a problem. But the others, the witch and her congregation, would have to be dealt with as well.

He could be the only one.

★ ★ ★

Milena had been keeping track of the days she was locked up in the large mansion in a leather-bound journal, which she hid with her Bible, the one she had received from St. Anthony's Church eons ago. She wasn't sure why she had kept a journal but now felt her entries were vital to her survival. They helped her unload the fear and anger she harboured over her dire situation, seeing that she had nobody to confide in. And if she disappeared, this document could help the police find out what had happened to her, shedding light on her circumstances, her ultimate fate.

Hidden within her Bible's gilt-edged pages was the special medallion intended to ward off evil spirits. Milena doubted its effectiveness, still wondered what the relic was for. The pendant had failed to protect her from her husband, who must have evil coursing through his veins, through his soul. She could feel the evil every time she looked into his emotionally void, black eyes. Maybe the medallion had protected her from turning into something akin to what Renner had turned into the night they had visited the chapel.

There was Paul and his strange visit, she continued to write in her journal. Paul had revealed that Renner justified locking her up by telling his coworkers and other acquaintances that she was suffering from a tumour that was turning her crazy. Had the whole visit to the research facility been staged to give credibility to his story? Had he drugged her? Fainting in front of everyone—true evidence that she was ill. Nobody would find her disappearance odd. Nobody would come looking for her.

But, he was the one that was really crazy.

Closing the journal, she tucked the book, along with the Bible, between her mattresses, pulling the blue flowered quilt over top in concealment, and then knelt down at the side of her bed in an act of prayer, another habit she had gotten into as of late. Not rehearsed in any formal prayers, she let her pleas fall out heartfelt and unstructured.

"Dear God, please give me the strength and courage to get through this. Help Renner to realize what he's doing to me, and to let me go. Please keep Brigita safe, and don't let her feel abandoned by me. Amen."

Completing her prayers with the sign of the cross, Milena was interrupted by a distant sound—a car door slamming, muted words yelled in hysterics but from a great distance. A woman's voice.

It must be coming from the front gate, but who could be there?

Two surprise visitors in the same week? This was unheard of as nobody ever came to visit. And the visit didn't sound to be a friendly one, either. There was no way to view the driveway before the gate to see who was hollering except through Renner's monitor. All of the windows in the house were angled in the wrong direction or blocked by thick stands of pine trees ensuring privacy for those within.

Renner was presently at work, not able to accommodate the angst-ridden woman. Milena hurried to the main entrance, hoping she would find the door unlocked as it had been two days ago. But the lock was secured and held firm.

Milena moved over to the monitor, and perching on her toes, inspected the screen from her low vantage point. She had seen Renner change the view many times but by hitting a button on his remote that was always kept on his person. Secure and out of Milena's reach. The monitor would show a clear view of the gate and who stood there yelling but only if Milena could get the monitor to work without the remote.

She dragged the cumbersome piano bench over to the monitor hanging at the front door, climbed on top, and started randomly punching buttons.

At first nothing happened. The shouting outside continued, rising until she could almost decipher what the woman was yelling. As Milena kept furiously pressing random buttons, she grew concerned that she was messing up the monitor, and when Renner discovered this, he would punish her. She didn't want to go through any more of his punishments, but she had to take the risk. This could be her chance to escape.

Just before relinquishing her attempts to activate the monitor, something she pushed finally worked, illuminating the screen with grey static. The picture flickered, and then focused. However, the view was all wrong. She could see her wilted flowers, the empty pool, and a sky crowded with bruised clouds.

Again, she jabbed all the buttons until she found one that shifted the view. The picture changed, displaying views of other areas on their property. The garage. The wine cellar. The panic room where she had been imprisoned.

So, you were watching me, you filthy bastard! The thought made her stomach sour.   The screen then flicked once more, revealing the front gate and Milena could see the woman who was hysterically shouting.

It was Wendy.

Tears coursed down Wendy's cheeks, and she was furious. But, Milena still couldn't clearly hear what she was screaming. Occasionally, she could read her lips, making out some of what she was yelling: Renner's name and a few fragmented sentences that made little sense.

"____ know____, Renner. Open ____. ____ did it!" Wendy quietly shrieked.

Milena palpated the surface of the monitor again, reaching behind, groping along the sides of the box until she found a button. The volume control? Pressing in, she heard a click as the button engaged, and then rotated the dial until she could finally hear what Wendy was yelling.

"Renner, you stupid bastard! Let me in! I know you did something to Paul. Where the hell is he? I know he was coming here. He told me!" She reached her face right up to the camera that was monitoring her every move as if she knew someone was watching. Spittle flew out of her mouth with each syllable as she continued to holler. "Did you hear that? He told me he was coming here. Nobody has seen him since. Let me in or I'll call the police!"

"Wendy!!!" Milena screamed back, hope building. "I'm in here! Renner has me locked up! Yes, call the police!" she shrieked. But Wendy continued on with her own screaming, unaware of Milena's pleas for help.

Over and over again, she kept screaming about Paul and his suspicious absence. Had he been missing since he showed up at the mansion, and broke into Renner's lab?

Finally realizing Renner probably wasn't even home, Wendy slammed both fists down on the hood of her car, climbed back in behind the wheel and sped off in a shower of gravel and dust.

Milena felt defeated. If only Wendy had heard her. But, there was a fragment of hope after all. Maybe Wendy would call the police.

"Please, Wendy, please call the police," she pleaded aloud.

But, what if the police believed Renner's story about her having a brain tumour that rendered her paranoid and delusional? All her wounds had healed, and thankfully she hadn't endured any more. She had a tiny pink scar on her abdomen where Renner had violated her in a way she still didn't understand, but he would probably find some medical reason supporting his tumour theory to explain the incision. No, having the police come probably wouldn't be enough. She needed some kind of proof that Renner was up to no good. That he was psychotic and needed to be behind bars.

Again, she remembered Paul, and his desire to get into Renner's lab. What was Renner hiding? Why did Renner spend so much time in there? What was the real reason he kept the lab under lock and key? Was he hiding stolen equipment inside, or was there more?

She had to get back into the lab.

It was risky. If Renner caught her before she found any evidence, she would be punished. He had made it clear that the lab was off limits. And she would never find a key, certainly having the only copy with him. As she walked down the stairs, her heart started racing, and a hot sweat crept up her spine.

How would she get in?

There would be no easy way—she would have to try the method Paul had used. Unfortunately, she didn't have any credit cards. Only Renner possessed them, and they were tucked safely in his wallet, wherever he went. She would have to find something else suitable that would do the trick.

Going back upstairs, determination washed away her caution. She rummaged through all of the drawers in their bedrooms and the living room until she came across a deck of playing cards. *Could it work?* The size and shape of the cards were similar to credit cards but was a playing card thick enough to disengage the lab's thick lock? She took the cards downstairs with her, decided at the final moment to use two cards pressed together and slipped the cards into the crack between the door and the doorframe. She wiggled the cards back and forth, but the lock held firm. She tried different angles, starting to get discouraged, the cards ripping, and tearing, but then finally she heard the click of the lock disengaging.

Fear suffused her body, but she had gone too far to turn back now. Turning the doorknob, she pushed the door open and entered.

The lab looked similar to the previous day minus Paul's developed Polaroid pictures and camera that he had left behind on the counter in his hasty exit. Also, certain pieces of equipment were no longer there, more specifically the ones Paul had been targeting with his lens. The room looked typical to any other lab, clean and sterile. The odour of bleach was strong.

She hadn't had much of an opportunity to get a good look at the lab when Paul broke in, due to their haste and Renner's interruption. Surveying the room now, she absorbed every detail. Two long, steel tables rested in the middle of the space with sinks implanted in them. The chrome sparkled when Milena flicked on the fluorescent overhead lights, the brightness reflected off the polished surface. Glass cabinets lined the walls. She walked over to them, and saw they were filled with beakers, test tubes, microscopes, empty glass slides, boxes of chemicals, and other lab paraphernalia. Two large freezers stood at the back of the lab, also chrome and shiny. Beside them were mustard-coloured filing cabinets. Milena walked cautiously through the room, not even sure what she was looking for, her eyes probing. Finally, she settled on the filing cabinets, an adequate place to start.

Assuming they, too, would be locked, she was astonished when they trundled open with ease. Renner had labelled the files within, most of them with titles she didn't understand, scientific jargon that was beyond her comprehension. But, one file in particular caught her eye.

In Renner's neat handwriting, he had labelled the file *Milena—Results.*

She removed the file from the cabinet. Flipping the cover open, she scoured the front page, which appeared to be blood work results.

She remembered the tests Renner had performed on her blood after she had fainted at his office, and regularly after the diagnosis. Were these the diabetes test results and monitoring samples? There were several numerical values listed, but in her limited scientific knowledge, deciphering what they indicated was difficult. Then a few words popped out at her, ones she had learned in school. Estrogen, progesterone, luteinizing hormone. Renner had measured all of these levels. As far as she knew these were female hormones, most likely not relevant to a diabetes diagnosis. Flipping ahead a few pages, she saw what appeared to be a fertility chart. Renner had marked on the chart Milena's menstrual cycle, mapping the days she would be fertile for the next several months.

What was Renner doing mapping her cycle when he didn't want to have children? The findings were bizarre and confusing.

She flipped another page. Again, the jargon was beyond her understanding. A hair sample analysis, as the title described, but the genetic information below the title meant nothing to her. The next page displayed another genetic analysis but, again, it could have been written in Chinese with how much she understood. Could this be used as evidence to incriminate Renner?

As she flipped the next page the file shifted, and the contents spilled onto the floor, fanning out across the room.

"Shoot," she uttered aloud. She had been hoping to keep things in order, so Renner wouldn't be wise of her entry. She cursed herself for her clumsiness. Somehow, she needed to clean up the papers on the floor and try to arrange them in the same order. Getting down on her hands and knees, she shuffled the papers back into a pile.

That's when she noticed strange marks on the floor. Long, thin scratches on the tiling, as if something heavy had been dragged across the floor. Looking for other marks, she found a few more scuffs and scratches leading up to the freezers. Standing, she walked to the chrome freezers, again predicting they would be locked. But the right fridge door popped open with an airy wheeze. The shelves contained numerous samples, labelled, and stored in beakers. Her name and Renner's name appeared on several. Closing the door, she then opened the door on the left.

She jumped back in shock, eyes stretched wide.

Trying to stifle a scream with her hand, a screech still managed to escape her lips.

If she was looking for evidence against Renner, she definitely found it.

Crammed inside the fridge, sealed within a transparent plastic garbage bag, was Paul's bloody body. He was contorted into impossible proportions. No human body would be able to maintain such a position and still be alive. Cold, dead eyes stared back at her, glazed, unseeing. A large gash on his forehead gaped open, covered in frozen blood.

Repulsed, she inched backwards from the horror, her mind desperately searching for her next course of action.

"I really wish you hadn't seen that."

The colour drained from Milena's face. Her breath caught in her throat, her lungs refusing to expand. Spinning around in slow motion, she faced Renner in the doorway.

An eerie calm filled his dark eyes as he pulled on a pair of rubber gloves. Slowly, he approached her. "You know, there's a reason I give you rules, Milena, but you just...keep...breaking them."

"Renner, I..."

He held up a gloved hand like a stop sign, freezing her words mid-sentence as he continued to edge towards her.

"I know what you're thinking. Where's a yellow rug when you need one?" he cackled maniacally.

Milena moved backwards, now practically touching the gaping door to the freezer. She emphatically shook her head in the negative.

"Yes, you were. You think I'm like my father. But, I'm not. Paul was an insect. He needed to be squashed. He threatened all that we have, all that I've been working on." He shifted his attention to the frozen cadaver. "What's that Paul?" He poked the stiffened cheek with his forefinger. "Nothing to say? No rude comebacks?" He paused, leaning an ear in, listening. "Ah yes. Finally. Silence."

Milena looked desperately at the door. Renner blocked her access.

"I'm a reasonable guy, but Milena, you keep forcing my hand. Now, what am I going to do with you? I have no choice but to teach you a lesson. One you will never forget."

Lurching forward, she attempted to dash past Renner and make a run for the door, but he blocked her exit, effortlessly grabbing her by the neck with inhuman strength and throwing her against the wall. Her head connected with the corner of a cabinet, warm blood trickling down her ear. Wrapping his fingers tightly around her neck, he choked her up against the wall with one hand, her legs dangling, her windpipe crushed beneath his iron grip. She gasped for air, fingers scrabbling to pry Renner's fingers from her neck, scratching him until he bled. But, his fingers were iron pipes. Completely immoveable.

Renner's black eyes analyzed her as she dangled in front of him. Her vision blurred as capillaries burst in her eyes and as her oxygen ran short. She almost blacked out. Renner released his grip just in time and she crumbled to the floor on hands and knees coughing and hacking as blessed air seeped back into her lungs. Gasping, dry heaving. Black spots exploded in front of her eyes like ashen fireworks.

That's when Renner kicked her in the stomach, his foot coming up from underneath her. She moaned and doubled over again from the impact. She felt her rib crack. As she coughed again, she spattered blood on the tiling beneath her.

Using his foot, he flipped her over on to her back like a capsized beetle. "I didn't want to do this, my Liebchen, but I must. You understand that, don't you?" he asked her so calmly, as if what he was doing was a completely normal act, one she truly deserved and would be willing to accept as punishment for betraying him.

He had finally come undone.

Straddling her torso, Renner pummelled her head, her face, her fractured rib, like a robot programmed to do his duty. Expressionless. "You must learn to mind your own business," he paused long enough to explain. More shots to the head, and she felt something crack in her jaw. "This is to ensure you never betray me again."

The beating continued, more intense and bloodier than before. Like a machine, over and over again, the punches kept coming. Milena's whimpering and pleas for mercy were ignored. Renner was relentless, and she felt her body surrendering.

Her vision wavered again. This time, she believed, Renner was going to kill her.

Chapter 33

At work the following day, Renner was only mildly surprised when the police showed up at his lab door on the Geneticode Laboratories' tenth floor. He was more annoyed than worried, truth be told. Renner had viewed the surveillance video at his house, witnessing the footage of Wendy's hysterical howling, blaming him for Paul's disappearance. She went right to the police as promised. Always a whiny, prattling pest, he never did care for her. Unfortunately, he couldn't get rid of her too. Her disappearance in the grand scheme of things would look far too suspicious.

The police stormed into his office, faces grim, pistols at their sides, ready to take down the culprit. Did they find the missing lab equipment? Once they did, they would conclude that Paul fled town due to his guilt or perhaps took his own life to avoid being charged for stealing from Geneticode Laboratories. Whatever conclusion they came to, either would do.

"We have more questions for you, Dr. Scholz. You're to accompany us to the precinct."

"I'm rather busy. Can't we do this here?" Renner suggested, as if he didn't have a care in the world.

"You can come down with us voluntarily, or we can arrest you. Your choice."

"I'm not sure what charges you would have against me, but that's not necessary. Of course, I'll come voluntarily."

Leaving his paperwork on the desk, he followed the policemen out into the hall. His colleagues gawked—shooting covert glances at each other—as he was led into the elevators and then out the front entrance of the facility as if he was already proven guilty of a crime. His jaw clenched, his teeth threatening to shatter beneath the surface of his cool veneer. He couldn't lose his temper, not now. Not in public, not in front of the police officers. They had no evidence against him, nothing to charge him with—save the ramblings of a little annoying rat. And, they would find nothing incriminating. Milena had unintentionally done him a favour. He hadn't realized he had been careless, leaving the body, his genetic samples, and test results in the lab. Assuming that his lab was discreet was a mistake. Now the evidence was gone; Paul's body dissolved in a barrel of heated lye, the lab samples and test results hidden in a much more remote location this time. Nothing linking him to Paul's disappearance or the missing lab equipment.

Everything would be fine.

He rode in the back seat of the police cruiser, like a criminal. As the police car drove in silence, Renner detected the stale smell of cigarette smoke ingrained in the fibres of the seat fabric, felt the tug of longing, a craving. Why had he quit smoking? He couldn't remember anymore, the events of his life before visiting the chapel more of a dream than reality.

The police cruiser pulled into the station, and the officers opened the rear door of the vehicle to allow Renner's large frame to unfold out of the confined space. Guiding him into the building, they placed him in an interrogation room painted eggshell white with brown laminate flooring. Bolted to the wall was a rectangular white-topped table with a steel frame, surrounded by plasticbacked chairs. All that was missing were the two-way mirrors that Renner had seen in the movies. Instead, there was a large window embedded in the wall. No pretense here.

He wondered if his father had been taken to a similar room for questioning after his mother's murder. Or, was he thrown directly into a jail cell, complete with bunk bed and stainless steel commode bolted to the ground? He was sloppy. Renner was not.

They took seats around the white-topped table, Renner conscious of leaving his legs and arms uncrossed to give the policemen the air that he was being open and honest, with nothing to hide.

"Are you aware that Paul Barrington has gone missing?" the first officer grilled Renner, his dark moustache twitching as he waited for a response. His hair was thinning on top, unlike his paunchy belly that was furrier than a gorilla's, seen through gaps in his overstretched buttondown uniform. Hazel eyes bore into Renner as he leaned forward in an apparent act of intimidation.

"No, I wasn't. I haven't seen him at work in a few days. Is he OK?"

"We were hoping *you* could answer that for us, because you were the last person to see him."

"I'm not sure what you're talking about. The last time I saw him, he was fine."

"When *was* the last time you saw Paul Barrington?" the same officer grilled.

"I guess three or four days ago at work. He passed me in the hall at Geneticode."

"You don't look so sure," the other officer piped in, this cop taller, muscular and more menacing. Renner simultaneously noticed another officer now watching from the window, coffee mug in hand, scrutinizing his every move. "We have a witness that claims Paul went to your house the day he disappeared."

"That's strange. He never came over. Hasn't been over in ages, as a matter of fact. Not since the day we moved in. Paul and I, we're not that close. We're just colleagues. Occasionally we chat at work, you know, superficial conversations about the weather and whatnot, but lately he's kept mostly to himself. Behaving nervous and distracted. If you ask me, I think the investigation was getting to him. You know, the one concerning the missing lab equipment?" He paused for effect. "Hey, you don't think he had something to do with that, do you?" Renner suggested, leading the horses to water. Now, all they had to do was drink of that water and come to the conclusion that Paul was guilty of stealing the lab equipment and probably fled.

The original officer took over the conversation again. His several gold teeth glinted in the harsh lighting, "You leave the questioning to us," he geared the interview back on track.

Renner didn't think the combined IQ between the two officers totalled 120. The pigs from his IQ experiment would probably score higher than them.

"We understand that you have been working together for years, and actually lived together while attending BIT University."

"Yes," Renner replied compliantly.

"And, you worked on your graduate thesis together?" Renner was surprised the officer even knew what a graduate thesis was. Someone must have written that question out for him. Renner nodded in response to the question.

"So, if Paul stole equipment from the research lab at Geneticode, is it safe to say that you also may be involved?"

"No, I would definitely not say that!" Renner denied defiantly, sitting up straighter in his chair, brows furrowed.

"And perhaps Paul was headed over to your place to let you know he was going to tell the police everything he knew, including your involvement. And maybe you had to take him out before he ratted on you." The policeman leaned back in his chair, looking smug.

So, they had searched Paul's home and discovered the missing evidence. But, Renner didn't fancy this turn of events. They were sniffing closer to the truth than he had anticipated.

"That's a lot of maybes," Renner responded. "An imaginative theory, I'll give you that."

"Our witness said that Paul was headed over to confront you about something. Paul told the witness that you broke into his house and stole something from him. Is this true?"

"Of course not!" Renner acted incredulous. "What an absurd accusation. I'm a doctor, not a thief."

"How did you get the bruises on your knuckles?" the muscular officer interjected, eyes glued to the fresh wounds on his dominant hand.

He rubbed at them absent-mindedly, his mind turning away from the truth, away from Paul and then Milena, and towards the prevaricated tale he had prepared as soon as he'd seen Wendy's ugly mug on his surveillance footage, knowing the police would come calling. He even had the foresight to provide evidence for his theory. That morning, before the officers arrived, he had reported a work-related incident, claiming his right hand had been crushed in some lab equipment, causing extensive bruising and swelling of the finger joints. Now he had documents to support his story. A paper trail. He relayed the tale to the police officers, who promised to verify the claim with his supervisor.

"And we have a search warrant for your estate. We'll see for ourselves what you're hiding."

Renner felt a tsunami of panic crash in his gut. Although there was no longer anything incriminating to find there, the police bozos were more intuitive than he had originally assumed.

"We're sending officers over there as we speak. We're going to hold you here until their search is complete."

Renner continued to act unaffected. "A search warrant wasn't necessary. I would have let you search the premises without one. I have nothing to hide."

"We'll see about that." The policemen concluded the interview and left the room. Renner assumed he was to remain confined to this room until the search was complete so as not to be able to interfere with the investigation at his home. He had been extra careful to remove all of the evidence: the files, samples, stolen equipment not planted at Paul's because he was still using them, the body, and especially the blood, Milena's blood.

At some point, Renner was served a bitter mug of brown sludge, leftovers from the morning brew. Different officers intermittently popped in. He was given a washroom break.   Finally, three painfully long hours later, Renner was released. Although there was no apology from the officers, he noticed they weren't acting as cocky, now unsure of his guilt or involvement in the case. As an afterthought, the larger officer commented, "You have a lot of security at your home."

"The security system was there when I bought the place," Renner replied. No doubt, the cops were familiar with the previous owner of the home and knew this to be true. Any additional measures he added would simply blend into the pre-existing system.

"The surveillance cameras?"

"Yeah, those were also there when we bought the house. They are disconnected. I have no use for them." Thankfully, he had disconnected them after Wendy's visit.

"I thought you were married. Where's your wife?"

"She was diagnosed with a brain tumour and developed schizophrenic tendencies. She's currently in Switzerland undergoing therapy. She'll be gone for a few months. I can give you the information to contact the facility if you wish."

"No, that won't be necessary."

Renner was released, a taxi transporting him back to Geneticode Laboratories.

The pointing, whispering and stares from his colleagues continued as he re-entered the facility. But that was not the end of it.

Returning to his lab to clean up the paperwork he had been working on when the police arrived, he was interrupted once again by a knock on his door. At Renner's invitation, Dr. Westbourne entered the office with a look that was simultaneously solemn and fearful.

"What can I do for you, Dr. Westbourne?"

"I'm sorry, Renner, but this facility can't take any more bad press. I know you probably weren't involved in any of this, but all of this suspicion has forced me to terminate you from your position here at Geneticode Laboratories. I'm truly sorry. I know you've had a lot going on at home with Milena's illness, but my hands are tied. The entire staff and stakeholders are in agreement that you be relieved of your position immediately."

"I understand," Renner stated, a coldness steeling his body.

"I'll have to escort you off the premises."

"Just let me gather my belongings." Renner grabbed some personal effects he had spread about the room and followed his boss out of the building. More gaping from his now ex-coworkers. He stared straight forward, avoiding all eye contact. Dr. Westbourne escorted him all the way down into the garage parking space.

When he reached his BMW, Renner turned to face his former boss who practically flinched under his gaze, and expressed in a sickeningly sweet voice, "It was a pleasure working with you, sir."

"Yes, well sorry again about the circumstances," Dr. Westbourne replied, clearly more relieved to be rid of the scientist, than sad at his parting. "You take care."

As Renner left the building for the final time, his anger slowly waned. They were fools for letting such a talented mind escape them, and they would be kicking themselves when he unveiled his experiment, his research, his massive discovery, and they would realize they couldn't take any credit. Stupid imbeciles.

And, most importantly, he now had completed the final stages of his experiment. He had already removed his secret genetically altered specimens from the genetics lab and brought them home, hiding them in a secret place where nobody would ever find them.

★ ★ ★

Milena cracked her eyes open. That was all she could manage, the skin on her eyelids tight and puffy. Excruciating pain wracked every muscle, every bone in her body. Her mouth was swollen, and after exploring with her tongue she noticed one of her teeth was missing—her right incisor. Her mouth tasted metallic from blood, and her throat felt bruised and crushed.

But she was alive.

The cell was familiar, her previous prison of solitude and punishment. Her heart plummeted. If the cops did indeed come as she had hoped, they would never find her down here in the well-concealed panic room.

How long had she been unconscious? If she screamed, would anybody even hear her? Her guess was that the room was soundproof, but she still hollered for help, shrieking at the top of her lungs. Because, maybe the police were there, as per Wendy's promise.

If so, had Paul been found? Renner was no dummy. He would have disposed of the body after confining her to the panic room.

Then she had another thought, this one even bleaker than the thought of staying Renner's prisoner. If Renner was arrested and nobody knew of her whereabouts, she would slowly starve to death in this vault. Would this be her final resting place? A coffin made of concrete walls?

She recalled the story about the drug kingpin that had previously owned the house, Emiliano Spinelli. She knew now where he had been hiding all that time when he went off the grid. He must have run low on supplies and stepped out of hiding for a second, but that was enough to be caught.

She wished she had the option of stepping out. For now, she would have to wait for her captor to come and feed her, if he hadn't been arrested after all. She didn't have any other choice.

Standing was exhausting in her battered state. Her vision wavered, an after effect of drugs or from the beating, she was uncertain. Hopefully, she hadn't sustained any brain damage or internal hemorrhaging.

Bile rose in her throat, but she managed to choke the burning liquid back down. Throat raw and bruised, she was reminded of her husband's vice-like grip locked tightly around her neck. Coughing, she felt a sharp pain stab her gut. With trepidation, she raised her blood-soaked turtleneck to check and saw what she dreaded. A new incision had been made where the former one had healed into a pink scar. Fear spiked her heart. More bile shot up the back of her throat, and she unloaded her stomach contents onto the floor.

What is he doing to me? Why didn't he just kill me?

She almost wished he would have.

Chapter 34

When Milena was finally released from her holding cell, it was in the same fashion as before. Out of nowhere, the door unlocked and swung wide open, releasing the stale air within like a mummy's sarcophagus.

Disoriented, Milena peered through squinted eyes, hoping her rescuer was anyone other than her husband. But, there he stood, his coal, black eyes glowering back at her, full of accusation. Boring through her soul. She had betrayed him, and her stint in the secret chamber wasn't sufficient enough to warrant forgiveness.

Would he attack again?

Seconds crawled by at a sloth's pace, neither one of them moving, but finally Renner simply turned and drifted away leaving the door agape. There was no pretense of escape this time. She was his prisoner for life.

Tentatively, she slipped out of the room, stumbling up the stairs as fast as her wounds would allow. Her injuries were more severe than the first time and she feared he had done some permanent damage.

At the top of the staircase, Renner disappeared down one of the many corridors in their mansion, leaving Milena on her own. She didn't bother checking the exits this time to see if she could escape—she knew they would be securely locked. Instead, she rushed straight to the guest room she had occupied and locked herself in the adjoining bathroom. Cranking the shower onto the hottest setting, she stripped off her filthy garments and submerged her battered body beneath the scorching water. Feeling violated, used, her dignity raped from her, she stayed in the shower, scrubbing every inch of her skin, taking extra care around the damaged tissue and new mysterious incision, until the spray turned cold and her skin erupted in goose pimples. Even after turning the shower off, she lay shivering in the basin in a delayed state of shock, trying to process what had happened. Figure out her options. But, after several moments, she nodded in acceptance. The answer was clear. She had no options.

Eventually she crawled out of the shower, cocooning herself in a thick, pink towel. Peeking out of the bathroom door, accumulated steam escaped from around her into the bedroom beyond. A quick scan told her that Renner wasn't there, waiting. A slight sigh of relief, but still feeling unsafe, she dragged an end table up against the door, barring Renner entry if he decided to pay her a visit. Pressing her ear against the varnished wood, she listened. No sound of footsteps approaching.

Once she established that Renner had left her alone for the moment, she dried off with the towel, and then studied her wounds in the improved lighting. Mostly bruising that had already started fading from purple and black to a yellowish-brown. Sitting at the vanity, the image staring back at her from the mirror looked haunted. She examined the gap where her tooth once rested. The puffiness around her eye had receded almost back to normal, but a black doughnut of bruising still lingered.

Limping over to the closet, she carefully slipped on a pair of black jogging pants and a fleece-lined grey sweatshirt. With the realization that she was out of options still sinking in, Milena burrowed groundhog style under the flowered quilt draped over the bed, and remained there, motionless, the last shred of determination to survive finally slipping away from her.

She lay there for days. The days stretched into weeks, blending together until she knew not when one day began and the other one ended.

She only stirred when absolutely necessary. With stiff-jointed movement, she would peel herself off the bed to fulfill her basic needs for survival—going to the washroom and sliding over the table barring the bedroom door to grab the food left there by Franc or Renner. She ate enough to sustain her, no more or no less, quickly shifting the table back in front of the door, retreating back into bed. Into her mind, into her memories, she'd hide. Slipping into an imaginary refuge of safety and security, a place where life wasn't so dark, and riled with insanity and pain. She imagined she was back at her home in Poland with her parents and sister, before Brigita's illness. Living out the seemingly insignificant routines of their daily lives in her mind, she sadly realized that these moments that she had taken for granted were more valuable than gems such as garnet, diamonds, emeralds and sapphires, and she clung to them now for dear life like a pirate who has found a lost treasure.

Picturing her *Mamilka* humming as she stirred a pot of porridge over the stove, her *Tatko* chopping wood in the backyard and showing Milena exactly how to hold the axe to get the log to cleave just right, Brigita sitting on the floor with her as they played with hand-sewn dolls, giggles erupting from their innocent mouths.

Milena felt a glimmer of peace in the memories, a fragment of her sanity that she latched onto like an infant with a pacifier. She purposely resisted returning to reality, to the turmoil around her, although there were times when clarity would dawn on her, unannounced.

During these brief moments of clarity, she would reassess her situation. She knew she had sunk into a deep state of depression, had adopted a state of learned helplessness. Like a rat in a cage that learns that if he tries to escape he will receive a jolting electrical shock, so eventually he simply stops trying. Renner had ironically been the one to teach her such things.

Thoughts of her family and her newfound faith in God were the only things that prevented her from taking her own life.

After several weeks had passed this way, Renner entered Milena's room, without warning, uninvited. Pushing the barred door open as if a piece of paper held it shut, he traipsed in one morning as if nothing was wrong, as if he hadn't beaten the living daylights out of her and invited Milena to come to the dining room for breakfast. She could smell the enticing aroma of bacon and eggs, heard the bacon fat sizzling and the toaster pop. There was the familiar clinking of plates, glasses and cutlery as Franc set the dining room table.

She did not stir.

The next day and the subsequent three days, Renner repeated the gesture. In response to his intrusions, Milena became increasingly creative, determined to prevent Renner from entering her room. Her barrier transformed from the small end table, to an entire bookcase, to finally the bed itself, her emaciated body driven by hatred. But, each day Renner pushed past whatever barricade she set up with minimal effort. His strength had multiplied, she had noticed. His demeanour was pleasant, even jovial as he extended his invitation for her to join him for breakfast, and now also lunch and dinner each day. When she continued to ignore his requests, he attempted a new strategy.

On the fourth morning, Milena heard him enter the bedroom and, looking up, saw that he had a fully stocked tray in hand.

"Wake up, my beautiful Milena. I've brought you some breakfast. If you won't come to the dining room to eat, I'll have to bring the meals to you."

Milena knew she looked anything but beautiful. She had limited her showers to once per week, and barely bothered to comb her long tresses; they lay mounded atop her head in matted knots. Her skin and eyelids felt puffy from too much sleep. Her muscles had atrophied beneath the jogging pants and sweatshirt she still wore, unwashed and wrinkled.

Renner was unrelenting. When Milena failed to move, he flicked on the overhead lights and set the tray on the bed. Milena slowly struggled into a seated position, squinting in the sudden brightness. Rubbing the sleep from her eyes, she finally looked up at Renner with pure loathing. He was scrutinizing her, intrigued, as if he was studying a novel organism under the probing lens of his microscope.

She didn't want to eat the food he had brought her. He might be trying to poison her or drug her again. Isn't that what he did before? How could she have been so naive as to trust this lunatic? To think he was helping her? Why hadn't she seen through his ruse?

"Come on, Milena, you have to eat," Renner hovered over her, waiting. He was still stunningly attractive, his golden brown hair long and feathered back, a goatee and sideburns worn short and perfectly groomed on his heart-shaped face. But his eyes were eternally black. Whenever she accidentally looked into them, her insides would clench in fear.

However fearful she was of Renner, she refused his offers. Perhaps she would eventually die of starvation. At this point, she didn't care.

Until she got sick. Each morning and sometimes even throughout the entire day, she would experience debilitating nausea, and vomited on a regular basis. She was losing too much weight, on her way to anorexia, and she could literally feel severe dehydration settling in.

Noticing her illness, Renner grew more insistent that she eat, promising that the food would make her feel better.

One evening, an untouched dinner tray of spaghetti and meatballs, fresh crusty buns, and a tall glass of milk sat untouched on the bed. Milena glared back at Renner, defiant as usual, unyielding.

"Milena, don't be stupid. You have to eat or you're going to starve to death."

"You can't force me."

"Milena, you're hurting more than just yourself. Come on, my Liebchen, take a bite."

353

"How dare you call me that! I'm anything but your Liebchen! I'm just your prisoner now."

"Milena, eat something already."

She crossed her arms defiantly across her chest, clamped her lips shut and turned her head to the side as if she were a spoiled child.

"Milena," Renner shook his head in frustration.

She held her position.

"Look, if you don't cooperate, my Liebchen, I will be forced to hook you up to an IVdrip. Is that what you want?"

Before she could stop herself, she plucked a crusty roll from the tray before her and flung the bread at Renner's head, where it bounced cleanly off his cheek.

There was a lengthy pause. Milena's heart ceased beating. Her throat ran dry.

A flicker of annoyance flashed across Renner's face but quickly transformed into amusement. "All right, Milena, suit yourself. But, you'll feel so much better after you eat. The food will make the nausea disappear." He left the room.

The meal smelled fantastic and a gnawing in her gut begged her to eat.

Finally, she couldn't hold off any longer. With a fork, she broke off a tiny piece of meatball and plunged the morsel into her mouth. Just a small piece at first. Her taste buds approved, and she immediately noticed her stomach settled. Next, a forkful of spaghetti noodles, and her stomach settled some more. She was already starting to feel full, her stomach shrinking over the past weeks of near starvation.

But, she felt good, better than she had in a long while. The little food she had, perked her up, gave her energy, and pushed the nausea aside.

Reluctantly, she reached a decision. She would eat whatever Renner brought her as the feeling of nausea was so unbearable she was even willing to risk eating contaminated or poisoned food instead of going back to that horrible feeling. And, at this point she didn't care what happened to her anymore. If he wanted to poison her, he could go right ahead.

After a few more weeks had passed, she noticed an odd tingling and swelling in her breasts. Not the kind that came before her period but a significant sensation, finally solving the mystery of the incisions on her abdomen.

She remembered the strange file, labelled with her name, which she had found in Renner's lab. He had been tracking her fertility cycle, measuring her hormones. There was only one reason she could think of that would lead him to do so.

I can't be pregnant! It's impossible! She hadn't been intimate with Renner in ages.

And, besides, Renner had made it clear that he wasn't the slightest bit interested in having any children.

But, the more she thought about the situation, the more she knew she was right. The nausea and vomiting, the tender breasts, and the file she found in Renner's lab all told her so.

She lacked the elation she should have felt over getting what she had always wanted, because she feared what the incisions meant. This was no normal pregnancy. She had heard about artificial insemination, Renner himself being the one who told her about the massive breakthrough in science, the new technique that would allow women who had trouble getting pregnant to be implanted with a fetus. The incisions on her abdomen finally made sense.

The hair strand genetic test she had found in Renner's filing cabinet was also a vital piece to the puzzle, but she couldn't figure out where it fit. Surely, what he was doing was unethical, using her as a lab rat.

Was the baby a lab rat as well? If Renner's job was altering the genetic makeup of an organism, could he have done something to the baby's DNA? What if he had tampered with the baby's cells before implanting them inside of her? Why else would he go through all of this trouble impregnating her against her will, instead of the old-fashioned way, especially since he knew how much she had wanted a baby? What was growing in her womb?

Nevertheless, no matter what she feared grew inside of her womb, she couldn't attempt an abortion. Her morals and beliefs held her back. For all she knew, the child she carried was perfectly normal. Also, she didn't know how to abort the baby without seriously injuring herself or bleeding to death in the process. She had heard horror stories of other women attempting to perform their own abortions. No, a forced abortion was definitely not an option.

The bottom line was that within her grew a baby, and regardless of how insane her husband was, the baby didn't ask for this.

To cope with her new condition, she went into denial, completely blocking the assumed pregnancy out of her conscious mind. In her head, she refused to accept the possibility.

As her belly swelled over time, she noticed Renner treating her again with love and respect, how he had when she was supposedly diabetic. She ignored him this time, and stayed hidden within her protective shell. Finally venturing out of her room, she roamed the halls, the massive rooms, searching for something to placate her. Her mind still reached for the solace of her childhood memories, of her loving parents and her sister before she became ill but they became increasingly difficult to return to. The changes in her body kept reminding her of her predicament. She would have to be more creative in blocking out her terrifying thoughts and fears. And what better way to go further into denial than to drink alcohol? She recalled her previous visits to the wine cellar to blur her plight before she was artificially inseminated. What did she have to lose?

Before she could talk herself out of it, she found herself standing in front of the wine cellar.

What to choose? So many bottles, so many labels stared back at her, enticing her. The stronger the better, she decided. Bypassing the wine bottles, she tugged a squat bottle of spirits from the top shelf, the oldest one she could find. Extracting the cork with her teeth and spitting it off to the floor, she took a hearty slug of the contents, several drops sloshing down her chin. The liquid seared her throat and stomach. She squished her eyelids against the heat, tears squeaking out between her eyelashes. She took another long pull from the bottle. When she exhaled afterwards, she almost expected to see flames shoot out of her mouth. Sliding down onto the floor, she continued drinking. After a while, she stopped having to brace herself against the searing liquid as the alcohol kicked in. Her mind and body numbed, her tension easing ever so slightly.

Halfway through the bottle, Renner appeared. Face grim, lips set in a thin line. "What do you think you're doing?" he scolded.

"Oops," she giggled, "how did you find me?"

She tried to take another gulp of spirits, but Renner tore the bottle out of her hand with such force that the amber liquid splashed all over her.

"Hey, giv' it back! I wuz 'ere first." She lunged for the bottle, but Renner held it out of reach.

He shook his head in utter disgust. Milena could sense that he was livid, but the spirits had done the trick. She didn't care.

Grabbing her by the armpits, he dragged her into a standing position, where she swayed on her feet. Her head was spinning, and she grabbed onto the brick cellar wall for support. She shook her head back at him. "Renn'r, what did ya think I w'u'd do? Huh?" she stumbled, regained her footing. "Didja think I w'u'd thank you? Huh? For locking me y-up...for beatin' the shitoutof me? For whatever else ya did to me?" She did a drunken flourish with her hand across her body, lingering at the area with the incision that was now protruding over the lump in her abdomen.

"Fine, Milena. You can pretend to deny that you're pregnant all you want. But, how could you risk damaging the baby? Isn't this what you've always wanted? A child of your own?" Renner blamed.

"I want'd a normal baby, not...thisss! A mutant! A frickin' monster baby!"

"I don't know what you're talking about. Why would you think the baby is a monster? This baby will be perfect, made from your egg and my sperm. The baby will have tiny hands and feet and smell of baby powder. He or she will have your eyes, and my hair or vice versa. The best parts of us combined into one."

Milena pondered his words the next day during her miserable hangover, and for days after that. The prospect forced her out of her denial and for the first time she touched the bump on her abdomen.

What if she carried a real baby, what she had always wanted? Her pregnancy appeared to be normal. The bump continued to grow. And, now that she thought about it, what she was trying to pass off as gas was really the first stirrings of life within her.

It could be a normal baby.

But, she was still afraid. What if it wasn't?

As the days passed by and the fluttering within her belly increased, she found she was starting to bond with the fetus. She would rub her warm hands over the lumps and bumps that would protrude here and there, wondering, *Is it a foot or a hand?*

She started speaking aloud to the baby, words of love and hope. She even sang traditional lullabies in Polish, ones her mother and grandmother had sung to her when she was a little girl. And for a time, her situation improved. She felt a hope she hadn't experienced in a long while. Found the confines of the house becoming more bearable. Could even be around Renner without feeling intense revulsion and wanting to kill him dead. And she need not worry that he harm the baby once it arrived, because he now treated her like a goddess simply for the package that she carried. A precious cargo that she carried for them both.

The anticipation and excitement over the baby brought them one degree closer again. Nothing like before—she still detested him beyond belief—but they had a common connection, a common thread of interest.

Renner kept saying he had done this for her, and although she knew that was untrue, she did accept her pregnancy as a gift.

So, for a short time, all was well.

Chapter 35

Renner Scholz filled his tumbler with scotch and placed the glass on the teakwood desk in his library. Lighting a cigarette, an old habit he had recently embraced again, he then eased onto a leather recliner, and snapped open the Boston Globe newspaper to the article he most anticipated.

For eight months now, he had been following the news daily, searching for this. Closure. And here it finally was, the headline announcing his greatest hopes. The search for Paul was over.

Without a body, his ex-roommate remained missing, but the incriminating evidence at his house led the police to believe he was guilty of stealing from Geneticode Laboratories and had fled. Renner's name was cleared for good, and the police would be bothering him no further.

Loose ends tied up into a neat and tidy bow.

Same as with the old psychic and her faithful followers. He had returned to the chapel. Paul had already granted them their initial invitation to attend the ritual that first and fateful night, so Renner naturally assumed he would be granted access anytime he desired. And he was right. The graffiti marking the chapel's entrance welcomed him with open arms. Traversing the tunnels, he reached the chapel mid-ritual, the entire space full of hooded participants, the old desiccated woman glancing up in surprise.

"Renner, I see you have returned," she announced in her gravelly, inhuman voice.

Without much effort, his powers unrivalled, he pinned the entire congregation to their seats to observe as unobtrusive statues. The psychic was the one he wanted.

The subdued witch struggled beneath Renner's power as he stalked up to the altar, grabbed her by the hair and yanked her head back.

"I need answers."

"And why should I tell you anything?" she snarled.

Renner leaned over the old woman's face, smelling moth balls and decay. "Because if you don't answer my questions, I'll kill you."

"But, you'll kill me anyways."

"Hmm, you got me there." He grinned maliciously. "But there's a whole lot of hurt I can deliver before that happens. So, if I were you, I'd start talking. Now."

"What do you want to know?"

"What do you know about Paul Barrington? Why was he hell bent on sabotaging everything I touched? Why steal my research and then have the joint project we were working on destroyed?"

"So many questions."

Renner punched the old woman in her chair, strands of white hair freeing from her bun as her head flew back. Hovering over her, he waited until she regained her composure, which didn't take long.

She grinned up at him through bloodied lips. "There is only one answer."

"Well, spit it out!"

"Paul was acting on his orders."

"Orders? From whom?"

"The voice."

"What voice?" he asked, but deep down he knew.

"The voice, like the one inside your head. The Guardian Angel Spell has its rewards, but they come at a great cost."

"That's enough!" he cuffed the woman again. "So, if Paul was acting on orders, was he told to kill my professor?"

She looked back at him proudly. "You can thank me for that one. Paul came to me asking for help. I performed the spell that led to your professor's illness and death. It was all part of the plan."

"What plan? Who's plan?"

"Haven't you been listening? The voice. We are all part of his plan." She paused. "I believe you play a larger role. Paul's job was to bring you in. My job was to keep you here."

The plan. Renner knew the plan, had been slaving over it for years now. But, it was his plan, wasn't it?

"How many more of you are there?" Renner asked.

"Besides Paul, we are all here. There are no others."

And there will be no more.

With a sinister grin, he withdrew a flask from his coat pocket and doused the pews in alcohol. The congregation watched gravely, still pinned to their spots by Renner's power, unable to escape. A flick of a lit match and the pews ignited. He bid adieu and left the chapel, barring the one exit. The memory of their screams still echoed in his skull, even though several months had passed since the time of their demise.

He smiled contentedly, swirling the scotch in his glass before taking a sip. Yes, everything was falling into place.

And to top it all off, Milena appeared in better spirits. He had made her happy again by giving her a baby. Maybe if he had talked to her about his plans in the first place she would have understood. Would she have gone along with his plans without the need for deception? Maybe he didn't have to trick her into believing she was diabetic so he could give her the fertility hormones. He needed her to produce more eggs so that he could harvest them. Being a doctor, he knew that antidepressants could sometimes mimic the symptoms of diabetes and had been sneaking them into her food. Once she had presented with the symptoms, he stopped, of course, and then was giving her injections of hormones instead of insulin.

But, would she have gone along with his plans if he had simply asked? She had shown strength in character that he had not predicted. For her to be able to rise above what had happened and behave as if there was no longer an issue was commendable. He was happy about her present boost in morale.

He hadn't wanted to attack her the first time. That part was a mistake and he knew that had made her disenchanted with him for a while. The plus side to that blunder was that he was given the perfect opportunity to harvest her eggs, a careful procedure. He then stored the eggs, along with his sperm, in the freezer at Geneticode as his mislabeled experiment. He still had a storage freezer in a hidden location filled with specimens in case this worked. Or in case it didn't.

Initially, Renner's goal was to alter their DNA so that the balanced translocation was found on chromosomes nine and eleven. Some of the sperm and egg samples already had the deletion, inherited from their own DNA. In the end, they all possessed the genetic code that would increase DMT production, and subsequently supernatural abilities. But then he thought, why stop there? Why not enhance other characteristics by splicing animal DNA into the sperm and egg cells? The potential offspring would be stronger, larger, smarter, and have powerful psychic abilities, unlike any other human. He randomly attached different characteristics to different embryonic cells, so each cell held a unique combination of enhanced capabilities.

The second time he attacked Milena, he hadn't a choice. She had found Paul's corpse and violated his trust. She needed to be punished. Deserved to be punished. Obviously, she hadn't learned her lesson the first time, so he made sure she did the second time. A silver lining in the whole ordeal—the timing was opportune, as he was ready to transplant the newly manipulated embryonic cells into her uterus. He used several eggs to ensure at least one of them would take, as is typical of any artificial insemination procedure. He was thrilled that the procedure was successful the first time, one of the embryos implanting and continuing to grow and develop inside Milena's womb.

So, did he need to jump through all of the hoops to get to this stage? Or would Milena have gone along in the first place? He would never know. The main thing was that the end result was what he wanted.

Milena now carried within her a new species of man—a potential superhuman with capabilities far surpassing that of any average human being. He would be solely responsible for the single most amazing discovery in history. Had he actually contemplated handing over this finding to Geneticode Laboratories if the experiment was successful? What a waste that would have been. No, this finding was his alone, for him to use in whatever way *he* desired.

He was to be the father of a new race.

★ ★ ★

Milena bolted upright in bed. Her back muscles immediately bunched up in protest to her sudden movement, the added weight of her eight-month pregnancy-belly like having an eighty-pound boulder strapped to her waist. Rubbing her lower back gingerly, she tried to make sense of the disturbing sounds that had so abruptly awakened her.

The darkness pressing up against the blinds told her the hour was still late, the clock on the nightstand confirming her assumptions, declaring the time was 2 a.m.

Alarmed, Milena peeled off the sweaty sheets tangled around her body and swung her swollen legs over the side of the bed, planting her feet on the cool hardwood floor. She hesitated, listening. And there the sound was again, unmistakable.

Renner, shrieking in terror.

Creeping quietly to her door, she pressed her ear against the grain, and listened.

More shrieks, fear filled and pleading, a slurring of words that were indecipherable, disjointed, incoherent. A loud bang and the ceiling shuddered. More yelling and screams, again followed by incessant babbling. She could detect only one voice, that of Renner, her husband.

Milena's veins flooded with ice. Uncertain of what to do or whether she should do anything at all. She didn't want to put herself and her unborn child in any danger. She had seen Renner during his rages and wanted no part of that.

But, this sounded different.

As if on cue, Renner released another string of unintelligible dialogue, and to Milena, the sounds appeared to be coming from his bedroom, the room they once shared.

She mustered enough courage to check on Renner to see what tormented him so, but, not without protection. Easing herself down onto her hands and knees, she fished out the heavy flashlight kept beneath her bed.

Taking a ragged breath, she entered the hallway, cautiously climbed the stairs to the second floor, and crept with bare feet towards Renner's room.

Please, God, protect us!

She paused outside his door, cracked open a sliver. Grasping the flashlight with white knuckles, she nudged the door with her big toe, which creaked open loud enough to awaken the neighbours living a few kilometres away.

"Renner, are you OK?" she asked.

He stood crouched on his bed, hair and nightclothes rumpled, the sheets in complete disarray beneath him. His body trembled, and perspiration coated his brow. He appeared to be alone in the room. Sheer terror filled his eyes.

"HELP ME!" he cried in anguish, the blood draining from his face. He sputtered and gasped as if he were choking, trying to get air.

He pointed into the corner of his room, into the shadows, causing her hair to stand on end. Milena wanted to flee, but she was rooted to the spot, watching her husband be consumed by his inner turmoil.

She couldn't see what he was pointing at, but whatever he thought he saw, it horrified him.

He began ranting again, but for most of what he said Milena couldn't make any sense of. Finally, she understood a fragment of his speech.

"Yes, it's him! He is so hideous, my eyes, they hurt." He rubbed at them furiously. "MAKE IT STOP!" Renner moaned.

She didn't know if he was speaking to her or to someone else. Suddenly, his body started convulsing. Luckily, the softness of his bed protected him from harm, although several times he came close to toppling right over the edge. White foam gathered at the corners of his mouth. His eyes rolled back in his head.

"Renner, it's me, Milena," she spoke a little louder, in a trembling voice. He acted completely unaware of her presence.

Protectively, she wrapped her free arm around her fetus, and with flashlight raised, entered the frigid room, shaking legs carrying her towards Renner. The air felt dense, her breath seen in plumes of mist with each exhalation. Her eyes flicked from Renner to each corner of the bed chamber, ensuring they were alone before she reached out and touched him—hoping to snap him out of his delusional, dream state.

He was ice-cold, her fingertips chilled the moment they made contact with his arm. Her hand recoiled instinctively. She thought of the ancient pendant hidden in her Bible, the one that was supposed to ward off evil spirits. Why hadn't she thought to bring the relic? Before she could make up her mind whether to run back to her room and quickly grab the pendant or not, Renner ceased thrashing, and for a moment was still. Although, he was silent, his lips still moved as if speaking to someone.

Up close, his eyes appeared red rimmed as if he had been crying for a great length of time, and still, tears streamed down the sides of his face. His features contorted again with fear and revulsion.

Suddenly, his eyes flicked over to her, seeing her for the first time. "MILENA, YOU HAVE TO HELP ME!"

Recoiling, she reflexively took a step back.

"IT'S HIM!" He raised his head and pointed again, frantic, towards the corner of the room. Then, he flipped over and on all fours, crawled towards the top of his bed, cowering upright against the wall in a fetal position, perched on the balls of his feet.

"HE'S COME TO GET ME!"

Realization sunk in, and Milena's shoulders dropped in resignation and defeat. She shook her head slowly. "No, Renner. He already has you," she whispered sadly, and turned to leave.

"DON'T LEAVE ME!" he cried after her.

Chapter 36

Daylight flooded Milena's bedroom through the vertical blinds, painting shadow lines on the wallpaper. Struggling to a seated position, she was surprised she had slept in, that sleep had finally claimed her after last night's episode.

Rolling out of bed, she grabbed her white, flannel robe and slipped the soft fabric over her shoulders. Franc was clanking pans in the kitchen. Otherwise, no other sounds were evident.

Was Renner up?

She exited her room and pattered into the main living room, glancing out the double deck doors as she passed by. The sight brightened her countenance immediately as she detected tender blooms stretching up toward the sky. Tulips and other perennials announcing the onset of spring, starting to poke through the soil, unbidden. A glorious surprise. The month had been a rainy one and the weeds were thriving as well, but the blooms towered above them beautiful and strong. They were survivors.

Even though she wasn't due for another month, she was enormous. Walking around was beginning to be a challenge, her massive belly pressing against her sciatic nerve, causing her back and leg to ache uncomfortably. Today was worse than usual.

Maybe she would give birth to a sumo wrestler, she thought chuckling. Absentmindedly, she massaged her lower back, wandering over to the base of the staircase, hovering, listening. No sound from above.

Had Renner survived his torment?

What she witnessed the night before wasn't a complete shock. Evil had been lurking beneath her husband's skin ever since they went to the abandoned chapel. And with every use of the hallucinogenic compound, the drug he initially smoked from the witch, the evil intensified, strengthening until the darkness bludgeoned his conscience into submission. The man he once was, now consumed.

Possessed?

She had briefly entertained the thought, but after she spoke with the priest at St. Anthony's Church, she dismissed the notion. Assumed she was just overreacting to Renner's changed behaviour. Now, she revisited the idea as an actual possibility. Although bizarre, she could find no other explanation.

She wished they had never gone to that God-forsaken chapel, but Renner was determined to go and see the witch perform the Guardian Angel Spell, promising any desire to be granted. Renner's one desire was to get past the block in his research. Was the spell successful? Was the quest worth losing his sanity, his soul?

Again, the worry niggled at the base of her spine. What was the secret research he had been working on? What if Renner had implanted her with something he had created in the lab— an abomination?

No, it can't be!

She had grown to love her vision of the baby, and fervently held fast to Renner's promise that the baby was normal. She could picture her little boy with curly black hair, a pale face with a spattering of freckles over the bridge of his nose, bright red lips, and her azure eyes. Inadvertently, her vision of the baby didn't include any of Renner's physical characteristics.

Retreating to the bathroom, she brushed her teeth, and scrubbed her face. She decided to keep her roomy pyjamas on for the day. Nothing else fit her properly anymore, even though Renner had regularly provided her with new maternity clothes that increased in size and could harbour her massive form.

Renner still hadn't come down, and he wasn't one to sleep in. Finally, she decided to go and check on him. Cautiously, she climbed the stairs and walked the length of the hallway to Renner's room. The door stood wide open, the room bright, curtains drawn back to allow the sunlight to reach each corner of the empty room. Milena breathed a sigh of relief. Renner must be up and back to normal. Well, whatever normal was for him these days.

Padding down the cream carpeted stairs in her pyjamas and bare feet, she was preparing to devour the entire kitchen when her water broke. At first, she thought she had peed herself as she watched the pinkish liquid spill down her leg and onto the stairs.

Then the first contraction hit. The pain was startling, intense, forcing her to cry out in anguish. She sat at the top of the stairs, doubled over, trying to catch her breath.

Renner immediately came sprinting into the room, concerned. "What is it?"

"What, do you have bionic hearing? Where were you hiding?" She flinched as the pain intensified.

"I was having coffee in the dining room." Then he saw the water on the stairs and Milena's face contorted in pain. "Is the baby coming?"

She nodded vigorously.

"The baby's coming!" he exclaimed. "Finally!" He swept Milena up into his arms, a difficult feat due to her increased weight and girth and carried her all the way to the basement lab. He had transformed the lab into a make-shift delivery room, complete with bed, heart rate monitor, and incubator.

"Renner, could we go to a hospital, please? I'd feel so much better there, you know, in case anything goes wrong," Milena pleaded.

"What could go wrong? You're perfectly fine here. You know first and foremost I'm a doctor. I've delivered hundreds of babies as part of my medical internship in Germany. Don't insult me."

"Yes, but the baby..."

"The baby will be fine."

After laying Milena on the bed, Renner donned a lab coat and gloves, and encouraged his wife to breathe as they had been practicing for weeks now. Promising her the breathing would ease the pain but it did nothing of the sort.

The labour progressed quickly, her contractions coming closer together. She knew what that meant. A quick exam from Renner and he confirmed her thoughts.

"You're already ten centimetres dilated. When you feel the urge to push, bear down and push with all your might."

She had a brief moment where the pain subsided, and she rested her head back on the pillow, relieved. But the relief was short lived. Almost immediately, the next contraction hit, and she felt a severe urge to push, in fact found her body was reacting automatically. She pulled up her torso by grabbing her legs and pushed down as hard as she could. Her legs burned but pushing helped make the contractions more bearable.

"You're doing great," Renner encouraged. "Just relax now, and then with your next contraction, push again."

Relaxing was not a possibility. Between contractions, anxiety squeezed at her heart. This isn't how she wanted to deliver the baby. She would feel much more at ease being in a hospital, the fact they were sequestered in Renner's basement lab further supporting her suspicions that this was not a normal pregnancy, and that he had something to hide.

The next contraction came on with a fury, and she bore down, grunting and panting until her strength waned. She was already exhausted.

An hour later, Renner's voice finally grew excited. "I see the crown of the head. Just one more big push, Milena."

Pushing as hard as she could, she finally felt a release, a gush of fluids, as the head came through. The rest of the baby slid out into Renner's waiting arms.

All was silent. Renner's face grew serious. Milena held her breath.

"What is it?" she gasped.

Was the baby stillborn? Then tiny mewls from Renner's arms told her the little one was alive. Renner's excitement was still extinguished. "Well, what is it? It's a boy, isn't it?"

Renner nodded distractedly without making eye contact. Milena smiled. A boy, exactly how she had imagined.

But, before she could see the little baby, now bundled in a white towel inside a plastic walled incubation cart Renner had ordered for the occasion, another contraction seized her.

This surprised Renner, almost more than her.

Twins? Automatically, she started pushing, and Renner's excitement resumed.

She pushed and pushed, and when she thought she could push no more, baby number two entered the world. They had no idea she had been carrying twins, her massive abdomen finally making sense.

Renner was quiet again. This baby came out howling, distracting Milena from Renner's strange reaction to the births.

"It's also a boy," Renner said as he wrapped the newborn in another towel and placed him in the incubator beside the first one.

"I want to see them," Milena gushed. She was overwhelmed by emotion. Thinking she was already blessed by having one child, now she had two. What an unexpected miracle.

"Let me clean them up first. I'll be right back." Renner wheeled the incubator into the bathroom next to the lab. Several minutes passed, when Milena was seized by another contraction.

"Renner, come back!" she cried in confusion.

Triplets?

The third baby came with great difficulty. She pushed again for over an hour. She could hear the babies crying in the other room, and her cries joined theirs. Just when Renner decided to prepare her for a C-section, the baby came out backwards, quiet and still. Milena could tell something was wrong. She had felt more pain with this delivery, as if her pelvis had cracked. From what she could see of the baby, the skin appeared blue. She did not hear any cries. And Renner panicked.

"No, not this one," he grieved. Milena watched as he grabbed the baby by the heels, and while hung upside down, repeatedly patted the infant's back. Renner's face was strained.

Then finally, a loud yelp and the baby's cries filled the lab. Milena stopped holding her breath, and she cried happily.

Three babies! And Renner quickly told her, this one also was a boy.

How was this possible?

Renner took baby number three from the room to clean him up with the others. He was gone for a long time, much longer than it would take to clean the babies from the amniotic fluid that had nourished them and protected them all these months. Milena grew impatient. The waiting was intolerable; she wanted to see her babies, their beautiful little faces, embrace their tiny warm bodies.

When he returned, he held three little bundles wrapped in clean, white towels. They were wrapped so tightly into little burritos, she couldn't see them.

He hesitated before bringing them over.

"Well, what are you waiting for? I want to see my babies." Milena's eyes welled up as she reached her arms out to embrace them.

He brought them over to her, and as he laid them down on her stomach, she carefully removed the towels covering their tiny faces.

Milena's heart shattered into a thousand pieces.

"Why? How…how could you do this?" tears now overflowing. "HOW COULD YOU DO THIS?" she shrieked.

Startled, the babies started crying.

"Why would you want this?" she added as if talking to herself, shaking her head.

"This isn't how it was supposed to be," Renner tugged at his hair. "But, you'll see Milena. You'll see. Everything will make sense soon enough."

Many years would pass before the triplets' powers and their terror would reign down on humanity. Now, it was merely forethought as they settled again, sighing contentedly against their mother's

breast, unaware of the budding hatred for them that had already
· blossomed within her heart.

Epilogue

My sons.
Three perfect sons.
Truly a part of me, of my loins, so to say.
And there will be others, many more,
All gifted, all flawed.
But, I am particularly fond of these three, the first of their kind.

We have a mental connection,
A constant psychic link.
No static interference like a truck driver's CB radio,
Not like it has been with Renner.
No moments of resistance or rebellion,
Also, not like it has been with Renner.

Just complete trust, worship, and loyalty.
Don't be mistaken, I have needed the scientist,
Still need him now,
The vehicle through which my offspring have come to be.
The problem with Renner,
Despite his genetic enhancements from my DNA
Is that he is still so inherently human.

His emotions sometimes well up,
Get the best of him.
In these moments I feel my grasp on him slip,
In these moments he makes mistakes.
Thankfully this does not happen often,
But still…

I realize I would not be where I am today without his help.
Still unsure how I possessed him so deeply,
Altering him at a cellular level.
Only heard of once before
Back when men first populated the earth.
My rebellious brethren and I,
Fallen angels turned demon,
Able to sneak into the souls of men
Possessing in such a way that we, the Sons of God,
Were able to mate with the daughters of men:
Mere mortals.
Creating a legion of humans magnificent in proportion.

Giants.
Biblically referred to as the Sons of Anak,
They corrupted the human spirit,
Unleashed sin and contention amongst the masses,
Such a magnificent time in history…
Until the great flood.
The Nephilim, the Anakim,
A combination of both man and demon.
Lost.
Like a reset button was hit,
The taint in the human genome eradicated.
The earth wiped clean of my sons,
Our sons.

Now, does something similar occur?
Once more able to pass my genes through a mortal man?
But how?
Was the DMT acting as a portal between our two worlds?
Renner's lack of belief in a deity
Or his disturbing experiences as a child that left him weak to my
claws?
The never-ending quest to prove himself or the Guardian Angel Spell
Leaving him pliable to my will?
Perhaps a combination of all these,
An impossible alignment of the right circumstances.

Renner must continue.
Manipulating the pineal gland to secrete more DMT is successful,
My offspring, supernatural beings with immense power.
Renner's contract ultimately fulfilled.
And, although he may view these creatures as his own,
They are really mine.

For the first time since my creation
I feel affection for another human, three to be exact.
But they are not actually human, now are they?
They are my sons, are they not?
My offspring, the beginning of a new race.

The human seed, once again tainted, corrupted
By my seed, my DNA.
My family grows and will continue to do so.
And I will not stop
Until my new and improved race consumes humanity,
Swallowing it whole.
Until every last person on earth and beyond will bow down to me,
Worship me, adore me,
And only me.

All. Will. Follow.
At last.

—Ruler of Demons

THE END

Acknowledgements

For inspiring me to create this book, the first in my four-part series, I want to thank God for giving me an overactive imagination and vivid dreams that were screaming to be made into a story. And for the Scooby-Doo episode that helped me realize the disjointed stories from my dreamscape were all part of a whole.

For their constant love, patience and support while I toiled away on the computer for hours on end, I want to thank my husband Lee, my son Erik, and little Chihuahua, Batman.

Without my parents, this book never would have happened. It would still be a jumble of thoughts stuck in my head. Thank you so much for your love and support throughout the years, and for truly believing that this book was meant to be and helping me to bring it to life. And to my sister: my Jell-O to her Caviar, the inspiration for the content of so much of my writing.

And I could never forget to thank my friends (my unrelated family) who kept me sane throughout this process—Karen, Lindsay, and Vivien—for always checking in to see how things were progressing and never judging when nothing was progressing. Love, love, love you all!

A few quick additional words about this book. Some elements are based on reality and some are completely fiction, like the university town of Barbora Bay and BIT University. The studies that Renner was conducting may sound familiar to any science buffs out there. As you know, neither of Renner's thesis endeavours made it to fruition, but in real life some did. The cancer rat model was based on the very real oncomice study by Rudolph Jaenisch and Beatrice Mintz (1974). Studies with human growth hormone in animals have also been studied extensively. These scientists are the real pioneers in using recombinant DNA technology, and they deserve all the credit, laying the groundwork for the treatment of so many diseases.

Any opinions voiced in the story were meant to reflect those that people held in the 1970s when recombinant DNA technology and artificial insemination were starting to rear their heads. In no way did I intend to offend anyone.

Finally, many liberties were taken on scientific techniques to make the story flow. Could Renner really have his entire genome memorized, and be able to see changes in his DNA by studying his blood under a microscope? Probably not.

And finally, a special thanks to you, the reader, for purchasing this book and taking a journey with me through time, science and beyond the realm of our physical earth. I hope you enjoyed the ride.

Will the triplets fulfill their father's quest to corrupt humanity?
Or will something even more powerful stand in their way?

Find out in

GUARDIAN OF ANGEL

Book II in the Father of Contention series
COMING SOON!

About the Author

Lanie Mores has her Honours Bachelor of Science Degree and a Master of Arts in Clinical Psychology and is a certified hypnotherapist and personal trainer. She lives in Ontario with her husband, son, and forever barking Chihuahua, Batman.